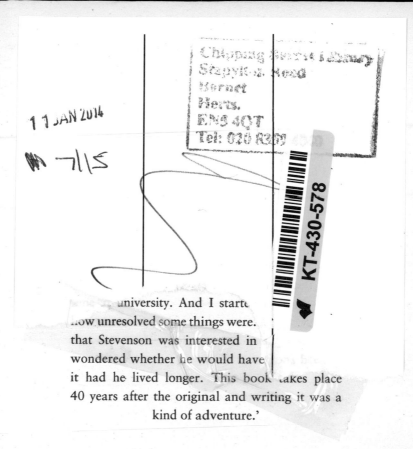

... university. And I starte
...ow unresolved some things were.
that Stevenson was interested in
wondered whether he would have
it had he lived longer. This book takes place
40 years after the original and writing it was a
kind of adventure.'

ANDREW MOTION

Silver

Return
to
Treasure
Island

VINTAGE BOOKS
London

Published by Vintage 2013

2 4 6 8 10 9 7 5 3 1

Copyright © Andrew Motion 2012
Illustrations copyright © Joe McLaren 2012

First published in Great Britain by Jonathan Cape in 2012

Vintage
Random House, 20 Vauxhall Bridge Road,
London SW1V 2SA

www.vintage-books.co.uk

Addresses for companies within The Random House Group Limited
can be found at: www.randomhouse.co.uk/offices.htm

The Random House Group Limited Reg. No. 954009

A CIP catalogue record for this book
is available from the British Library

ISBN 9780099552659

The Random House Group Limited supports The Forest
Stewardship Council® (FSC®), the leading international forest
certification organisation. Our books carrying the FSC label are
printed on FSC®-certified paper. FSC is the only forest certification
scheme endorsed by the leading environmental organisations,
including Greenpeace. Our paper procurement policy can
be found at: www.randomhouse.co.uk/environment

MIX
Paper from
responsible sources
FSC® C016897

Printed and bound by CPI Group (UK) Ltd, Croydon, CR0 4YY

FOR OSCAR FEARNLEY-DERÔME

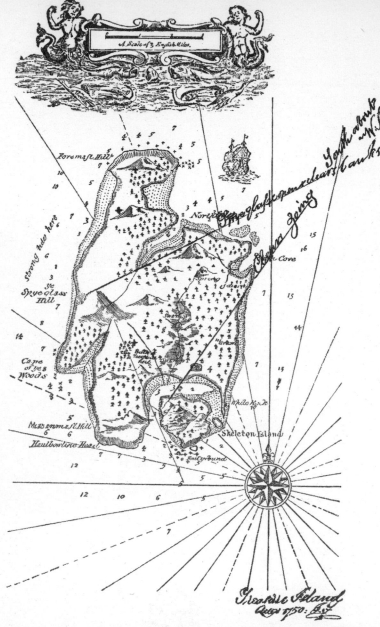

CONTENTS

PART VI

THE WRECK

PART I

THE TEMPTATION

CHAPTER I

My Father's Orders

In those days I did my father's bidding. I would leave my bed at six o'clock every morning, tiptoe past his door so as not to disturb his slumber, then set to work as quietly as possible among the foul tankards, glasses, plates, knives, gobs of tobacco, broken pipe-stems and other signs of interrupted pleasure that awaited me in the taproom below. Only after an hour or so – when everything had been made straight and the air was fresh again – could my father be trusted to appear, cursing me for having made such an intolerable racket.

'Good Lord, boy' was his reliable greeting. 'Must you dole out headaches to the entire *county*?' He did not look in my direction as he asked this, but slouched from the doorway to a freshly wiped table, and collapsed there with both hands pressed to his temples.

What followed was also always the same: I must look sharp and fetch him a reviving shot of grog, then cook some rashers of bacon and present them to him with a good thick slice of brown bread.

My father gulped his rum without so much as blinking, and chewed his meal in silence. I see him now as clearly as I did then – almost forty years distant. The flushed face, the tuft of sandy hair, the red-rimmed eyes – and melancholy engulfing him as palpably as smoke surrounds a fire. At the time I thought he must be annoyed by the world in general and me in particular. Now I suppose he was chiefly frustrated with himself. His life had begun with adventure and excitement, but was ending in the banality of repetition. His consolation – which might even have been a positive pleasure – was to finish his breakfast by issuing me with instructions he thought might keep me as unhappy as he felt himself.

On the day my story begins, which is early in the month of July in the year 1802, my orders were to find the nest of wasps he thought must be in our vicinity, then destroy it so our customers would not suffer any more annoyance from them. When this was done, I must return to the taproom, prepare food and drink for the day ahead, and make myself ready to serve. I did not in fact object to the first of these tasks, since it gave me the chance to keep my own company, which was my preference at that time of my life. I need not say how I regarded the prospect of further chores in the taproom.

Because it was not my habit to entertain my father by allowing him to see what did and did not please me, I set about my business in silence. This meant nodding to show I understood what was required, then turning to one of the several barrels that stood nearby, pouring a drop of best beer into a tankard, and taking this tankard outside to the bench that ran along the front of our home, where it faced the river. Here I sat down and waited for our enemies to find me.

4

It was a fine morning, with mist already burning off the banks and creeks, and the whole panorama of our neighbourhood looking very delightful. Beyond the river, which at this point downstream from Greenwich was at least thirty yards wide, olive-coloured marsh-land faded into lilac where it reached the horizon. On the Thames itself, the work of the day was just beginning. Large merchant ships starting their journeys across the globe, stout little coal barges, ferries collecting men for work, humble skiffs and wherries were all gliding as smoothly as beetles along the outgoing tide. Although I had seen just such a procession every day of my life at home, I still found it a marvellous sight. Equally welcome was the thought that none of the sailors on these vessels, nor the fishermen tramping along the towpath, nor the bargees with their jingling horses, would acknowledge my existence with more than a simple greeting, or interrupt my concentration on my task – which, as I say, was merely to wait.

When the sun and breeze, combining with a drowsy scent from the emerging mudbanks, had almost wafted me back to sleep again, I had my wish. A large and inquisitive wasp (or *jasper*, as we called them along the estuary) hovered cautiously above my tankard, then clung to the lip, then dropped into its depths with a shy circling movement until it was almost touching the nectar I had provided. At this point I clapped my hand over the mouth of the tankard and swirled its contents vigorously, to create a sort of tidal wave.

When I had kept everything turbulent for a moment or two, like a tyrant terrifying one of his subjects, I removed my hand and care-fully tipped the liquid onto the surface of the bench beside me. The jasper was by now half-drowned and half-drunk, its legs incapable of movement and its wings making the feeblest shudders. This was the incapacity I wanted, because it allowed me to delve into my pocket and find the length of bright red cotton I had brought with me, then to tie it around the waist of my prisoner. I did this very gently, so that I did not by accident turn myself into an executioner.

After this I continued to sit in the sun for as long as it took the jasper to recover his wits and his ability to fly. I had meant to rely on the breeze to accelerate this process, but when I heard my father clumping around his bedroom above me, I added my own breath to the warming; I did not want a second conversation with him, because I knew it would result in my receiving further orders to fetch this and carry that. I need not have worried. In the same moment that I heard his window shutters folding back, and started to imagine my father squaring his shoulders so that he could shout down to me, Mr Wasp tottered off from our bench.

The best he could manage was a low, stumbling sort of flight, which I thought might take him across the river – in which case I would have lost him. But he soon discovered his compass and set off towards the marshes, congratulating himself no doubt on a miraculous deliverance, and steadily gaining height. I ran quickly after, keeping my eyes fixed on the vivid thread that made him visible, and feeling relieved that he did not find it an inconvenience. Once my home and the river had fallen behind us, and the outhouses where my father kept his puncheons, and the orchard where we grew apples for cider, we came to open country.

To a stranger, the marshes would have seemed nothing more than wilderness – a bog-land crossed with so many small streams tending towards the Thames that from above it must have resembled the glaze on a pot. Everything was the same cracked green, or green-blue, or green-brown. There were no tall trees, only a few bare trunks the wind had twisted into shapes of agony, and no flowers that a gentleman or lady would recognise.

To me the place was a paradise, where I was the connoisseur of every mood and aspect. I relished its tall skies and wide view of the approaching weather. I loved its myriad different kinds of grass and herb. I kept records of every variety of goose and duck that visited in spring time and left again in the autumn. I especially enjoyed its congregation of *English* birds – the wrens and linnets, the finches and thrushes, the blackbirds and starlings, the lapwings and kestrels – that stayed regardless of the season. When the tide was full, and the gullies brimmed with water, and the earth became too spongy for me to walk across it, I was like Adam expelled from his garden. When the current turned and the land became more nearly solid again, I was restored to my heart's desire.

Meandering was always my greatest pleasure – which I was not able to enjoy on this particular day, with my captive leading me forward. While he flew straight, I jinked and tacked, crossed and returned, leaped and veered, in order to keep up with him. And because I was expert in this, and knew the place intimately, I still had him clearly in sight when he reached his destination. This was one of the stunted trees I have mentioned – an ash that grew in a distant part of the marsh, and had been bent by storms into the shape of the letter C. As soon as this curiosity came into view, I knew where my friend was heading; even from as far away as fifty yards I could see the nest dangling like a jewel from an ear.

A jewel, that is, made of paste or paper and moulded into a long oval. For that is how jaspers manufacture their nests – by chewing tiny portions of wood and mixing them with their saliva until they have made a cone; within this cone they protect their hive and their queen especially, who lays her eggs at every level. It is remarkable: creatures that appear confused to the human eye, and are always buzzing in different directions, or no direction at all, are in fact very well organised and disciplined. Every individual has a part to play in the creation of their society and performs it by instinct.

As I drew closer to the nest, I began to admire it so much I wondered whether I might return to my father and tell him I had obeyed his orders without in fact having done so. I knew he would never search for the thing himself: it lay in a part of the marsh that felt remote even to me. I also knew I would then have to live with the lie, which I would not enjoy, while the wasps themselves would continue to pester us.

These two reasons might have been enough to make me stick to my task. In truth, there was a third that felt even more compelling – albeit one I hesitate to admit, because it appears to contradict everything I have said so far about my likes and dislikes. This was my *desire* to destroy the nest. It intrigued me. I was fascinated by it. But my interest had quickly become a longing for possession – and since possession was impossible, destruction was the only alternative.

I therefore began to gather every fragment of flotsam or small stick the sun had dried, so that by the time I stood beside the ash tree at last my arms were filled with a bundle the size of a haycock. I placed this on the ground beneath the nest, then stood back to fix the scene in my memory. The tree itself was very smooth, as if the wind had caressed it for such a long time, and so admiringly, the bark had turned into marble. The nest – around which a dozen or so jaspers were bobbing and floating, all quite oblivious of me – was about a foot from top to bottom, and swollen in the middle. It was pale as vellum, with little ridges and bumps here and there; these I took to be the individual deposits, brought by each wasp as he worked.

When I had stared for long enough to feel I would never forget, I knelt down, pulled a tinderbox from my pocket, and set fire to the material I had collected. Flames rose very quickly, releasing a sweet smell of sap, and within a minute the whole nest was cupped in a kind of burning hand. I expected the inhabitants to fly out, and thought they might even attack me since I was their destroyer. But no such thing took place. The wasps outside the nest simply flew away – they appeared not to care what was happening. Those within the nest, which must have been many hundred, chose to stay with their queen and to die with her. I heard the bodies of several explode with a strange high note, like the whine of a gnat; the rest suffocated in smoke without making any sound.

After no more than two or three minutes, I felt sure my job was done; I knocked the nest down, so that it fell into the ashes of my fire and broke apart. The comb inside was dark brown and wonderfully dainty, with every section containing a wrinkled grub; the queen – who was almost as big as my thumb – lay at the centre surrounded by her dead warriors. They made a noble sight, and filled me with such great curiosity, I did not notice how nearly I had scorched myself by kneeling among the wreckage and poring over them.

Eventually, I stood up and faced towards home, knowing my father would soon be expecting my return. After a moment, however, I decided to please myself, not him, and changed my direction. I walked further into the marshes, jumping across the creeks and striding this way and that to avoid the larger gullies, until I had quite lost my way. There, in the deepest solitude of green and blue, I fell to thinking about my life.

CHAPTER 2

The Story of My Life

I was never a wicked child, but a disappointment to my father all the same. Thieving, deception, cruelty – I left these to others. Mine were faults of a less grievous kind, amounting to no more than a streak of wildness. I often ignored my father's wishes and sometimes his orders. I resisted the plans he made for me. I preferred my own company to the society he wished me to enjoy.

On reflection, *independence* may be a better word than *wildness* for what I have just described. In either case the question remains: what caused it? In our early days we are blinded by the heat of moments as they pass, and seldom pause to consider. Now my youth is a distant memory, and I have a wider view of my existence, I am drawn more strongly to explanations.

The first is that my mother died of her trouble in bringing me into this world – which bred in me, as surely as if it had been one of her own characteristics, a tendency to regard myself as someone for whom the whole of life is a battle. Where no fight exists, I am likely to invent one in order to reassure myself of my own courage.

The second, which was solidified by my having neither brother nor sister, was the country in which we lived. By country I do not mean the nation, England, but rather the country-*side* – being the north shore of the river Thames, at a point of no particular consequence between London and the open sea. How this landscape appears now I can only imagine, not having returned home for many years. Most likely it is overbuilt by everything that is necessary for the business of docks and docking. But I can tell how it was then, exactly.

On the landward side of our house, the marshes stood a mere quarter-fathom above the surface of the water, and the quarter of a quarter at high tide. Any buildings thereabouts were hardly buildings at all, but rough arrangements of timber in which fishermen kept their gear, and other more secretive visitors dropped off or collected things that were precious to them. If the mist allowed, these shacks made an impressive silhouette, with spars protruding at strange angles, roofs slumped forward like fringes, and windows completing a lopsided face. To my young eyes they resembled a community of ogres, or at least warty witches all rubbing their hands over a cauldron. None of them stood upright for long. Whatever the wind did not knock flat, the marsh swallowed. As for the tracks that wandered between and beyond them: these soon forgot the destination they had in mind when they began their journeys, and ended in confusion or nothing at all.

If I have made the place sound fearsome, I have good reasons. Many times, walking alone under its vast sky, I heard footsteps behind me where none existed, or felt silence itself seizing my collar like a hand. Yet to tell the truth, the voices of the marsh, and of the river in particular, were never entirely one thing or the other;

they were a mixture of sounds, pitched between sighing and laughter, as though they had never decided whether they meant to convey sorrow or joy. Perverse as it may seem, this is what I especially loved about the place; it was always in two minds.

The picture I have already painted of my father will make him seem straightforward by comparison – and so he was in certain respects. In others he was as contradictory as the landscape that surrounded him. I shall now show why, from the beginning.

My father's own father had also been an innkeeper – of the Admiral Benbow in the West Country, around the coast from Bristol. Here he died young – whereupon my father found himself at the start of the great adventure that it has been my fate to continue. This adventure began with the sudden arrival at the Benbow of Billy Bones, a battered old salt who once upon a time had been the first mate of the notorious buccaneer Captain Flint, and whose sole possession was an even more knocked-about sea-chest. For a week or two, the presence of this rascal caused no great difficulty at the Benbow – until the appearance of a second stranger, a pale, tallowy creature who, despite his ghostly countenance, went by the name of Black Dog – and soon after him a blind man named Pew, whose effect was so shocking that poor Bones fell dead almost the instant he saw him. To be particular, Pew tipped him the Black Spot; a man cannot long survive, once he has received that fatal sign.

There soon followed a whole history of dramatic episodes: an assault on the inn by pirates; a miraculous escape; the discovery of an ancient map; a perusal of the map; the understanding that treasure had been left by Captain Flint on a certain island; an expedition planned in Bristol and launched to recover said treasure; the treachery of the crew, and especially of a smooth-talking rogue named John Silver, who came ornamented with a parrot in compensation for missing a leg; a very dangerous and thrilling sojourn on the island; the discovery of some parts of the treasure; and a subsequent return to England and safety.

I have mentioned all this in summary, omitting the names of most of the principal characters and even some parts of the adventure itself, for the important reason that I have heard it told so many hundreds of times by my father, I cannot bear to write it down at greater length. Even the most celebrated stories in the world, including perhaps that of Our Lord himself, weary with the retelling. I will only add, in the interest of illuminating what follows, that close attention should be paid to the phrase *some parts of the treasure*, in order to encourage the idea that certain *other parts of it* were left undisturbed. I will also point out that when my father eventually quit the island, three especially troublesome members of the crew – whom my father called *maroons* – were left behind to meet whatever fate they might find. Much of what remains to be said will depend on these details.

Once my father had returned to Bristol he received his share of the wealth, which was valued in total at the astonishing sum of seven hundred thousand pounds. He often boasted of the amount, using it as an excuse to moralise – in a rather more ambiguous way than he intended – on the wages of sin. Of his own portion he never spoke precisely, referring to it as merely 'ample' before running on to say how Ben Gunn, a wild-man he discovered on the island and helped to rescue, had been granted an allocation of one thousand pounds, which he contrived to spend in nineteen days, so that he was a beggar again on the twentieth and given a lodge to keep, which he had always feared.

Whatever the precise amount of my father's treasure, it was clear that he need lack for nothing so long as he did not follow the example of this Ben Gunn. Accordingly, he returned to his mother, who was now in sole charge of the Benbow in Black Hill Cove, and helped her to manage the place until he gained his majority. At that time, being tired of living in such an out-of-the-way spot, which contrasted very markedly with the excitement he had known on the high seas, he departed for London and devoted himself for several years to the pursuit of his own pleasure.

It is hard for any son to imagine the youth of his father – to the son, the father will generally be a creature of settled habits and solid opinions. Yet it is clear that throughout his time in the city, my parent lived more dashingly than I ever knew him do in the course of my own existence. Released from the burden of caring for his mother (who now rested her head on the shoulder of an affectionate and elderly sailor, who would shortly become her husband), and provoked by a million new temptations, he became by his own admission a *figure about the town*.

This was before the period in which a man of fashion would be able to cut his cheek upon his own collar if he turned his head too sharply. But it was nevertheless a time of increasing opportunity in our country, when a man of means could easily footle his way through a fortune if so inclined. My father was never one to spend the best part of a day patrolling the Strand just so that a young lady might notice the tension in his trouser-leg, and the particular shade of a canary glove. He was, however, of a disposition to enjoy himself – and it is evident from the gradual slide in his fortunes that a period of living in fine lodgings, with good pictures on the walls, and expensive china on the table, and servants to bring him whatever comforts he required, was sufficient to consume a large part of the wealth he had dug from those distant sands.

Whether he would eventually have slithered all the way into poverty I cannot say. What I know for certain is this: before his third decade was very far advanced (which is to say the first part of the 1780s), he encountered the steadying influence that was my mother. She was the daughter of an ostler who ran a successful business on the eastern edge of the city, where day-visitors from Edmonton and Enfield would stable their horses, and often stay for dinner before completing their journeys home. Her experience in this place had turned a diligent child into a thrifty young woman. She soon persuaded my father to moderate his ways, and set him on the path that led to respectability in the world. He surrendered his cards and dice. He abandoned certain doubtful connections. He regulated his hours. He made himself a more pleasing prospect. And when he had showed the steadiness of his resolve for almost a year, she accepted the sincerity of his feelings and they were married.

It now became necessary for my parents to find useful employment. The obvious choice, given the history of both of them, was to run an inn – which soon they did. Not, however, an inn lying close to either of their previous connections, but one that proved the spirit of independence I would like to claim as my inheritance. The inn I have already mentioned, and will now give its proper name: the Hispaniola.

The place was at once marriage-bed, home and livelihood. And one more thing besides. For it was here, after only a year of bliss, in a room more like a fo'c'sle than anything on dry land, with a timber ceiling and walls, and a bay window overlooking the river, that my mother gave breath to me and was deprived of her own life in one and the same instant. I had, of course, no immediate knowledge of this. But from my first moment of remembered consciousness, which occurred some three years later, I was aware of what I had lost. To speak plainly: I grew up in an atmosphere stained by melancholy.

The weight of bereavement must nearly have broken my father. If the evidence of my own eyes had not told me this, I would have understood it from those who drank in our taproom, and had known him before the tragedy occurred. In the accounts they gave me, what had formerly been spirited in him was now subdued, what had looked for excitement now longed for moderation, and what had imagined the future now clung to the past.

You might wonder how the Hispaniola managed to survive these changes in my father. Sadness, after all, is not the common fare of inns. Yet survive it did – for reasons that shed some light on the variety of pleasures men seek in the world. Some individuals, it is true, did not appreciate his sombre character, and these my father dismissed with directions to other establishments on the waterfront, which they might find more to their taste. But there were few ejections of this kind. The majority of our neighbours looked on the Hispaniola as a welcome relief from the raucousness and vulgarity of the world. They considered it a haven.

In saying this, I realise that I might appear to suggest my father had an unfriendly and withdrawn character. Yet while he could certainly seem fierce he also understood the need for human beings to live in the world – which I saw in his determination that I should have a better education than any he had received himself. The school he chose for me was in Enfield; I was dispatched there at the age of seven, and remained a 'boarder' for a large part of every year until I was sixteen.

This establishment, which was proud to describe itself as a Dissenting Academy, was managed by a liberal-minded gentleman whose good qualities deserve great praise. But I do not propose to divert myself from my story in order to dwell on this part of my existence. Suffice it to say that when I eventually returned home again I had 'the tastes of a gentleman' in reading and writing, and a clear idea of what it means to behave with decent concern for others. Also, and in spite of the influences to which I had been exposed, I had a quickened appetite for what had always pleased me most: my own company, and the life of the river and marshes.

I must mention one further thing before I continue any further – and that is another paradox. In his sadness after my mother's death, my father often seemed the opposite of grieving. This was thanks to his habit of reliving the adventures of his youth, as I have already mentioned. Sometimes this was done at the request of new customers who knew his reputation and wanted to share a part of his history. But when no such requests were forthcoming, he was inclined to tell the stories anyway, pausing sometimes to expand on a moment of particular danger, or to digress into the background of an especially striking individual or event.

Indeed, it would be fair to say that long before my boyhood was over, the story of Treasure Island had become almost the whole of my father's conversation. Its inhabitants were more companionable to him than the customers he served, and more vivid to me. They were not quite inventions, and not quite figures from history, but a blend of these things. This almost persuaded me I might have met them myself, and had seen with my own eyes the wickedness of John Silver the sea-cook; and glimpsed the Black Spot passing into the hand of Billy Bones; and even watched my father himself when he was a child, climbing the mast of the *Hispaniola* to escape Israel Hands, then firing his pistols so that Hands fell into the clear blue water, and finally sank onto its sandy bed, where he lay with the little fishes rippling to and fro across his body.

With the mention of these ghosts, I am ready to begin my story. I will therefore ask you to remember where we stood a moment ago – on the marshes behind the Hispaniola – and then to jump forward a few hours. My solitary day had ended and I was reluctantly wandering home. Darkness had fallen. The moon had risen. Mist crawled along the river. When I stepped indoors from the towpath, candle flames burned still and straight in the warm air of the taproom, where my father's adventures were once again approaching their crisis before an audience of visitors. I kept in the background of the scene, slipping upstairs to my bedroom so that I did not have to follow him through the final windings of his tale.

A moment later I had reached my own space under the roof. This was the least comfortable room in the house – hardly a room at all, but infinitely precious to me because it was like a cabinet of curiosities. Every wall was covered with shelves, on which I had arranged the feathers, shells, eggs, pieces of twisted wood, rope, skulls, curious knots and other trophies I had collected from the marsh in the course of my short but busy life. And in the middle of this cabinet, my crow's-nest – which I might properly call my bed, where I lay every night to survey the rolling universe. Here it was that I lay down at last. And here it was that I turned my face to the window.

The towpath was deserted, patched by a large square of yellow light falling from the taproom window. The marshes all around had been simplified by moonlight into an arrangement of powdery grey and greens. The river seemed a richer kind of nothing – a gigantic ingot of solid silver, except that now and again it crinkled when a log rolled silently past, or a dimple appeared and then vanished.

I lay staring for long enough to feel I was entranced, and so cannot tell exactly when the boat and its occupant arrived. One moment the water was empty. The next it featured the crescent of a hull, with a figure sitting upright in the centre, oars in both hands, holding the vessel steady against the current. What sort of figure I could not say, only that it appeared slim and youthful; the head was covered with a shawl and the face was invisible.

It was an unusual sight so late in the evening. More remarkable still was the way the figure seemed to stare at me directly, even though it could not possibly have seen me in the lightless window. I propped myself on my elbows, but gave no other sign of interest. As I did so, the figure released the oar from its right hand, allowed the boat to spin a little, lifted this hand in a solemn salute, then beckoned for me to come near.

CHAPTER 3

My Visitor

So great was my astonishment at being invited to meet my shadowy visitor, I could not obey, but continued to lie unmoving on my bed. After several minutes, during which nothing in the world seemed to change, I grew uncomfortable and sat upright. At this, the long oars immediately plunged downwards, the boat turned round, and the silhouette disappeared as moonlight shuddered across the surface of the water.

What had I seen? A prank of some kind? Something not meant for me, but for a customer in the taproom below? Or was there a less comfortable explanation – namely, that I had seen a sprite or a vision. When I eventually rolled onto my back, I lay awake until the last of my father's customers had made his farewell and departed along the towpath, without reaching a definite answer. The clear light of morning, I hoped, would make everything obvious to me.

It has been my habit since childhood to rise early, no doubt because my father required me to help him prepare the Hispaniola for her voyage through each new day. (I say *help him*, though generally I worked single-handed, while he dozed.) On the morning after my visitation, my eyes flew open so suddenly I thought someone had called my name. Possibly they had, since when I peered through my window again – there was the boat come back. Suspended in the current as if it had never left.

Because the sun had just risen, and although mist was curling over the water, as well as lying more thickly across the marshes in the background, I could make out the detail of things more definitely than I had been able to do the night before. The boat was a wherry, with the wood of the hull well maintained and polished, and a name painted in flowing black letters around the prow: the *Spyglass*.

In the stern of the boat, covered by a plain orange cloth, was a domed object like a large thimble, about two feet tall, which I could not explain. The figure seated at the oars was also very puzzling. The whole upper part of the body was swathed in a tartan blanket, whose reds and greens made a powerful contrast with the grey of the river. Another blanket, this one sober brown and small enough to be used as a shawl, was drawn around the head and shoulders and concealed the face entirely. I guessed, rather than knew, that the eyes were turned towards me, which produced a strange sense of reversal: I was in hiding (behind the protection of my window) but felt in full view. The thought unnerved me, and as I steadied myself against the wall of my room, the figure did as I half-feared and half-hoped. It raised a hand and beckoned to me for a second time.

I did not need a third invitation. Stamping into my boots without tying their laces, and descending the stairs with my feet unnaturally wide apart to avoid falling over myself, and at the same time as quietly as possible to avoid waking my father, I passed through the smoke-scented air of the taproom and outside onto the towpath. I did not pause to think how foolish I must look, nor to imagine what dangers I might be courting. Although my visitor was full of mystery, there was no menace that I could detect.

The sharpness of the air made me cough – which produced an answering chuckle. I took this to be a form of mockery, and spoke more rudely than I might otherwise have done.

'What do you want?'

The words hung heavily in the stillness, and after leaving a decent space for reply but receiving none, I stepped forward – half-expecting to drive my visitor away again. In fact the wherry immediately veered towards me – and as the prow hissed into the grass over-hanging the bank, I bent to collect the mooring rope, pulled it tight, then took the marlin-spike tied to the end and pushed it into the earth. I felt I was obeying an order, although none had been given.

When I straightened again, the figure had arranged itself to look at me, still facelessly, with water trickling in silver links from the oars he held poised above the surface of the river. Once again I was startled into boldness.

'Who are you?'

Without any more to-do, the figure slowly took hold of the hem of the shawl, raised it, and showed its face. This was all done in the manner of a play, and I was immediately delighted – making a theatrical delay of my own, so that I had time to notice the hair crowning the face was very dark and cut short, the skin a warm olive-brown, the lips broad and the nose less so. I decided that it was beautiful, though whether it belonged to a boy or a girl I still could not be sure. More certainly, I knew it was a face with the power to lead me on, and to give instructions I could not easily ignore.

Later, I would understand how the seclusion of my childhood was being exploited for a purpose of which I had no knowledge. At the time, I was purely and simply flattered that such an appealing creature had sought me out. Squatting on my haunches, I brought our eyes level in a way that would have seemed intimate had it not been so innocent: I wanted to look into her eyes to understand my situation better. A girl's eyes, I was now sure. Deep brown, with scratches of green in them. Eyes which showed amusement, yet also withheld something nearly opposite.

When she spoke, I heard the same qualities in her voice. It contained a smile as well as severity. 'You refused to come down to me last night, Jim Hawkins.'

'I did not know I was invited.'

'I beckoned to you.'

I protested that I had not seen in the darkness, and reminded her it had been very late. Then I tried to regain some of the advantage her questions had taken from me, by asking one of my own.

'Where did you spend the night? Surely not on the river?'

'Why not on the river?' she came back at me. 'It is summer. I have my blanket.' She settled the shawl more smoothly across her shoulders, then patted the springy wires of her hair.

When her hands returned to her lap, I glanced at them and saw she was not telling the whole truth. The tips of her fingers were wizened with cold. This made me wonder whether I should ask her to come inside and warm herself in the taproom, but on second thoughts I decided that she belonged in the open air. 'Can I fetch you something to drink?' I asked. 'For your breakfast?'

'A noggin, thank you,' she said. Although the answer was one that my father's more ancient customers might easily have given, I went to do her bidding without delay. This was partly because I wanted to collect my thoughts in private. It was immediately apparent that my visitor was unlike anyone among our neighbours. While this drew me to her, it was also baffling. She was certainly mysterious, with the air of being engaged on a secret mission, but she was also steady – and this was the strangest thing of all. When I looked through the taproom window of the Hispaniola, while pouring our grog into two glasses, I found that she was not glancing round or showing that she was on guard in some other way; she had calmly settled herself on the farther side of her seat, so there would be space for me to fit beside her when I returned. All this might have seemed unaffected, and so in a way it was. Yet it was also done with an air of planning, and left me pondering her larger intentions.

When I came back outside, I stepped into the boat and passed her the grog as though it were the most sensible thing imaginable to drink hard liquor outside at six o'clock in the morning. Then I sat beside her with a show of conviction that was meant to match her own. As we began talking, alternately sipping the grog and chewing the two pieces of bread I had also produced, some of the mysteries of the *Spyglass* lifted. The name itself was taken from the inn owned by her mother and father – in London, close to the docks in Wapping. Her own name was Natalie, often shortened to Nat or Natty, since (she said with her characteristic air of simplicity) it sometimes suited her to pass as a boy. I wanted to question her about this, wondering what could require such a measure, but delayed in case I stopped the run of her confidences. Her age, for example; I wanted to know her age. All she would say was it was not much greater or less than my own, which at the time was a few months short of eighteen.

Throughout this conversation Natty glanced from time to time at the object she had placed in the stern, and then towards me, as if challenging me to ask what it might be. The truth is, I had already decided – thanks to the whistling and warbling that occasionally floated through the cloth. I recognised them as the sounds made by a starling, and assumed it was a bird she kept in a cage for company, and the amusement of its imitations.

I now did as I felt I had been invited to do, and asked if I could see the bird. Natty immediately bent forward to remove the cloth – and revealed not what I had supposed, but the starling's larger relative, a mynah. I had never before seen one except in drawings, and felt at once that none of these had done justice to the reality. It was a most impressive bird, with very glossy black feathers, a large yellow bill, and a shrewd red eye. On seeing my face for the first time, it cocked its head on one side and said in a rasping voice, 'Leave me alone! Leave me alone!'

I laughed at this, which the bird did not find at all entertaining; it stabbed fiercely at the bars of its cage.

'This is Spot,' Natty told me, anticipating my question. 'Take care what you say in his hearing. He will most likely remember it.'

'Good morning, Spot,' I said solemnly – which started some banter about the origins of the bird, its age, its repertoire, and suchlike. By the time this had run its course, I was in a kind of daze – for which the grog should probably take some responsibility, as well as Natty herself. Her voice had entered me, carrying its meanings into my mind and heart, yet also seemed to play over me – like light or water. In between her words, I heard the sound of the river fingering the planks of the hull, and felt the growing warmth of the sun as it destroyed the last rags of mist on either side of us. Every so often another little gang of vessels would glide past, and our talk would be interrupted by the creak of oars or a sail. At other times it was footsteps along the towpath, and a voice calling down 'Good morning', as my neighbours set off to their work. Occasionally the interruptions were my own – when I lifted my eyes to the windows of the Hispaniola, for example, and wondered whether my father would wake, and see us, and come down to demand an introduction. More generally, though, I kept my eyes fixed on Natty's face, or on the little pools of water that lulled and glittered among the duckboards beneath our feet. It is strange to admit, but the initial surprise of our meeting had already given way to a feeling of complete trustfulness. It seemed that our friendship was new in nothing but name.

When we reached the more precise reason for her visit, this sense of intimacy was to some extent explained. I have already described how my father had repeatedly been drawn into telling the story of his boyhood adventures; the character he most often invoked was the one-legged buccaneer John Silver. *Long* John Silver to his friends, as well as his enemies, who was also known as Barbecue on account of his being a sea-cook. At the end of each telling and retelling – with Captain Flint's coins rescued from the sand of Treasure Island, and my father and others (including Mr Silver himself) safely ashore in Spanish America – my father always gave the same detail. Mr Silver, he would say, had given his companions the slip, taking with him a part of the hoard, which was worth some four hundred guineas.

My father did not only mean to shock his audience when he revealed this. There was generally a note of admiration in his voice, to indicate that he and Mr Silver had a kind of sympathy because, during the course of their adventures, each had saved the other's life. Perhaps this was the reason he liked to speculate about the later existence of his hero. Some evenings, depending on the amount of drink he had taken, and the enthusiasm of his listeners, my father would imagine Mr Silver dragging through Mexico and into the south of America itself, perhaps to sink at last into an inland sea of rum, as Captain Flint had done before him in Savannah. Or perhaps to become a buccaneer again, and take to the high seas in pursuit of further adventure. Perhaps even to return to England and the wife he had left there.

The name of the boat in which I was now sitting should have told me that only one of my father's speculations was likely to be true: the inn where my father had first met Mr Silver was called the Spyglass, which was also the name of a hill overlooking the site of the treasure on the island and, I now supposed, the name of Natty's home. I blame my failure to see the significance of the letters curling around the prow of the boat – almost under my hand! – on the distractions created by my companion. That said, the basis of the connection I had felt with Natty now grew increasingly clear, as our talk veered into more open waters.

If it is not already obvious what I mean by this, let me speak plainly. Natty's father was John Silver – which she now told me as a matter of fact. My first response, I am embarrassed to say, was to glance down at her legs, and be sure she had not inherited his disadvantage. To hide my foolishness, and any nervousness I might have felt about her kinship with so disreputable a man, I said:

'And your mother?'

Natty pursed her lips, then began speaking fluently. As I listened, I felt the sunlight strengthening across my scalp, and saw wisps of steam rising from the roof of the Hispaniola, as if it were about to catch fire.

Silver had first met his wife on one of the islands of the Caribbean Sea, where he had courted her in his rough way before returning with her to Bristol. She was younger than him, being really no more than a girl when they first met, but already bold enough to fulfil the role he required of her, which was to join him in the management of the Spyglass. The same Spyglass in which he would eventually meet my father, and from which he would sail to Treasure

Island. When this momentous journey took place, Mr Silver's wife did as she had always done during such absences: stood guard for her husband and repelled those who tried to take advantage. (As Natty told me this, she gave a sharp sense of her mother's beauty as well as her courage.)

On this particular cruise Mr Silver was away for many months – so many, in fact, that his wife began to imagine the sea might have swallowed him, or some other tragedy had struck. But she knew better than to feel convinced of this, and in due course her husband returned to her – in disguise, in so far as any man minus a leg, and whose constant companion is a voluble parrot, can ever be said to be in disguise.

Natty told me this last detail with a smile that showed all her small white teeth, and proved that she regarded her father not merely as a parent, but as a *character*. It was a further example, I decided, of how she stood a little detached from life, observing its ebb and flow as if she did not entirely care whether events had one outcome or another.

'What sort of disguise might that have been, I wonder?' I said this hoping to surprise Natty into something candid – but she immediately slid back into the smooth current of her story, as if she were reciting a speech learned by heart. The changes her father had made to himself were more a matter of alterations within than without, in the sense that he had reformed himself during his absence. He had left Bristol a buccaneer, with a skill in pretending to be far nobler than he ever was, and returned denouncing his former habits. He had asked forgiveness for his trespasses. He set himself to his old business, of running the Spyglass, as though to manage such an establishment were all he had ever wanted to do in the world.

Natty herself was the living proof of this new steadiness, and as

I watched her pause for a moment, tear another piece from the bread I had provided, and place it in her mouth with a contemplative slowness, I felt our sympathy increase still further. I told myself that although the story of our two childhoods appeared to be very different – mine solitary and natural whenever my schooling allowed it, hers lived in a perpetual hubbub – in truth they were similar, because a shadow lay across them both. The shadow of our fathers' adventures.

At the same time, I did not know how much of his past Mr Silver might have revealed to his daughter. In particular, I found it difficult to believe that he had told her about his history as a buccaneer. His treacheries and murders. His double-dealing. His slippery pursuit of wealth at any cost. Alternatively, Natty might be perfectly familiar with the whole story of his life, and not care what it had contained. This left me with a deep question: was my companion an innocent, sprung from ancient corruption? Or was she an expert in the art of dissembling, as her father had also been?

I did not want to decide – not on our first morning together. I was too interested in knowing what purpose Natty had in coming to find me, beyond establishing what we had already discussed. I knew that everything we had said so far was nothing but a kind of scene-setting, and realised that my original question ('What do you want?') had been deferred. Now I returned to it again.

'Why have you come here?' I said.

Natty evidently felt, as I did, that we had enjoyed ourselves long enough, and had reached the time for business. 'My father sent me,' she replied very directly.

I was about to ask how he knew where to find me, when she continued without any encouragement.

'He has not liked to inconvenience your father, although he has known for a long time that you are living here. He did not want to disturb an old acquaintance who might not believe him to be the man he has become.'

It was now my turn to smile, imagining how reluctant my father would have been to change his opinion of Mr Silver. I began to confirm this, saying, 'I think –' But I was interrupted.

'My father wants to meet you,' Natty said. 'He has asked me to fetch you.' She paused as suddenly as she had begun, and her right hand lifted to brush a speck from my shoulder. The gesture was meant to soften me, and it succeeded. Rather than denying her request, or putting some difficulty in its way, I merely said:

'Today?'

'Today if possible,' she replied. 'Though not you alone. My father has asked me to say: does your father still own the map, and if he does, would he allow you to bring it to him?'

At this, sheer astonishment at her boldness overwhelmed everything, and I could not help half-shouting, 'The map! My father's map! Borrowing it!'

Natty said nothing but sat with her shoulders slumped, staring along the river to the point where it swerved out of sight towards London. It was clear that she had expected my incredulity, and knew it must run a course. The effect was to make me feel I had been reproached, when in truth I knew I should be reproaching her. It was extraordinary to think that her father – a pirate, a *murderer* – should approach my father in so casual a way. Worse than extraordinary, in fact. Insulting and impossible. As far as my father was concerned, Mr Silver was a monstrous impostor; he deserved jail or the gallows, and not cooperation.

I debated with myself how best to sink Natty's request so that it would never rise again, also staring downriver and concentrating very fiercely on a family of moorhens that were fussing around their nest. As I did so, my mind began to change. Natty's remarks, when I considered them, were not addressed to my father. They were addressed to me. Would *I* take the map. Would I, in fact, be willing to enter into dealings that my father would think were nothing less than criminal?

Natty began to hum a tune under her breath; I recognised it as 'Lillibullero', a melody I have always liked. I made no comment, but continued gazing ahead, as if I might find the answer to all my questions in studying the moorhens as they dived for food, then bobbed to the surface again with water breaking in jewels across their feathers. When I was tired of this, I turned to examine Spot once more. He was not in the least interested in my cogitations, but preened the feathers of one wing with smooth and steady tugs.

The map, I understood, was the map of Treasure Island. I had never seen it. I was not even certain that it was still in my father's possession. But I knew where it would be, if he did still own it. In the chest that stood at the foot of his bed. The chest that – as he had told me a thousand times – once belonged to Billy Bones. (It had remained in the Admiral Benbow following the death of that reprobate, and was claimed by my father as a reward for his troubles, when he returned to the inn after his journey to the island.) My father had nowhere else to hoard his valuables, which explained why he guarded this chest with a special vigilance, keeping its key tied at all times around his neck on a piece of string. I had never laid a hand on this key, much less turned it in the lock of the chest. But I accepted that if I were to do so, I would in all probability find the article that Mr Silver wanted.

The second and larger mystery, of whether I dare take it, remained to be solved.

'Do you know why your father wants this map?' I asked at length, in a voice that I hoped would convey a sense of general bafflement.

Natty broke off her humming and dipped a hand into the river; the water closed round it with a faint clucking noise, as if it were thick as treacle. 'Of course,' she said, at exactly the same moment as I spoke myself, and followed my original question by saying, 'I can guess.'

The coincidence of our speaking together was enough to end the solemnity that had crept over us, and we smiled again. This lightening, however, did not help me settle what answer I should give. I decided the best I could do, and the course of action least likely to cause harm, was to tell the truth.

'I do not know whether my father has a map,' I told her.

'I said *the* map,' Natty replied, with a note of impatience.

'*The* map, then.'

'But if . . .'

'But if he did have the map,' I said, taking up her words, 'I know where it might be found.' As I spoke, a cloud sailed across the sun and the sparkle died on the river, turning its traffic from a joyful bustle into a melancholy procession. A ferry-boat taking passengers towards London suddenly appeared to be on its way to the under-world. A coal barge, carried by a single ashen sail along the centre of the current, broke a black wash against the side of our wherry. If I had not been so thoroughly seized by the gravity of what I was now contemplating, I might have laughed at the thought of the world so obviously judging my behaviour, and finding me wanting. As it was I merely frowned.

Natty would not allow matters to rest. 'And where might that be?' she persisted.

'Oh,' I said, then hesitated again. I was imagining how I would creep silently to my father's bedside as he slept, slip the key from around his neck, open the chest, riffle through its contents until I found the map, remove it, lock the chest again, return the key, then make my escape – and all in complete darkness, without making a sound!

It was a preposterous idea. Preposterous because dangerous. And preposterous for other reasons, as well. Because the deception – no, the theft – would be a betrayal of my father. He had done nothing to deserve such treachery. Making me toil in his taproom? Leaving me too much to myself? Boasting? Wasting time on former glories? These were hardly unnatural sins that justified unnatural actions.

'Oh?' said Natty, echoing me.

'I'm not sure,' I said. And then, as if I were speaking for a ghost that lived inside me, or was being manipulated by Natty herself, I added, 'Map or no map, I should like to meet your father.'

It was not just curiosity that made me say this, but a sense that something so merely inquisitive could hardly be counted a crime. I was of course denying to myself the possibility that it might be a step towards crime.

Natty straightened her back, as if a burden had been lifted from her. 'When?' she asked.

'Today,' I told her, full of confidence. 'Now. I shall go inside to my father, and tell him not to expect me until this evening.'

With that I collected our two empty glasses, and stood up so abruptly the boat dipped and rasped against the bank – then stepped onto the towpath. When I paused in the doorway to look round, Natty had already untethered the *Spyglass*. She sat with the prow pointing towards London, the oars in her hands, and her face filled with the satisfaction of someone who is doing what they have always expected to do. Spot was looking in the same direction, and when he began talking, his words reached me very clearly. 'Hoist the mainsail,' he said. 'Hoist the mainsail.'

CHAPTER 4

To Wapping

Nothing was said or done on our journey to London that suggested my life had abruptly changed. Yet as the river carried us forward I felt I was not so much setting out from home as leaving it. The wide marshes smoking in the early sun were a sight that I had known all my life, but now they seemed as bewildering as images in a dream. Even before the Hispaniola sank below the horizon, I had started to think that ghosts might feel as I did – being intimate with the places they haunt, while remaining separate from them.

Natty took charge of the journey for our first few miles; I sat in the stern beside Spot, who tilted his head to observe me through the bars of his cage and made a continuous low hissing noise, which proved how greatly he resented my company. It was not in the least surprising to see Natty so expert in everything she did – strong as a boy in her handling of the oars, and like a boy too in the way she hardly seemed conscious of herself, but only of the task she performed. When sweat trickled from her forehead along her nose, she pouted and puffed it away; if other craft dared show any sign of wanting to cross her path, she shouted at their pilots to have a care. I understood she did not want to speak to me while she worked, and contented myself with watching. Although I often threw her a smile, and wished her to know I admired her dexterity, I felt the looks she gave me in return were intended to cut directly through me, in order to concentrate on some invisible thing that followed behind us.

I soon settled for living in a kind of trance. The marshes slid by as if a hand had descended from heaven to unroll a canvas of infinite length, on which everything seemed static and a picture of itself. Here was a piebald pony, clambering onto a shingle-spit as though debating whether to take a bath. Here was a boatyard where boys melted tar in a bucket – the heavy smell crawled over the river like a shadow. Here was a knot of sailors' homes around a stagnant inlet, and here a complete large village, where the inhabitants were beginning their day of chattering, bargaining, working, cursing and comforting. Each of them took as much notice of the *Spyglass* as if she had been a water-bug. Likewise the sailors looking down from their high decks, or the oarsmen in their rowing-boats that were more nearly our equal. They had their own business to attend to, and concentrated on that.

The estrangement continued even when my manners revived (I mean: when I had new orders from Natty) and I began to share the work of rowing. This was accomplished with a minimum of talk, as though we were old comrades dropping into familiar routines, and our silence continued for the final part of our journey. The effect was to make the beginning of my adventure seem inevitable. Our shoulders and arms (her right, my left) rubbed together with a soft friction. Cold river-water dripped onto our knees, and puddled around our shoes. Our lips blew out steady gasps, whereupon our breath mingled in a wake that (had we been able to see them) would have imitated the curling signatures left by our oars on the surface of the water.

In as little as an hour – such was the force of the current working in our favour – we had travelled through Greenwich and reached a part of the river I barely knew. Here, watching the houses crowd together on the bank in much greater numbers, I had better reason to think I was entering a new phase of my existence. This was not because I had never been to London before: I had several times accompanied my father on trips to provision the Hispaniola, and to pay our respects (before their death) to my mother's parents in Shoreditch. It was more a matter of this being the first expedition I had made on my own account, fulfilling my own wishes.

If anyone had asked me to say precisely what those wishes might have been, I could not easily have told them. The pleasure of sitting beside Natty would have been one honest answer. More than that, my journey showed a willingness to see her father – but a willingness that was accompanied by a great deal of doubt. I had yet to decide, for instance, what I would say to Mr Silver when he questioned me about the map. I reached the same point of indecision when I debated with myself whether I might be able to steal it. In my surrender to Natty's invitation, I assumed that appropriate actions would occur at appropriate times.

As we came close to Wapping, the safety of the *Spyglass* required all our attention. It also persuaded Natty to break her silence, and give me instructions about how to avoid obstacles by swerving now this way and now that. Although I had lived on the river for most of my life, I did not feel in the least demeaned by this. So long as Natty presented us to the world as equal partners, and did not embarrass me by suggesting otherwise, I was content to do her bidding, and bide my time until my own initiative might be required.

In spite of her cleverness, the dangers of traffic squeezed so tightly together in this part of the river were a good reason to think we might be rammed and sunk at any moment. The distractions of the quayside made our risk all the greater. At home in the Hispaniola, staring from my father's windows, I had often seen ships returning from the four corners of the world, and let my imagination play among the bales of silk and boxes of spice they carried in their holds. Now, to look up from my seat in the *Spyglass* and contemplate the towering walls of such vessels – to see the scars inflicted by their voyages across enormous seas, to watch the sailors with their skins browned and hair bleached by the heat of exotic suns – made me feel that the dream into which I had fallen was spiralling downwards still further.

When Natty eventually lifted one hand and pointed towards the shore, I saw a pair of tall warehouses that appeared so nearly on the point of collapse they had leaned together and formed a kind of tunnel. I understood this was our destination, and pulled more sharply on my oar, as I was told to do. The *Spyglass* slid between two ships, entered much calmer water – and Natty's fist landed in my chest to push me backwards, so that we could more easily approach our landing-place by slipping beneath a web of mooring-ropes. In this way I had the appearance of a sleeper, as well as the drowsiness of one, when we reached the end of our journey.

I should more properly say: reached the end of one part of our journey and began the next. For as soon as we had tethered the *Spyglass* to a ring attached in the quay, and climbed a slimy ladder onto solid ground (which meant following Natty, and passing up to her the cage containing Spot, who objected loudly to this change in his circumstances), it was immediately obvious that I must sharpen my wits. In the space of a moment, I was entirely surrounded by men and women who did not care if they knocked me with their elbows, or struck me with their baskets, or trampled me with their clogs, or in some other way encouraged me to disappear over the side of the quay and into the river to drown.

Natty signalled to me, and we set off beneath the arch of warehouses. By now I was accustomed to behaving obediently with her, and soon found myself passing through a sort of labyrinth made of greasy walls and billowy washing-lines. When we escaped at last – which happened in a sudden blaze of sunlight – she turned towards me with a strange catch in her voice.

'This is my home,' she said.

It was a house backing onto the river: that much was obvious, since beyond it to left and right lay a glimmer of water. But a house built on what method was difficult to say, since the entire construction contained little of anything that is generally accepted as being necessary in a house, and much that is not. A single door was squeezed to one side of the façade, windows were scattered here and there (some oblong, some round, some square), the roof was pitched high over one side and dwindled almost to nothing on the other, and several chimneys (all breathing smoke) stuck out at unexpected angles like gigantic whiskers.

The composition of the thing was more peculiar still. For rather than being made of bricks and mortar, the walls were comprised of planks, spars, logs, branches, roots, pieces of barrel, and every other sort of wooden material the river happened to have carried within reach – some of them with barnacles and hanks of dried weed still attached. It was impossible to explain, unless the Thames had hoarded every scrap of its flotsam and jetsam for an appreciable time, then been provoked into flinging the whole collection into an upright position, where it remained thanks to a miracle of balance.

Hard wood and soft wood, dark wood and light wood, carved wood and plain wood had been hammered or bound together, without regard for any principle except that of chaos. Only one thing immediately made sense: the ancient brass telescope hanging above the door, which gave the building its name – the Spyglass.

I gazed at all this with such rapt attention, I only realised Natty had taken hold of my hand when she released it. Whether she felt cheered by the sight of home, or alarmed by the idea of how it might appear to me (and therefore wanting to set me at my ease), she now became more talkative.

'You will ask my father how he built the house,' she told me. 'He becomes quite expansive on the subject.'

'I can see why he might,' I replied. 'But tell me yourself: when did he first come here?'

'Before I was born. With my mother.'

'You have said only a little about your mother,' I said, thinking I must soon meet her and needed to know as much beforehand as I thought I knew about Mr Silver.

'Does a person have to say much about their mother?'

'They do not,' I said. 'For instance, I will most definitely not even mention my own mother, because I do not have one.'

A shadow came over Natty's face, which made me regret I had spoken so crisply. 'My mother you shall meet soon,' she said. 'My father you will not see for long.'

'What do you mean?' I asked, but she did not answer immediately, only looked at me with a frown. It occurred to me then that her silence during our journey upriver had not been a result of indifference, but rather of absorption in herself – a kind of anxiety.

'My father . . .' she began at length, then faltered. I could see from the confusion in her face that a host of different explanations were clamouring for precedence. In the end she settled their argument by giving a sigh, and saying no more than this: 'My father is a very old man.'

Although I now felt more bewildered than ever by what Natty was trying to explain, or perhaps to conceal, I told her that I understood – and to make this answer seem as warm as I wished it to be, I reached forward and touched her arm. The upshot was the opposite of everything I meant. Natty flinched as if I had waved a flame at her, and backed away.

'Understanding, understanding,' she said impatiently, and avoided meeting my eye. 'So long as you are ready, that is all I need to know.'

With this she turned her back, pushed open the door, and invited me to follow as she began climbing the stairs that rose before us. I could not help noticing that Spot hopped from the floor of his cage onto his perch as she did so, and closed his eyes so tightly that wrinkles appeared among the feathers around their sockets.

The whole interior of the house was dark, and smelled strongly of damp and mould. It made the place rather disgusting, though whether I would have felt the same if we had entered any of the rooms we passed on our ascent, I had no way of knowing. When we had reached the landing on the first floor, I heard a rumble of conversation and laughter which suggested the taproom was nearby. On the second floor, beyond a door where Natty stopped and pressed her finger to her lips, then whispered, 'My mother,' I heard a woman singing. The music was a kind of ditty, a jaunty sound, although the strangeness of its setting made it seem melancholy. One verse in particular came through to me, which I have never forgotten:

> Take my heart, sweet Jesus, take my life,
> I borrowed them from you, now have them back.
> Come down to me, possess me as your wife,
> The breath I lose in you I never lack.

I tilted my head, meaning to enquire whether I should enter and introduce myself, but Natty's eyes widened as though the very idea were ridiculous. Once again, I had no choice but to agree – and so on we went, following the stairs upwards for several more flights in a succession of zigzags until I began to wonder whether we had reached a height that was actually dangerous.

I say this because I could not help noticing as we climbed that a gentle swaying movement began to affect the whole building. Gentle – but definite. It occurred to me that since entering the Spyglass we had somehow contrived to pass from a house onto a ship. Onto the top of a mast, in fact, from which there would be wide views over the river and the city, if only we could find a window to enjoy them. The murmur of the wind, as it tumbled all around us, added to this sensation of being at sea. It was at once absurd and thrilling, and gave me a shiver of excitement.

As we began the last and narrowest flight, Natty glanced over her shoulder and waggled her left hand (while still keeping hold of Spot's cage with the other) to show I must not make a sound. She meant well, I am sure, but the gesture reminded me of the shadow which had crossed her face when we had been waiting in the street a moment before. Whatever pleasure she had in carrying out her father's orders was accompanied by a good deal of nervousness, or perhaps even fearfulness. It gave a peculiar urgency to all her actions.

I took some comfort from this, since it suggested that Natty's feelings about Mr Silver might after all resemble those I had inherited from my own father. And for this reason it did not surprise me that my father now rose into my head like a spectre. 'Long John Silver,' I heard him say very distinctly, in the booming voice he used to attract the attention of customers in the fog of the Hispaniola. 'Long John Silver with his peg leg and his parrot and his plausible ways. Oh, he was a charmer, certainly, if lies and flattery can ever be called charming. At the end of everything, he was the most damnable villain in the world. I would as soon speak to him again as give my soul to the devil!'

If there had been a chance to think about these things more deeply, I would have seen that my presence in the Spyglass now damned *me* as a villain – and probably as a fool as well. But I was travelling too fast in the stream of my self-importance to feel the reality of such ideas. When Natty at last reached the head of the stairs, and turned to encourage me with a smile of the most melting sweetness, I had no thought in my brain except this: everything we did, we must do together.

CHAPTER 5

I Meet a Ghost

When Natty threw open the door to her father's room, I expected to find myself in some sort of aerial burrow or bolt-hole. The narrowing stairs had predicted this, and so did my father's opinion: Mr Silver would only have made his dangerous return to England if he had been sure of hiding in shadows.

I found nothing of the kind, but rather a deluge of such brilliant light that for a moment I was dazzled. When my sight returned, I saw I had entered a large cockpit, of which one wall was made entirely of glass, held together by the slenderest bars of wood. This window had been constructed in order to bulge outwards, and gave such an exceptional sensation of looking I could not decide whether it was *like* an eye, or whether I was actually *inside* an eye. In any event, I thought I might as well have been an eagle, because I was now able to scrutinise the city and everything it contained with the same clarity.

By the time I had taken this into account, and stepped forward to enjoy a precipitous view of the quay directly below me, where I could see our wherry lying like a seed among the larger ships, Natty seemed to have forgotten me. She had moved away as we entered the room, slinking along the wall furthest from the window as though she disdained its vistas, and coming to a halt alongside the figure I now turned to see for the first time.

Thanks to my father's stories of Treasure Island, Long John Silver had first come into my mind with the appearance and habits of a demon. His only saving grace was the trick of expediency; in all other respects he was entirely evil – a 'horror', my father used to say, 'of cruelty, duplicity and power'. The screech of his parrot – 'Pieces of eight! Pieces of eight!', like the clacking of a tiny mill – was a refrain of my nightmares. Another was the tap-tap-tap of his wooden leg, his left leg, which replaced the original he had lost in his country's service under the immortal Hawke. Whenever I felt liable for any sort of punishment, and often when I did not, I had a dread of feeling the stab of his wooden crutch, which he would aim and fling with extraordinary ferocity, like a thunderbolt between my shoulder blades.

With the passage of time these childish fears receded – in the way of such things – and in some cases even modified into images I paraded in my mind's eye, in order to calculate how much braver I was becoming. It impressed me that whenever I belittled Mr Silver my father would call me an ignorant boy who knew nothing of the world. But while these reprimands reduced me to silence, they did not alter my opinion. Long John Silver, I am ashamed to say, had gradually been diminished by familiarity into a feeble form of his original self.

As my eyes lit on him now, I knew at once that I had been a fool to ignore my father's judgement. I say this in spite of the ways in which time had eroded the contours of the man's body. He was lying on a chaise longue covered in faded green cloth, the velvet patched here and there with darker swatches, wearing an immense blue coat, thick with brass buttons, that would have hung as low as his knee if he had been able to stand; the high collar rose up around his ears and pushed them outwards.

To call this body *emaciated* does not do justice to the ravages it had suffered – especially since he had detached his wooden leg (from close by the hip) and laid it on the floor beside him. It would be better to say that his form seemed to be *disintegrating*, even as I looked at it: the collapsed folds of his trousers, the speckled brown stalk of his single leg, where it protruded beside its absent partner; the chest sunk beneath the grimy flounces of his shirt: all these led me to marvel that the spirit governing them was still active, and to suppose it could not endure much longer.

It was the head, and not the body, that made me recognise the menace my father had so often complained about. According to him, Mr Silver's face had been as big as a ham – smooth and plain and pale, but intelligent and smiling. Now it was shrivelled and sunken, and capped with hair that had become so extremely sparse it was more like an arrangement of threads than anything natural, and hung greasily from his crown as far as his shoulders. This itself seemed to imply a sort of abandonment, and was made all the more alarming by the fact that his eyes, which I had expected to see fixed on my own with a seductive intensity, boiled from side to side and were completely clouded over. Mr Silver was blind.

While this affliction might have produced an appearance of pathos in other men, and a mood of dependency, in him it had only inspired rage – which he was continually trying to control. His head rocked on the gold cushion that supported it, while his left hand clenched and unclenched beside his absent leg, as though searching for a dagger he might hurl instead of a greeting.

'Are you there? Are you there?' he demanded, scratching the air with his right hand. The voice was not so much exhausted as weathered – scrubbed and ridged and whitened.

'I'm here, Father,' said Natty, whose own voice rang very sweetly, although its mollifying tone had no effect. Once again the hand rose impatiently, and now that I looked more closely, I saw it bore the faded mark of a tattoo, blue and purple, running upwards from the knuckles and disappearing beneath the untidy shirt-cuff. I thought it might be a snake, with the mouth open and fangs about to strike.

'I'm here, Father,' Natty repeated.

Since entering the cockpit I had been so preoccupied by the magnificence of its view, and the mingled decrepitude and threat of its sightless inhabitant, I had not paused to consider Natty's behaviour. Now a host of questions rushed into my mind. Why had she not introduced me to her father? Did she want to give the impression that she was alone? She was certainly ignoring me, avoiding my eye as she set down the cage for her bird (on a small round table that was evidently its regular home), and tugging her shawl more tightly around her shoulders. As I watched a frown begin to cloud her face, it seemed there was an element of subterfuge in her actions, as well as of reassurance.

I was confused by these thoughts, which made me wonder who was the governing authority in the room? My uncertainty soon deepened. Instead of taking her father's hand and planting a chaste kiss on his skull, Natty bent to the still-twitching figure and rubbed her cheek against the side of his face like a cat. At this the old man finally lay still. 'My love,' I think he said, although it may have been

'My *life*'. When this was done, he inched his sparrow-body across the chaise, making a space for her to lie down next to him. This she did willingly, sliding her arm across his chest. I could not see her face, which was buried in the material of his topcoat. His own face continued to stare directly towards the invisible view; it was a mask of bliss.

The embrace continued for at least a minute, during which father and daughter lay in each other's arms without any acknowledgement of my presence. I have thought about the scene a thousand times since, often unhappily, but however I change the angle of my regard, I end with the same conclusion. The question of control was exceedingly vexed. Mr Silver had no remaining physical power to carry out his wishes, yet he still possessed a determined mind. Natty's intelligence was not yet independent, but her youth and energy gave her a kind of domination. They appeared to have settled the contest between their abilities by developing an exceptional devotion. A *love*, indeed, that I saw at once might mean the rejection of anyone else who wanted their attention.

As if to confirm the unease provoked by these thoughts, Spot now began to fidget very nervously, scraping his wings against the bars of his cage and repeatedly opening and closing his beak as though about to regurgitate a word or two. When he finally succeeded, he began the same phrase I had heard him utter before, when I first made his acquaintance outside the Hispaniola: 'Leave me alone! Leave me alone!' In the same instant that he began to speak, Natty suddenly sat upright, keeping her place beside her father's shoulder, and patted her hair like someone waking from a refreshing sleep.

Although she smiled directly at me, it was her father she spoke to: 'Now,' she said quietly, 'we must get to business. I have brought Mr Hawkins to see you, Father, as you asked.' Her tone of voice was absolutely even, and the look in her eye absolutely steady, as if she were daring me to object that I had seen anything strange or disconcerting.

'Mr Hawkins!' the old man cawed, as if he were a bird himself, and extended both his arms towards me. The idea that he might expect me to embrace him was something that filled me with revulsion, and I stood my ground – which of course he did not actually see. 'Mr Hawkins!' he said again, in the same crooning tone. 'My-my, boy, here's a treat for an old man. Come here. Come here and sit by me. Let me *see* you.' He pronounced the word *see* with a drawling slowness that made me want to shrink away – but as if I had lost the command of my faculties, I now moved forward until I found myself sitting on the chaise longue across from Natty, almost touching the bare brown skin of her father's leg. At this proximity, I could not help noticing the smell hanging over him – very musty and dark, as if he had lain underground for a while and recently been resurrected.

I sat still as a statue, accepting with a kind of passive sorrow that everything I now did, every breath I inhaled, was either a betrayal or repudiation of my father. I felt incapable of taking any other course. Natty, meanwhile, had kept her place on the opposite side of the chaise and gave me another of her sweet smiles, with her head bent slightly forward in encouragement.

Returning her look, I said: 'I am here, sir.' My voice was hoarse and small, so I thought to repeat myself, but this time managed to drop the 'sir' in deference to my father.

As the memory of my father continued to flash across my mind, I lowered my eyes. It was extraordinary to think the emaciated body before me had sailed the Seven Seas with my own flesh and blood. Bewildering, too. Not just in the difference between then and now, but because the past seemed at once infinitely remote and intensely

47

present. I thought that if I were to lay my hand on Mr Silver, he would quicken into his former self, and my own fingers would become my father's, clutching at him for help, or to repel him.

'I am here,' I said again – eventually.

I expected some further warm outburst to greet my words, but Mr Silver did not answer. Instead he fixed his milky eyes upon me, let one arm drop into his lap, and ran the other over every feature of my face; his nails felt sharp as claws as they scraped over my skin. He touched my hair, my brow, my eye-sockets, my nose, my cheeks, my lips, my chin, and the beginning of my neck – all the while making a low ruminative humming noise with his mouth tight shut.

'Yes, you are Jim,' he said at last, and snatched his hand away with a surprising suddenness; I saw the snake wrinkle across his wrist.

'I am.'

'I would know you in the street or anywhere. You are your father's son exactly.'

'Thank you,' I said, somewhat foolishly as it seemed, but Mr Silver did not notice.

'You are young,' he went on. 'But of course you are – very young. It is a pleasant thing to be young, and have ten toes, you may lay to that. When you want to go for a bit of exploring, you just ask old John, and he'll put up a snack for you to take along.'

'Thank you,' I said again, feeling still more awkward, but once again Mr Silver seemed to ignore me and to be talking to himself.

'Young, and an educated boy, I should wager,' he said. 'I had a good schooling myself, in my own days. I could speak like a book when so minded. Genteel. That's what the captain called me. Genteel. You know whom I'm speaking about?'

'Captain Flint, sir,' I said, remembering what my father had told me.

'Captain Flint exactly!' Mr Silver sighed, a dry rasping sound in the bottom of his throat, then broke into a weak sing-song. 'First with England, then with Flint, that's my story. Here's to old Flint. Here's to ourselves and hold your luff, plenty of prizes and plenty of duff.' He paused again and swallowed. 'But that was long ago, long ago. I have not spoken with your father since he was a lad even younger than you are.' The eyes hooded as he said this, which showed he must be calculating how many years had passed since their last encounter. His frown showed he did not like the number that occurred to him.

'Does he talk of me – your father?' he asked.

'Very often,' I said, which sounded more like a common courtesy than I meant.

'Does he!' Mr Silver exclaimed. 'Does he indeed? Did you hear that, my dear?' – this, turning to Natty – 'Mr Hawkins often speaks of me!' He nodded a few times, while Natty and I exchanged a shining look. 'Well,' he continued after falling still again. 'It is no great wonder, I suppose. Your father and I had great adventures together.'

'So I have heard,' I said stiffly.

'I'll warrant you have,' he said; 'I'll warrant you have' – and then, after a pause: 'I have often sailed past your haunt the Hispaniola. A quaint old place, very shipshape and busy, I dare say. Very convenient for yarns and news and all sorts. Very handy for *a bottle of rum*.' He leered when he came to the word 'rum' and then, turning to include Natty, straightened his face and continued, 'Isn't that so, my darling! We have often looked in through the windows along the estuary, and wondered whether we might call in and surprise Jim Hawkins. Old Jim and young Jim.' He gave a dusty cackle. 'But who wants to see a ghost and have their happiness shaken – eh, Jim? Who wants to see a ghost?'

I could only nod at this, which of course meant silence to Mr

Silver, while my brain began to understand what he had told me. It made me feel that my entire existence, which I had hitherto believed to be my own affair, might in fact have been an open book, of which Mr Silver and Natty had turned every page as my story developed.

'But I am not a ghost, am I now, lad?' Mr Silver cackled again, and lifted his revolting claw to nip my cheek between two of his talons. 'What flesh is left of me is real flesh. Real flesh! And real blood running in my veins, eh!' His hand dropped into his lap with a soft thud. 'Pieces of eight! Pieces of eight!' he said suddenly, in a kind of scream. 'I'm not done for yet! Not by a long chalk.'

When I heard this, I thought Mr Silver might actually have lost his wits, and was not surprised to see Natty run her hand across his brow to calm him. 'Hush, hush, Father,' she said, in a soothing voice. 'Hush, hush' – then, more briskly: 'Remember why Jim is here, and what you have to say to him.'

Mr Silver breathed deeply two or three times, bringing himself to order; I suspect he was remembering a drill that he and Natty had devised for just such a moment as this. But when he began speaking again, it was evident that his mind was still rambling; he only gradually arrived at the point Natty had indicated.

'Your father was a most valuable friend,' he whispered. 'A brave boy. A clever boy, too – a lad of spirit. The rabble that surrounded me in those days – he saw they were worth nothing. Outright fools and cowards. He gave them what they deserved.' He reached forward and searched for my hand; when he had caught it, he gripped it very tight, squeezing my knuckles. 'But with me he was always understanding,' he continued. 'He saw we were gentlemen of fortune – the both of us. And I told him, "Jim, I'll save your life – if so be as I can. Then see here," I told him, "tit for tat – you save Long John Silver from swinging."' With this, he withdrew his hand, and set about heaving himself more nearly upright on his chaise, squaring his narrow shoulders and shaking his head as if tossing hair out of his eyes. 'Really,' he said, in a slow and dignified voice, 'I might say he was like a son to me.'

These last few words sank into me as heavily as stones. And as often happens at moments of especial intensity in our lives, I became conscious that a part of my mind had withdrawn, and was observing its own operations. I began thinking that some of Mr Silver's fascination came from the fact that his voice, with its rolling vowels and comfortable patterns, showed he had been born in the same part of the West Country as my father's family. This meant his talk had a kind of familiarity, and the air of comfort, even when he was saying astonishing things. Truly, it was outrageous to hear this man, whom my father had called the devil, recollect him as a son – and yet it was convincing as well.

'My father –' I began, with no clear idea of how I might continue.

'Your father!' Mr Silver interrupted. 'Your father would have understood the reasons for what I am about to ask you. I always liked him for a lad of spirit, and the picture of myself when I was young and handsome. A brave boy and a clever one, as I say. Very brave and very clever. Clever enough to know the value of an adventure, at any rate, and brave enough to carry it out!'

As Mr Silver finished speaking, he clenched his jaws and stuck out his chin. The effect was to show how collapsed his mouth was, over gums that had long since lost their teeth. Yet the impression of defiance was unmistakable.

'What adventure do you have in mind?' I asked, although I already knew the answer.

'Why the map, of course, boy!' His voice rose once more into something like a scream, which completely destroyed the impression of gentleness he had just given. 'The map and then the treasure across the sea! The beautiful silver! All the beautiful silver we left there in the old days, with the old captain.' He paused and struggled for breath, then continued more softly. 'You know the story, boy, and don't say otherwise. Your father and I only took what we could carry – us and the rest of them. But there's more. All the beautiful silver. Silver lying in the ground and the map will tell you where!'

'Supposing I refused?' I said. In my heart, I already knew how I would respond to Mr Silver, but thought I owed my father at least this show of loyalty.

'Suppose nothing!' the old man flashed back at me, shuddering as he spoke. 'Think! Do not suppose! Think of the fortune waiting for you! Think of who is speaking to you! It is me! Long John Silver as was. Old Barbecue as was. But neither of these any more. Not for many a day. It is Mr Silver now – the same man but different. Like music set in a different key, you might say. Your father will understand that. O yes, he will understand that, being subject himself to the same changes. The changes that govern us all.' The voice was beginning to fail now, although in these last words there was still a hiss of steel, like a sword being pulled from its sheath. He then added two more words, both as sharp as stab-wounds. 'Bravery!' he said. 'Cleverness!' When this was done, as if he had spent his last drop of energy, his head sank onto the gold pillow, and his face relaxed into a smile. I thought he might suddenly have fallen asleep.

Natty evidently believed so, and leaned towards me across her father's body. 'You know what he means,' she whispered, with an unnecessary candour. 'He wants you to find the map of the island, and make the voyage to bring home what remains of the treasure. You might say it is his dying wish.'

A plaintive note came into her voice with this last sentence. I disliked it, for making me understand how palpable were her designs on me. But because I could not easily resist her enthusiasm, I fell back on complaining it was impossible for practical reasons.

'How would I manage?' I asked. 'I am too young. I have no ship, and no crew, and no money. It is a hopeless cause.'

Natty was not in the least put out by these objections, but only leaned closer still, until I felt her breath on my face.

'My father has settled it,' she said, then straightened again, as if there were no more to add.

'What do you mean, he has settled it?'

'He has a ship waiting. And a crew. And a captain. He has paid for everything.'

I was astonished to hear this, feeling once again that my future had presumptuously been decided for me.

'All that remains,' Natty added with a smile like a cat, 'is for you to give us our destination.'

'Us?' I said.

'I shall come as well,' Natty said. 'I shall be my father's representative.'

I had hoped she might say this, without quite believing she would, and the effect was to turn my discomfiture into something like relief. 'Supposing I *were* to come,' I replied, with a shrug that I hoped would give the impression of indifference, 'then I would be *my* father's representative. It is the same thing.'

With this I pushed myself to my feet, stepping back from the chaise longue and turning towards the window so that I could debate more clearly with myself. My dilemma was very stark. If I declined to help, I would be asked to leave the Spyglass and would never see Natty again; it would mean I had refused the great adventure of my life. If I accepted, I would betray my father and damage for ever my idea of myself.

When faced with a puzzle at previous times in my existence, I had always been able to ask others to help me towards a solution. Now I had to decide for myself – the only other noise in the room was not a human voice, but a curious soft snapping that came from Spot in his cage, as though he were swallowing flies.

I ignored this as best I could and kept my back turned, staring at the panorama of the city below – the Tower with the dark door of Traitors' Gate looming above the waterline; the great dome of St Paul's floating above higgledy-piggledy streets; and the river rolling through everything, gathering its strength to the east and disappearing past Rotherhithe towards my home and the open sea beyond. Just as I had done when first coming into the Spyglass, I thought the wind pressing against the window might as well have been blowing against my face; the creak of the timbers might as well have been a ship's deck beneath my feet.

Without taking my eyes off the scene before me, I gave Mr Silver and Natty my answer.

CHAPTER 6

The Woman of Colour

After I had given my decision, which made me a traitor and free in the same breath, I expected Mr Silver to stretch out his arms and once again embrace me as a son. But his only response was to open his milky eyes, turn towards Natty as though he could really see her, and give an inward sort of smile. I understood this to mean: 'We never doubted him, did we?'

Natty brushed his hand with her own, then came to stand beside me at the window. With the light now falling on her more directly, I noticed a fine dew of sweat sugaring her nose and top lip. It was a strange comfort to feel I had given her more anxiety than she could admit.

'My father is very pleased,' she told me in a soft under-voice. 'You will see him again when we return with the map.

But now we should leave him to rest – we have tired him.'

I wanted to remonstrate with her, saying something to the effect that I had been wrestling with a greater difficulty than either of them knew, and deserved some consolation myself. But I reckoned this might sound heartless. Besides, the news that Natty would return with me to the Hispaniola had softened all my other considerations.

'When do we leave?' I asked, trying to sound matter-of-fact.

'Now,' she said. 'To get there before sunset.'

'No,' I explained, 'when do we leave for the island?'

'Oh', she said airily. 'Tomorrow. The day after tomorrow. Whenever the wind will carry us. Everything is ready.'

'I understood that,' I told her. 'But is it true he knows the crew? Are they good men? Is the ship a good ship?' I did not ask these questions because I felt troubled by the haste with which I had been swept up; I wanted reassurance that the men chosen by Mr Silver belonged to the later and more nearly decent part of his life. I needed to know, in fact, that they were not *pirates*.

Natty seemed to think I was making a fuss about nothing. 'Yes, yes,' she replied, with a flap of impatience. 'All good men, especially the captain. And a good ship too. There is nothing that need concern us – not in respect of men and sailing, at least.'

'What do you mean?'

Natty put her hand on my arm – I felt its warmth through the cotton of my sleeve. 'The world is very wide – that is all I mean. It is full of dangers we cannot predict.'

Instead of alarming me, the admission was a sort of assurance; it reminded me that I could rely on Natty's honesty, even if her expertise might sometimes be in question. Encouraged by this, I decided to be forthright myself, and said, 'Supposing I cannot find the map – or find it but for some reason cannot take it?'

'You will find it,' Natty said, with a curious flat emphasis. 'You already know where it is, and know you will take it. It is the only way for us.'

With that she let her hand drop, and suddenly became brisk and amused. 'We had best be on our way,' she said, tipping her head backwards to include me in the joke.

'What?' I asked her. 'What is it?'

Natty would not answer, but quickly crossed the room and said goodbye to Spot by tingling her fingernail across the bars of his cage and then to her father by kissing his forehead, which she did with her eyes tight shut.

The old man barely stirred. I took this to mean he was finally asleep – and then as Natty stepped away I moved into her place to look down at him once more. The crumpled body was like a rag covered in rags; its energy had entirely faded. But when I looked at the face I felt another flutter of fear. Beneath their waxy lids, Mr Silver's eyes moved with a bulging energy, as though they were hunting prey, and his thin lips closed and parted to give orders or curses – I could not tell which. I thought if I looked on him for more than a few moments, I would begin to hatch ideas I had never previously dared to imagine.

This confusion vanished – or rather, *changed its character* – when Natty ushered me away, led me down two or three flights of stairs, and I began to hear the same singing that I had noticed before, on our climb towards Mr Silver's room. The voice sounded softer now, and had a more definite wistfulness.

> Mary's son, the King in Heaven above,
> Has taken me for wife and made me his;
> My song has told the rapture of his love,
> My heart has burst the gates of Paradise.

When we reached the door where this singing was loudest, Natty paused and knocked – which produced a rapid scuffling sound and then, as the door slowly opened, the sight of a large Negro woman. She was some sixty years old, with long grey hair wound tightly into braids, and wore a white dress that included so many petticoats and whatnot, she might as well have been enveloped in a cloud. Her face showed flickers of the light that must once have shone from her, but was now too heavy to be called beautiful.

'My mother,' said Natty, with an ironical bow that proved she thought her relation was ridiculous, or at least strange. In fact I felt nothing but curiosity. This was the same *woman of colour* who had appeared in my father's stories – the woman with whom Mr Silver had shared his early life in Bristol, and to whom he had evidently returned following his exile in Spanish America. Like her husband, she was a fable come to life.

Mrs Silver stared at the hand I was offering her to shake, as if such a courtesy were unheard of. Her own right hand was pressed to her bosom, which rose and fell very quickly. When I glanced beyond her I understood why. One entire wall of her room was a shrine, a gigantic plate of shimmering metal, into which various hooks and holders had been screwed to support candles. These were all casting their yellow light onto a table where more candles stood – surrounding a complicated silver crucifix, embossed with animals overlapping one another in a writhing dance. Mrs Silver had been at her prayers, and was breathless because she had been prostrate in front of her altar when we happened to disturb her.

I wondered why Natty had not been more circumspect. The explanation came when Mrs Silver recovered her composure and finally grasped my hands in both her own – which were peculiarly warm and moist. She did not consider us to be intruders, and never would have done; she seemed as uncomplicated in her friendliness as her husband was devious.

'Master Jim!' she exclaimed, in a rolling West Country voice. 'Natty told me you would be here. Come in, my lover, come in' – and before I even had the chance to hesitate, she clamped one heavy arm around my shoulder, the other around Natty, then swept us across the room to an ancient settle, where we sank in a single swooping collapse as though glued together, and listened to her talk.

Barbados (where she had been born); harbours; sea-sailing; tuna fish; salt; bunks; disagreeable biscuits; storms; phosphorescence; starlight, sunshine, following winds; the smell of vegetation; the River Severn; and the great old port of Bristol were all subjects she touched on, and then abandoned, as she ferried us with her from her native land to her first home in England with her young husband. His subsequent journey to Treasure Island she passed over, except to say it was 'a cruise' that left her alone for longer than she expected, but had allowed her to take on the management of the Spyglass. Since her husband's return, she wanted me to believe, they had worked quietly and happily together, *blessed by the arrival of our angel* (here our shoulders were given a terrific squeeze) – although now their existence was overshadowed by her husband's ill health.

As this sad subject came into view, Mrs Silver redoubled her efforts to be cheerful. 'Thanks to Jesus,' she declared, or I should say *sang*, for she drew out the name of her Saviour into a long steady note. 'Thanks to Jesus we are still able to count our blessings, and look forward to greater ones in the time that remains to us.'

This speech had taken several minutes to complete, and for most of this time I kept my gaze fixed on the altar in front of me. I could see now that it had been cleverly made to create a wholly irregular surface, which reflected the candlelight at unpredictable angles. Because thick curtains blinded every window in the room, and the other walls were hung with dark shawls and drapes of various kinds, she had created an impression of unusually concentrated devotion – and also of considerable danger, since the slightest gust of wind would certainly fan one of the many flames and set everything on fire.

This possibility meant I kept very still. Mrs Silver, by contrast, quivered and shook and fluttered while she spoke, and gradually convinced me that she resembled everything around her, and the altar especially, in blending rapture with recklessness. The longer I reflected on this, the more uncomfortable I became. My original response to her had been a kind of relief after the strangeness of her husband. Then I had felt puzzled that two such different people might actually be man and wife. This in turn had led me to speculate that her amiability was in fact a sort of tyranny: her story was designed to entertain us, but also to assert her control. The possibility had become more and more convincing as she continued talking, with the weight of her arms across our shoulders steadily increasing, and her grip steadily tightening, so that by the end we were more nearly her prisoners than her audience.

For Natty, who must have heard her mother's speeches countless times before, the detention would have been especially tedious. So I supposed, at any rate – and as her mother began another long paragraph of thanks to Jesus for blessings past, present and to come, I decided that I must bring our captivity to an end.

'Mrs Silver,' I said loudly, wriggling away from her and jumping to my feet. 'Natty and I have something to do, which we must begin immediately.'

The effect of my announcement was instantaneous, and much more powerful than I had expected. All the buoyancy that had filled Mrs Silver, all the bounce and assertion, escaped like air from a balloon.

'Something to do?' she said weakly, as if flabbergasted.

'It is a task,' I told her. 'A task your husband has given us.'

A second change now took place in Mrs Silver, which was like a hardening after the recent deflation. She folded her arms across her bosom, and disappointment stiffened her face. My first thought was: I have annoyed her by interrupting her. But as she began speaking again, I realised at least some of her irritation was directed towards her husband, either because she did not understand his mind, or because she disliked what it contained.

'I know your task, Master Jim; I know your task,' she said, with the sing-song note in her voice now distinctly sinister. 'Whether it is God's will or the devil's is another matter. Ye are the children of light, and the children of the day: we are not of the night, not of darkness.' Mrs Silver unfolded her arms and placed her hands upon her knees, before adding with a defiant emphasis and a glare at both of us, 'The First Epistle to the Thessalonians, chapter five, verse five.'

At this Natty also rose to her feet and edged away from her mother – glancing uncertainly from me to her and then back again. Mrs Silver ignored this. 'Go to your task then,' she continued. 'Go to your task, young man. Come back when it is done and I shall decide whose work you do. And you, young lady' – she darted another look at her daughter, which had nothing of a mother's love in it, but only jealousy and disdain – 'you go with your young man and do your father's bidding. It is your practice, after all.'

In the agitation of the moment, with candlelight shifting across every surface, it was impossible to see what effect this little tirade had on Natty. Outwardly she remained calm, extending a hand to help her mother stand. But I do not think it was in my imagination that I saw the colour of her face deepen, and a strange low fire – more like coals than flames – burn in her eyes.

The blaze continued for a moment, then receded as Mrs Silver heaved upright. Whether or not she had noticed Natty's discomfiture, she wanted to end our interview as suddenly as it had begun. Although I had no experience of what it meant to have a mother, this struck me as nothing less than unkind. The rapid changes in the temperature of her mood, and the remorselessness she now showed, might have threatened the happiness of any childhood. When such things combined with the influence of such a husband, they might shipwreck it altogether.

There was no time to dwell on these thoughts, since Mrs Silver was suddenly all business, shooing at us as if we were chickens, while the folds of her dress quaked and its hems hissed along the floor, which made the candle-shadows sway about us even more violently. As she scuttled towards the door there was no word of goodbye, no blessing for our journey, only an absolute determination to see us gone – as though she had just remembered a matter of far greater importance than anything our plans could represent.

My own desire to leave the house was equally powerful; I did not even wait for Natty, but quickly bounded down one flight of stairs, then along the landing past the taproom, then down the last flight and so into the street. Until she caught up with me, I was glad to be alone. In the last few hours I had grown so used to others knowing my future, it was almost shocking to realise I still had the chance to reject everything Mr Silver had offered. I told myself it would be the easiest thing in the world to melt into a side street, find my way home to the Hispaniola, and ignore any further visits and instructions from the Spyglass.

The easiest thing – but impossible, since all my ties of loyalty to my father, and all my instincts for safety, were as nothing compared to the feelings that now worked against them. To speak plainly: Natty had caught me in a bewitchment far stronger than any of the reasons

I had to shun her. The more doubtful I felt about the character of her parents, the more willing I was to think of her as their *victim* – the prisoner of their wildness and eccentricity. Yet such was her power over me, and my desire to please her, I did not feel inclined to rescue her from her father's designs – but rather to accept them. I now see my reasoning was casuistic, and I cannot admire it. At the time I was content, since it allowed me to suppose that my betrayal of my own father was not an act of selfishness, but of kindness.

When Natty appeared from the darkness behind me her face was cheerful again: eyes bright, mouth settled into her cat's smile. Such brave composure confirmed everything I had been thinking. I was not a traitor but a redeemer.

CHAPTER 7

Downriver

I shall not rehearse the details of our return to the Hispaniola, except to say the river, in which the tide had turned, and then turned again, made us labour hard to reach our destination. As we toiled along, with the light of day beginning to fade around us, I felt we were also brought together. By this I do not only mean to acknowledge my willingness to steal the map, but also to show that we needed to combine our efforts, and help one another, in order to complete our purpose. Our oars made untidy splashes as they propelled us through the water; our backs and arms ached. My consolation was to imagine the lights of ships and boats around us (much less numerous than in daytime) winked like partners in our conspiracy. Men and women tramping home along the towpath, heads down and intent on their own purposes, persuaded me that we were invisible to the rest of humanity.

Arduous as they were in certain respects, these circumstances encouraged Natty to speak about her parents more freely than before. As we passed through Rotherhithe, and began to tackle the widening stretch towards Greenwich, she told me that Mr Silver's ill health and her mother's religion, which might easily have united them as patient and nurse, had in fact led them into rather separate existences, him in the crow's-nest of the house, her in the midships. It was Natty who cared for her father, while her mother managed the business of the inn.

At this time in our knowledge of one another, I hesitated to press Natty for more details of her life, since my questions might easily have given hurt when they only meant to show interest. I felt no such reserve in mentioning our adventure – so when I thought we might have exhausted the subject of her father for the time being, I asked, 'Supposing we find our island. Supposing we find it, and afterwards come home safely and rich. What do you see after that? What do you want?'

I expected a bright reply, but Natty surprised me by speaking very gravely. 'I don't expect to come home,' she said.

'Not come home?' I repeated, looking into the narrow fields that now began to open on either side of us.

'No, never come home.'

'You mean not survive?'

'Oh,' she said, with a weary relaxation, 'I expect to *survive*. I mean not come home to England. You have seen my life here.'

This invited me to make a judgement that might offend her, so I replied evasively. 'Both our lives have their frustrations,' I said.

'Mine are more than frustrations,' Natty replied, with the same air of steadiness that characterised all her conversation. 'This adventure will allow me some liberty, at least.'

I thought her admission proved she would not mind me speaking more directly. 'Does your father know this?' I asked.

'What does my father know of anything? He rambles – you've heard him. He knows the past but not the present. Perhaps your father is the same?'

I agreed vigorously with this, and Natty continued.

'He speaks about how he has changed, which is true in certain respects. He is not a pirate any more. He is a law-abiding gentleman – for as long as he remains in the world. But he cannot change entirely, because he cannot forget the island. He must have that map of yours. He must have the map, and then he must have the silver.'

'Well,' I said, somewhat dully, because my mind was still fixed on practical things. 'At least that should mean he has found us a reliable crew.'

Natty nodded, and despite the gathering darkness I saw that her face was flushed – which I thought had more to do with the heat of our talk than the effort of our work. 'We shall not have the same experience as our fathers,' she said in a low voice. 'I can assure you of that. I have met this crew and their captain. They are all good men – Captain Beamish especially.'

'You know them all?'

'I said I have met them. The hands have all been hired by the captain. He is the only one I *know*. But I assure you we shall be safe. My father wants his treasure too much to allow it otherwise.'

'But how will he have it, if you do not return to England?' As I asked this question, I already knew how Natty would reply. She would tell me that once she had found the silver she would send it home with this Captain Beamish, then take her life in her own hands and strike off in some other direction.

I could not decide what this meant for me. It was an uncertainty that lay too far beyond other uncertainties. Because I did not want to imagine them yet, I was relieved when Natty did not answer me, but left a pause in which I heard nothing except the sound of our oars biting into the water. My question drifted for a moment on the surface like a leaf, then slipped out of sight.

'Of course,' said Natty, after a while, with a sharp note in her voice that showed she was changing the subject, 'I shall not be sailing as myself.'

I looked at her blankly.

'I shall be there,' Natty said. 'I shall be with you. But I shall be travelling as a boy. It is my father's idea – for my safety. Captain Beamish knows me for what I am, but the crew are already convinced that I am Nat.'

'Nat?' I echoed, with a smile.

Natty raised her eyebrows, pretending she was not in the least amused. 'I could not possibly go as myself,' she said. 'That is what I believe. And what my father believes. Our shipmates would not allow it. And supposing we run into any trouble . . . It is better this way.'

I assured her that I understood the good sense of what she had decided, but in truth my response was a little more complicated than I allowed. I felt a sort of annoyance at not being consulted, and thereby included, in her decision. I also realised that Natty's disguise meant no demonstrable affection could possibly develop between us during our journey – although I was so far unwilling to address this idea in any detail.

'Very well,' I said briskly, copying her example. 'This evening you are Natty. Tomorrow you are Nat. That is all we need say on the subject. But I have a question that is connected.'

Natty raised one eyebrow in a pretty arch.

'Will the crew know who *I* am?'

'You mean, will they know you are your father's true son?'

'Exactly.'

'Only the captain.' Natty paused, then added with the confidence I had come to admire in her, no matter how much it took my consent for granted: 'We thought it for the best. The men would only bother you for stories, and you have already said you do not enjoy such things.'

'Very good,' I said, knowing she spoke nothing less than the truth. My reward for this degree of understanding was to see Natty give me her sweetest smile; as it left her, we fell silent to complete the work in hand.

I have said that we reached our destination fairly easily, by which I mean our talk continued fluently enough. In fact we took considerably more time returning than we had done setting out. Perhaps we were tired. More certainly, I was loath to complete the crime I had already begun – partly out of respect for my father, and partly because I feared discovery. In any event: by the time we were past Greenwich (which was about nine o'clock, if the churches of that village could be relied upon), and beginning the last slow sweeps of the river that I recognised as the beginning of home, the moon had climbed into the sky, and the first stars were gleaming above the marshes.

Because I knew my father would be serving his customers until midnight, and was therefore likely to notice my arrival, or have it reported to him, Natty and I had no choice except to lie up in secret for a while. I therefore suggested we pull into a creek some distance away from the Hispaniola, and wait until the inn was quiet. The place we found was a water-alley that several seagulls had already chosen for their roost; they complained very loudly as the nose of the *Spyglass* turned out of the main river and drove them away.

Once this hubbub had died down, it was replaced by the sound of a million oozings and bubblings that were the ordinary conversations of the marsh. This was comforting for me, because it was the sound of the earth itself; yet it could not help but remind me of everything I was about to offend. I tried to ease these guilty feelings by keeping up a constant flow of chat with Natty – in whispers, of course, so the sense of conspiracy was never far away.

Our talk led us from earliest memories (avoiding the subject of mothers and fathers); to schooldays; to the difficulties of the Latin language; to hopes (of happiness); to fears (of *worms* for her, and of more abstract things, such as *failure*, for me); to birthdays; to foods liked (beef) and disliked (hard biscuit); to the stars and moon, which shone so brightly above us it might have been the door to another world, made entirely of light; to schooldays again and the teachers we had most enjoyed; to books (where Natty would not follow me, calling them *dull*); and so on. Occasionally a bird would approach, take fright, and clatter away again. For the most part the river was deserted – although now and again quiet barges sailed past, with lamps fore and aft, their sails and hulls a beautiful soft charcoal colour. The water lapping against their prows was like the noise of sleep itself. All these things helped to control my sadness. Had the air not grown steadily colder, I believe we would eventually have closed our eyes and leaned together, then resumed our gossip when the dawn broke.

I calculated that midnight had already gone when the last of my father's customers staggered out from the Hispaniola and home along the towpath. We knew this because we heard a tipsy farewell, and a few bars of his disappearing song.

> Good night, my sweet ladies, goodnight, my dear friends,
> The moonlight shows clearly where this journey ends –
> In sleep and in dreaming of countries not seen,
> Where loving is easy and no man has been.

A profound silence succeeded the fading of this ditty – swelling through the emptiness like a wave of black water. Yet instead of drowning me, the effect was to splash me awake, so that suddenly all my senses revived, and my brain concentrated. Everything I had previously done – all my book-learning, and in particular my time studying the creatures of the world – appeared to me like a preparation for this moment. I had no need for Natty to wish me good luck. After I had waited a few minutes more, in which I imagined my father taking himself upstairs and falling asleep, I merely touched her on the shoulder and climbed out of the boat. She, in return, said nothing I might have taken with me as comfort – except what I most wanted: 'I shall stay here.'

It is the strangest thing, to stand outside a childhood home and feel unknown to it. In my own case, the sense of division was all the more shocking after the last few hours, in which Natty and I had entertained ourselves with the history of our past lives. When I slipped in through the side door of the house, its familiar curly handle and the squeak of the latch were merely cold facts.

This feeling of strangeness deepened as I stepped further indoors. The pale stone counter in the taproom, daubed with moonlight; the larder door with its metal grille in the central panel; the worn-away hollow in the red bricks of the threshold to the hallway: these were suddenly objects of curiosity, and not the fabric of my exist-ence. I moved on – *floated* on, I should say, since I felt no more substantial than a wraith from the marshes. Up the narrow stairs. Along the corridor where the faces of huntsmen and hounds and horses regarded me impassively. Down the three steps of which the middle must be avoided because it would creak if stepped on. And here was the door to my father's room – left ajar – and the sound of his snores rising like bubbles through mud. These would have directed me to my father's bedside even without the help of a lantern, which he had left guttering on the floor beside his shoes, and which I now silently retrieved.

As I lifted up this light, a fresh sense of trespass poured through me, because I could not recall the last time I had entered my father's room. When I had been a child, no doubt, woken by a bad dream and stumbling for comfort. My exile at school in Enfield had brought an end to such visits, not by eradicating the need for them, but by creating a coolness between my father and myself. This grew steadily whenever we lived together during my holidays. He had his work in the taproom, and I had my life on the marshes, and my habits of botanising and collecting. By the time my school days had ended, and I had become a daily servant in the taproom, my body remained in the Hispaniola but my mind was elsewhere.

For these reasons, I now found myself looking round his room as inquisitively as a stranger, very grateful for the glow of my candle. My first thought was: my father kept his possessions remark-ably neat and tidy. The shirt and trousers he had been wearing that day were folded on a wooden bench, ready to be put on again tomorrow. The single picture on his walls – the sketch of a working vessel entering an estuary under full sail – was hung exactly above the Windsor chair, in which he evidently sat to look through his window at traffic on the river below. A pitcher and ewer stood on a marble-topped table in one corner, their whiteness strengthening the lantern-light. All perfectly orderly, all perfectly settled. Like a ship's cabin, I thought, and not just because I was thinking about the low roof above my head. In a part of my mind, I was already on the high seas.

At the foot of his bed, standing square and black, and locked with a most ingenious-looking and ancient device, was the chest I had come to open. The chest that had long ago been trundled into the Admiral Benbow with Billy Bones, and had remained there when

Billy Bones went to meet his Maker – for my father to redeem when he returned from Treasure Island. In my own childhood, I had been encouraged to venerate this object as though it contained relics that made the grave-cloths of our Saviour as insignificant as kitchen rags. But in truth it had not been so much the contents that attracted my attention as the thing itself. Running my small hands over its pitted planks, touching the scars in its iron bands, and the initial B burned on the top of it with a hot iron, I felt that I could trace the exact course and drama of the stories my father told me, with a far greater sense of conviction than any of his words engendered. The cannon-smoke of battle still hung around it, along with the gleam of blades, the blood of wicked men, and the glamour of their feuds. When I reached it now, I set down my lantern on the floor and laid my hands flat on the domed lid as if expecting something like human warmth to pass into my fingers.

I felt nothing but dust and cold – which my father also seemed to think was disappointing, for he suddenly stirred in his sleep, broke off snoring to open and shut his mouth with a succession of loud smacking noises, then resumed his dream. In the course of this disturbance, as his head rolled on the pillow, I saw round his neck the dark string on which was tied the key to the chest.

Up to this point in my raid, I had told myself that if my father were to wake, I would say that I had come to bid him goodnight, and report myself safely returned from my visit to London. But as I crept forward, and the night-winds pressed more loudly around the house, sending unexpected creaks through its timbers, I felt the weight of my actions more heavily. I was about to reach the point where my excuses would run out. The point where I turned from being a prodigal returning, into a prodigal departing.

So gravely did this thought strike me, I came to a dead halt and stood regarding my father for a full minute, as he lay softly illuminated in his unconsciousness. I examined his face and the hair thinning across his scalp. I saw his lips shake loosely as his breath came in and out. I studied the folds and ridges of his ears, and their long lobes, as if I were poring over a trophy I had brought from the marshes to add to my cabinet of curiosities.

This was my father. My father, who as a boy had enjoyed a greater adventure than any I thought possible in my own life. My father, who had never lifted a hand against me. My father, who had offered me advantages of schooling and suchlike that he had never known himself. My father, who had kept honourable the memory of my mother. My father, who had raised me in his loneliness, and whose only fault had been to expect hard work and too much loyalty. No doubt if he had not done so, I would have said he was ignoring me! I can honestly say that I had never loved him more than I did in the moment before I betrayed him.

This might explain why, as my fingers set about the work they were required to do, they appeared not to belong to me but to a stranger who had taken possession of my body. Mercifully, they did not have to be busy for long – because my father was now lying flat on his back, his night-shirt open at the throat, with the string loose around his neck and the key sunk into his right armpit, where it lay half-buried in damp black hairs. Gently I teased it out. Tenderly I felt along the string, which seemed gilded in the yellow lantern-light and was warm with the heat of his body. Gladly I found the knot. Deftly I picked at the knot to loosen it . . .

And failed. The knot was pulled tight and, having been left undisturbed for many years, had hardened into a solid mass. I knew what I must do next. I also knew that if I delayed for a moment longer I would be overwhelmed by fear, and lose my capacity. It was at this moment the thought of Natty burst into my mind – how the night would be sighing round her, how she would scorn me if I returned to the *Spyglass* empty-handed. So vividly did she appear to me, in fact, it might almost have been *her* head that I slid my hand beneath, and lifted. It might also have been her warm throat I brushed with my palm, as I reached for the string and drew it upwards, gripping the key between my thumb and forefinger.

In the middle of this operation my father appeared to stop breathing for a moment, opening his eyes wide and staring directly at me. I stood still, returning his gaze. But whereas my eyes were able to understand what they saw, his were blind – or fixed on some object that lay inside me. For a moment I also held my breath, with the uncomfortable sensation that I was being searched and found wanting. It was the crisis of my visit. I understood that if I dropped the key now, I could return to my old ways. Alternatively, I could proceed – into adventure and danger.

I do not need to say how I decided, or how quickly I finished my work. As my father closed his eyes again, I slipped the string over his head (which I then laid back gently on the pillow) and stepped away until I was able to crouch down beside the sea-chest. Thanks to the lantern, my work was much easier than it would otherwise have been.

To my surprise, the key entered the lock very smoothly and also turned very easily, with a pleasant heavy click that told me my father had often used it himself, for reasons I did not want to consider – they would have made its contents seem more important to him. The lid opened with an almost silent sigh, and released a faint whiff of tobacco and tar as it rested against the end of the bed. I bent forward as though I were peering into a well, and might at any moment lose my footing and fall headlong.

Mementos that we collect in the course of our existence are bound to have a value for ourselves that is unaccountable to others. So it was in my father's treasure-chest. Among the objects that I found, and held to the lantern so that I could see them clearly, were a quadrant; a tin canikin; several sticks of tobacco; an old Spanish watch; a pair of compasses mounted on brass; five or six curious West Indian shells; a leather pouch holding coins (which I assumed to be the residue of his share from the island); a loop of brown hair, braided and coiled; a green eyeshade; assorted notebooks, which were filled with columns of numbers, and must have been the business accounts of the Hispaniola; several articles of clothing, including a grey shawl and a pair of matching gloves; another small pouch containing three or four milk teeth; a very handy pistol with a label attached to it, on which a childish hand had written 'the weapon used to dispatch Israel Hands'; a sealed envelope on which was written, in the same hand, 'the Black Spot, as given to Billy Bones by Blind Pew: do not open'; several newspapers as frail as cobwebs; an empty scabbard; the large fang of a creature, on which had been scratched the image of a ship; and, where I expected it to be, at the very bottom of the chest, a small satchel made of green silk. This had a strap of braided string attached, so that it could be worn round the neck as handily as my father's key, and was held shut by a ribbon tied in a neat bow.

I immediately guessed this satchel would contain what I had come for – and I was not disappointed. Indeed, when I lifted the satchel closer to my face, and touched the ribbon that held it shut, the material crumbled into dust, and the sheet of yellow paper inside seemed actually to *give itself* into my hands, rather than requiring me to remove it. I hurriedly knelt down and held this sheet towards the lantern. As I remember it now, it seems extraordinary that I did not fear my father would awake at any moment, and call me a traitor. But I did not. My good sense, like my conscience, had been entirely consumed by curiosity.

The map had evidently been very often folded and unfolded in

years gone by, and was grimy with the print of many hands. Yet it
was still strong, and the drawing sharp. The island was about nine
miles long by five across, and had two fine harbours, and a hill in
the centre marked 'the Spyglass'. There were several additions that
appeared to be of a later date; but, above all, three crosses of red
ink – two in the north part of the island, one in the south-west,
and, besides this last, in the same red ink, and in a small neat hand,
very different from the tottery characters elsewhere, these words:
'Bulk of treasure here.' Over on the back, the same hand had written
the further information:

> Tall tree. Spyglass shoulder, bearing a point to the N of NNE
> Skeleton Island ESE and by E.
> Ten feet.
> The bar silver is in the north cache; you can find it by the bend of
>   the east hummock, ten fathoms south of the black crag with
>   the face on it.
> The arms are easy found, in the sand-hill, N point of north inlet
>   cape, bearing E and a quarter of N.
> J. F.

My head dropped as I reached the end of these words, and for a
moment the map seemed to swim before me. Then, with a strange
slowness, as though the air around me had suddenly become dense
as water, I raised the map towards me again and my eyes roved to
the topmost edge of the sheet. I found what I wanted. A statement
of longitude and latitude, which was branded on my brain in an
instant, but shall never be repeated. My relief was so intense I think
I may actually have gasped aloud. But it would have been a gasp
that faded quickly into a smile, as I noticed the artist had taken the
trouble to underline his information with irregular blue lines, as a
child might do to indicate the waves of the sea.

The fascination of all this was so immediate I might as well have been holding a page of the Gospels. The map was a sacred thing – a source of primitive knowledge that had been mentioned time and again throughout my childhood, but always kept out of reach. My father and everything in his room fell absolutely quiet as I gazed on it. At the same time, a sensation crept out of the document and passed into my hand, and I could not tell whether it was like weakness or strength. My hand trembled yet felt strong as iron. Still wondering at this contradiction, I folded the map, replaced it in the satchel, slipped the braided strap around my neck, tucked the satchel inside my shirt, then set about returning everything to the chest as quietly as possible, and in the original order, so that my father would not know the contents had been ransacked.

When this was done, and the chest was locked again, I tiptoed back to my father's bedside and once more lifted his head from the pillow, so that I could restore the key to its place around his neck. Often in my childhood I had silently condemned my father for sending himself drunk to bed. On this occasion I thanked him for it very profusely – although in total silence: his only response to my interference was to give an especially loud snore. When everything was settled again, I stared down at him for the last time.

In spite of all the recent disturbances, he seemed to have moved into a different chamber of sleep, and now lay more deeply below the current of the world than when I had first come into his room. His forehead was smoothed clear of trouble. His jaw was set as if nerved for a long journey. 'Goodbye, Father,' I heard myself say – which I had not planned to do. The words fell on him as lightly as snow and he did not feel them.

I returned the lantern to its place beside his shoes, and left the room quickly without looking back. I had not expected such sadness to be a part of my leave-taking, but now I felt it, I could not ignore it; it meant that when I came downstairs I paused in the taproom and wrote my father a message. Using the slate he kept to remember orders of food and drink (and wiping those away), I wrote that I was resolved to make a journey, as he had done when he was my age, and that I would be home again later in the year. I said nothing about the map, nothing about my destination, and nothing about my companion and her ancestry. In this way I both confessed and dissembled. When I was finished, I left the words basking in the moonlight.

It was the work of a minute to cross the marsh again, and find the creek where Natty was waiting. As I stepped into the *Spyglass* and sat down beside her, she looked into my face without speaking, saw my expression, then put her arms around me. It was the first time we had embraced, and the warmth of her body, with its faint scent of sweat, almost overwhelmed me. I hardly had the wit to notice she did not mention the map – and I was grateful she did not. In fact we did not speak at all. We let one another go, took an oar each, and rowed into the river, then a mile towards London. There we tethered our boat to a jetty and slept until morning. When the sun rose we continued our journey, with my treasure still hidden inside my shirt.

CHAPTER 8

Reading the Map

My father advised me never to pick over the reasons for a decision once it has been taken. As a young boy I thought this meant he always knew his own mind. By the time I left for Treasure Island, I had come to believe he preferred not to look at past mistakes.

Perhaps this change of opinion proved nothing except the doubt I felt about my own behaviour. Certainly, when I woke head-to-toe with Natty in the *Spyglass*, and lifted my head to inspect the marshes warming in the early sun, I imagined that each mist-wraith I saw wandering across them had come to accuse me. The whole shimmering panorama spoke directly to my moral sense – and I clutched nervously at the satchel inside my shirt, where I found the map safe enough.

When a fuller consciousness returned, I realised not even a whole army of accusers could now force me to return my prize to the sea-chest from which I had stolen it. Accepting this, I also understood that henceforth I would do better to keep looking forward, contemplating my future, rather than sneaking guilty glances over my shoulder. I therefore made a silent promise that in due course I would return to my father with a share of whatever I brought home from my adventure, but – until that time – think of him no more than was absolutely necessary. How well I succeeded in this endeavour will appear in the pages following.

The moment Natty awoke she gave a wide yawn that showed the pink inside of her mouth, and wiped her hands over her face. She then looked at me very boldly, as though refuting any accusation of having slept at all.

Because this was our first experience of beginning a day together, we were shy of one another, and spent the next few moments in silence. But after we had splashed the Thames over our faces, reassured ourselves the tide was running in the direction we wished to proceed, rowed away from our mooring, travelled a mile or two upstream, eaten our breakfast at one of the inns that offered food to sailors and bargees and suchlike, and settled our plan for the day, we were comfortable again.

The rest of our journey unfolded very easily. The strong propulsion of the river carried us swiftly back to Wapping. We safely escaped the traffic of merchant ships and barges to find a mooring where we wanted. We happily scrambled ashore and found a lane that led us directly to the Spyglass inn. The creaks and whispers of that building swept us rapidly up the stairs towards Mr Silver. By this time it was midday, and the haze of morning had long since burned away, leaving the sky as blue as a blackbird's egg; when I opened the door, I was once again so dazzled by light from its large window, I actually shielded my eyes as if I were staring into the sun itself.

Our host began speaking to me immediately, calling out my

name in a high, imperious whisper: 'Jim! Jim!' I could not see him yet, being still blinded, but it was obvious from the direction of his voice that Mr Silver's chaise longue had been moved into a different position since my last visit, and was now alongside the window. The change was a trifling thing, but enough to shake my confidence that I knew what to expect from my host.

Indeed, when I had lowered my hand and blinked a few times, I saw Mr Silver was leaning so far towards me he had almost fallen onto the floor. Natty moved quickly to his side, and knelt to straighten him; his only response was to batter her lightly with feeble hands. Spot did not like being passed over by his mistress in this way, and began calling his name very angrily from his cage on the table, which convinced me that I should intervene. I went over to run my finger along his bars – whereupon he spluttered like an ancient and outraged gentleman, then fell silent.

Now Mr Silver was settled again, he began hissing at his daughter. 'Do you have it? Do you have it?'

'We have it, Father,' she interrupted. 'We have it safe.' As she said this, she beckoned for me to stand beside her. Mr Silver was wearing the same blue sailor's coat and ragged trousers as yesterday, although his face was even more collapsed, if such a thing were possible. It was extraordinary to remember that my father had described him as looking 'like a ham'.

'Let me see it,' he whispered, rolling his eyes feverishly to and fro in their sockets. 'Let me hold it in my hands again.'

I glanced at Natty, searching her face for a sign of what I should do, and again she acted for me, indicating that I should take the map from its hiding-place. It occurred to me as I did so that this would be the first time she had seen it herself. Whatever excitement she felt was well concealed, which I thought was proof of her trust in me.

While I began to undo my shirt, Mr Silver clawed the air as he had done during our previous visit. 'And what of yourself, Father,' Natty said gently, ignoring this. 'What of yourself?'

The old man did not reply. He merely clenched up his face like a fist so that all his wrinkles were emphasised, and looked at her with disdain. Natty affected not to notice, and ran her hand over his forehead. There was nothing more than goodness in the gesture, which was a relief to see, but Spot evidently suspected otherwise. As her hand pulled back again, the bird hopped from the floor of his cage onto his perch and clung there with his bright yellow feet, rocking backwards and forwards. 'Leave me alone! Leave me alone!' he shouted, with enough defiance to keep us all still for a moment.

'I have it here, Mr Silver.'

It was my voice that spoke now, and my hands that were holding out the map. I had already unfolded it, which meant I was seeing it in daylight for the first time. The underlinings appeared even more childish than when I had glanced at them in my father's room. Yet the *names* – the names and the rusty cross-marks – held such extraordinary power, the air seemed to shiver around me.

Mr Silver did nothing for a moment except stare, his milky eyes narrowing with an effort of concentration, his brow tightening, and his head lifting an inch or two from the pillow.

'Give it to me,' he said. 'I need to be sure.' His voice was very thin and scratchy, but had a note of command that Captain Flint himself would have obeyed. When I did as he ordered, he laid hold of the paper with great delicacy, as if he feared that it might melt between his fingers. When he had stroked it a few times, and reassured himself of its robustness, he raised it close to his face and breathed in two or three times very deeply.

'Do you smell it, boy?' he asked in a much quieter voice, when he had allowed his head to sink back onto the pillow again. 'And you, my girl, do you smell it? The sea and the earth and all that in them is!'

Neither of us answered, but watched in amazement as he returned to touching all over the map with his finger-ends. To and fro they wandered, to and fro, as though he had transported himself from his bed and was in fact strolling around the coves of the island, exploring its valleys and forests, drinking from its streams and hauling himself up its hillsides. Eventually he settled on the words 'bar silver' and seemed to pluck at them, teasing them upright. When he had satisfied himself in this way, he caressed the whole surface of the map with a most lingering fondness, which made the snake tattoo writhe along his arm. Next he performed the same action with his face, sliding the paper backwards and forwards across his white bristles, over his nose and forehead. Finally he held it to his lips, and puckered them into a tender kiss.

It was a revolting performance, as well as a spellbinding one, and by the end of it Mr Silver's mouth had filled with saliva, so that he had to swallow not once but twice. Natty took this to be a sign that she should bring things to a close, perhaps fearing for his health. She therefore leaned forward and prised the map from between his fingers, all the time murmuring, 'There, there, Father; we will take it back now. There, there.'

When she had returned the paper to my safe keeping, Natty sat down on the chaise longue beside her father and took both his hands in her own. 'Listen to me,' she said, in the voice of sweet reason. 'We have come to show you the map, and now you have seen it. We have also come to say goodbye to you. You know what we must do. We must begin our journey. Will you give us your blessing; and say you look forward to our safe return?'

'My blessing? Why of course you have my blessing,' said Mr Silver; his voice was very quiet, as if he were speaking in a church. 'You have my blessing and my prayers – my prayers for your safe return, and your *success*.' He drew out the last word so that it sounded like a serpent's hiss, then collected himself, which showed he was about to say something he wanted us to remember. It was this: 'Your success will be the end of everything. It will set me free. It will set all of us free. Bring me the silver and I will be able to die.'

'Hush, hush, you must not say that,' Natty told him quickly, but her father would not respond, except by tightening his jaw.

This made an awkwardness in the room, which I felt I must end for Natty's sake. 'Before we set sail,' I said, 'I have a request. I was not able to say goodbye to my own father – for reasons you will understand. Can I ask you: will you give me a memory of him that I might have instead?'

I thought Mr Silver would ignore my request or brush it aside, so contemptuous was the expression on his face. But as the words sank into his brain they exerted a most curious influence. His eyes widened, his features relaxed, and a smile spread through him that was as warm as sunlight. It gave me a glimpse of the sweetness my father had witnessed many years earlier – the sweetness that was always false, and expedient.

'Jim!' he said, as though suddenly astonished. 'Dear boy! You saved my life and you kept your word. We were two of a kind. We wanted to save our skins and get rich, didn't we lad? Liberty and riches, they were the things.'

These were sentiments I had heard before, at our first meeting, but now they were uttered with a deeper sense of recognition. And my response to them was the more uncertain, because although I understood that Mr Silver was speaking of my father, I could not help gaining the impression that he thought of me as his own child.

This was not the memory I had requested, but it gave me a re-assurance about the journey that was very welcome – at the same time as it troubled me.

So welcome, in fact, and so troubling, that for a moment I stood quite still and felt nonplussed. When I was able to move again I surprised even myself. I stepped forward and kissed the crown of the old man's head; it was a thing I had neglected to do when leaving my own father a few hours earlier, for fear of waking him. The threads of white hair felt ticklish against my lips and the skin very tight.

'You are a good boy, Jim,' he murmured as I straightened again. 'You are a good boy and you must take care of Natty. You must . . .'

But the voice cracked as he spoke, so whatever he intended to say was lost. Instead, and with an awkward gulp, he lurched out to grasp his daughter's left hand and my right, holding them together in the grip of his claws and shaking them slowly up and down.

With the light pouring over us, and the wind pressing against the window, and the immense silent pageant of London and its river spread out below, it was a moment of the most complex solemnity. A wedding and a farewell at once. And when it was finished, Mr Silver threw our hands into the air, making us understand that he was sending us on our way, and if we stayed any longer we would offend him.

It was a sudden conclusion, although no doubt for the best. It allowed Natty the dignity of seeming trustworthy to her father, and us both the privilege of feeling united in a common purpose. I waited a moment while Natty once more laid her hand on her father's brow, closing her eyes as she did so – as if, by a great effort of concentration, she could absorb all the knowledge preserved inside his skull. Then she moved swiftly to collect Spot (who was now settled more calmly on his perch) before joining me again.

We walked slowly backwards out of the room as if departing from royalty, and kept our eyes fixed on Mr Silver for as long as possible. He never stirred – except, as the door closed, to lift one long hand and so repeat the blessing we had asked for.

CHAPTER 9

The *Silver Nightingale*

As I look back today from the vantage point of my later age, I am astonished that so much remained unsaid during our final interview with Mr Silver. Very little about my father. Next to nothing about the adventure they had shared. Nothing whatsoever about their later lives. Our haste in setting sail was partly to blame for this – and also my reluctance to ask questions, having already heard so many answers at home. The main reason, however, was my youth. I showed insufficient curiosity about the means of arriving in a particular situation, and excessive concentration on the situation itself, and my importance in it.

I was equally complacent about the preparations for our journey. In fact, as I followed Natty downstairs from her father, I had the same expectations of removing immediately to our ship that a gentleman might feel on leaving his house for his carriage – except I did not have any of my own possessions for the voyage. When I asked Natty whether we should fill a trunk with things we might share, she brushed me aside: her father had sent ahead with everything we could possibly need. What about her mother then? Should we not say goodbye to her? Natty frowned as if dismissing the idea, then changed her mind and led us to the taproom of the Spyglass.

Unusually for such an establishment, this was on the first floor of the building, as though to escape any floods that might occur – as well as other kinds of unwelcome visitation. When I opened the door, I found a low-ceilinged, smoke-filled den where everything was brown as a kipper: chairs, tables, floorboards, hands and faces. The ebb and flow of talk, which broke occasionally into arguments or laughter, filled my head with memories of home. But to say this was my chief impression would be to underestimate Mrs Silver. While we made our way among the customers (who were a very rough crew bundled up in old sailors' coats, with pipes fuming in their mouths and neckerchiefs pulled round their ears), she rose from behind a trestle table that filled one end of the room. Her face flushed a deeper mahogany with the effort of standing, and she spread her arms wide.

'My children!' she exclaimed, so loudly that everyone around her fell silent; I noticed especially one lanky fellow who seemed fiercer than the rest because a part of his right ear was missing – sliced off, I supposed, in a sword fight. He flicked a glance in my direction, then chewed his quid with an insulting slowness and spat on the floor before sinking back into his chair.

Natty and I stood as still as truants brought to book. This only encouraged Mrs Silver, who now shook her arms and fiddled her fingers in the air. 'My children,' she said again, 'come to me' – and she folded us strongly to her bosom. A sigh rose from our audience, accompanied by the banging of tankards on tabletops.

'My brave children,' Mrs Silver continued in a quieter voice. 'The Lord has told me what brings you here. You have come to bid farewell to your mother, and then to leave these shores in the pursuit of your fortune. "We must appear before the judgement seat of Christ; that everyone may receive the things done in his body, according to that he hath done, whether it be good or bad." The Lord has told me this. And the Lord has told me that he is satisfied. I therefore give you my blessing and let you go. Be gone! Be gone! Find your happiness and, when you are ready, return with proof of it to your mother.'

Any objection that I might have made – to the effect, for instance, that she was *not* my mother – would have been futile. I was clasped too close to do more than nod my head, which was in effect to rub it against her skin.

Natty was making more vigorous attempts to escape, which I knew because I heard Spot's cage clanking in her hand, and the bird himself give a raucous shout: 'Hold steady, my hearties!'

'Thank you, Mother,' Natty said when she had regained her freedom, sounding very relieved. This was a cue for Mrs Silver to weaken her grip on me, at which I also sprang back, breathing much faster than usual. When I looked around to get my bearings, I saw our audience in the taproom had already begun talking among themselves again – all except for the lanky man I had noticed earlier, who was now slipping towards the stairs that led onto the street, taking his mangled ear with him.

'We will be very glad of your prayers,' Natty was saying. 'We will remember you in our own, and often think of you.'

Few as they were, and softly spoken, I heard in these words what I supposed was the whole history of Natty's feelings for her mother. There was enough courtesy to show gratitude, but also a coldness, which reflected the lack of warmth she must have known all her life.

As if proving the point, Mrs Silver then closed the scene very abruptly. She waved her hands at us again – this time ushering us away – and busied herself with her customers, filling their tankards and laughing with them even before we had turned our backs. It made me impatient to be gone, but I was delayed another minute by noticing something I might have seen sooner, had I not been so distracted.

Set on a wide shelf above the lintel, and arranged in a large glass case with its wings outspread, was a magnificent parrot. The wings and body were brilliant green – green as spring grass – shading to soft yellow along the belly, from which protruded two extremely wrinkled black legs that ended in talons of a prodigious size. These grasped a fragment of mossy log, behind which rose a background of leaves to represent a portion of jungle.

The eyes of this marvellous creature were made of glass and seemed very malevolent – as did the beak, which was open to speak or bite, and was exceptionally thick, so that its layers of nail appeared separately towards the edge, like levels of rock along a coast. It was a weapon that could easily have taken a lump as large as a chicken's egg from any man's arm.

'Captain Flint,' whispered Natty.

'*The* Captain Flint?'

'The very same. Two hundred years old if a day, when your father met him. Parrots live for ever, mostly.' Natty paused to let me admire this interesting fact, then continued. 'The same Captain Flint who sailed with the great Captain England, the pirate. Captain Flint who was at Madagascar, and the Malabar, and Surinam, and Providence, and Portobello. Captain Flint who was at the fishing-up of the wrecked plate ships – that's where she learned "Pieces of eight!": three hundred and fifty thousand of them!'

Because of the eagerness with which she told this brief history, I might easily have thought Natty felt some affection for the bird. But I noticed that all the time she spoke, she kept her fists clenched tight – as if she were fired more by anger than fondness. For my own part, I could only repeat the name to myself in a state of astonishment. In all my father's stories of Treasure Island, the bird had been a constant presence – perching and fluttering on Mr Silver's shoulder, and shrieking his dreadful cry. 'Pieces of eight!' He had become as vivid to me as Israel Hands himself, or Blind Pew, or any of the rest of the buccaneers.

'Will *he* pray for us, do you think?' I asked Natty with a sort of smile.

Natty did not reply, but lifted her face and stared into the bird's unblinking eyes as though daring him to fly through the glass and attack her. It occurred to me that she was remembering times when she had felt these very talons nipping at her flesh, and this very beak. As I considered this, I decided she might in fact be the reason why Captain Flint was inside the case, and not still alive.

Eventually, and still without saying a word, Natty hoisted the cage in which her own bird crouched mutely on his perch, and led me downstairs into the street. Here, instead of heading directly towards our ship, she surprised me by turning into an alley that ran adjacent to the Spyglass, and re-entered the building through a side door. I found myself in a dim parlour where the bricks of the floor had been deeply gouged by barrels rumbling across them.

'What now?' I wondered aloud, but Natty would not tell me.

'Wait,' was all she would say. 'Wait and look after Spot.'

I did as she told me, but this was evidently not what the bird wanted, since as soon as I took hold of his cage he began calling the command 'Stand by to go about; stand by to go about' – while Natty disappeared into a narrow passageway. I had no choice except to remain alone, doing my best to calm the bird by repeating his name in what I hoped was a soothing voice. My efforts seemed only to deepen his dislike of my company.

When Natty returned, it was my turn to be speechless. The young woman who had left a moment ago, with her brown shawl and her plain woollen dress and her short black hair, had come back transformed into a boy with knee-length white linen trousers, a smart blue sailor's jacket, and a large cocked hat that slumped conveniently low over the forehead and concealed much of the face.

'Nat Silver,' she said, with her usual simplicity. 'I don't believe we have met.'

'How do you do, sir,' I said, recovering myself and giving her my hand to shake. Her own hand felt very slim in my grip. This, combined with the softness of her skin, and the beauty of her face, on which there was not a single whisker but only a faint down, made me certain that her attempt to live in disguise would not go undetected for long. I did not want to say as much, thinking she would be disappointed.

'How old are you, may I ask?' I said, still with a pretend gentility.

'This is not a game,' she replied – and frowned, which made her hat sink still further forward.

'I know that,' I said. 'But I must tell you: I think that if you claim to be younger than you are in fact, you might be more credible.'

Natty threw me an irritated glance, then saw that I only meant to make myself useful.

'Sixteen,' she said.

'Too old,' I replied.

'Fifteen, then.'

'Fourteen,' I told her. 'Admiral Nelson was at sea by fourteen. I doubt whether he looked any older than you.'

'Very well, fourteen', she said, after a pause – then rubbed both hands over her face as though to coarsen her cheeks, and cleared her throat to roughen her voice as well. With that, she evidently felt she had taken enough advice, seized Spot's cage from my hand, and strode outside into the sunlight with a rolling sailor's gait.

As we dodged westwards, along streets that lay parallel to the river, the sight of Natty now looking so gallant and handy prompted me to a question I had not previously liked to ask – though it had been much in my mind. Would we have any protection in the ship, in case we came under attack?

I expected Natty to look down her nose and accuse me of being a coward, so felt relieved when she merely said, 'I have asked my father about this.'

'And what did he tell you?'

'He told me we do not live in a barbarous age, and need not fear that kind of danger.'

'You mean there are no arms on board?'

'I did not say that. I believe there are a few. Pistols. Swords.'

Natty's reticence suggested that she herself thought our supplies might be insufficient, but was not willing to admit her father had given bad advice. I suspected this even more strongly when I heard a note of chiding come into her voice.

'I have told you before, Jim. Captain Beamish is an excellent fellow. My father has settled everything for the boat. He has paid for everything. It is very good of him.'

This made me feel put out. 'I did not suggest otherwise,' I told her – although when she did not answer, I knew I should not say any more. Indeed, I felt our adventure was so tainted by my own guilt in stealing the map, I should not quibble with any of the other arrangements, but generally follow where Natty led. I did not even feel it proper to mention that our map showed there were arms buried on the island, since I did not want to strengthen the idea we might need them. I had raised the subject in the first place and now I regretted it; I held my peace.

Perhaps Natty reckoned my silence was a proof of speechless excitement, because we were about to set sail. And I admit: by the time we reached the dockyard I was once again almost tongue-tied. Although I had lived beside the river (I might almost say *on* the river) all my life at home, and considered myself an authority on tides and currents, boats and shipping, and every kind of man, woman and creature that splashed along its banks, I had never before seen such a prodigious concentration of watery energy.

The smell of tar and freshly cut wood was wonderful – as wonderful as the figureheads of the ships all around me which had looked at the other side of the world, and now were jutting above my own head, and also above the heads of sailors with rings in their ears and whiskers curled into ringlets and pigtails. If I had seen as many kings or ambassadors I could not have been more delighted. The whole purpose of humanity seemed suddenly to be the exchange of one element for another, because the Great Flood would soon begin, and anyone who did not find a way of living *on* the water would shortly be drowned *in* it.

A dozen – more – individual quays extended from the dockside, and along each were sailors loading, unloading, haggling, cursing, heaving and sweating. The number of ships crowded into my view was too numerous to count – some sparkling with new paint, some drab from long voyages, like migrant birds that had suffered in their journeys. Above them rose a myriad of masts – some slender, some brutish, some as high as steeples, and all supporting so many hundreds of pieces of rigging the sky actually seemed dark with them.

I would have liked to stop and admire, but was so instantly caught in a great current of busy-ness, there was no time for reflection. Indeed, it would be better to say that Natty and I entirely *surrendered* to the place, since we soon felt as helpless as corks in a stream. This meant I passed the last part of our journey in a strange state of passivity – and was not in the least surprised (though at the same time astonished) to find that after swirling through assorted eddies and rapids we should come to rest at last beside a ship that seemed even more elegant and interesting than the dozens of other beauties we had already passed by.

She was a breed I had often admired from my perch in the Hispaniola: a Baltimore clipper, some hundred feet long, with two masts (both distinctly raked), a bowsprit made like a dagger to cut the waves, a flush deck, a beam rather great for her length, but the most graceful and easy lines. Had my father been at my shoulder, he would have said she was *sired by war, mothered by piracy and nursed by cruelty* – except that her nature had evidently been tamed and turned to peaceful ends, since a roundhouse had been added close to the wheel. This looked to have a clear view of every horizon, and gave the suggestion that a cruise would be preferable to warfare.

My impression grew stronger as I approached the stern, and saw a bo'sun's chair was rigged over the rail. In this sat a man who was stripped to his trousers, and working with a pot of paint to change the original name of the ship, the *Nightingale*, so that it read: the *Silver Nightingale*. The word 'silver' was there, of course, to manifest her owner, and to make him almost a member of the crew.

'The *Silver Nightingale*,' I said aloud, in a state close to wonder. 'This is ours.'

'The *Nightingale* is ours,' Natty repeated, with a similar kind of awe in her voice, which I dare say owed something to pride in seeing how well her father had provided for us. 'I told you; you need not have worried. Everything is prepared. The captain is waiting here now.'

Even before she finished speaking, Natty launched up the narrow gangplank to land herself in the stern of the vessel. Had she arrived in a more forward part of the deck, she would have remained in plain view; here, however, an arrangement of weatherboards and railings had been added to form a barrier against the waves, and this concealed her entirely.

Without any further hesitation, I followed where she had gone, and dropped down into the ship. Away to my left, a gang of men had formed a human chain, conveying boxes and chests and trunks and all manner of containers up from the quay – and I shall return to them in a moment. For now, my eyes were fixed on the *Nightingale* herself. A well-scrubbed deck of broad planks, with the shadows of rigging swaying gently back and forth across them. A low bulwark, painted fresh green. A hatch shaped like a tortoise shell that shielded steps leading below deck. An old brass long-nine gun – which was evidently more for ornament than use, since the scuttle where her cannon balls were once stored was now used for oilskins and ropes, which I saw in sleepy coils. At the foot of one mast – nothing. At the foot of the other – a large barrel, filled with ripe rosy apples. The roundhouse which I have already mentioned, and now saw was very snugly fitted out with a table and benches. No wheelhouse, but the wheel itself studded and strapped with shining brass. And beside the wheel Natty, or Nat, as I reminded myself to call her, speaking to a man the size and shape of a bear on his hind legs.

'Jim,' Natty called. The new rough note in her voice made me smile, which I hoped would be understood as nothing more than a friendly greeting. 'This is Captain Beamish.'

I walked up to him and gave my best salute, which he returned much more smartly, then removed his hat – an ancient tricorn – and

tucked it beneath his arm. Cropped brown hair and whiskers.
Wide handsome face. Bright blue eyes that might have been made
of salt water and sunlight. These narrowed very shrewdly, inspecting
me from top to toe. Whatever estimate he made about my sea-
worthiness seemed to satisfy him, for after a while he solemnly
extended one hand.

'Mr Hawkins,' he said in a warm voice.

'Captain Beamish,' I replied, sounding as expert as I knew how.

'I never knew your father,' he said, which was bolder than I
expected, and left me a little uncertain how to reply. Seeing my
confusion, he pressed on. 'I never knew him but I honour him.
In silence.'

'Thank you, sir,' I said, recovering myself. 'And it is my own wish
to travel as myself, not as anyone's relation.'

As I said this, I wondered whether I was offending Natty, who
was known by the crew to be Mr Silver's child, although not his
daughter. But she seemed to think our cases were different, and
smiled at me.

So did the captain. 'Very well,' he said. 'I am glad we are all of
one mind. We will tell the crew you are on board as a friend and
companion to Master Nat. Are you happy with that description?'

'Perfectly, sir,' I said, and dared not turn aside to see what Natty
herself might think. The fact she said nothing was a sufficient answer
for me.

'Very well,' the captain said again – then paused and lowered his
voice to a whisper. 'But I must ask you at once, my lad: have you
brought us what we need?'

CHAPTER 10

Captain and Crew

Our captain was a man whose good heart showed in his kindly face
– but what of the others aboard the *Nightingale*? Natty had insisted
they were not the same kind of men that had sailed on the *Hispaniola*
with our fathers – but the dozen or so now working behind me
seemed *a motley crew*, as the saying goes. The eldest was the bo'sun,
a brown old sailor with a barrel chest and a smooth beard like a
badger's coat; he was overseeing the proceedings. Beside him was
a much shaggier fellow, with earrings in both ears and a snub yellow
pipe that poked through the wild grey fuzz engulfing his face.
Another, whom I took to be the cook because he wore an apron
already stained with gravy, seemed so thin and delicate I wondered
whether we should ever get enough to eat. A fourth who caught
my eye was working beside the steps that led below decks, and

when the others began singing a stave, he turned his head aside to show he was not inclined to join them. As he did so, I noticed his mutilated ear and recognised him from the taproom of the Spyglass. I told myself I must have misjudged him there, since I could not imagine the captain employing the kind of person I had originally supposed him to be.

I have made this sound like a long scrutiny; in fact it was nothing of the sort – just a glance that ended as the captain released me from his handshake.

'Very wise,' he said, in a rolling voice that belonged to the West Country. 'Our business can wait a while. Just so long as you have what we require; that is all I need to know. Hold it by you a moment longer.'

He meant the map, of course, which it had never been my intention to deny him. But now that I had been given credit for keeping it secret, I pretended that discretion had always been my aim – and changed the subject.

'You are from Bristol, sir,' I told him.

'Close by. Do you know it?'

'My father's family is from there,' I said. 'He speaks as you do.'

'Your father,' the captain said slowly, relishing the word as he had done a moment before. 'Well there's a man who must have the sea in his veins. What do you have in yours?'

In a different voice, this might have sounded like a challenge. In fact it was gently spoken – though still with enough snap to make me look at Natty for reassurance. She had been watching my exchange with the captain as if she were my sponsor, and now the feel of her eyes sweeping over my face, reading my thoughts, made me take care not to claim more than my right; she would only have reproached me later.

'Not so much salt,' I said. 'Fresh water, perhaps.'

The captain laughed and clapped me on the shoulder – which I took to mean he expected I would soon encounter all manner of things that were strange to me, and had better prepare myself.

Natty, feeling this had been a sufficient introduction, now broke in. 'When do we sail?' she wanted to know.

The captain narrowed his eyes, as if not used to such forthright-ness, then bit back whatever he might have first thought to reply; he was remembering she was Mr Silver's daughter, and his repre-sentative on the ship. This made me conclude the captain was his own man, but nevertheless had respect for higher authority. And good humour, too, since he now made a play of looking at the sun, then along the length of the deck, at the height of the masts and across the rigging, and finally into the direction of the wind, before turning back to Natty again and telling her, 'Within the hour' – as though he had only this moment made his decision.

'So soon?' I said, which did not sound as enthusiastic as I meant it to be.

'We have everything we need,' the captain said. 'Now that we have you, Mr Hawkins, we have everything we need.'

With this, he took a step closer, as if he could no longer contain his curiosity, then checked and looked round about. I followed suit, and saw the crew was still occupied with the task of loading. Only one pair of eyes watched us, which belonged to the same scarred fellow who was lurking beside the hatch that covered the stairs. I would have preferred him not to be there.

'The coast is clear,' the captain murmured, despite this scrutiny. 'Perhaps we could share our secret safely. After all, if we are to set sail, I need to know my direction.'

Natty laughed at this, which was a kind of tease, but I pretended not to notice and went about my business very seriously. I opened the front of my shirt, removed from around my neck the little satchel containing the map, and handed it to the captain without a word. I could not help noticing it felt warm from contact with my skin.

The effect on the captain was extraordinary. His smiling manner evaporated and his whole face seemed to tighten and concentrate. He laid the satchel on the palm of his left hand, opened the flap, and very carefully withdrew the map. First he held it away from his face, narrowing his eyes; then he lifted it close to his eyes with such trembling caution the paper seemed to vibrate.

This was enough to excite our silent spectator so much, he gave a gasp – at which the captain and I whisked round to see a smear of white as he disappeared down the companionway, like a rabbit vanishing into a burrow.

If this troubled the captain he did not show it. Taking up where he had been interrupted, he began to pass one hand gently over the map, tracing the shape of the island. The contrast with Mr Silver was very striking; there was nothing but wonder in this touch, and nothing but delight when he scanned the paper first on one side and then the other, and mouthed some of the names he read: Captain Kidd's Anchorage, and Spyglass Hill, et cetera. The bar silver, I noticed, he left unmentioned. Also the arms.

When he had done enough admiring, he closed his eyes. Here, I thought, he was imagining his approach to the island, and the currents that might sweep us from the fairway, and the sandbanks and other obstacles he must avoid. Then he opened his eyes again and gazed with a particular intensity at the measurements of longitude and latitude, written across the top of the chart. Without these, as I knew very well, the map was a mere curiosity, though admittedly one of a very tempting kind. With them, it was a key to open the world.

'Good lad, good fellow,' said the captain in a reverential voice, turning back towards me. 'You'll have no objection if I keep it in my possession – for safety's sake?'

This jarred somewhat, since I had already begun to think of the map as my own property, but I soon saw that the captain's proposal was quite sensible. He had the authority and the experience, which meant he was much better able to protect it than I had been.

'Of course,' I told him – and then, as an afterthought that really should have been my first thought: 'Perhaps you will give it back to me when we leave the island? Then I can return it to my father in the fullness of time. You might say it is on loan from him; I am sure he will be pleased to have it again.'

The captain adopted a very serious expression, as if he did not know how guiltily I had obtained the thing. 'Very well,' he said, 'we have an agreement' – and folded the map as carefully as he had opened it, before returning it to the satchel again, looping the strap around his neck, tucking it beneath his topcoat, and finally inside his shirt, where it lay against his heart as it had formerly done against mine.

'Now that we have concluded that piece of business,' he went on, with a brisker note in his voice, 'we have to begin the next. I must ask you to inspect your lodgings below decks, and get your-selves acquainted with everything. All hands! Mr Allan!'

The last two commands brought forward the thin fellow I had supposed was the cook – though he had now taken off his apron. Behind him, in a boisterous rush that showed they knew what was required of them and did not need orders, several other crew also appeared. These very quickly finished what little loading remained to be done, then formed into two gangs: one went forward and another aft, where they stood ready to untie the ropes that held us to the quayside.

Mr Allan, meanwhile, stood with his head tipped to one side like a dog waiting to be told 'Fetch'. 'Ah! Cookie!' said the captain. 'Now, make these lads at home.'

Natty did not move immediately, as the captain wished her to do, but made the same guess as I had done and said to Mr Allan, 'My father was a ship's cook. He also had a nickname. It was Barbecue.'

The poor fellow rumpled his hair with an embarrassed expression; he evidently felt that to be mentioned in the same breath as Mr Silver was more than he deserved. 'So the captain has told me, sir,' he said. 'And very expert too, I am sure. I don't have his skills, I dare say, in barbecuing or anything else. But how could I, being the age I am? Never mind, though, never mind. You'll not go hungry so long as I'm on the *Nightingale*, I promise you that. We've plenty of vittles, don't we, Captain? Plenty of vittles. Your father himself has taken care of that, and very generous of him too, most generous in fact. We've got biscuit, and pickled fruit, and salted pork, and salted beef, and the largest bunch of grapes you ever saw, and some grand old pieces of cheese, and a whole cage of chickens, and . . .' he rushed on, without giving anyone a chance to interrupt or reply. 'You go ahead, sir, and you, sir' – looking at me – 'straight ahead, mind you don't crack your heads, and I'll follow. Take an apple as you pass. We'll none of us be hungry on this cruise, that's for certain, not so long as I'm in the galley.'

This patter continued, without Natty or me paying it much attention, until all three of us were across the deck and down the stairs into the stomach of the ship. Here we wound along a dark and narrow galley that led towards the stern and a plain wooden cabin. Two bunks had been built against the curving outer wall, one above the other, and were linked by a short ladder; these bunks, we understood, would be our beds for the journey. After glancing at one another in silence, Natty decided she would sleep on the lower level while I had the top. The crew, Mr Allan explained, had their quarters towards the prow, beyond the galley, which acted as a kind of barrier between us.

Once this had all been settled, we were left to inspect our home. I would have done this more thoroughly if I had not been so keen to return to the light and bid farewell to London – but I did stay long enough to notice that my bed was extremely small and dark, like a coffin with one side removed. Also that I would have to reach it every night by climbing past Natty's face, in order to lie directly above her. This idea brought a flush to my face, which I did my best to ignore while saying the arrangement suited me very well. With that, I went back on deck and found a place behind the wheel in the stern of the *Nightingale*, where Natty soon came to join me.

As though he had been waiting for us to admire his skill, Captain Beamish now ordered the crew to set us on our way. They did this immediately, with some men untying the *Nightingale* fore and aft, then pushing us away from the quay with long poles, and others working the capstan to raise our anchor – chanting as they did so:

Haul away you sons of Neptune – haul away;
Say goodbye to all your lassies – haul away;
For we're leaving dear old England
And we're bound across the waves;
Haul away, you sons of Neptune – haul away.

They sang this three or four times, and when the work was done we were already a yard from the dockside. The crew fore and aft now laid their poles on deck and began setting the jib, which took the breeze with a delightful clean smacking sound, so I felt the *Nightingale* quicken like a living creature. 'Have a care! Have a care!' shouted the captain, as the booms of both masts swung across deck – but the hands knew how to dodge, and in a trice everything was under control again, and we were making our way towards the river. As we found our place among the traffic heading downstream, I noticed the water made a beautiful low humming sound. This was our prow 'talking', as sailors say – treading the innumerable ripples with an incessant weltering splash.

The waterfront of London quickly vanished – docks and warehouses turning into open country, then a panorama of fields and cattle, until we reached the fancy houses of Greenwich and the little mole of the Observatory. I had seen these things only recently, rowing to and fro with Natty, but from the greater height of the *Nightingale*, and with the stronger feeling of purpose that now possessed me, they had an extra freshness and significance. Everything told me that I was leaving, that my boyhood was slipping behind me, and that I was choosing the terms of my own existence.

These feelings, I dare say, were all the more intense because Natty stood beside me. At any rate, I gave this as the reason why tears swelled into my eyes as we entered a bend of the river that I recognised as the beginning of my home stretch. It was a remarkable moment, even though it came so early in our voyage, with the blackened old timbers of the Hispaniola, and the low red sweep of its tiled roof, appearing on the horizon – as if I were returning to it as a ghost. It put me in mind of a sentence I remembered my father using in his stories, which he heard used of the pirate O'Brien, whom he called 'a rank Irelander': 'Do you take it as a dead man is dead for good, or do he come alive again?' I saw in minute detail the dozens of winding tracks I had walked since childhood, and remembered in a single instant the hundreds of lives I had seen there – the moorhens and geese, the summer visitors, and the foxes that preyed on them. It was an immense variety, but all squeezed into something like a keyhole, and set my heart racing because I knew it was passing away from me even while it came closer.

Exactly when we reached the inn – as if it had been ordained by fate – the front door opened and my father appeared. He was wearing the old blue sailor's cap he had kept as a memento of earlier days, and carried in his right hand a pail of water. My first instinct was to duck down below the bulwarks out of sight, but I thought this might draw his attention, so I stood still, without making a sound, and watched him. He walked towards the bed of roses that formed the border of our property where it met the towpath, and poured his pail of water over the flowers very studiously, making sure not to miss one. I saw the earth darken. Then he straightened, his free hand smoothing the small of his back, and glanced around him. Although he looked directly at the *Nightingale* and seemed to admire her, he did not change his expression, which to my eyes had a sad severity. Then he turned away with a shrug, and after that I saw him no more.

PART II

THE JOURNEY

CHAPTER II

The Sailor's Farewell

The Thames had been a close companion all my life – its marshes were my nursery and its tides my education. Yet once the *Nightingale* had passed my home, I soon found myself sailing through a country I had seldom visited before. The horizons felt almost infinitely far off, and on this particular evening, as daylight faded, and clouds thickened, they made the world appear very empty and dreary. Houses dwindled from few to occasional to none at all. The banks on either side slumped into mud-heaps. The water roughened as it met the open sea. From my lookout in the stern, I imagined the waves rising to meet us were an imaginary armada, made of all the enemies England had ever known – Vikings, Romans, Danes, Normans, French, Spanish, Dutch – advancing upriver in a single force towards London, where they would spread misery and grief.

Natty seemed not to notice this change in my mood, but kept looking round brightly and remarking on every twilit field and barn and farmer with a kind of astonishment. This told me that however much she loved her father, she was very glad to be free of him, and had soon found a way of putting him out of her mind. Spot, whose cage she had hung from a peg in the roundhouse, so that he swung with the rhythm of the ship, seemed equally at ease, and whistled at shipmates as they passed, or made occasional requests for 'A little bit of cheese; a little bit of cheese'.

Captain Beamish on the other hand was practical in everything he did and said; his concentration, as we slid down the crowded current, restricted him to speaking only when he had orders to give. Once we had left the estuary, however, and were riding the steadier pulses of the channel along the coast of Kent, he began to mix his instructions with remarks about our progress (which was apparently good) and anything that happened to take his fancy on the shore – including some sort of fair, or circus, that had set out its stalls on one particular strand, and flicked its lights very prettily over the dark water.

The crew continued to go about their work with such enthusiasm, it seemed second nature to them. This was especially evident the first time they set all our sails – main, top and gallant on both sticks, and even the bowsprit to give us dash. Nothing in my acquaintance with the river had prepared me for such a grand performance, since I had previously been occupied merely with rowing-boats and such-like. Here, suddenly, the whole sky seemed carved into solid squares and oblongs, each of which had a mind of their own and yet belonged to us – filling and heaving as we commanded, and putting a skip into our step so the *Nightingale* seemed to fly across the surface of the waves rather than cut through them.

Once this was done, it required several hands to keep an eye on the weather, ready to make changes if the need arose. The rest of the crew now had more liberty to do as they pleased, which meant that after evening had fallen several gathered in the forward part of the ship, where they hung two or three lanterns and began talking among themselves. They did this with so much affability, I began to trust what Natty had told me about their good character.

This was especially striking since, when all was said and done, our cruise was nothing other than a treasure hunt, and therefore bound to stir an unusual degree of excitement. And it is true to say that most of the conversations on deck, including this first one I overheard, always ended with the same subject, which was the bar silver. My shipmates knew from the captain that the majority of it would be given to Mr Silver, our patron; they had also been assured that a percentage would be shared among them as payment and reward when the trip was finished.

The badger-bearded fellow I had seen supervising the loading of our supplies, and whom I now gathered went by the name of Bo'sun Kirkby, was at pains to dampen expectations on this score. He insisted (which I understood was true enough) that the great bulk of treasure had been removed from the island during my father's visit. Several others were reluctant to believe this, or interpreted 'a modest amount o' bounty' as a considerable hoard – none more so that the party who said least, but whom I saw repeatedly clasp his fingers together, then unknot them to touch the scar beneath his mutilated ear.

'Who is he?' I asked Natty, with a tilt of my head. By this time we were off the coast of Sussex and well under way, with our sails fairly bulging.

'Jordan Hands,' she said at once, and pulled down her hat until the brim was touching her eyebrows. 'He is the nephew of Israel Hands.' She spoke with no great emphasis, and might have been telling me the price of herring.

'Israel Hands?' I repeated, astonished. 'The man my father killed? Israel Hands who was Captain Flint's gunner in the old days?'

'The same.'

I stared at her, still incredulous, but she would not meet my eye and continued quite calmly. 'Jordan is a careful young seaman, and you have nothing to fear. He is not the same man as his uncle. He bears you no ill will, my father assures me of that. Besides, my father has chosen him to come, so come he shall.'

'But you told me the captain had selected all the crew,' I protested.

'And so he has,' Natty replied. 'All excepting Jordan.'

'He must know who I am,' I continued. 'He will tell the others.'

'That cannot be his plan,' Natty said. 'If it was, he would have done so already. You are making a fuss, Jim; there is no reason to worry. The captain is content.'

This was said with a rather haughty air, as if I were foolish to think there might be anything untoward. But I could not help my surprise turning into something like anger. 'How can you say he bears me no ill will?' I said. 'By the look of him, I'd say he wants me dead in my boots.'

Natty folded her arms and turned her back to the wind; her face glowed faintly in the light of the lanterns. 'He is melancholy,' she said, 'that is all. He gives the same greeting to everyone.'

'Which is no greeting whatsoever,' I replied. 'My father has spoken of Israel Hands more than any of the crew who went before us, apart from your father himself. He was a murderer, that is all.'

'Israel was a companion to my father,' said Natty. 'But he did not . . .' She paused, and bit the inside of her lip. 'He did not *adapt* like my father.'

'He did not adapt?' I said quickly. 'He could not adapt because he was lying on the seabed. Because my father killed him.'

I expected Natty would at least show some sympathy at this, preferably for my father and what he had done to save his life. But none was forthcoming. She merely shook her head, as if to show that everything I had said was an exaggeration she could not take seriously.

I shook my own head in return. I felt I had been tricked, and made to accept a danger where none needed to exist. But there was nothing I could do to lessen it, except be vigilant. Be vigilant and, if I did not want to sour everything between myself and Natty, let the matter drop, which I immediately did. At the same time, I reckoned it cavalier of her, and surprising of the captain, to assume they would have my agreement on so delicate a matter. It told me how much they were both in thrall to Mr Silver. The old man's force of personality was evidently still extraordinary, although his body had almost ceased to be.

When I turned my attention back to the rest of my shipmates, I found they had almost exhausted the subject of treasure, except to remind one another that the bar silver had been left by Captain Flint at the same time as he deposited the larger hoard – the one my father had already taken. The hushed tone in which they spoke of what they hoped to discover was quite unlike the rapaciousness my father had found on his own voyage. Instead, it seemed to bestow a magical quality, even a luminosity, on everything they said; I think they felt the words glowing in their mouths as they talked, in the same way they imagined the ingots themselves, shining in their hiding-place beneath the sand.

This kind of dreaminess ended when Mr Tickle (whom I had noticed before on account of his yellow pipe and fuzzy beard), brought up the matter of the *maroons* – the three pirates left behind by the *Hispaniola*. Mr Tickle wondered aloud what had become of them.

'Turned into skeletons,' said Bo'sun Kirkby very abruptly – which I thought showed that he did not like to think of their suffering.

'Turned into gardeners,' said another by the name of Mr Stevenson – a Scotsman and a wisp of a fellow, whose place was generally in the crow's-nest, where he acted as our lookout.

'Eating each other,' said Mr Allan, which – judging by their laughter – the others thought was a cook's prerogative. But when this merriment had died away, another voice added his thoughts, and this belonged to Jordan Hands; it was the first time I had heard him speak.

'More likely they'll have prospered,' he said. His voice was very quiet but at the same time definite, as though his remarks were based on knowledge and not conjecture (which was of course impossible). 'They were left a good stock of powder and shot, along with a few medicines, and some other necessaries such as tools, clothing, a spare sail, and a fathom or two of rope. Also, I believe, a handsome present of tobacco.' He broke off to swallow with a dry click. 'And the bulk of the salted goat, which they could eat before they set about the animals that are native to the island, and the berries, and the oysters. Oh, they'll have prospered, no doubt on that score. Prospered very nicely, I expect.'

This verdict cast a chill over everyone, and although daylight had now entirely drained from the sky, I was still able to see disappointment hollowing their faces, as they absorbed the idea that the island might not after all be theirs and theirs alone.

Mr Allan tried to rally them by repeating 'goat and berries and oysters' twice more, in an admiring murmur as any cook might. But his good cheer was now in vain, and the conversation was done. Within a moment, the men had found an excuse of work to finish, and the whole long deck was empty except for the captain at the wheel, and Natty at my side. Then Natty said she was going to our cabin, and yawned to show me why, before saying goodnight to Spot at his place in the roundhouse (by draping his orange cloth over the cage) and vanishing towards the companionway.

The suddenness of these departures was surprising. But the novelty of the situation, and my pleasure in having myself to myself, persuaded me I should feel grateful and seize the chance to take stock. Accordingly, I moved forward to the prow of the *Nightingale*, beyond the reach of the lanterns, where I could look over the glimmering water that stretched ahead of us.

A feeling of great solitude came over me – one that took no account of the captain at the wheel, or Mr Stevenson above, where he had climbed to keep the first watch of the night, or the dozen other warm bodies below, including Natty. I told myself this was because I had a proper sense of the largeness of the world for the first time in my life, and also of its indifference. Our prow broke through the waves with a grace that was wonderful, but knew nothing of wonder. The moon, which was now beginning to climb between the clouds, timed our progress but knew nothing of time. The waves produced a most delicate mingling of cream and brown, and blue and black, but knew nothing of delicacy.

All this might have been alarming, yet it filled me with a profound sense of quiet. I held my arms straight down at my sides and let the breeze rush over my face and chest, cleansing me of everything that had weighed on me during my previous life. As I did so I heard a tune strike up, which I turned to see the captain was squeezing from an accordion. It was a far cry from the 'Fifteen men on the dead man's chest' and the 'Yo-ho-ho, and a bottle of rum' they had sung on the *Hispaniola*. Drink and the devil had done for those endless old ballads. The captain's song was 'The Sailor's Farewell', a love-ditty that anyone might learn in their youth when they begin to follow the sea, and which he now played while leaning against the wheel:

> Goodbye, my sweet ladies of England and home,
> My thoughts will stay with you wherever I roam;
> In storms and in sunshine, in drought and in rain,
> My one hope is only to see you again.
>
> The loving you give me, the loving I take,
> Is done for your kindness and dear beauty's sake;
> The thought of it lingers, 'twill always endure
> Until water and starlight and land are no more.

The captain's voice was very deep and true, and his song made me think of ancient things – the thoughts I had known, or rather felt, about my mother and father and the land where I was born. These lived very vividly in me for several minutes, but soon their beauty became too difficult to bear. I called goodnight to the captain and quickly went below decks, where the darkness felt more comfortable. When I looked at Natty on the pillow she appeared to be asleep, so I continued gazing in silence for a moment, admiring the dark beauty of her face, and especially of her closed eyes, which seemed to tremble beneath their lids as though they were conscious of my attention. This gave me a delicious feeling of conspiracy, but was at the same time disconcerting. A moment later, I had climbed up my little ladder, lain down on my bunk, and closed my own eyes tight shut.

CHAPTER 12

The Death of Jordan Hands

The weather treated us kindly, and within two days the *Nightingale* lay off Start Point on the coast of Devon, which was our last view of old England. The crew came on deck around sunset, and stood in silence as I had once or twice in my schooldays seen the audience do at a theatre. Our entertainment was not in the foreground, which showed nothing more interesting than a few seagulls wheeling through the uncertain light, but rather in the background, where smoke rose from cottage chimneys, fishing-boats returned to their harbour, and miniature figures melted from the quays. None of these things showed much evidence of particular lives, yet they suggested an *idea* of life that we were sorry to lose – however great our reward might soon be elsewhere. It was my first apprehension of a reliable truth: that every sea-journey gives a presentiment of death, before allowing us to be born again. This discovery made me one of several who sat down very quietly to Mr Allan's food that evening, and went to bed early.

I dare say my shipmates were not surprised to see me do this. Because my place on board was neither precisely crew nor guest, I had already set myself apart from the flow of things. It was the same for Natty, who of course was universally known as Nat. In the days that followed, when the rhythms of our journey were established, we were confined to a role that might at best be called *skivvying* (coiling ropes, scrubbing decks, painting bulwarks, et cetera), and at worst *idling* (sleeping, staring, daydreaming). Natty, I might add, was often chided in a harmless sort of way for being a very girlish sort of boy as she set about her tasks – no matter how she bulked herself up and used a gruff voice. She took this in good part as though entirely used to such banter, which proved an effective way of concealing the truth of her situation.

It will be clear from everything I have said that Natty and I passed almost the whole of every day in one another's company – and almost the whole of every night as well. Yet in our proximity there was a kind of reserve. We could not allow anything we said to encourage the maturing of our friendship. To have done otherwise would have threatened Natty's disguise, if any of the crew had observed us. It would also (speaking for myself) have worked my heart into a condition I might then have found difficult to control. Besides, and despite the warm feelings that Natty provoked in me, it was rather in my disposition at that time of my life to withdraw than to come forward, for I was somewhat in fear of mockery by womankind. Reflecting on this after many years, I suspect I had found an exquisite recipe for frustration. At the time I only felt that my timorousness and self-discipline encouraged me to notice every-thing, and enjoy everything, while sparing myself some anxieties about *what might happen next*.

Ten days after we lost sight of England, the wind that had propelled us from London suddenly failed, and we sank into a dead calm. I would rather be stupid, and numb, or better still unconscious, than endure again the lassitude of that time. How long did it last? I cannot tell. Perhaps a week. Perhaps two. Perhaps eternity. Long enough, at any rate, for me to feel a sailor's life was the most desperate, the most tedious, and the most pointless, of any in Christendom. Our sails hung limp as grave-cloths. A rook that had followed us from the West Country, and evidently meant to emigrate to America, glued itself to our prow and closed its eyes. The Atlantic Ocean, which I had imagined to be made entirely of roaring billows, settled into a shimmering stillness, and was so seldom disturbed by any sort of activity that the appearance of a log, or a tuft of weed, seemed like a great event. And the men? Although the captain endeavoured to keep them occupied by setting them tasks such as mending sails and checking stores, they gradually subsided into a lethargy, and thence into something more sullen.

It was not difficult, even for someone as ignorant of the sea as myself, to realise this mood might easily spark into something troublesome. However much the crew respected their skipper, and notwithstanding they were generally good fellows and mindful of the rule of law, a certain insolence crept into their behaviour. A man who slipped in the rigging, and had to be caught one-handed by another, was more roundly chastised than he deserved to be. Spot, whose regular warnings to 'Keep away' and suchlike often rang out like banging metal, was threatened with the barbecue in voices that really made me fear for his survival. The games of dice and cards, which the men frequently played on deck in the shade of a sail they had arranged to make a tent, produced more vicious curses than seemed to fit the spirit of a game. Even when the captain entertained us by playing on his squeeze-box, only a few voices rose to join his

own – and these were very reluctant. I remember on one occasion
he sang the bawdy old fragment beginning 'Don't speak to me . . .',
in which he presented himself as a woman for our amusement – but
no one was amused:

> Don't speak to me of kindness, sugar-man,
> Don't give me all your sweetness and your charm;
> I know you want to take the most you can,
> I know you talk of love but mean me harm.

On another, he gave us the whole of the ballad called 'Mistress
Anne', without a single other voice joining him:

> When my love was young and comely
> I led her through the fields,
> 'Sweet maid,' I said, 'lie down with me' –
> But no, she would not yield.

> I led her next to a wood of oak
> Astir with singing birds,
> 'Sweet maid,' I said, 'lie down with me' –
> But I think she never heard.

> I led her next to a winding stream
> All full of smooth white stones,
> 'Sweet maid,' I said, 'cross with me here' –
> But she sent me on alone.

> 'Sweet maid,' I said, when I'd had my fill
> Of all these slights and 'no's,
> 'Will any words untie your heart?
> Take pity. Tell me how.'

Then 'Sir,' she said, 'the world itself
Is all I need to love.
Not feet of clay and hands of bone
But God in Heaven above.'

And this is why I sigh and moan
And keep no company;
I have but one true heart to give
And that remains with me.

As the captain sang this song, I found myself becoming thoughtful, as often happens when we hear sweet music. In particular, I began to reflect on a lesson that our becalming had taught me – namely, that every man has a natural tendency to decline. Another idea was equally alarming. I saw I was mistaken in supposing I had been born into a gentler age than my father. Governments and navies might have begun to root out the piracy he had lived among, and the crew of the *Nightingale* might have reckoned they represented a nobler sort of savage than Mr Silver. But nothing had been done to alter a fundamental fact about our human nature – namely, the appetite for savagery passes unchanged from generation to generation, and will always emerge when a suitable occasion arises.

The calm in which we languished was just such an occasion. That is to say, the crew's treatment of one another was soon worse than irritable; it had become a variety of sickness – and eventually the day arrived when Jordan Hands became an outright agitator. Natty and I heard this because we were sitting at our usual place in the roundhouse, with the door open, when Bo'sun Kirkby reported to the captain that, by sowing insults and fanning rivalries, Hands had set shipmates against one another, while always slinking away himself and pretending innocence. Although Hands could not easily be accused of a particular crime, the captain immediately summoned him to explain himself.

Hands went through his interview without so much as a glance at his accuser, and his whole attention fixed on Natty and myself – who must have seemed like jury members, sitting on our bench in the roundhouse. Although he said nothing of great significance, the repeated and unnecessary references to his uncle all struck me as definitely as if they had been a series of blows. 'My uncle always hated a calm,' he said; 'My uncle knew how to set a sail that would catch the breath of a butterfly'; 'My uncle' – he said this with a particular enthusiasm, looking directly into my eyes – 'knew how to aim a cannon so it would blow the head off a match at a hundred yards.'

When this interview had ended, the captain sent Hands away with a warning to keep a civil tongue in his head, and learn how to rub along with his fellows – at which the fellow merely smiled to himself before slouching below deck. The captain seemed to think this meant nothing beyond a touch of 'sea-fever', and it was not my place to contradict him.

I did, however, mention my concerns to Natty when the day ended and we were alone together in our cabin. I told her plainly that I thought Hands meant to do me some ill. She gave a snort of derision – then the advice that I should not consider myself so interesting that Hands would reckon me worth hurting. I felt I had no choice but to accept the criticism. At the same time, I was implicated in his story and knew that he resented me. The thought gave me considerable anxiety, and I lay awake that night, listening for steps on the stairs that led down from the deck, long after Natty herself had fallen asleep.

The consequences followed with surprising speed, since rather than acting as a kind of balm, the captain's advice to Hands in fact excited him still further. The next day I saw him early, swaggering around the foredeck in a most ostentatious fashion, stumbling into others when he might easily have avoided them, and whispering insults that he pretended were remarks addressed only to himself.

Natty, when I pointed this out to her, was at last inclined to think I had not been exaggerating the danger he represented. 'He has lost his wits,' she told me, which she evidently thought must absolve her from having made a wrong judgement about him. I told her I thought that was indeed the case. Hands rolled his head as he spoke, and his long fingers, with their red knuckles, plucked continually at once another.

Such unsettledness, though alarming, should really be a cause for compassion. The captain evidently thought so, which is why he did not straightaway put Hands under lock and key. If he had been able to observe the man more closely, he might have taken a different course – and great trouble might have been saved. But to speak plainly, the captain was often unsighted at this time in our journey, since the canvas shelter beneath which the crew played their cards, and where Hands often strutted and gyred, had been built between the two masts of the *Nightingale*; this made it only partly visible to a person in the stern, where the captain habitually stood. For this reason it was not he but Natty and I who saw everything exactly as it happened, since we often relieved our boredom by perambulating round the deck, taking in the scenery of greasy waves and glaring horizons.

On the day I am thinking about, half a dozen crew had formed a circle inside their tent, most of them sitting cross-legged and leaning inwards to place their bets, or slap down their cards, or gather their winnings. (These bets and winnings were made with marbles, and pieces of bone, and other tokens that represented the share of treasure they supposed would eventually come to them.)

Hands was one of this group – standing outside the ring as was his wont, keeping a watch on proceedings and making occasional remarks that were meant to be disparaging. The heat of the afternoon and the somnolence of our mood initially made these too insignificant to cause offence.

Natty and I continued on our patrol, stepping over the strips of tar wherever the heat had made them bubble up between the deckboards. Slop-slop came the sound of the ocean against our hull. Creak-creak went the rigging. Groan-groan said the masts. Down and down sank all our minds into a state of waking sleep, where our usual watchfulness was diminished. Diminished and then entirely suspended, since I did not for the life of me notice the transformation in the scene I was watching.

Later reports established that Hands had delivered an exceptional insult to one of his fellows, a gingerish man named Sinker, whose lack of humour was notable, perhaps as a result of teasing about his name. Sinker responded with an equally foul word – whereupon the card game was suddenly abandoned and the circle broken. Hands and Sinker crouched at one another, bare feet braced on the deck, arms hanging low, and each holding a knife.

The moment I saw this, I ran forward with Natty and Bo'sun Kirkby. The captain, who must have peered round the obstacle of the masts, soon joined us. By this time so absolute a silence had fallen over the crew, even the scuffle of the two men's feet over the planks sounded enormous, and the captain's voice, when it came, was like a trumpet.

'Stop this!' he bellowed, placing his hands on his hips and pushing back the edge of his topcoat, to show the sword hanging from his waist. His face wore an expression of complete command, which reminded everyone the *Nightingale* was his ship, and subject to his enactments of the law.

The fact that neither Hands nor Sinker paid him any attention only deepened his anger. 'Stop this!' he repeated, even more loudly. 'Stop this now, and we shall hear no more of it.'

I was aware (because I saw a flash of black, like a shadow leaving us) that our companionable rook had been sufficiently alarmed by the disturbance to leave his post at the prow, and float into the rigging. Sinker, who was beginning to recover his temper, stood still. Hands, however, seemed to have slipped beyond the reach of his own intelligence, and continued his prowling. Perhaps this should not have surprised me, given what I already knew of his ancestor. Perhaps, too, I should not have been taken aback by his next action – which I admit did knock me very hard. He turned quite leisurely towards everyone watching, scanned our faces, then singled me out and gave me a sarcastic smile as if to say: 'It is you I am punishing, Jim Hawkins. You. No one else.'

Hands then swung round to Sinker again, shaking the hair out of his eyes and tossing his weapon lightly from palm to palm. After a few moments of jabbing and feinting, he said – more to me, I felt, than to Sinker – 'You cheated me.' His voice was not in the least excited but quite factual. Indeed, he might not have been disappointed by the murmur that arose round him, and perhaps believed it was a show of sympathy. There was certainly a moment when he stood more nearly upright, and rolled his shoulders – which seemed to me like the prelude to peace, and a handshake, and the remainder of the card game.

I was quite wrong. Hands was not standing himself down. He had merely sensed an advantage. Dipping to the left and gripping his knife more tightly (which I saw by the whitening of his knuckles), he threw it quickly forward.

Sinker's shirt-front, which until this moment had hung loose from his bony shoulders, was suddenly pinned above his heart, as though it had snagged on a thorn. Around the thorn, a blossom of blood appeared. Sinker stood still, with his neck twisted to look down at his wound, and seemed to be astonished by it – as were we all, to judge by the stillness that seized us. Eventually, with a marvellous slowness, he grasped the knife handle and attempted to remove the blade from his body. When it would not come, a frown of annoyance passed over his face, but only of a mild kind, which suggested that he would slip downstairs to the galley in a moment, and comfort himself by eating a biscuit. Then this expression changed into a mask of sadness and his legs gave way beneath him. He made no attempt to protect himself in the fall, whereupon the back of his head banged loudly against the deck, and two of his shipmates rushed forward, kneeling at his side. One took his pulse, then looked round at the rest of us and pursed his lips.

My first dead man.

I had been so caught in the scene while it unfolded, I had no sense of what might follow. But as I stared at Sinker where he lay, I realised I should now be concerned that Hands might turn on the rest of us, and on me especially, to continue in his madness. I could think of nothing except how the soles of Sinker's feet, where they were angled towards me, were blotched with soft buttons of tar, and fissured like the dried bed of a stream. When I lifted my eyes, I found that Hands himself had fallen into a similar kind of reverie. Far from chasing after other victims, he stood still and exhausted, with his whole body as useless as the sails that drooped above our heads.

In such a state of torpor, it was very easy for one or two of his shipmates to lay hold of him, which the captain now ordered them to do. Easy as well for them to lead him below decks and imprison him there, while others collected the body of their friend and laid it on a long sack, after tugging the knife from his chest.

When this was all done, I found some of my energy had returned

– enough, in any event, for me to take Natty by the arm and lead her to the starboard side of the *Nightingale*, where we could contemplate the clean water lapping beneath us. Our silence was not so much a matter of our having nothing to say, but of having too much – although, for my own part, I was not certain what *too much* might actually be. I had seen Death for the first time. I had felt the warm surface of my life split open, and glimpsed something cold beneath. These things were self-evident, but a question remained. Had I been the witness to a kind of aberration, or a reliable truth?

Natty's face, with the greenish light of the swell reflected across it, gave no indication of whether she was debating the same question. Exactly as she had done when rowing me upriver, and again when we had sat with her father in his cockpit, she kept her thoughts to herself. I could permit myself to feel we were in broad sympathy with one another, but understood that if I wanted her to feel for me more deeply, I would have to make a more active demand on her interest.

It might seem unnatural for such thoughts to have occupied me so soon after the murder. But if I am to give a true account of my adventure, I must admit that in this particular circumstance I felt more curiosity than tenderness. And my curiosity grew to fascination when the captain, having spoken to Bo'sun Kirkby, came aft to interrupt the peace that I was enjoying with Natty, and informed us that he required our attendance.

I bridled somewhat at the phrase, since it had the ring of an order about it, and I was used to speaking with the captain in the language of friendship. But I understood this was an emergency, and went willingly with the bo'sun until we were in the waist of the ship, where the body of Sinker had been laid out. This had been done with as much reverence as possible, but the effect was still very humdrum: the man was wearing the clothes in which he had been killed, with the blood still wet on his shirt, and his lank hair blowing about his face. His right eye had not been perfectly closed, so that he seemed to be taking a final sly look at the world, and therefore to be noticing that the sack on which he lay was very dirty, and sprinkled with pieces of the grain it had lately contained.

The captain stood on the further side of the body, while the rest of us formed a semicircle opposite. He informed us in a very straight-forward way that he had two offices to perform – the first being a burial. He produced from a pocket of his topcoat a small prayer book, which I noticed was much thumbed and had several loose pages. Having found the service he wanted, he lifted the book close to his face and began to read. His voice moved quickly over the words, which showed he was not enjoying the task in hand, and when he reached the passage that mentioned committing the body of our shipmate to the deep, he positively glared at Bo'sun Kirkby and Mr Tickle. At this signal, they picked up poor Sinker, and made him as good as his name. They lifted him on his sack and swung him over the side and let him go. The rest of us knew he had begun a better life when we heard the splash.

Before silence could settle again, the captain quickly put away his prayer book, straightened his hat, cleared his throat, and called for Jordan Hands to be brought on deck. As he did so I realised that his haste was not the result of a lack of feeling for the office he had just performed, but a sign of nervousness about what came next – since it involved a more complete sort of test and confrontation.

A moment later, Hands was standing face to face with the captain; his wrists were bound, and Bo'sun Kirkby and Mr Tickle were close on either side of him. In spite of this, Hands tipped his head back-wards and stuck out the tip of his tongue. I noticed that since he had last been on deck, he had wound a bandage round his thumb, where he had cut himself in his fight.

The captain continued to look flushed and serious, as I saw when he removed his hat and tucked it underneath his arm, in a way that suggested he was not merely in command of the *Nightingale* but of the entire world. In that instant a frail breath of wind – the first we had felt for many days – bloomed into the sails and made them tighten. The ship immediately began to yaw about, and the line of the horizon behind the captain disappeared then heaved into view again. Although I felt engrossed by the scene before me, I could not help noticing one of the crew (a very dainty man named Mr Lawson) peel off from the crowd and trot aft – to take a hold of the wheel, I supposed, since it was obvious that our becalming had ended, and we would soon be under way again.

The change sent a ripple of talk through the men, and several turned to look behind them, where the sun was already curtained by clouds. The captain ran the fingers of one hand through his hair, and demanded we listen to him and finish the business we had started. He then began speaking in the same rapid voice as before, which at least now had the excuse that his ship needed him to hurry.

'Gentlemen,' he began, which made one or two of the crew raise their eyebrows, since none of them assumed themselves to be any such thing. 'Gentlemen, I shall be brief but I hope not careless. With the power invested in me as captain of this ship, I ask you to witness that Jordan Hands stands accused of the murder of Robert Sinker, and to notice that I intend to keep him a prisoner in chains until we return to England, when he will be delivered to face the sentence of the law.'

Another darker ripple of comment now ran through the men, which I could not so easily interpret. My first thought was: they did not appreciate the captain's judgement, although it seemed quite reasonable to me. My second, which was re-enforced by the fact that Bo'sun Kirkby and Mr Tickle pressed against Hands more urgently, was that they wished to see an immediate punishment. I must confess, although it does me no credit, that I myself felt uneasy at continuing our voyage with a murderer lurking in our midst – ready to escape at any moment, or likely to do us further harm.

As for the prisoner himself: he seemed to have inflated since committing his crime, and to be standing his ground, and looking about him with greater confidence. It made me reflect that in becoming wicked he had become himself, which I took to be a dreadful possibility.

'Remove him below,' said the captain, which conveniently ended this line of reasoning. He had interpreted the restlessness of his men as a sign of agreement, and had not noticed or chosen to care about the change in Hands himself. Without waiting to see his orders carried out, he crammed his hat back upon his head, checked the buttons of his coat, and made his way towards the stern, where he took charge of the wheel from Mr Lawson.

As he went, the majority of shipmates also scattered to their duties, since by now the *Nightingale* was rolling scuppers under in the swell. The booms were tearing in their blocks, the rudder was banging, and the whole hull was creaking and groaning and jumping like a manufactory. Some men set about tightening ropes, some slammed the bolts on doors and flaps, some vanished to their quarters to make everything secure below decks. Natty and I took up our place in the roundhouse, where Spot greeted us by saying, 'Have a care, have a care' – to which I should have paid more attention than I did.

Although it was only a moment since the court scene had ended, the sky was now entirely overcast. The ocean, which had been as still as the surface of an eye, and possessed the same sort of density, had begun contorting into waves, some of which were already fringed with white. A steady wind, flecked with rain, had taken every sail that was set – and the sound of their stretching and straining seemed delightful. Only our resident rook was put out by these changes, since he had been dislodged from his place in the rigging, and now circled us making a series of very offended remarks. Spot, who must have heard them as clearly as we did, closed his red eyes and pretended to feel indifferent.

This sudden business gave Hands the opportunity he needed. To have seen him during what I must call his recent *arraignment*, any observer would have thought as I did that the ropes binding his wrists were held by those standing either side of him. In fact they were not – which allowed him to retain a great degree of freedom, even as he began his journey towards the companionway. So much freedom, in fact, that instead of following meekly where he had been directed, he astonished us all by giving a sudden leap sideways, and landing on top of the gunwales that ran round the *Nightingale*. There, and in spite of the quickening movement of the ship beneath him, he kept his balance and squared his shoulders like an orator. Each of us stopped whatever we were doing, and gazed at him.

For a moment I thought he might be about to unmask Natty, and reveal her to be the young woman she was, or else to expose me as my father's son. But his tirade was more general. 'Why?' he demanded of us all. 'Why should I suffer in the dark, only to die in England?' His voice was loose like his body, and slid from word to word with a strange languor, as though he might be drunk. 'My life is my own,' he continued. 'I choose to keep it or lose it, not to give it over for any one of you to manage.' As he paused he glared at the captain, and in particular at his throat, as if he wanted to slit it open. After this moment of loathing, he then scoured the deck with his eyes until he found my face inside a window of the roundhouse. The effect was to make me cringe like a child before his master.

'Jim Hawkins,' he called to me, in the same watery drawl. 'I had hoped our lives might run along side by side for a while, so our enmity could have been resolved – as I decided.' His eye fixed on me as he said this, which in the confusion of the moment I barely understood.

'Be that as it may,' the voice went on, with a sincerity that made it terrifying, 'I still have enough breath to curse you. Which I do, Jim Hawkins. I curse you. May everything you desire be a torment to you, and everything you get be poison.'

With that, when he seemed to be warming to his subject and likely to continue for several more sentences, his mouth closed, the red tip of his tongue disappeared, and he lifted into the air as though the wind had caught him. He hovered for a moment with his shirt-tail flapping behind him, then dropped silently out of view.

Every one of us that could rush forward now did so; because I was one of the last to arrive at the place where he disappeared, I had to push a way through the men to see the last act of the drama. Hands was upright in the water like a wooden statue, bobbing among the steep grey waves. His eyes were wide, and looked quickly from face to face as the current carried him along the broadside of the ship. After this moment of interrogation, he began speaking again, or rather shouting: 'I curse you. I curse you. I curse you. I curse you.'

Not one of us made any attempt to throw him a line, which in any case he would not have been able to take, but stared in silence as the wind carried us quickly away from him. I had half a mind to run aft and watch him vanish entirely, but as I began to move Natty put her hand on my arm. 'Leave it be,' she whispered to me. 'Leave it be.'

A moment later he had been swept from our view, and we had nothing to see but the wide wilderness of empty water.

CHAPTER 13

A Universe of Wonder

The earth remembers us. We are generally survived by the homes we have lived in – and our improvements, like our desecrations, leave marks on the landscape that curious historians may study. When we no longer live and breathe, headstones show where our journey has ended. In all such ways, the solid ground resembles a book, in which our stories are recorded.

The sea is the opposite. Rolling waves eradicate everything written on them, whether it is the wake of a ship, or the passage of the wind, or a log, or a bottle – or a man. After every kind of interruption, water wants nothing more than to be its simple self again.

Such thoughts preoccupied me after the death of Jordan Hands. When I had finally pulled away from Natty, and gone to the stern of the ship despite her protest, I kept my eyes fixed on what I thought must have been the exact spot where he had jumped – but within a second or two I could no longer be sure whether it lay in this hollow or that. Then I concentrated on the idea of his body sinking through various levels of darkness. This also proved a failure, since my imagination could not reach as far as the seabed, but became distracted by the question of what creatures, such as jellyfish and sea horses, might survive at such depths. Eventually – which was only a matter of minutes afterwards – I resolved not to stare downwards or back, brooding on the violence I had seen, but instead to look up and forward, and so anticipate whatever new trials would soon come. The decision gave me a distinct sense of relief.

A relief, I admit, that was accompanied by a paradoxical feeling of anxiety. Before I had stolen my father's map, I felt superior to those who first set sail for Treasure Island. Brooding on my crime persuaded me I had been overconfident. And because I knew I was no better than them, I also knew I would be no safer than they had been.

In my heart, and without a word to Natty or the captain, I began an apology to my father, and a prayer for his forgiveness. I did this in solitude, continuing to stand for a while in private in the stern of the *Nightingale*, and as I watched the waves wrap round one another, I could not help recalling the story of Noah. My prayers circled like the rook, which flew to and fro while the waters covered the earth, and could not find a place to settle.

Superstitious readers will already have speculated that our better progress had been allowed by the demise of Hands. Like Jonah (I am now remembering a different part of scripture), he appeared to have been responsible for our becalming. Yet as I finished these orisons to my father, good sense persuaded me that no man, however malevolent, could claim such a great control over nature. When I turned to face the midships again, and looked at the crew, I noticed a similar stubbornness in them as well. They might have become more sensible of our situation, but they were also more galvanised. There was a new eagerness in the work of setting sails, and a new determination in Captain Beamish.

Indeed, from this point onwards the captain was seldom away from his place at the wheel. The map he kept with him at all times, tucked within its satchel and hidden inside his topcoat. I was content with such an arrangement, since I was sure that whatever dangers we might encounter, they would not begin with him. Nor did I expect them to come from the sea. Although the blow that carried us forward did sometimes gather strength and threaten to become a storm, for the most part we felt the same kind of gentle pressure that a child knows when a parent's hand pushes between his shoulder blades and encourages him towards his goal. We *pranced* through the waves – and as we extended our journey south and west, the cold skies of the old world gradually rolled away behind us, and were replaced by a depth of blueness and of warmth that I had never experienced in my life before.

In my own opinion, we had entered a universe of wonders. Among the herring gulls and black backs that occasionally appeared overhead, and were familiar from home, I began to notice more extraordinary kinds of bird, that were only known to me from books. On one occasion, an albatross attached itself to us for several hours, hanging off our starboard side and keeping pace with very few and easy strokes of its enormous wings; because we remembered the story that these birds are the souls of sailors who have drowned, we watched it with a melancholy reverence, and were almost pleased when it abandoned us. On other days marvellous kinds of tern appeared – some very small and quick, others as large as gannets. Increasingly I saw birds whose names I did not know at all – one (pure white, with a speckled breast like a thrush) had the odd habit of leaving its long green legs trailing behind it as it flew, so that when it made passes over the deck of the Nightingale, some shipmates would jump up and attempt to catch them, saying they would be eating well soon.

The sea was even more remarkably full of novelties. By night, when the moon turned the waves into a bolt of velvet that ridged and collapsed in almost complete silence, we noticed what seemed to be chains of light – like water turned into fire – decorating the hollows as we cut through them. My first idea was: it must be a reflection of the moon or stars, but a nearer look (achieved by hanging giddily over the side of the Nightingale, until the spray flicked my face) revealed it to be natural phosphorescence.

By day we had an equal share of marvels. I found each wave, instead of being the big, smooth glassy mountain it seems from shore, was full of peaks and smooth plains and valleys. Very often a school of dolphins appeared among these slopes and summits, giving the impression – thanks to the curved line of their mouths – that they kept us company, and leaped in and out of the waves, for no reasons except their own pleasure and our entertainment. Sometimes we watched a piece of driftwood, or a tonsured head that turned out to be a coconut, tumble over and over in the swell: no great thing in itself, but in the heat of midday, with a soft wind blowing, and the deck sweetly rolling, enough to induce a kind of trance.

I lost many hours concentrating on nothing other than the movement of waves themselves – the long surges of the mid-Atlantic, which are much larger in their stride than the waters around any coast, and swept towards us like the glistening backs of legendary monsters. And one day in particular I was occupied with monsters themselves – right whales, which came close enough to make us feel a part of their fraternity.

It was a morning of unusual brilliance, with the sky almost purple blue, and the sea a very intense yellow. This yellow, when Natty and I came to examine it, was produced by many millions of small seed-like objects, each a miniature bright sun; they were entirely mysterious to me, but familiar to the crew as 'brit' – being, I suppose, a truncation of 'bright'.

This yellow was delectable to the whales, as we could see because every one of them grazed on it hungrily, pushing forward with slow lashes of their fins. They kept their mouths wide open as they did this, so the brit clung to the fibres stretched between their jaws, and was in that way separated from the water draining away at the lip. It was a most beautiful sight, made all the more so for being accompanied by a soft slicing noise, as if the whales were harvesters in a field of wheat – which indeed they seemed to be, for behind them they left clear tracks of green water, showing where they had been and what they had consumed.

Had we not kept a very definite idea of our purpose in setting out from London, and a strong desire to return home in safety, we might have spent several months examining such things, and regarded them as an end in themselves. As it was, we enjoyed them while we were able – and then, as our destination drew close, suddenly abandoned them.

I suppose they were nothing more than a diversion for us. Yet the memory of these weeks, with their long periods of quiet, and their slow disclosure of nature's mysteries, have remained in my mind as clearly as the events I shall soon describe. I believe they taught me as much about the infinite capacity of things to be surprising – and a great deal about the power of beauty.

CHAPTER 14

Land Ahoy!

Our pleasure in travelling on board the *Nightingale* was more certain than our knowledge of how close we might be to our destination. This was because the captain kept such information to himself – which I thought was only sensible – while more and more often disappearing into his cabin to labour over charts and quadrants. Because it was impossible for any of us to gauge our progress by his comments (of which there were very few), or by landmarks (of which there were none but indeterminate waves), I relied instead on the gradual intensification of the suspense in which we all lived, and the greater appetite we had for gazing at the horizon.

The captain fed this appetite by keeping Mr Stevenson in the crow's-nest, where he swayed over our operations like a god in his cloud, making occasional observations about whales or flocks of birds that happened to be passing. Once or twice he brought us to a halt in whatever we were doing by calling 'Land ahoy!' – but on such occasions the captain quickly answered that it could not be *our* land, since we had not yet sailed sufficiently far into the Bay of Mexico. On several other occasions Mr Stevenson threw down comments about other ships he had seen, and especially slavers. I am glad to say none of these came close enough for us to have any communication – glad, because everything in my education (and, I would like to think, my character) had already persuaded me the trade was repugnant. I can say with confidence that I did not need the support of laws to reach these conclusions, although I have since been mightily pleased to see such laws come into existence.

When night fell, the captain generally called Mr Stevenson down from his perch and changed him with another man, who had rested during the day; Mr Stevenson would politely resist this, saying he knew his place, and enjoyed his work – which he would then resume as soon as possible the following morning. On the evening of which I am about to speak, the exchange was Mr Tickle, who to mark the occasion had pressed a fresh plug of tobacco into his pipe, and dressed his head in a red cap that appeared to be made of pieces of carpet.

As was the custom, shipmates gathered round the foot of the mainmast when this changeover occurred, with some congratulating Mr Stevenson as he stepped onto the deck – where he flopped like a puppet whose strings had been cut – while others patted Mr Tickle on the back and wished him good luck. Then we watched him disappear into heaven.

Darkness falls very quickly in the Caribbean; one moment the sky is full of dying glory, the next it is cloaked with stars. At such times of change I especially enjoyed lying on deck beside Natty, so that we could more comfortably gaze at the universe sailing above.

Night is a dead monotonous period under a roof; but in the open world it passes lightly, with its stars and dews and perfumes. What seems a kind of temporal death to people choked between walls and curtains is only a light and living slumber to the man who sleeps under the sky.

With the gentle wind blowing across our faces, and the quiet slashing of the waves against our hull, both of us would soon be hesitating on the boundary between waking and sleeping – wondering whether the stars were real, or the product of some idealising dream into which we had fallen. For my own part, I am sure I would have continued happily in such a state until morning – had it not been for the occasional accident of my hand brushing against Natty's arm or thigh, which always brought me back to myself again. Whether or not she welcomed these occasional contacts I could not decide, since she never mentioned them or returned any obvious sign of affection. In different circumstances, this would certainly have troubled me. Here I decided it meant nothing, since we had already agreed that discretion was the better part of her disguise.

So it was on the night of which I am speaking: darkness as soft as moss overhead, thickly inlaid with stars; the moon hanging as large and clear as a plate; breeze urging us onwards; Mr Tickle in his nest overhead, where I imagined him sucking his pipe and occasionally patting his beard to extinguish the sparks he had ignited there; and the captain coaxing a sweet melody from his squeeze-box, singing quietly as he did so:

> Do you miss me, sweet ladies,
> Do you keep me in your heart?
> As for me, I'm always with you,
> Never mind how far apart.

Starlight shines on me like dewfall,
Sun or rain is what you see;
Though the world keeps us asunder,
Love remains eternally.

Deepest loss means sweetest greeting,
Deepest vows mean sweetest pain;
So miss me dearly, all you ladies –
Then wrap me in your arms again.

When Mr Tickle first called down to us, the dying strains of
this song almost drowned him out – which made him shout
more urgently:

'Land ahoy! Land to starboard!'

'Come again, Mr Tickle?' called the captain. 'What can you see?'

'Land ahoy!' came the cry another time, and much more loudly.
'Land to starboard! A mile off or I'm a liar!'

In a second the captain braced himself completely and, while he
spun the wheel a few clicks to the west, the deck suddenly became
frantic with shipmates crowding along the side of the *Nightingale*.
When Natty and I joined them, most were already pointing into
the distance, cursing and laughing to themselves. Such performances
had happened before, when other islands had appeared on our
horizon, but this time the captain did nothing to dampen the excitement. Indeed, when I turned to look back at him, he was leaning
forward and smiling very broadly; his squeeze-box, I noticed, had
been passed to Bo'sun Kirkby, who let it dangle in his hand, where
it gave occasional mournful sighs.

When I faced the horizon again, I thought Mr Tickle might
have been deceiving himself – and us; although I narrowed my
eyes like the most seasoned mariner, I could not find any kind of

interruption between sky and sea. Yet such was my eagerness, I soon persuaded myself yes, there was some vague outline in the extreme distance, although in truth it was no more definite than a breath on a window pane.

Once I had noticed this, however, a kind of miracle occurred. The breath became a substance – an almond shape, like half an eye. Then the eye became a mountain. Then the mountain became three mountains, running up clear in spires of naked rock until there was no doubt left in my mind. We had found Treasure Island. Although I had only the light of the moon to guide my eye, I found Spyglass Hill – like a pedestal to put a statue on, just as my father had told me. There at its feet and a few hundred yards out to sea was the smaller bulk of Skeleton Island, and the little bump of the White Rock. There was the channel and bay that would accommodate a ship of our draught.

On my father's map, this bay was known as Captain Kidd's Anchorage – and it was here that I assumed our own captain meant us to drop anchor, since he now beckoned me to his side at the wheel. I tapped Natty on the shoulder and whispered that she should come with me.

'You see where we are, Jim?' said the captain, speaking in a low voice.

'I do, sir,' I told him.

'And you, Nat – do you see where we are?'

She nodded – a curt bob with no words, which I took to be a sign of her strong feelings. I imagined her father's hand choking the speech in her throat, as she saw him making this same approach, through this same fairway towards this same shore.

'I propose,' continued the captain, 'that I should do as others before me, and lay up here in the Anchorage. If the map is telling the truth, which I have no reason to doubt, it is clear sand there.

We can go ashore in the morning; the stockade is only a short distance beyond the marshes.'

'If the marshes are not too marshy,' I said, and was immediately conscious that my excitement had made me sound childish.

'And if the stockade has not rotted away,' added Natty, with rather more dignity.

The captain grunted, which showed he understood what we both meant, then called over Bo'sun Kirkby and invited him to take the wheel. When this was done he ordered several of our sails to be taken down, so that we could proceed at a slower speed in case we encountered sandbanks not shown on our chart; after this, he set a watchman in the prow, then led us to the starboard side of the *Nightingale*, where we stood apart from the other men. Here he slid the telescope from his belt and, after placing it against his eye, swept the lens carefully backwards and forwards – searching, I thought, for a clear route into the Anchorage.

I took the opportunity to look more carefully at Natty. Her recent silence suggested she might have regretted the first part of our adventure was already over, because she was now face to face with a history she did not want to contemplate: her father's duplicity, and the evil he had done. But now that I could see her expression more clearly, with the moonlight pouring over her features, I decided she was not so much troubled as determined. While the rest of us were very eager to set foot on dry land, and claim what we had come for, Natty seemed almost desperate. Her head was thrust forward, her teeth were biting her wide bottom lip, and her breath was coming in quick gasps. I believe that if she had thought it would bring her to her prize more quickly, she would have dived overboard and swum ashore there and then, regardless of the danger. As it was, she was so resentful of having to remain on board, she had sent her imagination ahead. Her feet were already padding over the

wet sand, climbing towards the cabin where her father and mine
had decided their fate and – at a prodigious distance – ours as well.

When I looked away from her again, I expected to see the captain
had finished his inspection of the island, and was ready to give the
orders for our approach. Instead, I found he was still holding the
telescope, so that it concentrated on a particular spot. A weight
seemed to have settled on his shoulders. My first thought was: he
had noticed some obstacle to our progress, and would shortly order
the men to take any necessary action to avoid it. The longer this
did not happen, the more strongly I suspected a sinister reason –
and felt an immediate shiver of dread when he bent towards me and
said, 'You have young eyes, Jim. Tell me what you see.' He was
speaking quietly enough for his voice to be inaudible to the rest of
the crew, whose excitement on finding the island had now abated
somewhat, and who were going about their business, or staring
ahead, with a quiet concentration.

I took the telescope without a word and lifted it to my eye; the
brass was still warm. There was a moment of plunging wildly from
heaven to earth, then from wave to wave, before the dark mass of
land settled in my sight. At this time I suppose we were still approxi-
mately half a mile offshore. Such a distance, at night-time, would
have been impenetrable had the moon not been shining so strongly
above us. As it was, I saw everything simplified, but nevertheless
with startling clarity. Here were the trees that had sheltered my
father; this was the earth where he had left his footprints.

'Not in the hills,' breathed the captain, interrupting me. 'On the
shore. Look on the shore.'

I did as I was told, and swung down from the darkness of
Spyglass Hill until I came to a long thicket, which continued from
the top of one of the sandy knolls, spreading and growing taller
as it went, until it reached the margin of a broad fen, through

which several small streams and one larger river soaked their way into the Anchorage.

There was nothing else to it – no sign of life – and I pulled away past a band of more feathery trees until I came to a patch of open ground. The steady moonlight showed this to be dotted with what I first supposed to be large boulders. As I tightened the focus and looked again, it occurred to me that these shapes were in fact tree trunks that had been felled and left to rot, over an expanse of several acres. My heart immediately started to beat more quickly. It had been my father's recollection, and the captain's assumption, that only three maroons were left on the island when the *Hispaniola* had sailed away some four decades before. How could three men have done so much? More pertinently: why had they taken the trouble?

The answer began to emerge when my eye slid further towards the west. Hitherto this part of the island had been concealed behind the silhouette of Skeleton Island. Now our silent progress had brought us to the point where I saw it for the first time – and noticed a pale glow spreading along the foreshore, and out across the water towards the White Rock. I focused on this protuberance for a moment, finding it was topped with a shivering clump of what appeared to be large ferns, then went back to the island. The light was now creating long shadows and strange tricks of scale and perspective, but I could decipher more tree trunks lying among tufts of grass, and also ribbons of beaten earth that meandered here and there. It was not until I tracked several hundred feet still further to the west that the source of this light became obvious. I found a large bonfire, a regular blazing pyramid, such as people use to send messages across wide distances. But in this case there was no intention of communicating a meaning, since there was no expectation that anyone existed who might be able to receive it.

The fire had been set for the sole purpose of warming and lighting

– but warming and lighting *what*, I could not decide. In so far as the leaping shadows and the narrowness of my view allowed, I made out a large central area, like a forum, surrounded by a wall made of pointed staves. To the eastern and western sides, like square wings, smaller compounds had been built; one seemed to contain several crosses, arranged higgledy-piggledy; the other was full of animals.

These I could easily interpret as a graveyard and some sort of farm pen – but the palisaded area between them was more puzzling. In the centre rose a structure about twenty feet high, and shaped in elevation like a colossal fan; what purpose it served was obscure, since from my seaward position I could look only at the *back*. Beyond it, on the right-hand side of the square, stood a log-house that was punctuated by tight windows and fronted with a veranda. Opposite, on the left-hand side of the square, was a building of equal size but much dingier – without windows, and only a kind of porch shielding the door. The first of these matched my father's description of the cabin that had stood in his day, where Mr Silver had made his negotiations. The second, I supposed, had been built more recently.

So much construction – almost a little village! – struck me as remarkable. Much more astonishing (and which I noticed in the same giddy instant as the buildings) was the number of people who flickered through the scene – the majority very dark-skinned, so far as I could tell. Several lounged, or sat, or sprawled on the ground around the more comfortable cabin; I happened to tighten my focus on them first, and received such a surprise that the telescope jumped against my eye.

Although occasional thin clouds drifted off the crown of the island, there was still enough moonlight for me to form a definite impression of everything I saw. Five or six of the people who had appeared to me were European, and the rest were not fellows at all but women, which I could tell because none of them wore a stitch of clothes on the top half of their bodies, and not much below; their skin seemed to glisten in the slippery light of the fire. All these women, where they were allowed to remain so, sat very still. The men, by contrast, behaved with wild abandon, lurching and dancing and suddenly toppling this way and that, which made me suppose they had found a way of making themselves drunk. One of them, in the few seconds that I looked at him, stripped off his belt and used it first to taunt a woman lying before him on the ground, then to bind her hands before flinging himself down on her.

I flinched at this, and immediately swung my lens towards another part of the stockade. But here I found scenes of an even greater barbarity, such as I cannot bring myself to describe. Women (in the same state of undress) fetching and carrying, or sitting in groups with their heads bowed. Barefoot urchin-children scampering or trudging or sitting in ones and twos. Men in rags, some lying prostrate, others hobbling with such hopeless shambling fatigue, I knew they must be exhausted. Several dozen of them swam across my eye, appearing and disappearing like figures in a nightmare, as I tried to understand what I was seeing.

Before I could make any sensible decision, Natty was speaking to me. 'There are people here?' she said; it was a question but delivered with such flatness it might as well have been a statement.

I lowered the telescope, and was wondering how best to answer her when the captain spoke for me.

'There seem to be, yes,' he said.

'I can see their fire,' said Natty.

'Yes, they have a fire,' I said, still numbed by what I had witnessed.

'And will they see us?' Natty asked. 'Have the people seen us?'

This question brought me to my senses, and made me realise that I had been so compelled by everything I had discovered, I had not considered the question of my own visibility. Neither, apparently, had the captain – and now the danger had been pointed out to him, he hurriedly gave orders for yet more of our sails to be taken down as quietly as possible, so that we very soon came to an almost silent stop on the surface of the ocean. Although this emergency must have puzzled our shipmates, they had sufficient trust in their captain to do his bidding without question – and to go about their work very quietly, which he also commanded.

For a minute or two we hung still, scarcely daring to breathe, and wincing whenever the *Nightingale* gave one of her characteristic creaks or groans. It soon became clear, however, that the inhabitants of the island were so preoccupied, and so completely unprepared for visitors, that we were safe. Our silhouette, if it had been noticed at all, had been dismissed as a figment.

After a further interval, the captain himself confirmed this. Taking the telescope from my hand and putting it to his eye once more, he whispered, 'Thank God.'

'We are safe?' I asked.

'We are safe.'

'What does it mean?' I continued, speaking very low. 'What have we found?'

'I am not sure,' he said, in a distracted tone that showed that he was still concentrating on the stockade. 'Not sure at all.'

Natty was not satisfied by this. 'What are the people doing?' she said bluntly. The captain, who was again sweeping his telescope carefully to and fro, made us wait a long time before giving his reply – and, when it came, it was not precisely an answer.

'I have decided what we should do,' he said, suddenly compressing the telescope with a series of oily clicks. 'We should give ourselves time.'

With this, the dream-like slowness of the last several minutes ended and everything quickened again. The captain patted us both lightly on our shoulders, to make us feel we had done well as his advisers, then briskly returned to the wheel and ordered Bo'sun Kirkby to gather the men round him. They came as silently as ghosts, and when every face was fixed on his own, and all equally pale in the moonlight, the captain spoke to us in a peculiar sort of stern whisper, so that his voice would not carry across the water. 'We shall not land here,' he said. 'We shall head towards the northern part of the island, and arrive in a different place.'

A murmur arose when my shipmates heard this, because they had not seen everything that we had, and did not understand the extent of our danger. But the captain was very business-like, no matter how softly he spoke. 'Look sharp and not a word, if you please,' he said. 'We don't want to wake the mermaids that live here.' To show there would be no more discussion, he then took hold of the wheel and turned it several degrees, so that our prow began to swing from due west to north-west.

Treasure Island sank back into the darkness like an animal shrinking into its lair. Or perhaps I should say the *Nightingale* itself disappeared into the night, like a moth that had been drawn towards a flame but luckily escaped its heat. I found a place beside Natty on the port side, where I could imagine the breeze prowling across the exposed slopes of Spyglass Hill, and sighing through the fringe of its melancholy woods, as easily as I could hear the waves breaking against our prow. Because I feared that other dreadful events might be unfolding on the island, which the darkness benevolently hid from sight, I allowed myself to draw close to her as the moments passed, until at last our shoulders touched and a little warmth flowed between us. We said nothing. We were invisible. If anyone on dry land had looked in our direction, they would have seen empty waves riding towards them through the glow of their fire, then breaking in anarchy along the blade of their shore.

CHAPTER 15

Our Berth

I have mentioned that my father was fond of describing Treasure Island as a dragon rearing on his hind legs. I might reasonably say, therefore, that as we travelled north on the last part of our journey, we left behind the belly of the creature and came towards the heart, where the ground was entirely overgrown with trees. The moonlight was not strong enough for me to see what kind they were, but when I cocked my ear to the wind, which was blowing offshore, I reckoned they must be Scots pine – making the high dry note that everyone recognises.

After a further half an hour of sailing this whistling began to diminish – by which I knew the contours of the island must have folded into a valley. This was soon confirmed when a narrow inlet appeared on our horizon; a moment's thought told me it must

be the place where my father had found refuge, when he circum-
navigated the island before his final confrontation with Mr Silver.

As I realised this, I remembered that he had seen a very ancient
and broken-down hulk lying in this same river mouth. The thought
prompted me to interrupt Captain Beamish and ask permission to
borrow his telescope again. When I had found my range, the estuary
appeared to me in the half-light like the fulfilment of a promise,
and so did the wreck. It had been a vessel of three masts, but had
so long suffered the injuries of the weather, the hull was hung about
with great webs of dripping seaweed, and flourished thick with
flowers. It was a sad sight, but at least it showed the inlet was calm.

'We shall be safe here, sir,' I said to the captain.

'How can you be confident?' he asked me, peering into the gloom.

When I explained everything that I had just seen, the captain
accepted my judgement, for which I admired him almost as much
as I did for his skill in steering us comfortably across the whole
Atlantic. He then called the crew round him again, and told them
we had reached our destination. Their questions, which were largely
concerned with the safety of the place, showed that by this time
some stories had begun to circulate of what might be ahead of us.
Although the men had seen no more than fires burning along the
shore of the Anchorage, these flames had made them anxious –
because their suggestion that a significant population lived on the
island was entirely unexpected. The captain rallied them as vigorously as he could, saying that since the bonfire and the stockade
were no longer visible, and no other lights had been seen travelling
through the trees alongside us, it was fair to suppose our arrival had
not been noticed. He ended by urging us to feel we might therefore
enter the river mouth as cheerfully as children coming into their
parents' house.

This was enough to raise our spirits, but not to make us carefree.

In fact as the sails were trimmed, and the *Nightingale*'s pace slowed to a dawdle again, Bo'sun Kirkby hung over the prow and quietly called out the depth so that we could avoid any sandbanks. But there were none to trouble us, and no other kind of difficulty. Our ship slotted as easily into the estuary as a key into a lock, with the rustle of bushes close on either side. I did not have any chance to discover what variety these were, but the leaves were generally glossy, and made a low squeaking sound as they were blown together by the breeze; although somewhat nervous-seeming, this was not unpleasant, and gave a sense of lavishness and abundance.

My inspection ended with the splash of the anchor going down – which several sleepy birds thought a rude interruption, and criticised as they flew away through the undergrowth. This had the most striking effect on Spot, who had so far slept through our recent adventures at his place in the roundhouse. As the clamour died, he made his own contribution by uttering a sentence I did not know he had learned. 'What to do? What to do?' he demanded, scraping his bill backwards and forwards across the bars of his cage. This provoked several of our shipmates to laugh aloud, and reply, 'You tell me?' or 'What indeed?'

The answer to Spot's question was: wait until morning – which the captain soon told us. At this, Bo'sun Kirkby turned to Mr Stevenson, our angular Scotsman, and ordered him to replace Mr Tickle in the crow's-nest, and so become our eyes and ears for the night; he then recommended the rest of the crew to go below decks, and get the sleep they would need before tackling whatever the morning might bring.

I was about to follow when the captain called me back, and also Natty, and led us into the roundhouse. Here he draped a cloth over Spot's cage so we would not be interrupted, and invited us to sit beside him while he pulled a silver flask from the pocket of his breeches. After taking a swig he passed it across to us. Natty swallowed a nip and so did I, and the rum licked through me like a tongue of fire. I then handed the flask back to the captain, who took another long mouthful before sliding it into his pocket again. With such small signs of celebration, and the air flapping as softly as muslin onto our faces through an open window, and the blossom on the bushes around us glowing like lamps in the moon-shine, we might have been friends overstaying our welcome at an evening picnic.

Yet when the captain began speaking, his voice was very grave. 'What do you think you saw there, Jim – back in the Anchorage?'

I was surprised to be asked so direct a question, having expected the captain would first give his own opinion.

'I am not sure, sir,' I said. 'Men and women. Strange things.'

'And you, Nat, what did you see?' The captain used a gentler voice when speaking to Natty, which was his way of admitting who she was, without dishevelling her disguise. I liked it because it showed loyalty to her and to her father at one and the same time.

'I saw their fire' she said, with her usual straightforwardness. 'Jim saw people.'

'Indeed,' said the captain. 'People.'

'My father,' I added, wanting to make up for my uncertainty a moment before, 'my father told me only three men were left on the island . . .'

'Three men,' Natty repeated. 'No more than three.'

As she said this, I remembered my father telling me how, when he had left the island some forty years before, he had felt shocked by the sight of these men: Tom Morgan, a man named Dick, and another pirate whose name we did not remember. The three of them had been hunting in the undergrowth – distracted by the chase, my father supposed, and not aware they would soon be abandoned. Yet as the *Hispaniola* moved off through the narrows near the southern-most part of the island, they suddenly understood their fate and appeared all together on a spit of sand with their arms raised in supplication, begging to be taken back to England. He described it as a most pitiful sight, and had never forgotten any detail of it – including how, as the ship quickened on her course into open water, one of the three had glimpsed the desert of loneliness stretching before him; he had jumped to his feet, whipped his musket to his shoulder, and sent a shot burning over Mr Silver's head and through the mainsail.

These pictures glowed so vividly in my own mind, I could not help mentioning them to the captain and Natty – ending with the reflection that it had been a desperate act, performed by desperate men.

'And now more desperate still,' said the captain, 'if my eyes are to be believed. But this does not explain what else was there – the women and the other men.'

Neither of us felt able to reply to this, and apparently the captain had no further thoughts of his own that he was willing to share. These other men and women must have arrived from across the sea, that was all we knew, and the majority of them were evidently in thrall to a few of them.

'We should investigate tomorrow,' I said.

'Or find our treasure and make our escape.' That was Natty's opinion, or rather the possibility she offered – for when the captain replied, she quickly changed her ground.

'Those people we saw,' he said. 'Several of them seemed to be slaves. They were certainly in difficulties.'

'Great difficulties,' I said. 'Terrible difficulties.'

'Then we should investigate,' said Natty, after a pause.

'Certainly,' I said, to make my own feelings as clear as possible.

'We should take a look at them at close quarters, and then decide what to do.'

The captain did not give his own opinion. Instead, he clapped his hands on his knees and levered himself to his feet. Peering through the open window to see what kind of weather we might find in the morning, he said that rain was coming, and we had best close up the roundhouse before we turned in. With that we also stood, and he solemnly shook us by the hand before bowing goodnight, calling the same to our watchman in the rigging above us, and disappearing towards his cabin. Natty and I soon followed without any more words being spoken. I like to think it was not fear or confusion that kept us silent, merely the longing for sleep, now the first part of our adventure was over.

PART III

THE ISLAND

CHAPTER 16

The Other Side of the Island

When I awoke it was no thanks to daylight creeping through our porthole, but the result of an immense cacophony around the *Nightingale*. I left Natty pulling the blanket over her ears and climbed on deck to find Captain Beamish standing with his arms akimbo, scowling in outrage. Because a thick mist still hung over the inlet, it was impossible to see exactly what creatures were responsible for the hubbub, only to be sure they felt their proximity to one another was so disagreeable, it must be condemned in a steady barrage of whistles, grunts, squawks, flaps, rattles, whoops, skirls, snaps, laughs and watery ululations. For a moment I thought these were sufficiently offensive to explain the captain's annoyance. Then I understood more clearly. Had the island's other human inhabitants wanted to creep up on us undetected, using the racket as a protection, they might easily have done so.

The captain need not have worried. Soon after the sun had risen, every creature forgot its reasons for feeling insulted and the rumpus ended – or at any rate was replaced by the gentler chirping of countless insects. As the air steadied, and the vapour thinned, our new world was revealed to us. Both banks of the river were covered by the foliage of extraordinary plants – all growing together so densely, with such profusion of blossom, that after the predominant blues and greens and greys of the previous weeks they seemed unnatural as well as delightful.

Most I had never encountered before – although here and there were ferns that seemed related to smaller varieties I knew at home: these had furry trunks rising to the height of a man, and the tendrils of a gigantic octopus. Also camellias and rhododendrons – with pink, white, yellow, red and purple flowers of astonishing size. As their mixture of scents intensified with the sun it became actually overpowering – so that I soon felt a touch delirious, and wondered whether I might have arrived in the country of the lotus-eaters.

While I continued in this state of wonder, the rest of the crew emerged from their sleep in dribs and drabs – and eventually Natty, rubbing her eyes in amazement. They were not allowed to remain in their dizzy state for long.

'Good morning, men, good morning,' said the captain, clapping his hands when everyone was assembled. He then called each of us by name, to make sure we had not been carried off by wild beasts in the night – and at the end almost lost his hat when a flock of birds skimmed very low over the *Nightingale* and flew fast out to sea. I had the chance to notice they were as large as widgeon, but with gold feathers across their wings and back, and bills that were blue as cobalt.

The captain began by telling the men a little of what he and I had seen through the telescope the previous evening: enough to let them understand we might be close to danger, but not so much that they might be daunted. They responded with a show of courage that did them credit – clapping one another on the back, and boasting they were afraid of nothing. The captain smiled very broadly when he saw this, and moved on to other matters. He told us he had studied our map during the night and realised the inlet was only a short distance from the place marked as the site of the silver; once again, he made no mention of the arms. He said this discovery turned what had felt like an inconvenience on the previous evening into something that seemed like good fortune now – except that we faced a dilemma. Put simply, it was this: should we send a party to retrieve the treasure, then slip away from the island as stealthily as we had come? Or should we investigate the area around Captain Kidd's Anchorage, and intervene if we found that crimes were occurring there?

No sooner had the captain presented us with these questions than we answered them. He announced that four men would accompany him to the site of the silver, and to collect some fresh water (and if possible some fresh meat) for the *Nightingale*; some other men, including Mr Allan the cook, who was not built for exertion outside the galley, would stay behind to defend our ship if necessary, with Mr Stevenson still glued to his lookout post; and a third party would trek south to spy on the stockade.

This third group apparently had the hardest task, since the way was uncertain and the outcome possibly dangerous. It was therefore a surprise to hear the captain decide that I should be a part of the expedition, along with Natty and Mr Lawson, under the supervision of Bo'sun Kirkby. Mr Lawson was a dainty fellow, as I have already noticed – but taciturn, and for that reason I had not spoken to him much during our voyage. I now looked on him as someone who might shortly have my life in his hands – but he avoided my eye;

his face was badly scarred with smallpox, which I thought explained his shyness.

After considering for a moment, I understood the captain had made these divisions of labour in order that our duties should be more or less equal, and everyone should feel they were somehow responsible for the safety of us all. It seemed a sensible way of keeping us linked together, even when we were separate. If the captain had known a half of what I was about to see, I am sure he would have chosen differently and decided to keep me and Natty on board.

When the arrangements were settled, we set about fuelling ourselves with water and biscuit and apples, while collecting enough of the same to last a day's march. The captain also provided, from the chest in his cabin where they had been locked before we left London, a short sword for each of us, and a pistol for himself and Bo'sun Kirkby. The allocation of these items was undertaken with the formality of a solemn rite. The captain did not need to say that our weapons should be used only in extremity, nor did Bo'sun Kirkby have to support this by giving a speech of his own. One look from his badger's face, and I understood my duty was not to be courageous, but to be quiet.

The two parties disembarked at the same time, clambering down ropes over the side of the *Nightingale* then rowing the short distance to shore in our jolly-boat. I saw as I descended that the submerged part of our hull was covered in brilliant green weed; it was very slimy to the touch, and I thought must have attached itself as we came into the warmer waters around the island.

This was the first time for six or seven weeks that I had stepped onto dry land – if you can call it *land* when the ground bubbles, and wobbles, and shows an insatiable desire to take the boot off a foot. After so many days of rolling decks and plunging seas, even this degree of solidity was extremely strange, and brought on such a fit of giddiness that as I reached the vegetation I actually sank to my knees. This disappointed me, because I had meant to enjoy the moment I came to stand in my father's footsteps at last. Instead I could only think how wildly everything was heaving around me, as if the whole earth were suffering a convulsion. The consolation was seeing a small orange lizard, which seemed to have a divided tail, look me straight in the eye. I had never seen such a strange creature in my life before, but it vanished so quickly I thought I might have invented it, and therefore said nothing to any of my party.

After we had shaken hands with the captain and wished him good luck, I watched him and his men disappear into the undergrowth – and heard what I thought must have been a kind of macaw give an opinion of their prospects. It ended with a derisive laugh. No sooner had this faded than a similar verdict was shouted in our own direction: a riotous outburst of mirth and sneering, that was suddenly interrupted by a series of loud and clumsy-sounding scuffles.

I shall return to these noises – as they also returned to me – in a little while. At the beginning of our journey, it was the communication of plants rather than animals that most preoccupied me. The rasp of leaves against our arms as we pushed uphill from the river; the soft explosion of tubers under our shoes; the squelch of wet grasses as we sank into slushy ground and pulled free.

In several places the vegetation was so densely woven together we had to crawl forward on our hands and knees, taking it in turns to grapple with the tendrils of vines and other obstacles. Mr Lawson, being small, might have shown the initiative here, but seemed nervous of what he might find. Natty immediately took his place, and showed such adeptness in making our path that she became the leader we all preferred. To see her slither like an eel through tangled roots, and spring like a cat across the barriers of fallen trees, and worry like a dog at the knots of branches, made me think she must be a compendium of God's creatures.

The reward for our persistence was to emerge, as soon as we left the valley, into the pine wood we had previously seen (or more properly *heard*) in darkness from the deck of the *Nightingale*. The contrast was wonderful, especially since the trees were impressive specimens, with some standing fifty feet, some nearer seventy feet high. To walk between them was a delight, and also very easy, since the ground was covered with a bed of needles that was smooth as a carpet.

We now began to make rapid progress, which should have lifted our spirits. Yet as we pressed ahead a peculiar nervousness began to settle on us again. This was due to the scuffling sound I have already mentioned. My first thought was: it must be some kind of small deer that was native to the island, since the noise was always accompanied by a sense of speed. But as we pressed deeper into the pine forest, where there was no underbrush, this seemed unlikely. And the more unlikely it became, the more frightening the noise seemed – until our fear suddenly turned into amazement.

We had stopped to drink a mouthful of water from our flasks, and so for a moment were unusually silent, when we saw the tree-tops ahead of us shake violently, then open to reveal a red squirrel bounding towards us. A red squirrel quite unlike any I had seen in England, for the simple reason that it was ten times larger – the size of a spaniel, in fact – and apparently not at all well suited to its treetop existence. For as long as the creature did not see us, it blundered through the high branches shaking down a shower of needles and twigs, and sometimes snapping off small branches; when we did come to its attention, it careered away at the fastest possible speed, causing as much damage as a miniature tornado.

Although I felt almost stupid with astonishment, I nevertheless reckon this was the moment I first accepted a truth that had already begun to occur to me on the *Nightingale*: namely, that Treasure Island was the home to several creatures that were not to be found *anywhere else in the world*, let alone in England. Although this excited me very much, and made me feel there was a reason other than treasure for being where we were, it did not change my mood entirely. There was too much uncertainty in what else might be lurking around us, and too much fear of what more definitely lay ahead.

Judging by their faces, my companions felt the same. Once their pleasure in seeing the squirrel had faded, and the creature itself had thrashed off into the distance, I saw Bo'sun Kirkby fall into a melancholy stoop. I knew a part of the reason must be that he felt anxious about what we would find in the stockade. But I also suspected that he was influenced by our surroundings – by the drab country that opened in front of us as the pine forest ended. This was made of bare slopes coloured a uniform slate grey, that undulated like a frozen sea until they formed the foothills of the Spyglass, which ran up sheer on every side, then suddenly ended as if it had been hacked by an enormous axe.

The effect was extremely alarming, and found a natural accompaniment in the music we now began to notice – the boom of surf breaking along the shore on our left-hand side. When I first heard its thunder and foam, and the seabirds crying as they dived into its scrambling rollers, I immediately remembered my father saying how much he had come to hate Treasure Island. He insisted he never saw the sea quiet around its shores. The sun might dazzle overhead, the air be without a breath, the sky smooth and blue, but still these great rollers would be running along the eternal coast, thundering by day and night; he did not believe there was a spot on the island where a man could be out of earshot of their noise, and complained always about their *poisonous brightness* – the same that I now saw myself, as spray-light bounced off the rocks and boulders.

Whether Natty compared her own impressions with her father's, I could not tell. She had spoken so sparingly of Mr Silver since leaving England, it was not clear how much was strange to her, and how much she recognised. All I know is: she kept very silent as we continued across our shaly floor, with her shoulders slumped and her eyes fixed on the ground, as though she were being pulled forward by an invisible force. Whenever she shook off its authority, she dropped into place at my side and threw me a look that seemed like a request to confirm something she had just asked – but I had never heard the question.

After half an hour of this, during which we skirted the edge of Spyglass Hill and began a slow descent towards the south-east corner of the island, our suspicions deepened. The ground here was more fertile, and we found large stretches of azalea, mainly red and purple, with a few thickets of green nutmeg trees that mixed their spice with the aroma of the flowers. The effect would have been delicious if the walking had been easier; as it was, we picked a way around the bushes with some difficulty – and almost every footstep provoked a prodigious amount of scrambling and flapping from the creatures we disturbed in their lairs.

Sometimes we caught a glimpse of feather or fur, and these sightings tended to confirm that here at least we were unlikely to meet something larger than ourselves. On one occasion, however, as we paused in a patch of open ground, we heard a different and much more alarming sound. At first it was almost indistinguishable from silence – yet seemed a *heightened* sort of silence, rising from deep within one of the larger bushes. Slowly this sound developed, becoming first a soft scratching, then a definite shaking rustle. A part of me thought it might be some sort of spirit – a spirit of the place, if you like – but I could not entertain this idea for long, and told Natty and the rest that it must be a monkey. They gave me a blank look. We had neither seen nor heard a trace of monkeys elsewhere on the island. Certainly, whatever it was had the ability to move through thick undergrowth at great speed. If it had been impelled by fear, as seemed likely, I did not like to think how intense that fear must have been.

In later life I have often the chance to notice that people who discern a particular mood in others will soon feel it in themselves. So it was with us, as silence settled round us again. Hitherto on our march, any feelings of dread or sadness had been assuaged by self-congratulation: we were equal to the task our captain had assigned us. Now we were near our goal, I could not feel so optimistic. I knew in my heart that what I had already glimpsed in the stockade was enough to justify all the horror I felt growing inside me.

For this reason, it was a relief that Bo'sun Kirkby began to lead us much more carefully, repeatedly holding up his hand like a scout to indicate when we should halt in file behind him. As it turned out, we faced a more immediate danger than any we knew. For as we continued to creep forward, we suddenly found ourselves at the edge of what I can only call a ravine. My first indication of this was seeing our bo'sun fling out his arms and lurch wildly. When I leaned forward to offer him a hand (he gave me a scowl that said my help was not necessary), I saw over his shoulder a horrible gash in the earth, as if God himself had scratched a fingernail across his creation. It was not wide – only about six or seven feet – but about forty deep, with extraordinarily smooth sides that were interrupted here and there by saplings sprouting from small fissures and ledges. Jagged stones lay on the bottom, green with damp, and also the white ribcage of a large goat, or perhaps a pig.

A very peculiar sort of air rose from this ravine, which produced a feverish sensation of cold and damp as it entered my lungs. Natty must have felt it too, for while I was still intent on looking, she put her hand on my arm and urgently led me away – led us all away, in fact, so that we continued our descent along a path that ran a good distance away from any risk of falling. I say *path*, but in truth there was no such thing, only a floor of roots coated with moss, and clumps of flowers the same colour as bluebells, but like celandines in their shape.

At another time, I would have relished the chance to botanise among them; now, after we had continued for another minute or so, I found the wilderness had suddenly ended, and was criss-crossed by a number of tracks, some running true and purposeful, others circling as though they described the movements of someone who had no idea of where they wanted to be. Because we reckoned these had been made by human feet, and meant we might soon be discovered, we were very glad the ground-cover soon changed yet again, and concealed us inside a thick belt of rhododendron. Here we gratefully dropped onto our hands and knees, and took shelter in the darkness under their leaves.

Once we had got our breath, Bo'sun Kirkby pressed down a branch so that we were able to look ahead. Imagine a child opening a book written in a language of which he speaks almost nothing. Just such a book is what I saw when I looked a hundred yards down the slope ahead. I mean I saw confusion. Confusion slowly settling and resolving. The stockade, for example: I recognised that. Also the cleared area, and the cemetery, and the farm pen. Further off, a quarter-mile beyond the stockade, the marshes had been drained, and rice was growing in small fields divided by low mud walls.

All these things suggested order and were therefore reassuring. But then my eyes lifted towards Captain Kidd's Anchorage, and I found the entire harbour blighted by the wreck of a large sailing ship. She was a very desolate sight, lolling four-square against the backdrop of Skeleton Island, with the neat little obstacle of the White

Rock shaking its fronds fifty years astern. Her decks were as bare as one of the prison hulks I had often seen in the Thames at home, with all the masts and rigging torn away. Her hull was split in two and many of its planks were broken or missing. It may sound extravagant, but this ruin spread a pall of misery across everything that lay round about: whatever catastrophe had brought her to the Anchorage still lurked within her timbers like a tyrant in his castle.

Why did I feel this so certainly? Because of what I saw when I looked more carefully at the stockade. I reckoned it must be fifty yards long, and fifty wide. On either side of the open ground were the two log-houses, one much better built than the other, with a shack leaning against its side-wall for a purpose I could not immediately decide. Midway between them, and occupying the heart of the place, rose the large fan-shape I had previously seen from the *Nightingale*. Now that I was looking from the landward side I could see it resembled a court – with a chair (or throne) in the centre, a dock below, and on either side two benches that might be filled by a jury and an audience.

I might not have so soon deduced the purpose of this structure, had it not been in use – and as I began to comprehend this use, I also understood why other activities in the camp were all suspended. Seated on the bare ground before the court, and arranged into separate rows of men and women, were the Negro inhabitants of the island that yesterday I had seen suffering at the hands of their white-skinned masters. They were even more shabbily dressed than I had thought – wearing rags where clothes covered them at all – and all wretchedly thin and slumped and dejected. Even the few children struggling free of their mothers' arms had a listlessness that made them seem sickly. Sickly and terrified, since very often their rambles were blocked by the five or six white men (though their skins were very stained with dirt) who wandered around the compound. These men held long bamboo sticks, which they occasionally slapped against their legs with a menacing insouciance – or poked into the shoulders and backs of those huddled at their feet.

Natty, who lay beside me so quietly I had not even heard her breathing, now turned to look at me: our faces were inches apart. A leaf fragment had glued to her cheek, but in the movement of her skin when she whispered to me, it fell off.

'Is this a trial?' she said.

I nodded.

'Who are these people? Where have they come from?'

I gave a grimace and a shrug, which told her that I did not know, then said, 'The ship?'

Natty frowned, but slowly, to show she thought this was a possibility – then we resumed our watching.

At the distance of some thirty yards, we were too far off to hear exactly what was being said. The general sense, however, was easy to understand. In the high throne sat, or rather *lounged*, a judge – a large, foul-looking villain with a greenish cocked hat on his head and a fuzz of grey hair reaching as far as his shoulders. Directly beneath him, and previously unnoticed because he stood very still, was a figure in absolute contrast. This fellow wore sailor's trousers, a shirt that had once been white but was now brown as a biscuit, and a short blue jacket that flapped open to reveal a sword at his waist. His face showed a complete lack of expression and was as pale as a cadaver's – except for a russet smear that ran across his throat.

I assumed this must be some trick of the light, and turned instead to look at the accused. This wretch stood lowest of all in the construction, with his hands tied in front, and his eyes switching between the companions sitting on the ground before him, and a third and very confused-looking pirate, who paraded before the empty right-hand bench, tossing out occasional remarks and otherwise mumbling to himself; he wore a very battered old hat, with one of its cocks fallen down, and a handkerchief underneath to protect his neck from the sun. I thought by the way this man swayed against the rail that ran alongside him, he was probably drunk.

The whole spectacle was so sordid in its parody of justice, and so genuinely menacing, my first instinct was to scramble away, and return as fast as possible to the *Nightingale*. To judge by the soft groan she gave, Natty shared my feelings. We all did, I am quite certain. Yet we were bound to stay – to spare ourselves the risk of discovery, and because we were caught (though I am loath to admit it) in a web of fascination. What were we about to see?

I did not have to wait long to find out. As though he had suddenly tired of hearing so much mumbling from his 'barrister', the judge abruptly hauled himself upright in his seat, clapped his hands, and barked loudly enough for his words to carry to our hiding-place: 'Enough, Mr Jinks, I have heard enough.'

A gasp rose from the Negroes crouching on the ground, which made their guards move among them more quickly, lashing out with their sticks like boys knocking the heads off nettles. The meaning of this sound was entirely clear. It was a gasp of terror and disgust.

Everything now followed with a sickening appearance of regularity. The judge straightened himself once more, so that he was almost erect in his place, and shook his hair away from his face. He then leaned forward, tapped the white-faced fellow below him on the shoulder with his right hand, and with his left drew a line across his own throat.

The noise of the crowd now changed from gasping to groaning, despite the blows whipping down on them. The cadaverous man paid no attention. He descended the rickety steps of the court until he had reached the accused in his dock, then seized him roughly by the arm and dragged him forward until they stood side by side on solid ground. The contrast between them was dreadful to see. One slim and pale and passionless, but with a shine of purpose about him; the other dark and skeletal, with his knees pressed together and his head sunk between his bare shoulders.

The moment held them – and in my memory has never ended. In truth it finished soon enough, with the white man grasping the other by his wiry hair and forcing him to kneel, then drawing his sword with a flourish, pausing in an attitude of monstrous relish, then sweeping it downwards. While it fell, a great cloud of birds rose from the shore beyond him, screaming and circling in the air. The blade sliced through the victim's neck as if it were made of water.

All the breath left my own body in the same instant, and as my head sank forward I found myself looking closely at the earth – at the grains of mud, the leaves, the roots wriggling through the soil. This had the strange effect of making me feel I was a child, seeing the miracles of the world for the first time, with no sense of separation between them and myself. A moment later, being more than a child, I could not help looking upwards again. The body had collapsed sideways and was curled like a brown shrimp, with the head lying separately, a foot apart. The executioner, whose face was still entirely without expression, then thrust the tip of his sword into the flesh of the cheek to mangle it, before hoisting his trophy towards those still seated – or rather now *cringing* – at his feet.

Their sorrow rose and fell in a ragged wave, but his only response was to lift his chin and leer at them – which allowed us to see the long shadow across his own throat was in fact a scar. It ran from ear to ear, and made him seem like a man who had been killed, but refused to die.

'Now you may get back to work,' he squawked, in a high and finicky voice. 'All of you. Back to work.' The guards immediately began swinging their long sticks, and made sure the order was obeyed.

CHAPTER 17

Scotland

I said nothing – none of us did. I lay still – so did we all. But my silence and stillness revolted me, since they made everything I had just witnessed seem bearable. Where was my defiance, my outrage, my disgust? What had I begun, when I stole the map from my father? What had I become, stepping onto the island?

It was a strange kind of fortune that dragged me away from such questions. For while they were still fuming in my mind, Bo'sun Kirkby began to wriggle backwards through the undergrowth, beckoning us to follow. When I saw his eyes wide with fear, and remembered how steady he had been on the *Nightingale*, and also during our march towards the stockade, I did not need any further encouragement. He was a man who understood danger, and knew when it must be avoided.

While we were still close to the pirates, our escape was very slow because we did not want to draw attention to ourselves. But the moment we felt sure we would not be noticed, the bo'sun slapped Mr Lawson on the back, and the two of them set off as fast as their legs could carry them. I seized Natty's hand and we also dashed away – but in a wild zigzag, as though we expected bullets to strike us. For the next several minutes the only noise was our shoes pounding the earth, and our hearts thundering in our chests.

As I ran, all manner of questions began bubbling into my brain. We had seen a grotesque sort of trial, but what of the judge, the prosecutor and the executioner? Most probably they were the three maroons, who had been left on the island when the *Hispaniola* departed. What of the guards, then, and the prisoners? What kind of society had they made, that depended on cruelty? I could not be sure. I needed calm and the opinion of others to make a complete picture. Until I found them, I reckoned I would do better to remain as I was: like a fleeing animal.

After a few hundred yards we stopped again, beside a monstrous old azalea bush that had grown to the size of a church. We were not able to speak, but stood in a circle with our hands on our knees, panting until we had recovered our breath. If we hoped we would find our confidence at the same time, we were disappointed. For before we were quite ourselves again, Bo'sun Kirkby suddenly cupped his ear.

'What's that?' he whispered.

All my senses quickened: every gleam of sunlight on the leaves around us seemed to be the blade of a sword, every scuffling bird the footstep of an enemy.

'Ssssh,' hissed Kirkby, as if even these thoughts were outrageously loud.

In the deeper silence that followed, I caught a faint disturbance on the air, travelling from a distance I could not easily estimate. Not a human noise, I thought at first – more like the chattering of a creature. It seemed quite unselfconscious, which made me think it must come from some kind of rabbit, or hedgehog, that was feeding among the bushes. The longer it continued, however, the more strongly I became convinced that it was not so much careless as involuntary, and might therefore be the sound of terror.

Bo'sun Kirkby beckoned to us very cautiously, and we crept forward again, skirting the huge shrub that had blocked our way, and finding what appeared to be a foot-worn path among a belt of smaller bushes. When the bo'sun next raised his hand, we gathered round him in dread of what we might find, but also with relief that our suspense was almost over. Mr Lawson, I remember, took a handkerchief from his pocket and mopped his face; he did this very gingerly, as if the scars on his skin were still painful to him.

'What?' I asked the bo'sun, as quietly as possible.

He did not reply, but pointed and put one hand across his mouth. On the path ahead a large hole gaped open. We stepped towards it in line, taking strength from one another, and peered in. It was about twelve feet deep and ten wide, square-cut, with a few small stones and feeble roots protruding from its sides. A litter of branches and crumpled brown bracken leaves, which had evidently once been a kind of roof, now covered the floor.

If any of us had been inclined to speak, we would have done better to call it a 'pit' than a 'hole', and better still to say 'trap' than 'pit'. For a trap is what it was. And if it had originally been made with a view to capturing animals that might be killed and eaten, it had just as effectively caught a man. A Negro whom I saw must until recently have been among the prisoners in the stockade. He was now cowering on all fours, coated in dust and dirt and throwing up pitiful looks. The sound we had heard was his whimpering.

Because we were so astonished to see him, we stared for much longer than was kind – and watched the terror in his face change to bafflement, then to curiosity, then to a nervous hopefulness. The terrible noise of his fear stopped, and he stood up. A man about twice my age, but my own height and very thin, with bruises on his shoulders and back, and a shaven head that was also covered in scabs and cuts. He was barefoot and naked to the waist, and the number seven had been branded onto his right shoulder. The skin of this wound shone almost purple in the black skin surrounding it.

All of us now suddenly remembered our better selves, and leaned down so that we could pull him out of his abyss. It happened that my hand was one of those he jumped up to grasp, and the rough-ness of his palm shocked me; it might as well have been the root of a tree. After a quick scramble he was standing among us. Standing *over* us, I should say, since he was taller than I had supposed – until his legs folded and he sat down, whereupon Natty offered him her water-flask. He drank from it greedily, then poured a splash over his scalp. As this trickled down, it revealed a handsome face, although his cheeks were sunk with hunger, and flecked with numerous small scars and scratches.

Bo'sun Kirkby was the first to break the silence, indicating we should also sit, to show that we were equals. 'We are friends,' he said – very slowly, as if he did not expect to be understood.

'Where are you from?' the answer came back, in an accent I recognised to my amazement as Scottish.

'England,' I joined in.

'Your name is England?'

'We are *from* England,' I said. 'From London.'

'My name is Scotland.'

After so much anxiety, the comedy of these confusions seemed greater than it was, and we all broke into laughter – which Bo'sun

Kirkby stopped by speaking in a voice hardly louder than a whisper.

'Your name is Scotland,' he repeated, then began pointing to us in turn as he continued. 'My name is Kirkby, William Kirkby. This is Mr Lawson, this is Master Jim, and this Nat Silver. We are from England. Our ship is anchored at the northern end of the island, where we have other men waiting.' As he finished, we bent forward to shake hands, Natty being the last to do so and leaving her fingers in Scotland's grip for a second or two longer than the rest of us.

As she relinquished him, she asked the question that was in all our minds: 'What is this? What are you doing here?'

'I was trying to escape,' Scotland said in his rolling brogue – and gave a hopeless shrug. 'Impossible, of course.'

'Escape from the stockade, you mean? But where?'

'Anywhere,' came the answer. Then, like a weary afterthought: 'I knew I would have to return to them soon enough.'

'And this . . .' Natty paused, unable to decide how best to describe the trap. 'This thing. This pit. It was dug to prevent escapes?'

'To stop escapes, yes. And to catch animals. It's all the same. They would have found me eventually.'

'Surely not!' Bo'sun Kirkby broke in, as though he thought Scotland's tyrants might have considered eating him, if they had reached the trap before us. 'Well, well. You have no more reason to be frightened. We have rescued you.'

This was spoken in a very open-seeming and friendly spirit, but I could not help noticing that nothing had so far been said about our original reason for coming to the island. When Scotland followed these introductions by turning to each of us in turn, and fixing us with his large eyes as though to make a judgement about our trustworthiness, I thought that he too might be holding things in reserve. He did not show the exuberant gratitude of someone who feels that he has been entirely saved, but remained quiet and watchful.

I would like to think it was respect for this discretion, and not any baser motive, that prevented us from immediately bombarding Scotland with questions. The truth is: we still feared that men from the stockade might stumble on us and make us their prisoners. For this reason, we did no more than ask him whether he would return with us to the *Nightingale*.

'To work for you?' he wanted to know, but we assured him he would come with us as a friend, which was how we then continued.

Because Scotland had shown signs of exhaustion so soon after escaping his trap, I suspected we might have to carry him, or assist him in some other way. But his weakness was only a kind of cramp, and quickly disappeared. As we moved out of the undergrowth, and began the part of our trek that lay across the open shale and into the pine woods, he fell into step beside Bo'sun Kirkby and spoke to us easily.

Scotland, it transpired, was so called because, after his removal from Africa, he had worked from a young age on an estate in Jamaica which had been owned by a gentleman who had been born in Edinburgh and had run his business with the help of fellow countrymen, whose accents had influenced Scotland's own. When this man died childless, his estate was sold along with Scotland and the other slaves that lived on it. This new owner, it seemed, was converting the ground to a different kind of agriculture, and required fewer men to work.

In any event, Scotland and a party of some fifty other slaves (men and women, elderly and children) found themselves on a ship bound from Jamaica to a more western part in the Bay of Mexico. At some point in this journey their ship ran into a storm, was blown off her course, lost a mast, almost found a berth in Davy Jones's locker, and eventually was wrecked on Treasure Island along with the sailors, guards and suchlike that had also been aboard.

This ship was the *Achilles*, which we had seen in the Anchorage by Skeleton Island. Scotland indicated that when she had run aground about five years previously, he thought at first the winds of fate must have blown him to freedom, or at least into a place where he might be able to arrange a different kind of existence with his guards. From the way he explained this, I knew that he came from a family that expected to assume the responsibilities of leadership, and had retained this role during his enslavement.

Scotland said that his hopes of freedom were crushed as soon as he reached the island – because the slaves had landed in the exact spot where the maroons had made their camp. As I heard this, I remembered that when the wreck occurred, these maroons must previously have lived in solitude for almost thirty-five years – which gave me some idea of how wild they might have become. In any event, it was clear from Scotland's account that they had very quickly suborned the ten guards who survived the storm, and made them instruments of their will in subjugating the slaves. These poor wretches then became victims of the most barbarous appetites imaginable.

As we digested this information, Bo'sun Kirkby wanted to know how well armed the tyrants might be – which struck me as a sensible question, given the revenges we were already beginning to contemplate. Scotland replied that there were swords aplenty, and a few guns and rifles. These firearms, however, were very little used, since the weather on the island had made them rusty, and the original stores of powder and bullets were anyway almost exhausted.

This might have been a kind of comfort to us, except that Scotland then insisted any kind of weapon would be less fearsome than the men themselves. I understood from this that he meant the headman, Smirke (which was the name of the lounging beast I had seen in the judge's chair), the executioner, Stone, and their lackey, Jinks, were all so absolutely depraved, they kept the whole community in a state of passive terror. The maroons might be some sixty years old, but their demands and desires had been violently increased by their long isolation from humanity, and were insatiable. This thought alarmed me so much, I did not immediately appreciate the small mystery in what Scotland had told us. I mean: that the names these men used were not the same as those I had heard from my father. I could only assume that Smirke was the anonymous pirate, and that Tom Morgan and Dick had both chosen a new moniker which they thought suited their new life; Dick, I thought, was probably Jinks – for no better reason than the two sounds resembled one another – and Tom Morgan was Stone.

I kept those thoughts to myself, since they seemed trivial in comparison to what Scotland had forced us to consider – and felt all the more justified in doing so when I noticed that as Scotland reached this part of his story, his pace begin to slow and his footsteps to grow more erratic. I might almost say he staggered, as if remembering the weight of blows and other suffering he had endured. For five years there had been desperate labour for the imprisoned men, who were always viciously oppressed by beatings and insults of every kind; for five years there had been degradation for the women, who were deemed to exist for no reason except the pleasure of their masters; for five years there had been neglect for the children (even those whose fathers were their tormentors); and for five years there had been such impoverishment for the elderly, they passed their time begging that it would soon be at an end.

It was impossible to hear Scotland speak of such things and not feel compelled to show some signs of reassurance – which now we did. Mr Lawson set aside his shyness and became very eloquent with his sympathy; Bo'sun Kirkby and I patted Scotland on the arms, and said what we could. Natty took both his hands and rubbed them tenderly between her own. Scotland did not appear to notice any of these things, or to feel any good effect from them, but only produced more instances of the horror he had endured until his voice began to fail. Eventually he pulled away from us entirely, covered his face with his hands, drew to a halt, and wept.

By this stage on our march we had reached the backbone of the island and were among the pine trees, with the bare flanks of Spyglass Hill now falling behind us. By the standards of Treasure Island it was a kindly place, where the only surprising sounds were made by the squirrels as they crackled through their high branches. Although it would have been callous to say aloud that these things might benefit Scotland, I could not help but think so.

Whether Natty felt as I did was impossible to say. Ever since we had rescued Scotland her face had become closed, which was characteristic when she was debating a difficult question with herself. I knew her well enough to feel sure that if I tested her quietness, she would lock herself away even more securely. For this reason, I had tramped beside her in silence during the last mile or so.

Now, as Scotland began to recover, wiping a hand over his face and clearing his throat for conversation again, Natty seemed to have reached the end of her deliberations. She stepped forward and laid her right hand on his shoulder, where the smooth honey colour of her skin made Scotland seem all the darker and more injured with bruises. In my mind's eye, I saw her father lying on his bed in London, with Natty nuzzling his face. There was the same feeling of intimacy.

'You are safe now; you are safe now,' Natty said, as if she were speaking to him in private.

Instead of comforting Scotland, this seemed to jolt him; he rounded on Natty and stared at her with wide eyes; his face was glistening with tears.

'We are not the same,' he said.

'But my mother . . .' Natty began – and then paused; she did not know whether to finish her sentence.

'We are not the same,' Scotland said again after a painful interval. 'You cannot understand.'

Natty withdrew her hand. 'We will look after you,' she said, in the same crooning voice.

'I have a wife!' Scotland said. 'She is still there.'

Now it was Natty's turn to seem startled, asking, 'Where?' – as though Scotland might have meant Africa.

Scotland did not answer her directly, but kept with the story he had just begun. 'We escaped from Smirke and the others together,' he said. 'We ran into the bushes. But things separated us.'

'What things?' Natty wanted to know.

'We were confused,' Scotland told her. 'We had no idea where to be safe. Then I was trapped.'

'Where is she now?' said Natty, returning to her original question. 'Inside the stockade?' She seemed to have recovered from her surprise, and sounded nothing more than reasonable.

Scotland nodded again. 'Inside the stockade. If that is what you call it. We have another word.'

Bos'un Kirkby could not help asking what other word this might be, but when Scotland rolled his eyes, showing he was not inclined to spell out something so obvious, I thought it best to put a different question.

'How long have you been married?' I said. 'I did not think . . .'

'You thought it might not be allowed?' Scotland's interruption proved this subject was no easier for him. He lifted his head and looked at me proudly. 'Well, you are right. She is my wife to me, as I am a husband to her. What the law says is no matter to us.'

'We will find her,' I told him, more in hope than conviction, but with sufficient force to bring our exchange to an end. When I looked round at the others I saw they were nodding in agreement – Bo'sun Kirkby and Mr Lawson with a sincerity that proved they shared my embarrassment at not being able to put Scotland more quickly at his ease.

Scotland himself had his own solution to this awkwardness, which was to bow his head briefly against Natty's shoulder, and close his eyes. I told myself this was only a sign of gratitude, and meant to include us all – but when he opened them again and looked into her face, I saw a kind of recognition pass between them, in spite of what he had said a moment before. I have to admit this perturbed me, and I was on the point of urging us onwards again, when Nature herself came to my rescue. Five or six yards away, perched quite still in the shade of a pine tree, and watching us with eyes as dark as plums, was another of the squirrels we had seen earlier in the day.

This specimen was larger than the first, almost the size of a small pony, and with fur of such deep and glowing redness it might have been made of embers. Bo'sun Kirkby saw it in the same instant as I did, and by the sound of him felt as grateful as I was to have this distraction.

'Damn my lamps,' he said softly. 'What have we here?'

The creature was not in the least alarmed by the sound of his voice, which made me think it had seen so few people, it did not know how dangerous we are. I felt sure of this when I saw Natty take hold of a pine cone that lay on the ground close to her, and roll it forwards as though beginning a game. The animal allowed the cone to follow its curving course then stop within easy reach, whereupon it picked up the gift, raised it to its nose, considered for a moment, then re-placed it carefully on the ground with a distinctly apologetic air. When this was done it clasped its two front legs – which I might call *hands*, except their nails were thin and yellow and pointed – and gave a comical sort of bow. Mr Lawson, who had been chuckling throughout this performance, bowed back, which the squirrel appeared to think was permission to depart. He dropped silkily onto all fours and, with a speed that seemed truly astonishing because of his large bulk, scaled the pine tree behind him with a loud scratching noise, and rustled into the canopy and disappeared.

Scotland, when I turned back to him, was smiling broadly; the tears had dried on his cheeks, and the sad anger had lifted.

'You have seen this before?' I asked.

'The squirrels?' he said, rolling the 'r's very impressively. 'Yes, there are plenty of them about.'

'We have squirrels in England,' I told him, 'but this size' – and held up my hands to show what I meant.

'Very small!' Scotland stretched his eyes.

'No!' said Natty. 'Here they are very big. Gigantic!'

Scotland shrugged, as if to prove he was quite used to things being strange – which put a further question in my mind.

'Tell us,' I said, 'what are the other animals on the island, and the birds?'

Scotland spread his hands wide, palms upwards; this allowed us to see how pale they were, and also how deeply scarred and wrinkled. 'Plenty of birds,' he said. 'Plenty, plenty of birds, and plenty of animals. The doo-dah.'

We were listening hard now, craning forward since we thought he might be about to surprise us. When he said 'doo-dah', my first thought was he meant something like 'et cetera'.

'Tell us about the doo-dah,' said Natty, which showed that she already understood him better than the rest of us.

'Big bird,' said Scotland, stretching out his arms. 'No wings.'

'A big bird that cannot fly,' said Natty for the sake of clarity.

Scotland nodded vehemently. 'Cannot fly, but easy to catch. People like the doo-dah.'

Compared to everything else we had seen and thought and said in the last several hours, this exchange seemed very pleasant, and persuaded us that we now liked the doo-dah as well. We liked it so much, in fact, we made it the reason for continuing our march, in the hope that we might find an example as we went.

From this point, as happens with journeys of all kinds, our way seemed much shorter and easier than it had done when we were setting out. Within thirty minutes we had left the pine woods and come to the luscious undergrowth that led down to the *Nightingale*. And within another ten we had trampled through those thick leaves, and found the mudbank where we could hail our jolly-boat and so climb back on deck and be dry again.

Just as we reached the shore, and saw our captain looking towards us, with his cocked hat on his head and his large face creasing into a frown as he noticed Scotland among our party, Natty laid her hand on my arm in that tender way she had, which made my heart quicken.

'The doo-dah,' she said. 'You realise they eat it. That is why everyone likes it.'

CHAPTER 18

The History of the Maroons

Captain Beamish watched our approach, no doubt puzzled by how we had added to our party, but still interested in our safe arrival. If I had ever doubted his qualities, I should have known him for a good man the minute we stepped on deck. Instead of showing any suspicion of Scotland or interrogating him, he threw an old shirt across his shoulders and led him into the roundhouse, where he ordered Mr Allan to send up food and drink – explaining to us, after he had done so, that he had found plentiful fresh water and fruit on the island to add to our supplies. Spot, whose cage was attached to its usual place, seemed happy to have so much company gathered round him, and clearly announced, 'Welcome, welcome,' before settling down on his perch to listen.

There was a great deal of curiosity among other shipmates, who soon appeared at the windows and began peering and pointing until they were sent about their business. All this fuss was good-natured, but might easily have become a sort of insolence; the captain was conscious from the beginning of Scotland as a *man*.

Bo'sun Kirkby and Mr Lawson remained with us, since they were anxious to tell their part of our story, and also to hear what the captain knew about the silver. I had expected their chance to tell their tale would come after we had introduced Scotland, but since he began tearing ravenously at his meal the moment it arrived, the treasure took precedence. Even before the captain began to speak, I could see from his face that his news was not likely to be good.

The time of which I am now speaking was late afternoon and, although we had scarcely noticed it in the excitement of our return, the sun had disappeared behind clouds and the wind was beginning to blow more strongly. Several of the larger plants around the inlet knocked their leaves together with heavy slaps. When I faced down-river towards the sea, I found a mass of yellowish turbulence on the horizon, like an army waiting to advance. All this gave intensity to the captain's story. Whatever thoughts I had begun to develop about the change in our adventure, I could not deny the silver was still a part of it.

The captain, along with the four crew that went with him, had found the same difficulty as ourselves in leaving the valley: they had been obliged to crawl, weave, sidle and plunge when they wanted only to walk upright. Also like us, they had emerged from this primitive vegetation into a pine wood as soon as they reached level ground. But whereas our trees had been evenly spread, and were pleasant to walk under, theirs grew very sparsely and were stunted by fierce winds. If the island did indeed resemble a dragon on its hind legs, the creature could be said to be going *bald*, and to possess a head that was more pitted, weathered and ancient-looking than the remainder of its body.

These features gave the landscape an air of desolation that depressed everyone in the captain's party – especially when they found they had overshot their destination and come to the north-ernmost point of the island. Here they discovered cliffs that were carved into the resemblance of a human face. This gaunt profile, made of black basalt, stared pitilessly out to sea with one eye, while the other seemed to twist in its socket to gaze inland; the tragic expression suggested that no amount of vigilance could guarantee the safety of whatever needed protection.

As the captain expressed this geographical fancy, he prepared us for the thing he wanted to say next. Using my father's map as his guide, and setting a course south-west from the Black Crag, his party soon reached the site where the silver had been buried. They knew immediately they had found the right place – not because it seemed such a likely spot, and not because they saw ingots poking through the earth. But because the earth had been disturbed. Because the silver had been taken.

Worse than simply 'disturbed' and 'taken', in fact. The captain told us the whole flank of sand had been ripped and ruined by whatever spades and other implements, including bare hands, the thieves had used to open the ground. Now the place was merely earth again, although strewn with broken handles and sticks, and the footprints of scuffling feet. It was itself, but empty.

Our journey had been in vain! The shock of this flashed through me – but was instantly checked. Why, if his expedition was so fruit-less, did the captain not look more dejected? For, to tell the truth, he recited this story with as much equanimity as if he had been discussing a spoiled dinner. The shipmates who had accompanied him also seemed very phlegmatic, as did those who had stayed aboard with Mr Allan; they continued to go about their work, repairing sails, scrubbing the deck, et cetera, as if they were perfectly reconciled to their failure. It was only my own party that reacted with dismay, and Natty in particular. While Bo'sun Kirkby and Mr Lawson hung their heads, she gave a long and miserable sigh, a much deeper sound than it seemed possible might come from a delicate body, as if it were her father's breath and not her own that was squeezing from her lungs.

While they all seemed incapable of speech, I put the question that only I knew to ask, because I was the only one apart from the captain to have seen the map. Bending towards him I said, 'And the arms?'

'The arms also,' the captain said, and seeing how this made my face fall, went on: 'But what of that? The arms alone are nothing. It is the people who wield them we must think about. A dozen pirates – or whatever their exact number might be – is still a dozen pirates, however many swords they have. We do not need to worry about the arms.'

I understood the logic of this, but still could not understand why the captain was not more agitated about our treasure. One explanation might have been very simple: he knew where it had been taken, and would soon tell us. Another was: he felt compensated for losing the treasure by finding a ready means of replenishing our supplies. A third was: since seeing the stockade and the misery of its inhabitants, he realised that a better reason than silver might have brought us to the island. This seemed likely, given what I knew of his character – and was a response I felt sure would only strengthen when he heard Scotland's story.

I never had the chance to ask. As the captain began speaking again, saying that perhaps other pirates had stumbled on the cache and made off with it, Scotland himself interrupted. He sounded more confident than he had done on our journey across the island, which I thought showed he now felt securely among friends. The effect was to emphasise his accent; if I had closed my eyes, I would have thought myself among the mountains of Caledonia.

'You are talking about the silver?' he asked, turning his face towards us. The light off the river still gleamed in his eyes.

The captain nodded and held his breath – as did we all.

'We had orders for it to be moved,' said Scotland. 'I was one of the party that did the work.'

'And you know where it is now?' the captain asked. He kept his voice steady, as if to sound urgent would scare away the answer he wanted to hear.

'I do,' said Scotland.

'So will you tell us?'

'I will.' Scotland paused, which was only to create an amusing sort of suspense – but not even the captain could resist hurrying to the next question.

'And that is?'

Scotland slowly put down the piece of bread he was eating, and looked the captain in the eye. 'Where it is safe.'

I could tell by the way the captain's hands tightened in his lap that he thought this answer was insubordinate – but would not respond to it as such. 'And where might that be?' he asked. 'Pray tell us.'

These last two words had a trace of iron in them but Scotland did not seem to notice – or to care. He tore another piece off the loaf Mr Allan had given him, and chewed it thoroughly. After a full minute he swallowed, and then replied with a longer speech than any of us expected.

'Mr Captain,' he said. 'If I give you the silver you will have no further use for me. You will take it, and sail away, and leave me to my fate. And you have seen what that fate will be – or your friends have.' Here he looked at me and Mr Lawson and the bo'sun. When his eyes turned to Natty, and locked with her own, I thought she would come to his defence. Her lips opened and I saw her teeth. But as Scotland raised his head a fraction, and jutted out his chin, she changed her mind and stayed silent.

Instead it was the captain who spoke next. He felt thwarted by Scotland's stand, yet his voice held nothing but sympathy and understanding. 'Very well,' he said. 'Perhaps we might agree this: you will remain as our guest, while we decide how we can help you and your friends. And when that is done you will help us find our treasure.'

'*The* treasure,' Scotland replied.

'*The* treasure,' said the captain, which was the only time I ever heard him at a disadvantage. 'I meant *the* treasure. Everyone will have a share. There will be plenty.'

As the captain leaned back against the wall of the roundhouse, Bo'sun Kirkby and Mr Lawson murmured that they agreed with his plan, and so did Natty. Perhaps some of us reckoned we had no choice. For my own part, it seemed inevitable as well as necessary.

Now that he had been corrected, the captain seemed anxious to prove his mistake had not been deliberate. He moved quickly away from the subject of the silver and asked Scotland to tell his story. Some of what followed was a complement to everything we had been told during our march back to the *Nightingale*; it proved that Scotland's life on the island – and the life of all the prisoners – had been lived under the spell of the wilderness. He confirmed that Smirke was the chief man among the maroons, and described him as a monster who lived in a state of cynical disregard for his fellows. The administration of his justice, which took place in the structure he had named the Fo'c'sle Court, was especially terrifying, and especially feared. I would have liked to think it was such a long period of isolation that had made him so heartless, but from my father's evidence (and the fact the Squire Trelawney had not thought him worth saving on the *Hispaniola*), it was clear the origins of his bestiality were deeply rooted, and buried in circumstances of which I knew nothing.

That said, Scotland believed Smirke would not have been capable of creating such horror as existed at the stockade without the influence of his deputy – Stone. This was the executioner we had seen at work, whose face was so ashen it seemed all humanity had been bled out of him. When I mentioned this, Scotland told us something remarkable: some time before, there had been a rebellion in the camp and an attempt was made to overwhelm the guards. Stone had been captured during this episode and his throat had been cut – but he had survived, and now had the scar that ran under his chin like a strap. Scotland briefly covered his eyes with one hand as he remembered this, and said it gave Stone the appearance of a dead man. From this I felt sure he was the evil spirit of the whole island; it made me more convinced than ever that we should think differently about our reasons for being there.

Scotland told us the third maroon (the man who now called himself Jinks) seemed to be the least definite character – although, as the captain noticed, this was no reason to think he was harmless, since weak people have a dangerous need to prove their strength. We nodded at this, having seen Jinks in his role as inquisitor at the trial. I understood that if ever I were to encounter him alone, I would have a decent chance of saving my life; if ever I found him in the company of his fellows, I should expect him to be willing to do whatever they asked of him.

Scotland finished his account by telling the captain what the rest of us already knew: that he had been stolen from Africa when still a child, slaved in Jamaica, then blown to Treasure Island. This led him to the opinion that if Smirke and his men had not been as they were, the place would have been a paradise. When the captain pressed him about this, he gave some more instances of the cruelty that blighted everything – but also, and more surprisingly, said that for all the beauty and strangeness of the animals, it was also like the Garden of Eden in having a snake. Or rather many dozens of snakes, which lived in a particular region near the northern cliffs. The captain was very interested in this, for reasons I did not understand at the time; Scotland told him they were dull grey in colour, and no more than a foot long, but extremely poisonous. He knew this because one of his fellow prisoners (whom he called his 'friends') had been bitten and immediately died.

As Scotland came to the end of this description, the energy left him and his chin sank forward onto his chest. This happened so suddenly, I wondered whether he might have fallen into a daze. Events that followed later in the evening proved me wrong. Far from *sleeping*, Scotland was *thinking* – but keeping his thoughts private. Although he took no part in the rest of our conversation, he weighed in silence everything we said.

And the gist of this talk? It was led by the captain, who was not concerned to rush into action against the stockade, but to reflect and talk again in the morning. His suggestion, which was delivered in the kindly tone a parent might use, had the effect of making me feel as drowsy as I thought Scotland must be. I was somewhat embarrassed by this, since it seemed to prove my lack of experience compared to Natty, who was still bright-eyed and attentive. At the same time, the exertions of my day, and the sight of the moon climbing through the clouds outside, allowed me to feel that it would be reasonable to make my excuses.

I pushed back my bench from the table. Because the captain was so preoccupied with our difficulties he saw nothing unusual in this, although he did recommend I find some food in the galley before going to my bed, which I thought was also like a parent. As I closed the roundhouse door behind me, I tried to catch Natty's attention – but she was concentrating on Scotland, rearranging the shirt around his shoulders to cover the scar of his branding, and did not notice.

When I reached my cabin I looked around me very carefully, with a strangely exaggerated sense of being alone. The few books on their shelf beside our two bunks; the grain in the woodwork by my pillow, which resembled lines on the palm of a hand; the smell of wet leaves and mud creeping through the ship: all these were things I recognised, yet made me feel less like myself than a beetle who had crawled inside a log. This was consolation of a kind: it meant I could still exist in secret. Yet I knew I would never be innocent again. I had seen the wickedness of men with my own eyes, and heard it with my own ears. It was an impenetrable darkness.

It was at this point my father appeared to me. He was not holding forth in the taproom of the Hispaniola, where I knew he was likely to be at such a time of the evening, but sitting on the edge of the bed where I had seen him last. His head was in his hands, so I could not tell his expression. But I knew he was grieving, and understood the cause of his grief was the great wrong I had done him. My proof was the sight of Billy Bones's sea-chest, which gaped open at the foot of the bed. My father had searched it for the map of Treasure Island, found it stolen, and guessed at the reason for my absence.

If I had believed at this stage in my adventure that I would return home safely and soon with a portion of the silver, it is possible that his reproaches might not have weighed on me so heavily. As it was, I thought we would arrive in London empty-handed – if we arrived at all. This entirely transformed my reasons for setting out in the first place. I was nothing like a redeemer. I was a traitor.

I sat down with my own head in my hands, as I imagined my father was doing. The same fitful moonlight gleamed through my porthole as shone through his window above the Thames; the same atmosphere of the world pressed against the walls protecting us both. This was no comfort when weariness overwhelmed me at last, and I toppled backward onto my blanket and fell asleep.

PART IV

NATTY'S STORY

CHAPTER 19

A Walk at Night

I must now describe things I did not see with my own eyes, but have been told by Natty. When I suggested the account would be more truthful if she wrote it herself, she told me I have enough words in my head for the two of us, and might as well use them. I said I was willing to do so, on condition that she allowed me some freedom to *interpret*, as well as merely to *report*. She bridled a little, then accepted – saying the difference between our views would never be very great. I could not disagree.

When I had retired to my cabin, after failing to catch Natty's attention as I have just mentioned, the captain and Bo'sun Kirkby and Mr Lawson soon followed my example. Natty and Scotland were left alone together – and they decided, because the rain had so far held off, they would go on deck and see something of the moon and stars, which Scotland said would be pleasant for him after his long incarceration. Although our nightwatchman (who on this occasion was Mr Stevenson) was still in the crow's-nest, he did not notice their arrival because he was asleep – which they discovered by calling his name and hearing no answer.

I say the rain had delayed, but Natty could still dimly make out the large mass of turbulence on the horizon beyond the estuary. These clouds, which were now a sinister ivory colour, had been fluffed up by the wind into an enormous size, then hollowed out to give the appearance of a cave. In the centre of this cave, the storm was waiting to arrive, occasionally firing off impatient bolts of lightning.

Although it seemed this storm might now begin at any moment, Natty and Scotland decided they preferred to walk on deck rather than take cover again, and so began a slow perambulation of the ship. Natty maintains that despite their lack of an audience, they knew they made a peculiar couple – she with her hat still pulled down around her ears; Scotland wearing the captain's shirt and the threadbare rags in which we had found him. Neither of them felt any embarrassment. Indeed, I understand they talked quite freely – which at that time Natty had not often felt able to do with me, who knew her much better.

When I have asked the reasons for this candour, Natty has never given a clear answer. My own conjecture is: whatever feelings Scotland provoked in her were somehow akin to those she felt for her father. Ever since helping to rescue Scotland from his trap, she had shown an exceptional absorption in him – almost a fascination. This is because she was excited by proof of what I will call *experience in the world*, even when it could not always be condoned (as with her father), or when it was impossible to enjoy (as with Scotland). I knew my own place in her affections must be curtailed, because I had not yet lived variously enough. This was difficult for me, and stimulated feelings I do not like to name, but I dare say will become manifest in what follows if they are not already.

Their main topic of conversation seems to have been how the captain should proceed – and this soon led them into a greater danger than any we had faced, as I shall show. In Natty's opinion, the captain was so offended by everything he had heard about the stockade, he was bound to launch an assault as soon as possible. How he would manage this with so few men and such paltry fire-power she did not explain – but made do with imagining we would break into the pirates' log-house and then overthrow its tyrants like the populace entering the Bastille.

While Natty was still warming to this theme, Scotland interrupted her. Was she dreaming? Had she not seen the stockade was well geared to resist an attack? What was needed, he said, was not directness but guile. Surprise and guile. The former he proposed leaving to the captain – perhaps by launching his assault very early in the morning, when the maroons were still groggy with their pleasures of the previous night. The surprise, he said, he would manage himself. It would come in the form of encouraging his friends to rise against their oppressors in the same instant that the captain began his assault. And how would he guarantee this? By the expedient of returning voluntarily to the stockade, where he would become his friends' commander-in-secret.

It is easy to give Natty's reaction to this idea, in so far as it mixed respect for courage with dismay at risk. What is more difficult to describe is the clash of these things in her mind – and how her reply to Scotland fought to do justice to the greater good. That is, the good of the greatest number. If ever she strayed from this principle while they continued talking, Scotland held up his hand, or shook his head, and brought her round. And when she had almost agreed with him, he led her into complete accord by reminding her of his wife, whom he said he particularly wanted to protect from dangers she would otherwise have to meet without him.

In this way they decided – with the appearance of perfect good sense – a plan that seemed entirely unreasonable to the rest of us, when we eventually discovered it. And having achieved this feat, Natty then compounded it: she volunteered to accompany Scotland on his walk back to the stockade, and at some convenient point to part with him, before returning to the *Nightingale*, where she would tell the captain everything that was afoot. I can only assume she meant it as kindness, and an expression of the sympathy between them, and that Scotland took it in the same spirit. I have told her since that what she thought of as charity was in fact foolishness.

When they had reached their decision, the two conspirators quickly acted upon it. Not so much as a note was left behind – only the captain's shirt, which Scotland folded on a bench in the round-house. Once this was done, they slipped over the side of our ship, waded ashore (which they could do because the tide was low), and vanished into the foliage. If Mr Lawson had been awake at his place in the crow's-nest, he would have heard nothing but the slap of another wave against the mud.

The route that Natty and Scotland took across the island was the same we had followed with Bo'sun Kirkby a short time before – but darkness made it seem strangely un-like, albeit still very difficult. The very dense vegetation in the valley, which had previously appeared exciting and abundant, was now sinister and chilling. The leaves of plants appeared to rub themselves quite deliberately over their faces. Roots seemed too sticky, or too cold, or too mobile, whenever their hands touched them. The noises of animals, as they quacked, or snorted, or grunted, or growled in protest at being disturbed, were not merely curiosities but reasons to feel alarmed. It was here, Natty admits, so near the beginning of her journey, that she realised how long she had been without sleep, and how exhausted she would soon become.

This weariness ebbed when they reached the pine woods and found the walking easier. On the other hand, the wind now began to blow more strongly, and when they looked out to sea they found the ivory sky-cave had broken up, and a succession of more compact clouds was rolling over the horizon, which sometimes let through shafts of moonlight. Although these gleams were only intermittent, they were very bright (the moon being close to full), and showed the waves beneath had been churned into an overall creamy whiteness. These gave Natty a strong impression that certain things in the world had worked loose from their usual ties – and that she herself might also be hurrying towards a conclusion she did not want, but could not avoid.

The idea of catastrophe increased as the wind rose. Up to now, the two travellers had been talking to one another very easily – about such matters as how Scotland would lie low until one of the slaving parties went into the fields, when he might join them unnoticed. Now they fell silent except to warn one another of hazards – striding through the thickened air, often with one hand before their faces to deflect the dust and pine needles blown up from the forest floor.

Natty says that if the weather had not been so bad, she would have kept a better lookout for patrols sent from the stockade. As things were, she did not think the maroons would be bothered to stir from their sleep, but would rely for their protection on the traps and other defences they had laid around the camp. This was reassurance of a sort but also a warning, because it reminded her she would very soon have to leave Scotland and make her way back to the *Nightingale* alone.

To prepare for this separation she took shelter behind a large boulder, and pulled Scotland in beside her; they had reached the edge of the pine forest, with the bare black slopes of the Spyglass opening ahead, looking dull as charcoal when the moon was hidden, but like a frozen torrent when it entered a patch of clear sky. No sooner had they found this bit of quiet than Natty realised she could not give the message of hope she wanted. Less than two hours before, she had sat in the roundhouse and felt equal to any emergency. Now she was like a creature pushed back through history into a more primitive existence.

Whether or not Scotland noticed this, he confirmed that he must now leave her – and seemed to crouch down so that she thought he might actually be about to break into a run.

She could only nod.

'Remember,' he said, 'you must tell the captain to catch them off-guard. If you are successful, you will hardly need the rest of us to help.'

'And if we are not?' said Natty.

Scotland looked at her gently. 'If you are not successful, we will do what we can.'

Natty nodded again.

'You have not asked me about the silver,' Scotland said, in the same quiet voice.

Natty shrugged. 'We decided – you heard the captain. We will help your friends first. The silver can wait. It has waited long enough already.'

'That's true. But it will not wait for ever. You will see.'

'What do you mean?'

'It will find you.'

Natty felt puzzled by this, as well she might have been, and did not especially like the feeling that Scotland was teasing. She therefore changed the subject and made herself more practical. 'The attack cannot be tomorrow,' she said. 'We need time to prepare. Not tomorrow, but the day after tomorrow. Then you must listen for us and be ready.' She had no authority to speak for the captain in this way, but knew that whatever she affirmed now would be difficult for him to change later.

'Bright and early with the lark,' replied Scotland – which I have always thought was a strange phrase for him to use, since it conjured a feeling of England, where he had never been. It was evidently intended to reassure Natty, and at the same time make himself seem the master of the occasion.

Natty tells me she then laid her hand on Scotland's shoulder, and looked at his face for what she thought would be the last time this side of his liberation. He smiled, and when she glanced beyond him she saw a burst of kindly moonlight showing a way back through the pine trunks towards our ship.

Then she turned towards him again. Scotland had moved away from the boulder and was still facing Natty; the wind poured across the open shale and buffeted him so much, he was forced to keep moving his weight from one foot to the other. A yard behind him, a darker shadow than any produced by the clouds seemed to rise from the bare rock. A shadow with a cocked hat pulled back to show a wolfish face, and a jacket buttoned to the throat.

Natty recognised him at once. It was Smirke's man – Stone. A bare sword flickered in his right hand, and the forefinger of his left was pressed against his lips in a horrible gesture of conspiracy. Natty shook her head, refusing him, but Stone's pale face remained absolutely blank as he rested the point of his sword in Scotland's bare skin between the shoulder blades.

Scotland's own face crumpled – but he said nothing: he knew.

Natty also said nothing. They only stared at one another, with their unhappiness passing between them.

'I know this one,' said Stone, looking into Natty's eyes as if he were staring straight through her head; his voice was surprisingly high, almost squeaky, as she had heard it before in the stockade. 'But who might you be?'

As Natty returned his stare, she felt herself beginning to tremble. The man's hair was as white as his skin, and blew in revolting thin hanks across his sunken cheeks. He might as well have been a ghost, yet the hunger in his eyes spoke of distinctly human appetites.

'Who indeed might you be?' he said again. 'I shall enjoy finding the answer to that question.'

CHAPTER 20

Taken Prisoner

Here are Natty's own words, unmediated for once. 'Scared me to
death,' she said. 'Really, scared the life out of me when I saw that
old pirate, with the wind blowing dust in my face and Spyglass Hill
all black in the distance. Every drop of blood in me sank to my feet.
Although a strange thing. I felt on fire, like a tiger.' Does this mean
she made a run for it? No; even though Stone was a man in his
sixties, he was very lean and wiry and she thought he would have
caught her. Did she panic? No; she kept her eyes wide open. She
even remembers Stone's large metal belt-buckle, shaped like an eye,
which she saw when the moonlight poured across him in a sudden
flash; it winked at her from below the buttons of his jacket, which
he had done up very properly.

As for Scotland – he stood still as a rock. Natty reckoned this was sensible, but she saw a terrible change in him as well. All the confidence he had found in the last few hours was suddenly worth nothing. His shoulders sank; his face was closed. She remembered the sound of his fear in the trap, which had led us to find him in the first place, and knew he was imagining how he would be punished.

Natty's instinct was to put her arms round his shoulders and comfort him – but of course Stone would have none of this. As soon as she began to lift her hands, he withdrew the tip of his sword from Scotland's back and pointed it directly at her throat. 'As I was saying . . .' he began, then paused to lick his thin lips. 'As I was saying, who might you be?'

Natty has told me it was only when she heard these words that she fully understood how much danger her night-walk had made for others besides herself. In the first shock of Stone's appearance – his seeming to rise from the rock like a spirit – her only thought had been how to survive. Now there was room in her mind for larger ideas to appear. Ideas of how she must not betray her friends. And of how she must keep her identity a secret, or face a worse fate than already seemed likely.

'Dropped from a cloud, did you?' Stone went on, leaning the point of his blade briefly against her neck. 'Got carried across the sea by an albatross? If you lie to me I shall know – I have an eye for liars, don't I?' Here he glared at Scotland before lashing out with his boot, and landing a kick on the ankle that made his prisoner groan. This, despite the boot in question being as much like the spectre of such a thing as he was like the spectre of a man. The sole had long since parted company from the upper, and was bound to it by what seemed to be a length of string, but was probably a vine of some kind.

'I came here on a ship,' Natty said – and when she saw Stone jerk his head, knew that even so vague a statement was intensely interesting to him. In her mind's eye, she saw him rallying Smirke and the others, then the *Nightingale* under siege, then the crew overwhelmed, then the pirates sailing towards the horizon while she stayed marooned on the shore.

'Ah-ha!' said Stone, taking a step backwards as he relished the sound of her voice, and looking her up and down. It occurred to her as he did so that this scrutiny was fed by what must have felt like an eternity of longing for new sights, new sounds, and new company. His eyes hungered across her eyes and mouth and neck, devouring her as greedily as the moonlight allowed. 'A young English gentleman, if I'm not mistaken,' he said at last. 'Now that's something I haven't seen for many a year.' An expression of such bitter sorrow passed over his face as he said this, Natty almost began to pity him. But when the sorrow burned away, and was replaced by disdain once more, Natty remembered it would be very dangerous for her to feel anything for her captor except fear.

'A young English gentleman,' Stone continued, 'who has arrived here on a ship. A ship with others aboard. Well, well. Now that's an interesting set of facts to discover in the middle of a stormy night.' He gave a whinnying laugh, which had no mirth in it whatsoever, then unbuttoned the collar of his coat and wiped the long fingers of one hand across the scar around his throat. When he withdrew them, he suddenly began rubbing his sword-arm very vigorously. Natty realised he was cold, but had the idea it was the sort of cold no earthly warmth could remove.

'You'll forgive me,' he went on with a sneer, 'if I don't ask after the health of His Majesty. We live beyond his reach here, and make our own laws.'

Stone meant King George, who had recently ascended the throne when the *Hispaniola* first brought him to the island, and Natty understood that because so much time had passed since then, he must be ignorant of many recent changes. Had the guards from the *Achilles* told him, for instance, about the war with America? Or the bloody revolution in France and the liberation of the people? Did he know anything of the developments in science and agriculture? With one part of herself, Natty wanted to distract Stone with such things. Another and larger part reckoned it would not be wise to say anything, since the smallest utterance might be taken as provocation. Indeed, the longer she reflected on this, the less inclined she felt for conversation of any kind – only for thoughts about how she might save her life.

Scotland came to her rescue. 'I saw the wreck,' he said suddenly, without raising his head – at which Stone landed another kick on him. 'No one asked you to speak, you skulk,' he muttered. 'Speak when you're spoken to, if you want to keep your head on your shoulders.'

'It's true,' Natty said quickly, to deflect Stone from this line of thinking. 'We were travelling to one of the other islands, and were blown off course.' She did not want to add more, about who and how many had survived, thinking that every lie she told would soon require a hundred others to support it. Besides, she could see that Stone was already tired of standing in the open; a thin rain had begun to fall, and his eyes kept glancing away, in the direction of the stockade. This made her think that he must soon report to his captain – or seem mutinous.

'Blown off course?' Stone said. Repeating things was apparently a habit of his, to win control of everything by smothering it in sarcasm. He pushed Scotland roughly aside and lurched towards Natty. 'Not thinking of *blowing off course* again, are we, young man? Because if we are thinking of *blowing off course*, I'll have to prevent that happening, won't I? I'll have to hobble my pony and make my life easier that way.' As he said these last few words, he tapped the blade of his sword against Natty's leg, so that she felt its hardness through her trousers.

Natty opened her mouth to insist that no such thought had been in her mind, but Stone would not allow her to speak. He had fed some of his hunger for novelty by admiring her from an arm's length; now he crouched forward until his mouth was an inch from her own, and might be about to lick her skin; there was a horrible smell of meat on his breath. 'My, my,' he went on, peering especially closely at her lips. 'But aren't we a handsome lad. A very pretty lad. Very pretty indeed. My captain will be pleased to make your acquaintance and no mistake.' He continued to stare at her, panting like a dog, until Natty wanted to strike out. To suggest that she was in control of her feelings, but really to distract herself from these same feelings, she kept her attention fixed on his face. Even in so dim a light, it was possible for her to see that age had carved dozen of small deep lines around his mouth, which made it seem sucked inwards in a continual expression of disgust. Although his cheeks were covered in silver stubble, he had no eyelashes.

The longer Stone returned her gaze, the more Natty felt her powers of concentration fading. As they went, the rest of the world seemed to fall away from her as well. The strengthening rain, the wind, the glittering black rock, the pine trees, the surf making its melancholy boom on the rocks below: all these were nothing. Stone had drained her. He was a ghost whose ambition was to make her a ghost – and he would succeed, unless she could stay alert and wakeful.

'Heigh-ho,' Stone sighed eventually, but without any of the feelings a sigh might be able to convey; this was just an expulsion of foul air. 'I see we are getting nowhere, like ships in a mist. But no matter. There will be enough time for questions – more than enough time. So you had better start licking your answers into shape, you whelp, and considering how to serve them.'

He hesitated for a moment, as if expecting Natty to agree, and when she said nothing, began speaking more briskly. 'And as for this *we* you mention – I don't suppose your friends, if you have any friends brave enough, will come looking for you in this weather, at this time of night. Do you? No, I very much doubt that. And if I am wrong – well, they will certainly regret their trouble.'

With this, and in the same efficient manner that had suddenly seized him, he placed his free hand on Natty's shoulder and spun her round so that she was side by side with Scotland. 'You!' he barked, baring his teeth at the man's neck as if he were about to bite it. 'I had almost forgotten you. I suppose I should wonder what you might be doing here as well?'

Natty thought this might be the prelude to more of his rambling and rhetorical questions. But it was a non-existent sort of curiosity; Scotland was so insignificant to Stone, he did not want to waste any breath speculating about him. Instead, he ordered the two prisoners to put their hands behind their backs, then tied them together with a greasy piece of rope he pulled from his pocket.

This was done with a casual kind of ferocity, as if she and Scotland mattered as much to Stone as rabbits he had taken from a snare. When his sword began to prod them in their legs and shoulders, making them walk on, she thought the quick death of a trapped creature would certainly be preferable to whatever fate now awaited her.

I have often asked Natty whether she took the opportunity of their journey back to the stockade, which lasted a mile or two, to devise some sort of strategy for their survival – and perhaps also for their escape. Her only answer has been that she decided to show nothing but courage, whatever she might actually feel, on the premise that people tend to believe what they see.

It occurred to her that Scotland must have had a similar plan. She did not dare look at him directly, but saw in the corner of her eye that he had withdrawn himself from events as far as possible. He trudged with his head sunk down, his shoulders hunched, and his eyes fixed on the ground before him. This was a sign of how defeated he felt, but might also – she thought – be a sort of protection. He was becoming docile so that he could remain himself.

Their path was not a clear track but rather a line of least resistance, winding around the base of the Spyglass then slanting downhill between nutmeg trees and clumps of azalea. In daylight and fine weather, as I knew myself, it was fairly easy going. With the rain now falling heavily, and wind pummelling the foliage, it was difficult to make rapid progress. The two prisoners slipped and floundered, often losing their balance and sometimes falling down entirely – whereupon Stone would again lash out with his boot, or slap them with the side of his blade.

After half an hour of this, Natty felt it was not despair but anger that kept her moving forward. Anger with herself for her impetuosity, and anger with Stone for his cruelty. Also anger with the whole island, which she decided had made her sick with the poison of its story. For every insult she received from Stone, she wanted to inflict another on the earth itself – stamping the surface as if she might have been able to give pain that way, and kicking at stones.

When she heard Stone's humourless snigger, and realised she must be making a spectacle of herself, she stopped – not wanting to give him even this kind of pleasure. Their pace therefore quickened, and although this – combined with the deeper darkness, now that rain had driven the moon entirely into hiding – meant she had little opportunity to notice much that lay round about, she determined to stay watchful. She has told me, for instance, how little rain-puddles filled every blossom, and how the hollow whoops of night-birds sounded like children at play. She has also explained how her sense of the beauty in these things made her feel insignificant as a grain of sand, and yet determined not to die.

At which point, as if he were now the engineer of her mind, and controlled its movements as completely as he governed her actions, Stone broke in on her reflections. 'Whoa there, whoa there,' he called, twitching the rope that tied her hands together. 'Look where I have brought you. See what we have made.'

It was impossible to know whether Stone had planned to arrive at the stockade exactly as dawn broke – but this is what he achieved; it seemed to Natty to demonstrate his complete control of the island. At first she was sure of nothing except that she was standing on a high bluff overlooking the open sea; the horizon was marked by a bar of rust. But soon this bar split apart, and as the red eye of the sun began to open, so the rain also began to ease. Silhouettes that had previously been misty squares and oblongs in the clearing below her were changed into the two log-houses, the shell-shape of the Fo'c'sle Court, and the whole jagged wall of the camp. A cockerel crowed once, then decided it was another day not worth greeting, and fell to picking at the ground in front of the court. The earth here was still stained with blood, although the body of the accused had disappeared.

'Move on now,' said Stone, when he reckoned she had enjoyed the view for long enough, and clicked his tongue like a carter. 'We have people to meet. We have a busy day ahead.'

CHAPTER 21

Questions and No Answers

There was never a doorway or entrance of any kind in the old stockade my father and Mr Silver had known. The whole construction was a solid square of pine trunks six feet high, sharpened into spikes at the top, and anyone wishing to enter had to clamber over them at some risk to their person. When Natty approached the place now, she found a *gate* lolling open, which she supposed the maroons had made; as Stone prodded her through, she noticed the workmanship of its latch and hinges was very poor; the nails had been driven in crooked for half their length, then walloped sideways.

It was a suitable introduction, since almost everything inside the compound was either ramshackle or entirely spoiled. The original log-house was still pretty stout, fit to hold two score of people on a pinch, and loopholed for musketry on every side; the more recent building, the prisoners' log-house, was a sorry affair made of planks salvaged from the *Achilles*, and others rough-cut from the forest; the Fo'c'sle Court, though ingenious, creaked continually in the wind. The ground itself looked similarly exhausted. Tufts of greasy weed sprawled over the central area, which was otherwise pitted with black puddles that marked the places where trees had been grubbed up; half a flowerbed, dug alongside the gate, was nothing but a mound of snapped-off stalks. Rags of mouldy clothing were rotting there.

Even more disgusting was the sickly-sweet smell that crawled over everything, and seemed to drift from the shack which leaned against the maroons' cabin. Natty saw through its open door an apparatus of bamboo pipes that climbed up and down and eventually pointed into a large barrel: it was a primitive sort of distillery. She thought this contraption must explain the generally repellent look of the compound, and the invisibility of the maroons themselves. They were still sleeping off the effects of the night before.

As the gate slammed shut and its echo died across the yard, Natty expected it to act as a signal for the morning to begin. But nothing happened – except that Stone continued to drive his prisoners forward, whistling between his teeth and occasionally sticking the tip of his sword into Scotland's shoulder blades. The cockerel strutted up to make an inspection, then went back to his pebbles. The doo-dahs crowded towards the nearest wall of their pen and gabbled to one another, mingling their voices with the goats, pigs and other creatures that shared their confinement. Natty found these doo-dahs a very curious sight, with large heavy bodies the size of a Staffordshire terrier but covered in soft grey feathers, remarkably small wings, and curved red beaks they clacked together with a dry hollow sound when hungry – as now.

Stone noticed Natty slow down as she looked at them, and tugged at the rope around her hands. 'What's the matter with you, eh, my lad? Never seen a doo-dah before, is that it? Eaten all the doo-dahs in England, have they?'

She said nothing, struck by the strange beauty and great vulnerability of the birds.

'Look at them all you like,' Stone went on, apparently not in the least put out by her silence, and enjoying his own ramble. 'You won't be seeing them for long. Nor be eating them either. Not eating them at all, I should say.' He hauled at the rope again, until it bit into her skin. 'Nor you, you scum,' he added – which was aimed at Scotland. 'Worms and grass for you. Worms and grass.'

Scotland did not reply either, but continued walking patiently with his head bowed until they had reached the centre of the yard, and came to a stop beside the court. A single glance told Natty that this also owed a great deal to the *Achilles*, in the sense that certain items of furniture, such as the judge's chair (a captain's lounger), the witness stand (an arrangement of biscuit boxes) and the jury stall (the bench from a galley), had been looted from it wholesale. When I later saw the almost lunatic assembly of these different parts with my own eyes, I was reminded of Mr Silver's house in London – which I did not like to tell Natty.

Although very roughly made, the prisoners' hut was more sturdily built than this monument of sighs and groans. Natty herself has said it seemed like a box rather than a house – and no doubt it offered the same comfort as a box would do. But it was a box full of valuables, with a guard outside, who was slumped in a comfortable old chair with a battered tricorn on his head (pulled forward to cover his face) and his arms folded across his chest. He was fast asleep – and the empty pitcher at his side, with a tankard fallen over beside it, showed that he was likely to remain so for some time.

Stone had no intention of allowing this to happen. 'Jinks!' he barked, with as much irritation as if he had been speaking to his prisoners.

There was no response.

'Jinks!' he shouted again. 'Budge, you skulk!' – then he dragged Natty and Scotland closer, so that he could knock his mate's hat from his head with the point of his sword, revealing a state of complete baldness. Natty thought he deliberately mis-aimed, since he nicked the scalp itself, and let a trickle of blood flow across the bare and sun-blistered skin.

This brought the fellow to his feet in a swirl of hands, one of which eventually grabbed the sword hanging from his belt. When he saw it was Stone that had woken him, and not his charges escaping, his fury gave way to a cringing smile. It was not the look one friend gave to another.

'What's this, Ben, what's this?' Jinks said gruffly, sweeping his hat from the floor. He then pulled a foul handkerchief from his breeches' pocket, draped it across his skull, and fitted his collapsed old tricorn back in place – very gingerly, because of his sunburn. 'Wake a man from his beauty sleep, would you?' he said, once this little perform-ance was done. 'Wake him and deny him his rest?' He was still so fuddled, then so busy sliding his sword back into its scabbard, he had not yet noticed Scotland and Natty. When he did, his face cleared to a malevolent simplicity – and Natty recognised him as the accuser in the trial scene we had witnessed together. More nearly sober now, his bulging eyes were still red and swollen, and the flesh of his cheeks very flabby. When she considered his age, and the depriva-tions and excesses of his last forty years, she was surprised to find him capable of even the little energy he had already shown. It was clear, however, that wakefulness and thought were a burden to him. He wheezed heavily as he re-dressed himself.

When this operation was complete, Jinks put his hands on his hips. 'But never mind that, never mind that,' he said, looking very insolently at Natty. 'What have we here? Been hunting, have we, Ben? Brought us something to play with, something to beguile the time? This one I know' – here he spat at Scotland – 'but where did you find this one? We'll be drawing lots for him, I can see that . . .'

Jinks stumbled forward and chucked Natty under the chin as he finished speaking. There was such a horrible insinuation in this gesture – such a creeping weakness disguised as independence of mind – Natty wanted to knock him away from her. Stone, in his different way, also thought it was foolish, and growled as if he were chastising a dog. Then he twitched again on the rope attached to Scotland, and lugged him onto the raised porch of the cabin.

Natty lifted her eyes enough to watch, and wished that she had not. Scotland's back was entirely covered in lacerations, which Stone had inflicted during their march from the foot of the Spyglass. He had endured these wounds silently, with no sign he might retaliate, but it was clear a storm was raging inside him. His head, now bent until his chin almost touched his chest, bobbed uncontrollably – so that he seemed in perpetual agreement with something being said. The sight was very shocking to Natty, since it showed her how deeply Scotland had fallen into humiliation. None of his feelings were secret any more.

It occurred to her that Stone might kill him there and then, or perhaps order Jinks to do his murdering for him. But the man's disdain was so absolute, he did not think the trouble worthwhile.

'Take him,' Stone said, meaning Scotland. 'We can think how to punish him later. Throw him in the hole. This other one' – he pointed towards Natty – 'I'm keeping with me. I'm taking him to the poop deck and the captain.'

Jinks gave a tittering laugh, then set about the task Stone had given him. He hauled Scotland round and – once he had unlocked the door to the log-house – punched him once or twice in the kidneys before dismissing him with a heavy kick. This would certainly have sent Scotland sprawling onto his knees, had not several outstretched black-skinned arms appeared in the doorway to catch him and immediately drawn him inside. There was the sound of weeping, and a stifled cry. It was a most melancholy greeting, and yet at the same time comforting, since it showed how much Scotland was loved by those he lived with – his wife among them.

'Now,' said Stone, when the door was locked again and Jinks resumed guard with his silly hat flopped down over one ear. 'You come away with me, my English sparrow.'

The use of this word, which in other circumstances might have sounded like an endearment, made Natty wonder whether he had finally seen through her disguise, and was about to take advantage. This idea made her think very longingly of the *Nightingale* – where, along with the rest of the crew, I was just about now waking to find her gone. She knew her disappearance would be a mystery. But she also trusted I would know what she had done, and for what innocent reasons. I have not always been able to give her my reassurance about this.

Be that as it may. As far as Natty was concerned, two thoughts were now more important than all others. One was how to survive for as long as it took a rescue party to arrive; the other was how to give away as little as possible about the *Nightingale* and her whereabouts. Both were very difficult to calculate. The first because she could not be certain the captain would assume she was inside the stockade. And the second because Stone – now that he felt safe inside his camp – behaved with much less urgency than before. After leading her away from Jinks, he even allowed himself to untie her hands, then pushed her with his boot so that he could once again look her over at leisure. Natty suspected his eyesight might not be all it had once been – which was relief of a kind. But the inspection was alarming nonetheless, as well as disgusting, and she made sure to square her shoulders, and pull in her chest and stomach, to make herself as much like a boy as possible.

While she grew more certain that Stone had not seen through her pretence, Natty's confidence rose. During the march that had followed her capture, she had assumed the maroons would be desperate to collect information about her means of arrival on the island, the number of her companions, their arms, and so forth. But all she had so far discovered was a lazy kind of curiosity. This, she was beginning to realise, was the result of several factors, among them drunkenness and sloth in Jinks, and a sort of vicious complacency in Stone.

Stone was so completely accustomed to controlling everything on the island, he had forgotten the ways in which he might be overthrown. At this very moment, she thought, he was not examining her to decide whether she was male or female only to admire the fact that she was completely his creature. Furthermore, he appeared to think that because she had hitherto given him no resistance, there would also be no difficulty in capturing her companions – supposing she had any. This was his vanity, and although grotesque, she welcomed it with all her heart, knowing it might encourage delays in a course of events that would otherwise have meant the speedy end to our adventure.

'What do you think of the weather on our island?' Stone said abruptly, when he had finished leering. This was very unexpected, and the best answer Natty felt able to give was a shrug. She did not want small talk with a man who was considering whether to cut off her head.

'I can tell you,' he went on, 'I am heartily sick of it. This time of year, you see what we get. A few hours of sun, then a bucket of rain and enough wind to blow your topsail away. Give me your English skies any day, your beautiful English skies.'

Natty could hear this was said with real yearning, but continued to say nothing. The difference between Stone's white face, with its absolute lack of kindness, and the turn towards softness that his talk had suddenly taken was very confusing. It made her realise again that he was still suffering from simple needs, after so many barbarous years on the island. To put it simply: he was lonely. A new face, even if it belonged to an enemy, was irresistible to him.

This returned Natty to her earlier idea: she might still distract Stone by giving him news of home. For the moment, however, his talk ran on so quickly, in such a torrent of sentiment, she could not find a way to begin.

'Hideous rains,' he said, 'that's what we have here; hideous rains. Time was, I'd creep indoors and wait them out with a song and a glass of grog. And oh we have singing and grog here all right, precious little else but singing and grog. But they're nothing compared to what I mean.' A peculiar scratching noise came from his throat, which was his laugh. 'Hideous rains,' he then said again more gently, brushing away the strands of white hair that had drifted across his face, and seizing on the subject that had seemed about to elude him. 'Rains and blowing all night. Blowing so a soul can't get his forty winks but has to wander abroad.'

He drew breath once more, only long enough for a twisted flame to kindle in his eyes. 'But look what my wandering brought me to, eh? It brought me to you.' He lurched close to Natty, then swung away. 'That's right, isn't it, my pretty sparrow, it brought me to you, and now here's this beautiful morning. Wind and rain gone. Sunlight come. All magic and calm. But you'll see, you'll see. We'll sweat in the rain soon enough. We'll all roll round in the wheel.'

These last few sentences were not so much spoken as sung, and might have been the words of a ditty he half-remembered from his earlier life. They brought a glimmer of something like contentment into his face – but this vanished as soon as it appeared, and he slapped his skinny thigh to admonish himself for his levity. It had been an extraordinary performance. Natty no longer felt certain that she should feed him with any thoughts of home, because she might only nourish his madness. Nevertheless, she threw him a scrap to see how he would take it.

'This year our summer in England was perfect,' she said. 'Healthy crops everywhere.'

Stone looked about him very quickly as she spoke, narrowing his eyes and scrutinising the prisoners' hut, then back to the cabin where he slept with his mates (if he slept at all). He seemed to be looking for any small sign of change or disturbance. Finding none, he turned again to his habit of giving a shiver and rubbing his hands together, as if he were cold.

'Summer, you say.'

'I said it had been warm.'

This seemed a remarkable sentence to Natty, given her circumstances. For Stone, who now seemed to have forgotten everything he had been talking about, it was quite meaningless. His eyes roved over Natty's face with none of the wistfulness he had shown a moment earlier, but only the usual careless savagery.

'No one told you to talk,' he snapped. 'Here you never talk unless you're told to talk. Understand?'

Natty refused to say she was sorry but only waited for what came next. This was a cuff round the ear (which would have knocked off her hat if it had not been pulled down so tight), and a snatch at her arm, and a shove across the yard towards the distillery that leaned against the pirates' cabin. A foot-long metal spike had been driven into the ground close to the door – no doubt another bone from

the body of the *Achilles*; Stone now forced her hands behind her
back and attached her to this, so that she had no choice except to
collapse onto the ground. To judge by the gouge-marks in the soil
all around her, she was the latest of many who had been kept
prisoner here.

'The staging post,' Stone said, bending down so his foul breath
again swarmed across her face. 'You'll see soon enough what it's a
stage to.'

With that he straightened again and, after prodding her chest
with the toe of his boot, strode round to the door of the hut where
his fellows were still asleep.

Natty reckoned it must now be about seven in the morning,
because the sun was clear of the horizon and pouring its first ration
of heat over the camp. Enough heat, at any rate, to remind her she
was very thirsty. This drought was all the more painful thanks to
the tinkling sound that came from a small spring she saw rising near
the door where Stone had disappeared. It battered lightly against a
metal basin, mixing with sand like a porridge beginning to boil,
before draining across the yard and disappearing beneath the wall
of the compound.

Natty has told me that as the water cut into her brain, it also
carried her back to certain things she had heard from her father.
She saw him clambering over the stockade to sue for peace with
Captain Smollett of the *Hispaniola* – throwing his crutch across the
wall first, then scrambling after it. She followed him across the yard,
where – what with the angle of the slope, and the soft soil – he and
his crutch were as hopeless as a ship in stays. She watched him
sitting among the tree stumps – all cleared now – and refusing the
offer of help to rise again. She tracked him through a dozen scenes
of begging, then asserting, then begging again, with a full sense of
how put-upon he felt, and how insulted.

I have explained to her that this was a delirium, brought on by her lack of sleep, her hunger and her thirst. She understands this. Yet she always insists her father was beside her as plain as daylight. She says it was the lowest point of unhappiness in the whole story of her adventure. When a small lizard crept towards her from beneath the log-house – a pretty one, with red spots across its green back – she thought even this cold-eyed creature stopped for a moment to look at her with sympathy.

It might have been an hour before the camp came back to life; it might have been a few moments. She was not in a condition to know. Jinks, who had evidently slumped into his chair after Scotland had been returned to captivity, at last decided that he had rested for long enough – so stretched, yawned, took off his hat to rearrange his handkerchief, peered into the empty tankard that lay at his side, put his hat back on again, and finally stood to spit in Natty's direction, before rapping on the prisoners' door and shouting, 'Five minutes.'

This produced a multitude of soft scrabblings and scratchings, like mice under a bed. At the same time, more definite bangs and scrapes began in the pirates' house close behind Natty. From this, she realised that Stone had not immediately woken his captain when he vanished inside, but had waited for Jinks to give his reveille. It surprised her, and not for the first time, that so evidently heartless a man should be so respectful towards another – until she thought how this proved there must be even less humanity in Smirke himself than in his henchman.

How much less she soon saw, for Smirke was the first to appear from the pirates' cabin, dragging behind him an undressed woman, whom he hurled towards Jinks as if she were made of rags; Jinks opened the door and tossed her into the prisoners' hut without a word. Smirke then knelt on the veranda and washed his face in the spring, lapping at the water like a dog, before shaking his head so the water-drops flew off in all directions.

Once this ritual was finished, Stone also came outdoors, helped Smirke to his feet, and began whispering very urgently. For as long as this lasted, with Stone's right hand laid across his captain's back while he completed his story, Smirke often threw glances in Natty's direction – first in surprise, then in curiosity, then in anger, and finally in a sort of amusement that was more alarming than any of the rest.

Frightening as this was, it gave Natty an opportunity to look closely at her tormentor. When she had crouched beside me in our hiding-place, overlooking the trial, we had both noticed Smirke's cloudy grey hair tumbling about his shoulders. At this new proximity, she could also see how his life on the island had aged him, as it had the others. His skin was very crumpled and blotched with sores, and although he had evidently long since abandoned any attempt to shave with a razor, he had not grown a beard but only odd tufts, which sprouted from his chin and cheeks like eruptions of smoke. His mouth, likewise, gave him a very neglected look – the lips were cracked with sunburn, and his teeth showed very brown and haphazard. Taken all in all, he resembled a large and battered scarecrow – half human, half soulless.

This made it all the more astonishing that his first gesture towards Natty was one of kindness. He patted Stone on the arm to show he had heard enough, then slipped off the veranda of the log-house (*staggered* would be better, since he was still very unsteady on his feet) and with a great deal of groaning knelt down beside Natty to undo the rope that tied her.

'Well, well,' were his first words, spoken close to her face. Like everything he said, they sounded *wet*, as though there were always too much saliva in his mouth. 'Mr Stone told me he'd caught a pretty one, and a pretty one you are, no mistake.' His breath was so rancid, it was as much as Natty could do not to flinch away; but she was determined to keep her eyes fixed on his, to show she was not afraid. 'An exceedingly pretty one,' he went on admiringly, lingering over Natty with the same greed that Stone and Jinks had shown. 'Exceedingly pretty. Not quite a girl and not quite a boy by the look of you: a very strange bird. Or is this the way of the world, nowadays? I have precious little knowledge of the world, you know. Precious little. And precious little regard for it either.' He narrowed his eyes as he said this, breathing deeply and apparently inhaling the scent of her skin. 'And what's this?' he continued after a pause, which he filled with soft grunts and sighs. 'A smudge of brown as well as a smudge of white? Very choice. You'll be at home here, my lad; you'll be at home here all right. None of us cares who we are or what we do.'

Natty felt so disgusted by Smirke's closeness, and by the insult and insinuation of his words, it was almost impossible for her to stay silent – as she knew she must. But just when it seemed he would become intolerable, he suddenly lurched away, hauling himself to his feet and looking down at her with his hands thrust into the tops of his trousers. 'But we can come to all that in our own good time,' he said. 'Time is the one thing we've got plenty of, isn't that so, shipmates?' He leered at Stone as he said this, showing more of his ruined teeth, then continued – apparently speaking to all and sundry, but with the dreaminess of a man talking to himself.

'First things first is what I always say. First things first. So let's begin with the first of all. What shall we call you? I wonder. Shall we just call you *English*? Mr Stone tells me you come from the old country, and I would like to revenge myself on her. Or do you have a name of your own?'

Threatened like this, Natty felt there would be no harm in telling the truth, though her throat was so dry, her voice squeezed out sounding very pinched.

'Nat.'

'Nat,' Smirke repeated with a mocking fondness. 'Nat with a thirst, by the sound of it. Mr Stone! Fetch the lad a drink, if you would be so kind, and we can hear how he pipes.'

Stone did as he was told, which again seemed remarkable, by filling a tankard at the spring, carrying it carefully, and pressing it into Natty's hands and staring as though he had never seen a person drink before.

Natty almost choked as she swallowed, and swallowed again, thinking she was like a calf being fattened for the slaughter that must follow – and perhaps would have come very soon, if a distraction had not interrupted them. This was Jinks flinging open the prisoners' door, and ordering his charges to appear – which they did immediately, and formed into a column two abreast.

After the first few pairs had emerged, Stone backed away from Natty, ripping the tankard from her and throwing it onto the ground as Smirke bellowed, 'Look lively, men! Look lively!' A great commotion then began in the pirates' own cabin. This was the sound of bodies falling out of bed, cursing as they searched for clothes they had mislaid, complaining about their headaches, snatching a mouthful of food and water – then stumbling into the bright yard. The majority stood still and gaped – first at Natty, then at one another – but this rigmarole was soon ended by Smirke barking orders. At this, two or three of the men broke away and lolloped towards the prisoners like wolves discovering a flock of sheep.

The prisoners seemed to shiver as these guards approached, but not one of them faltered or looked up, their dejection was so great.

There were some fifty of them, men first, women following, and every one stooped and ashamed, with dull eyes fixed on the shoulders of the one before. All were naked to the waist, all were barefoot, and some of the last to emerge carried young children, or led them by the hands. The paler skin of these children showed their parentage; several, in fact, had hair as yellow as the sun, and one a tangle of red ringlets which reached halfway down his back. Everyone – child and adult – held either a shovel, or a mattock, or a fork, or some other implement in their unbound hands; only their ankles were tied together – with lengths of rope that made it easy enough to walk, but impossible to run.

Natty soon found Scotland among them, shuffling with the same cowed meekness as the rest so as not to invite attention. He refused to look towards Natty – although it comforted her a little to notice how the blows inflicted on him by Jinks, and the dozens of stabs and cuts delivered by Stone, had been cleaned since he had been thrown back to join his friends, and the blood on him wiped away.

Natty understood that she was watching a daily ritual, which Smirke and the others were also now closely scrutinising, eager to reprimand anyone who strayed from routine. Still in line, the prisoners approached the stream that ran towards the edge of the stockade. In pairs they knelt to drink and, when they had swallowed a few mouthfuls, rose and stepped across, allowing those behind them to do the same. When the last had taken their refreshment – which was never enough, and to the children was especially miserable (many of them began weeping) – those at the head of the column had reached the southern gate. From here they passed into the fields they had made, which were already shimmering in the heat.

As each pair of prisoners left the stockade they began to sing – a slow-paced song Natty did not recognise:

In the morning with the dew upon the field
Alleluia!
We will rise and find our injuries are healed
Alleluia!
We will greet the rising sun
As if a new world has begun
We will do our Saviour's work and never yield.

Eventually the troop was in full voice, swaying gently from side to side as they went, with the children now drying their eyes, and beginning to clap their hands. It was a most affecting sound, very beautiful in its sorrow, but at the same time full of dignity and defiance. Until they began to drop out of sight towards the shore, their music really seemed to fill the sky and cancel its emptiness.

When the song ended, which happened as the prisoners set to work, this emptiness returned, but now seemed larger, just as the misery of the prisoners' plight also seemed more engulfing. Plans that Natty had spoken about with Scotland – plans that had seemed so easily achieved when they were nothing but words – now felt impossible as she saw them translated into facts. Fifty friends, all of whom had shovels and suchlike to use as weapons, and thirteen enemies. Their uprising must surely succeed! Yet so broken were the prisoners, and so completely demoralising was the thought of sticks against swords, the battle seemed lost before it had begun. Natty had imagined a second storming of the Bastille. On Treasure Island, such a thing was impossible. Here was the old world still, stupid and brutal as ever.

Smirke saw nothing of this as it passed through Natty's mind – nor much of anything except his latest chance for cruelty: the prisoners were so familiar to him, they had no individual selves. In fact all the pirates seemed so completely used to their own barbarity,

Natty asked herself whether they might in fact prefer not to be rescued from the island, no matter how much they might say they missed England and her weather.

From this, Natty deduced that Smirke's *comfort*, if that is quite the word for such a diminished state of being, was so enormous, he could not be bothered to cut off her head. In this respect, she understood that he was filled with the same vanity as Stone. And once again, while being astonished by the lethargy it produced, she also felt a profound gratitude for it. Smirke was so convinced of his authority, so blinded by his habits of domination, he was not merely reluctant to search for the ship that had brought her to the island – he could barely stir himself even to consider the likelihood that it would have a crew opposed to his way of managing his affairs.

At the same time, it was quite natural for him to be very suspicious of Natty, and once he had finished his perusal of the slaves, he therefore began a bullying and laborious sort of interrogation. How many others had come with her to the island? Where was their ship if it had survived the coast? Were they here by accident or design? In the beginning, these questions were delivered with the same false kindness that Stone had shown in passing her the tankard of water. But the longer they continued, and the less helpful Natty became, the better she understood that he was not in fact expecting answers at all. He was performing a brutal charade that, thanks to his sense of invincibility, had nothing to do with a real curiosity about Natty's friends or the *Nightingale*. Instead, he was looking for ways to terrify her. It was for this reason and no other that he eventually grabbed her by the shoulder and hauled her across the yard until they stood in front of the Fo'c'sle Court.

'You know what this is, do you?' As Smirke hissed this into Natty's ear, he gave it a painful tweak.

She shook her head, which made Smirke continue even more fiercely. 'Very well,' he said, widening his eyes. 'I shall tell you what this is. It is our court, here on the island. Our court, where we see justice done. We are a reasonable society. We arrest, and we try, and we punish. And we've arrested you, haven't we, Master Nat? We've arrested you, and now we'll try you and punish you.'

He paused again – but when Natty stayed silent, decided he might as well lose control of himself. 'Still tongue-tied?' he spat, looking round at Stone for encouragement then lunging wildly towards Natty again, with the tufts of grey beard wagging on his face. 'By God, I'll shake you up, you miserable dog. We'll shake him, won't we, Mr Stone, we'll shake him until his bones melt. I don't care if he is no more than a boy – a boy's as insolent as a man, more insolent in fact. Much worse. Much more insolent. Where's your respect, boy, where's your respect? Ha! What are boys and men to me, they're all the same. A babe in arms or a doddering fool, they're all the same. I'll chop them up and fry them if I want – they're all nothing.'

Natty heard this with her head bowed, as though the words were blows, but when they ended and she looked up again, and saw the court arching above her, she knew that everything she had heard was the simple truth as Smirke understood it. The shock jolted her into speech.

'I have lost my friends,' she said, which made him gaze at her in utter bewilderment, as though she were an idiot.

'Have you not understood me, young man?' It was the strangled voice of a schoolmaster that Natty heard, and a schoolmaster's snatching hand that grabbed her chin, and pinched her face. 'This is our *courthouse*. Our courthouse, where we hold our assizes and punish all liars and other wretches. This is where we see *fair play*. Where we set *everything right*.' He released Natty, and bent close to her again. 'You see that, boy? If you see that, you will answer my questions and our justice won't trouble you. Otherwise . . .' He did not complete the sentence, but straightened and wiped his chin, to clear the saliva he had ejected there.

'I don't know what to say,' Natty told him, which was truth of a kind but really none at all.

'You don't know what to say?' Smirke repeated, much more quietly now, as if he were suddenly exhausted. In truth, he had remembered another way to enjoy himself with her. 'By my reckoning,' he continued, 'you need to look sharp and make it your trouble to know, if you want to keep your head on your shoulders.'

With this, he pushed back the sleeves of his jacket, in a gesture Natty thought must be the prelude to his drawing a sword. But no. Rather than that, he proceeded to wrap his arms round her and lift her up as if she weighed no more than an infant, and then to carry her in the same upright position until he reached the dock of the court, where he installed her like a peg in a hole. In this strange embrace, the fear that rose in Natty was continually checked by the foul smell of dampness, and rotten flesh, that rose from Smirke and filled her head to the exclusion of almost every other thing.

'This is where not knowing will land you,' he said as he released her. 'You will stand *here*' – he jabbed at her with his finger – 'and I shall sit *there*' – he pointed at the chair raised on its platform behind her – 'and Mr Jinks will be *here*' – he stabbed the air close to her head – 'and Mr Stone will be waiting *here*, in case we think you are guilty.' As he said this last phrase, he indicated the stained ground on which he stood, and scuffled his feet as if he were trying to colour his shoes with blood.

The performance was so bold, Natty insists she found it more farcical than anything, and actually had to resist a compulsion to smile. I have since told her this was merely an aspect of her fear, and nothing to be surprised at. Yet she was right in thinking Smirke was not about to put an end to her. He was enjoying himself too much for that, like a cat with its mouse. After frowning at her for a moment in her new place, and finding this still did not loosen her tongue, his hand went nowhere near his sword but only flew back to his tufts of beard again, from which he wiped the spittle and sweat a second time.

This scowling gradually became a long grumble, delivered more to himself than Natty, about the growing warmth of the sun, and the impossibility of working any more, and the need for Natty to 'consider her fate' and suchlike. From this, Natty understood that her silence had won her a victory of a kind: it allowed Smirke to remain convinced that not even a whole army of her friends would be capable of organising an attack on his camp. In this respect at least, she silently gave thanks for his degradation, which allowed him to remain complacent about the extent of his own power on the island.

At the same time, Natty understood the balance of his mind might very easily swing in a different direction. So when Smirke eventually turned his back and ordered Stone to put her in the distillery, she complied with the order in a way that must have seemed close to grateful. She followed across the compound without a word. As the door of the distillery closed behind her, and the key turned in the lock, and the smothering reek of the place wrapped round her like a cloth, she actually mouthed, 'Thank you' into the darkness.

CHAPTER 22

The Ravine

When I was a child helping my father in the Hispaniola, I very often saw men made drunk by the fumes of their grog, as well as by grog itself. Natty had found the same in the Spyglass; it is a common enough sight. Now she herself became like one of those topers. The distillery might not have been visited for several hours, and the barrel that was the climax of the operation might have been only half full – but every part of it smelled so strong, it quickly made her feel intoxicated. For this reason, you might say she began her captivity by seeming to celebrate.

Perhaps this was all for the good, since it allowed her the drunkard's opportunity of taking an excessive interest in matters that deserve only a moment's attention. Bars of sunlight, slanting between the planks of the walls, soon became objects of great sentimental interest as they illuminated the dust in the air, and turned it into a stairway for miniature angels. The scratching of birds' feet along the roof created a melody as fascinating as the music of the spheres.

At the same time, in the familiar paradox of drunkenness, Natty felt liberated from immediate circumstances, and able to concentrate instead on remote figures and places. Her father, for instance, whom she saw on his bed overlooking the River Thames as clearly as if she were lying beside him; when she pressed the hard ground on which she was sitting, she might have been touching the bones of his hand. She assures me that I also appeared to her, and by looking closely into her eyes showed how much I wanted her safe return. From this I conclude that she welcomed the thought of me – which, had I known it at the time, would have consoled me more than I felt able to comfort her.

Such dreams, alas, were never solid enough to occupy Natty for more than a few moments. Fear continually dragged her back to the present – fear stoked by the sound of the pirates' voices, which reached her through the wall of the shack that was also the wall of their hut. Every word of their conversation was audible, and its subject was mainly herself.

Smirke had begun talking the moment he went in through the door: Natty heard the clump of his boots across the wooden floor, then a terrific creak as he hurled himself onto a bed; the rest arranged themselves more gently.

'What kind of scrape have you got us into here, you swab?' he growled.

Natty understood this to mean that she was the scrape and Stone was the swab – which hardly seemed fair, despite her loathing of him. Stone, to her surprise, seemed almost contrite.

'I wish it had never happened, Captain. Just a lad. But a dangerous lad, seeing we don't know what comes along with him.'

'Give me the word and I'll tear out his tongue. That will make it start wagging soon enough.' This was a voice Natty did not recognise – perhaps another guard off the *Achilles*, who had stayed behind when Jinks and the other men left to oversee the prisoners at work.

'If we tear out his tongue,' replied Smirke, in a sarcastic parody of reason, 'how shall we ever hear what we want?'

This produced a burst of laughter, and a babble of voices all talking together, wondering quite what they did want, and whether it need involve words. Smirke stamped his foot to silence them.

'Quiet, you dogs. Quiet, and use your heads. There's a question we must consider. A whole heap of questions in fact, and I'll now proceed to lay them out for you, along with the answers. One: is the boy alone? I'll wager not. Two: who comes along with him? I'll wager a party. Three: what sort of party? I'll wager a party with weapons. Four: what will they want of us?' Here Smirke paused, and Natty imagined him widening his eyes to solicit opinions – for rather than continuing with his own next 'wager', there was a sudden outburst.

'The silver! The silver!' said half a dozen voices together. 'They'll want the silver!'

Smirke said nothing to this, which again allowed Natty to do some imagining. She saw much nodding of heads, and apprehensive rubbing of hands, and squaring of jaws, as the pirates reminded one another that nothing mattered more to them than their treasure.

'So there we have it, shipmates,' Smirke continued eventually. 'A question. What we might call a di-lem-ma.' He spoke the word trippingly, as if it were something too hot to swallow. 'And this di-lem-ma is: do we need the lad Nat to help us solve our difficulty? Or is he just . . . *in our way?*'

Although these last three words were slowly drawn-out, they also produced a squall of voices, which showed that, as far as the majority were concerned, the question had already been answered and the dilemma solved. 'Show him the sword!' they clamoured; 'Make him into pork!'; 'Hang him with a rope!'; 'Squeeze out his eyes!' – and other gleeful cruelties that came with such a wild clattering of feet the whole cabin shook.

When this fusillade had died away there was further pause before Smirke spoke again. 'Very well, lads,' he said, with a surprising lofti-ness, as though to remind them he was their captain. 'I'm obliged to you. I'll take your advice under consideration – indeed I shall. I'll do my considering, and I'll digest all these things that you've given me to chew upon, and I'll render you my verdict in my own good time.'

More mumbling followed this, rising into another ragged crescendo when the third voice (the voice Natty did not recognise) asked, 'Why not make him a hostage? We'll have his mates where we want them, if we have their pretty boy to trade.'

There was a pause, then a snigger. 'Course, if that's too much trouble we could just string him up now and be done with him. We'll deal with his *party* likewise, when they show – we'll –'

But there was no chance for Natty to hear what new violence might be proposed, since just as this voice began warming to its theme, Smirke interrupted. There was none of the dignity he had attempted a moment before – only a flash of anger. 'I've told you, Noser,' he snapped, 'I'll have no mutiny from you. Not from any of you shipmates. I'm your captain, and you'll do my bidding. And my bidding is: wait while I consider. Understand that?' Natty pictured him glaring round, his wide mouth half-open like a cod.

This outburst seemed to quench the pirates' appetite for more talk – and to confirm that he reckoned the debate was finished, Smirke now smacked his hands together and gave a decisive 'Very well!'

A turbulent silence settled inside the cabin – if it can be called silence when men are dragging off to lounge on their beds, and complaining about the temperature, and berating one another, and quarrelling about a bottle found beneath a table. In truth this sound-show was commonplace in all its details, yet it gave Natty such an impression of brute stupidity, she began to fear Smirke was more likely to kill her for entertainment than any other reason.

In this respect, the effect of the distillery became a kind of salvation: when the log-house was eventually quiet, Natty fell asleep. This might seem surprising, since it suggests she was not sufficiently terrified by the idea of death to stay awake. But in reality our bodies often choose to obey their own laws, rather than the operations of our minds. Many condemned men, when they wake and remember they will be hanged within the hour, take the trouble to eat their breakfast, and show concern for themselves as though they expect to live. Even Jordan Hands bound his thumb before leaping over the side of the *Nightingale*. To dignify this, I might add that Natty had not slept all the previous night, and was tired.

She woke again to the scrape of her door opening, and a flood of light in her eyes – through which appeared the silhouette of Smirke. Her first thought was: she had a foul taste in her mouth. Her second was: her head thundered, as if she had been drinking. Her third was: regret that she had not been awake to hear Smirke announce her fate. These first two made her sorry for herself. The third made her frightened.

'On your feet, lad,' he ordered. 'We must do this man to man, or I'll be thinking I've murdered a baby, and that will hang heavy on me.'

Given the number of Smirke's other sins, this seemed a strange concern – but Natty was glad to hear it nonetheless, since it suggested a grain of charity still remained in him. How much chance it had to develop was another matter, which Natty realised as her eyes grew accustomed to the brightness, and noticed that behind him stood Stone and the other man whom she had heard in the cabin saying he wanted to cut out her tongue. She assumed this must be Noser; he was the tallest of the three, with a very lean body, and childish goggle-eyes that were separated by the unnaturally large proboscis that gave him his name. This made him look odd enough. Stranger still was his dress, for he was clothed with tatters of canvas and sea-cloth, and this extraordinary patchwork was held together by a system of the most various and incongruous fastenings, brass buttons, bits of stick and loops of tarry gaskin. About his waist he wore an old brass-buckled leather belt, which was the one solid thing in his accoutrement, and squeaked very noisily whenever he moved. He might have been the jester in a medieval court.

Natty felt as certain there was no compassion in this man as she was sure there was none in Stone and Smirke. All the same, she kept staring bravely at each of the pirates in turn, and then around the yard as they led her forward, to give the impression that she was undaunted. Because the sun was two-thirds of its way across the sky, she calculated it must be late in the afternoon. By this time, as she knew, the evening storm would be brewing out to sea, and very soon would dispatch clouds to spew their rain and wind over the island. Whatever the pirates had in mind for her, it was clear they wanted it finished without delay – so they would not get a soaking.

Smirke kept his hand heavily on Natty's shoulder until they reached the open ground close to the Fo'c'sle Court – where he relaxed his pressure. 'Now,' he said, wiping his blubbery face. Natty understood from the new deliberation governing his behaviour that for the first time he was genuinely concerned to discover whatever secrets she knew – while still wanting to entertain himself with cruelties. 'Damn me if you don't know something I need to know, lad. Something we all need to know, which you're going to tell us.'

Because Natty had only just left her prison, she felt it reasonable to say nothing for a moment, but merely rub her arms and wrists until the blood flowed through them more easily. This silence, which in Smirke's mind was merely a continuation of her stubbornness, very quickly enraged him.

'Don't you keep playing the fool with me,' he bellowed. There was a flustered look on his face, which told her he had probably intended to lead up to this anger by a more circuitous route. However, having lost his temper immediately he took no steps to gather himself again, but instead ploughed on, drawing a gully from his belt. 'I've had enough of your silences, my boy. Give us the news of how you came here. And who came with you. And where you reckon they might be now – or maybe you think they've left you to your fate? Can't say I'd have done any different, if I'd been them. In any case; it's your words I want, or I'll take your tongue if I can't have them.'

Stone stood impassive as he heard this, but Noser lunged forward and slapped Smirke on the back, as if to say, 'Now we'll see some fun.' Smirke seemed not to feel it, but kept his rheumy eyes fixed on Natty's face and slowly rolled up one sleeve of his jacket. 'Here's luck' and 'Ted Smirke his fancy' were very neatly and clearly tattooed above the wrist, and on his forearm, which was leathery with age and completely hairless, there was a sketch of a gallows with a man hanging from it.

'I cannot tell what you want,' Natty said, looking away in revulsion. She thought her voice sounded light and frail – very like her own true voice, in fact, which she then struggled to disguise in what followed. This was not something she had practised, but a thought that came to her by instinct.

'Mr Smirke,' she said, using his name for the first time. 'You must put yourself in my position. You must ask yourself: would I save myself to betray my friends?'

Natty had expected this to be the start of a much longer speech, in which she would appeal to the spirit of common humanity. But the effect of even these few words was so dramatic, she had no chance to continue.

'Spare me your speeches!' Smirke said, slashing the air in front of her face. 'It's *news* I want from you, lad, not speeches. *News. And facts*. Now I'll ask you again. Will you give them to us, or must we frighten them out of you?'

If any fumes from the distillery still lingered in Natty's brain, this dispelled them. She knew that she had come to the end of excuses, and could not delay any longer. It was time to speak about the *Nightingale*, or else suffer and die.

She opened her mouth – and then suddenly closed it again, as the sound of singing rose from the land between the stockade and the sea. At first it was very faint, but quickly came closer and gained strength:

> Praise the Lord for the beauty of the field
> Alleluia!
> Praise the Lord for the seed-time and the yield
> Alleluia!
> Praise the Lord for earth and grain
> Praise the Lord for sun and rain
> Praise the Lord that hurts are healed
> Alleluia!

There could be no doubt what the song meant; it was the prisoners, returning from their work. And although this was a daily event, and might therefore have been tedious to Smirke and the rest, in fact it seized their attention. Natty thought this must be because it proved their authority, while reminding them of evening pleasures that would soon begin. When she looked again at Smirke, he seemed to have quite forgotten her; like Stone and Noser, he was agog to see the southern gate open, and the procession begin.

Although Natty was glad of the respite, what now appeared to her was very shocking. The prisoners were quite worn down with fatigue, so every head drooped and every foot dragged through the dust – which made their continuing to sing seem all the more remarkable. When she saw Scotland, she quickly closed her eyes. The skin of his shoulders was shiny with blood, and a long wound was open across the top of his head, as if the skin had been cut and deliberately pulled apart.

Jinks strutted at the head of the column, like a general who had marched his men up to the top of a hill and then down again; the other tyrants who had escaped the wreck of the *Achilles* patrolled on either side, waiting to snap at anyone who strayed. No one had the energy. As their singing stopped, which it did as soon as they came into the compound, the prisoners trudged in sullen weariness and obedience. This, to judge by the smile that now creased Smirke's wide face, was everything he wanted.

Onwards they shuffled, towards the porch outside their log-house, where a barrel had been placed, and a wooden trough such as might be used to feed pigs. It was filled with water, which each prisoner knelt to drink before delving into the barrel and retrieving a wedge of black bread. With this in their hand, they then sank into the same darkness that had disgorged them a few hours before. It was not the end of their day's hardship, however – merely a pause before the beginning of its second and more terrible part.

Natty did not expect to see any of these later cruelties, because she did not expect to be alive – as Smirke soon reminded her.

Watching the last few prisoners disappear, he lost interest in them as abruptly as he had found it, and remembered what they had interrupted.

'One final time,' he barked, turning towards Natty and tapping the blade of his dagger against the open palm of his hand. 'Tell us where your mates have got to. Have they left you, or are they coming for you?'

'I have told you as much as I can,' Natty replied, tearing her gaze away from the prisoners. To give an impression of indifference, she did not look at Smirke directly, but into the sky behind him. Smirke did not seem in the least impressed by this, but Natty could not have expected such a simple gesture would lead to the strangest exchange of their encounter. For as she continued watching the clouds travelling across the sky above the Anchorage, trying to distract her mind with their shifting greys and whites, she heard Smirke say, 'God's teeth but you're a stubborn piece of work, Nat. Don't you know who I am? Don't you know how I've lived? I've sailed with Captain Flint! I've been the friend of old Barbecue Silver!'

To hear her father mentioned like this, as if he were the devil himself, struck Natty a painful blow.

'And what of Mr Silver?' she whispered.

'What of Silver?' he ranted on. 'The coldest heart I ever knew. Silver's a dog, and he taught me my own dog's ways. Woof! Woof!'

Smirke threw himself against Natty as he made these noises, so that she felt his buckles and buttons pressing through her clothes. But he was not quite finished with her father yet.

'The last I saw of that rogue was his miserable face leering over the side of the *Hispaniola* and my musket ball parting the hair on his head. Another inch to the south and I'd have blown him to the flames he deserved! Not a day passes . . .'

Here Smirke seemed ready to continue swimming for some

while in the current of his hatred, and might well have done so if Stone had not stepped forward and tapped him on the arm.

'Yes?' he snapped, whirling round.

'The prisoner, Captain sir,' said Stone, speaking very properly like a good sailor but at the same time grinning. 'You are forgetting the prisoner.'

The effect of this interruption was startling. Smirke stood still, frowning at the ground as though he had forgotten where on earth he was, grinding his teeth and cursing. It was a terrifying glimpse of hatred, but Natty told herself she must take advantage of it. To hear her father condemned with such violence should have been outrageous – the man she knew bore no resemblance to anything Smirke had described. Yet in fact it invigorated her; by conjuring up her father, Smirke had given her an example of ingenuity, when she felt her own resources were about to run dry.

Her new resolve was tested immediately, for no sooner had Smirke composed himself than he became purposeful again, as Stone had encouraged him to be.

'You there,' he called across the yard, to a brace of guards who had recently returned the prisoners to their quarters. 'Robinson. Rawson.'

'Yes, Captain,' grunted one man, and the other, 'Aye-aye, Captain,' as they trotted towards him.

'You know your duties,' Smirke told them, thrusting his gully back into his belt, and suddenly smiling at Natty to show how much he was enjoying this new display of his power. 'Light the fire and make everything ready for my return. Noser!'

The goggle-eyed man lurched forward obediently. 'Aye-aye, Captain.'

'Kill us a doo-dah, and that will be our dinner. I expect to be hungry when I'm done with Master Nat here.'

'Gladly Captain,' said Noser, rubbing his proboscis and stamping off towards the farm pen. As he leaned over its low wall, the creatures beyond it began a most pathetic gabble, appearing to understand that he bestrode their world like Death himself.

'An excellent executioner,' Smirke told Natty, still smiling. 'We all say that about Noser. A very excellent and delicate butcher.' Then he turned to face Stone and continued in the same complacent voice. 'As you are yourself, of course, my friend; as you are yourself. So favour me with your company if you will, and walk with me so that we can attend to our prisoner here.'

By way of giving an answer, Stone ran one hand across his throat. As he did so, the sun disappeared behind clouds and the wind strengthened off the sea, flapping his trousers around his legs until he leaned backwards a little to resist the pressure. This tilt of his body, slight as it was, gave Natty the fanciful idea that even wild Nature had finally turned against her, since it supported her enemy, and now she would be taken to the Fo'c'sle Court, where –

But she did not have to complete the thought. For instead of heading in that direction, Smirke began goading her towards the northern gate of the stockade. She noticed that Stone seemed to understand what must follow; he gave a high-pitched chuckle as he fell in step with them.

The ground at this end of the yard was lumpy with old tree roots, so Natty sometimes stumbled as she went, and once even staggered to keep her footing, as a person might do if they were weak with fear. She regretted giving this impression, since her spirits were now suddenly higher – she insists – than at any time since her captivity began. I have often questioned her about this, finding such optimism hard to credit. Her answer is always the same: that what she felt was not optimism, but rather the impossibility of her own death. She did not think the foliage would suddenly part and reveal her rescuers – the captain and myself. She did not imagine Smirke would change his mind and show mercy, or decide to keep her as a hostage after all; he was too foolish and too vain. She very simply could not believe that she had reached her limit in the world. It was the mention of her father that made this possible; he seemed to have survived everything – why should not she?

Natty remained steadfast, or perhaps I should say *innocent*, even when the climb uphill from the camp began in earnest, along a track that wound between many large rhododendron bushes. Here, rather than contemplating Last Things, she says she began thinking that courage might not be an exalted state, but a natural and primitive thing that derives from our desire to die as we want to live – with dignity. Her life had not been a long one, but she had assembled it carefully. She felt that to vandalise it now with some sort of collapse would have been worse than giving Smirke a victory; it would have licensed her to become a little like him.

Before Natty could finish these thoughts, the fellow suddenly called her name, then followed it with a barrage of groans and curses. Evidently every practical thing was always done for him in the degeneracy of the camp, and although once a very strong man, he had become almost entirely slack during the passage of the years. Even marching this short distance had puffed him out. 'Damn me for a landlubber,' he gasped, between futile hoofs at the ground. 'Damn this earth. Give me a good ship and a following wind; I'll have none of this weight and clay.'

This outburst made Smirke so thoroughly exhausted, Natty thought for a moment she might be able to save herself – by plunging into the bushes and running away. When she felt Stone's sword in her back, however, and heard the steadiness of his silence, she realised he would easily overtake her, then overpower her, and then in all likelihood deprive her of the very dignity she had just been celebrating to herself. She therefore kept to the path and continued walking, trying to occupy her mind by noticing how suddenly some of the blossoms around her had begun to close, now there was no direct sunlight to encourage them, and how the raindrops that had started to fall made a light tapping sound on the leaves, like fingernails.

After another few minutes of hard climbing, they left the belt of shrubs and came to a little wood of Scots pine. Here they felt the wind blowing more strongly, bending the crowns of the trees so that some of them began to scrape together – except where they seemed to step back aghast, and left a patch of open ground. As soon as Natty saw this, she realised it was Smirke's destination – the great crack in the earth that ran down from near the summit of Spyglass Hill, the ravine we had found together with Bo'sun Kirkby on our reconnaissance of the stockade. Then we had been near the shore, where the depth of the thing was not more than forty feet, but still terrifying. Here it was more than twice as much.

'Stop here, lad,' said Smirke, pausing for breath between every phrase. 'This is as far as we go. And as far as you'll ever go.'

Natty turned round and saw Smirke crouched with his hands on his knees. Stone, on the contrary, stood cool and upright, swinging his sword like a pendulum; the blade was shiny with raindrops.

'We often bring our friends here,' Stone said, in his thin and piping voice.

Because this sounded reasonable, Natty thought for a moment they must come to see the view behind him, which was indeed beautiful. The stockade was entirely hidden by the bushes they had passed through, and the island seemed a paradise again. A stormy paradise, with loose purple clouds billowing up from the horizon, but gorgeous in the polished green of its vegetation and the prolific scattering of its flowers. If this was to be her final sight of the earth, she could think of nothing to match it.

When he had allowed Natty to gaze for a minute, Stone corrected her. 'Behind you,' he said with a snigger. 'The view is behind you.'

At this Natty turned – and found herself looking vertiginously into the black wound of the ravine. She lurched backwards.

'Not *back*,' said Smirke, wheezing loudly as he levered himself upright again. 'Not back, any more, my lad – not for you. Only forward and down, forward and down. That's the direction you're heading.'

Natty said nothing to this, hoping her silence would be the last answer she had to give. Her legs were trembling so violently, they actually shook the fabric of her trousers.

'But then again,' Smirke continued, 'you must be wondering: why here? Well, I'll tell you why here, my lad, since your brains may not be working as well as normal. We've brought you here because we don't want your friends to find you when they come looking. Always supposing you have any friends, of course.' He exchanged a glance with Stone, and a smile of congratulation, then went on with a quite unnecessary labouring of detail. 'If we kept you behind with the rest of the swabs, and dealt with you there, we'd look . . . *responsible for you*. I mean, your friends would know we'd chopped off your head, wouldn't they? They'd dig you up and take a look. If they exist, they would. Up here, they'll never think of looking. And if they do look, they'll never see. You'll be too far gone into the earth. Unvisited, you know. That's what you'll be. Unvisited.'

The wind was now strong enough for Smirke to raise his voice as he unburdened himself of all this, which Natty knew must be his definitive attempt to frighten her. But the shouting did nothing to dry the strange wetness in his voice. Quick dabs of spittle, warmer than the rain, dropped into the tufts of his beard or flew directly into her face.

It seems extraordinary, when Natty had already suffered so much that was insulting and terrifying, but this small annoyance ended her patience with him, and so in a sense with life itself. Quite suddenly, she could not endure Smirke's disgustingness any longer.

Two steps were all it took to prove as much – two steps that brought her to the edge of the ravine, where a steady draft of cold air suddenly blew upwards from its depths and fluttered against her face. She glanced across, wondering whether she might be able to jump and escape that way. But no, it was too wide, and the far side was too thickly forested with pines, all swaying in the wind, and shaking their hair like mourners.

She looked down. Twenty fathoms down and shockingly far, to where the pale green slimy walls, and the dribbles of white and grey left by roosting birds, ended in heaps of bone. Some of these had rags of clothing among them. They made Natty think: the world itself has died here. It is the end of everything. I know now how my own body will appear, when others come to look for me. Meaningless and forgotten.

'Damn you all,' she said, without so much as a glance backwards at Smirke and Stone. 'You will never hurt me.' Then she stepped into the empty air.

CHAPTER 23

Walking on Water

When Natty was a child comforting her father, she sometimes dreamed of launching from his crow's-nest overlooking the city of London, and letting the wind sweep her along its currents. This fantasy came back to her in the first seconds of her fall into the ravine – the glide, the hush, the cushion of air against her breast. It gave her the leisure to inspect everything that passed before her eyes, with as much attention as if she were looking through a microscope. The green weed covering the rock face, which had been carved by trickles of moisture. Ledges on which a skin of earth had formed, and dwarfish shrubs taken hold. The grubby tail feather of a pigeon, snagged on a twig.

Then the silence ended, and the light dimmed, and her plunge was no longer a glide but a cacophony, and a tightening, as if her body had been ordered to squeeze through a crack in the air but would not fit, and finally lost all sense of itself in a sudden and stinging halt.

I am describing this as Natty told it to me, but I am withholding something, a thing she herself had hidden from Smirke. While he was jeering behind her back, and Stone was poking with his sword, she had looked into the ravine – hoping to give an impression of preparing to meet her Maker, while in fact devising her salvation. Although the drop to the bottom would certainly have killed her, she saw that several pine trees, which storms had uprooted and tossed into the narrow opening, were wedged in it crossways. These made a very rough sort of *ladder*, on which a person might climb towards the distant floor, if only they could reach the first rung and so begin their descent.

Natty's intention, when she stepped into thin air, was to fling herself onto the first rung of this ladder, which was a tree she reckoned must have been felled by the recent strong winds, since the snapped wood around its base was still very white and clean; it lay some twenty feet below her. And this is what she managed to do. The fall I have just described, which seemed to last for a whole minute but in reality filled no more than an instant, ended not in the blackness of oblivion, but in the much more forgiving dark of pine branches. Their bark was the sudden halt she felt, and their needles the sting.

This might have been her salvation, but it knocked the wind from her lungs and the wits from her head. All the wits, at any rate, apart from those that told her to rouse herself as soon as possible, since Smirke and Stone were likely to peer downwards for evidence of her death. This made her wriggle through the branches until she had buried herself from view; when this was done, she waited quietly until her executioners lost interest.

When she was certain they must have returned to the stockade, she waited for the same period again, to make doubly sure, clinging to the branches like a squirrel. Her fear now was: the pine tree might be insecurely wedged between the two sides of the crevice, and tip her into the abyss – but its own weight had apparently been enough to guarantee it stuck fast. Her comfort lay in knowing the world above was growing darker and more heavily rained-upon with every passing second, and so less hospitable to prying eyes. Crashes of thunder were now clearly audible, along with the hissing of other trees that remained on the edges of the ravine.

Natty was inclined to remain hidden until dawn, but she expected Smirke might suddenly return to enjoy the scene of her disappearance, or more likely Stone. This meant she must escape their reach more definitely – and therefore, after yet another cautious delay, she nerved herself to crawl onto the bare trunk of her perch; from here she could dimly see other trees arranged like lower rungs in the half light beneath her.

Sliding herself over the side of the trunk she dropped through space a second time, only to knock the breath from her lungs a second time. As she recovered, with her head spinning and her face pricked and scratched by needles, the idea of a third fall and then a fourth became intolerable. There must, she thought, be an easier way to proceed – and set about finding toe-holds in the wall beside her, and finger-holds, and assorted small ledges and shelves and platforms and outcrops. With their help, and all the agility she could muster, she made her way downwards into the colder and darker air. When her feet eventually touched solid ground, she stood four-square for a moment, allowing her eyes to become familiar with the gloom. As the outlines of boulders and smaller rocks grew more definite, and their various shades of grey or black became separate from one another, she felt the gratitude of a traveller who has met Death on the road but brushed him aside.

This was an especially strange sensation, because Death in fact now appeared all around her, represented by the bones and skulls of prisoners who had been forced to share her fate without having her fortune. In her nervous gaze they appeared to glow in the twilight, as if they possessed an unearthly interior power. Several had lain among the rocks so long, they had been picked clean by birds – and also, she thought, washed by stream-water running over them, since they had been disarranged, and were now pointing in all directions. One or two, however, including one that must have been the body of a child – it was so small – were not yet disturbed.

Natty did not tell me this detail to prove her lack of sympathy, but to show how the mind, when it is shocked, retreats into a way of noticing that appears cold-hearted but is in fact the opposite. It places a value on everything, by paying attention to everything. This is a subject I might elaborate, since it interests me greatly – but I will resist the temptation, and mention instead that while Natty did not weep for the wretches around her, she saw enough of what they had endured to feel certain she would never forget them, and then turned away.

As the ravine jinked downhill, and the last flush of day faded from the narrow strip of sky overhead, and the walls gave back the reassuring sound of her own breath, Natty's fear of discovery and recapture began to disappear. It was replaced by something akin to dreaming. She no longer heard the thunder above her. The rain only reached her in flicks and dashes. Sometimes, because the darkness around her was thickening steadily, she thought she must have become a kind of sleepwalker, whose way ahead had already been cleared for her. Sometimes she seemed entirely outside the familiar boundaries of the world. All she knew for certain was that her walk did not resemble any she had taken before. The earth – which a short while before had seemed indifferent – was now defending her.

When Natty first told me this, I thought the effect of her imprisonment and hunger, and the marvellous shock of her escape, must have combined to produce a *hallucination of mercy*. But what if it did? For as long as she stayed in that secret cleft, with the spirits of dead prisoners padding over the rocks behind her, she considered herself safe. And when a large white owl appeared out of nowhere, and floated before her for several paces, she imagined she had seen her own soul set free from her body, so that it could act as a guide, and felt nothing else would ever frighten her.

It was for this sort of reason, if reason is quite the word, that Natty decided she would not immediately return to the *Nightingale* and her friends. On the contrary. As her walk continued east, parallel to the stockade, she made a second judgement I have always found very surprising, but realise she believed must have been for the best. She persuaded herself that if she turned towards the pine woods when she came above ground again, and set off towards our ship, she would probably meet Stone, who would kill her as soon as he had convinced himself she was not a ghost. Either that, or she would lose her way in the storm. Or else she would encounter some other danger – such as a pit of the kind that had trapped Scotland, or a ferocious animal. In any event, and guided by her unhappiness, she decided she must delay her journey back to us until sleep and sunlight had made the world familiar again.

So it was, when the walls of the ravine eventually shrank to nothing, and the chill air began to grow warmer, and echoes that had been her companions gave way to bullying gusts of rain and wind, she did not come in my direction, but kept on towards the coast. I would later suggest she might have been led by the spirit of her father, for reasons that will soon become apparent. She has never told me I might be wrong.

Natty had emerged on the northern shore of Captain Kidd's Anchorage, which she knew by seeing the curve of the bay to her right and – opposite the bulk of Skeleton Island – the walls of the stockade, and the roofs of the log-houses, all reddened by the fire that Smirke had ordered to be built before he led her away. The poisonous glow of its flames, and the leaping shadows they cast, were enough to convince her that if she had been able to put a telescope to her eye, she would have found the same scenes of barbarity that the captain and I had previously seen together, no doubt with a few guards set here and there as a defence against 'new arrivals' on the island.

This made her crouch down, in order to avoid being made visible by any moonbeams that might burst between the clouds, and then creep further round the bay. Only when she reached the next patch of cover did she dare stand upright again, and pay proper attention to where she was, rather than always staring at where she feared to be. The trees here were live oaks, all blown by the sea-wind into contorted attitudes; their leaves felt hard in the darkness, and shone in the rain like fragments of jade.

At this safe distance from the camp, Natty was again tempted to lie low and rest, knowing she would have fair warning of any approach. But as before, her instincts prompted her onwards, until she was through the trees and walking on softer ground. She had reached the rice-fields, which she saw had been made very neatly, and were fed by streams running off Spyglass Hill.

Natty understood Scotland and the rest must have been brought here that same morning, when she had seen them marched from the camp. Each trim plot was their devising and their work. The thought of so much care, given under the threat of so much cruelty, made her stop and cover her face with her hands – until she realised her silhouette must be visible against the open sea, and she had better cower down again.

The sound that now filled her head was no longer only wind and rain, but the surf as it folded in long rollers along the crescent of the bay. As she paused to listen, Natty found she was filled with a kind of reverence. The density of noise, and the strange inward luminosity of the waves, and the repetition of their self-gathering, provoked her into feeling she must drop onto her knees and give thanks to her Creator. Thanks for her escape from Death, and for the world He allowed her to enjoy. But even as this feeling dawned in her, she knew it was not the moment for any such reflection, and hurried onwards.

A hundred more paces and she came to another standstill – sensing immediately that she had found what she wanted, without having previously guessed what that might be. It was the beginnings of a sandbar, running out through the shallows towards the open sea. For the most part it was covered by the tide – but at the edge of vision, where she expected to see nothing but waves churning in the darkness, lay a sudden dark bump of land, obscurely crowned with ferns. It was the White Rock – the same that I had first seen myself from the deck of the *Nightingale*.

She stepped into the sea, where she thought the sandbar must be submerged, and felt it hard and ridged beneath her feet. This made her remember Moses walking through the waters of the Red Sea, and Christ himself gliding across the Sea of Galilee – but such ideas were soon washed away. Within a minute she was gripping long fronds of bracken that flopped over the edge of the Rock. Then she was hauling herself up the sheer sides and balancing on the rim, with the ferns and other plants swaying around her.

So far as she could tell, the little island was no more than half a dozen yards wide in every direction, and hollow like the mouth of a miniature volcano. But whereas a true volcano would have a crater as bare as the ravine she had just left, the declivity here was very spongy, because it was covered with the dead leaves of plants that grew above it.

When Natty stepped among these plants they seemed to embrace her eagerly, caressing her face with their long fingers, which had a delicious scent of rotten wood, and leading her down and inwards towards the centre of the nest. Here the noise of the storm was miraculously stilled, and the rain became a slowly falling dew. It was impossible for Natty to resist her weariness any longer; impossible not to stretch out and sleep. As she did so the latticework of leaves closed above her head, obliterating the storm entirely.

PART V

THE AFTERMATH

CHAPTER 24

The Captain's Plan

I shall now leave Natty in her nest and return to my own story –
which must begin with the account of how I occupied myself in
her absence. This was a bitter time, haunted by fears for her safety,
but I was not allowed to shrink from the world and fret in solitude.
On the contrary, I found things happening to me that I could not
avoid and cannot forget.

The birds in our estuary began their squawking and chattering
as soon as the sun came up. Yet I knew before I hung over the side
of my bunk, and saw the smooth pillow on the bed below me, that
Natty was not there. The silence in the cabin was too absolute. My
first thought was: she had fallen asleep on deck, where I knew she
had stayed with Scotland. But when I had pulled on my day-shirt
and clambered up the companionway, I found nothing except

footprints in the dew, which had covered the surface of the ship as thickly as a layer of paint. From this I learned they had paced the deck for a while, then padded towards the landward side of the *Nightingale* – where they disappeared. When I called up to Mr Lawson, to ask whether he had seen them, it was clear from the yawning that preceded his answer – 'No' – that he had been asleep for the past several hours. I cursed him and turned to scour the undergrowth, which sunlight was now heating into lurid yellows and greens. In my heart I already accepted I would not see them. They had gone.

Gone where? If there had been traces of a third set of footprints on deck, I should have thought one of the pirates from the stockade had taken them – or maybe some other inhabitant of the island of whom we presently knew nothing. But there was no evidence for this sort of kidnap. No sign of a stranger, and no trace of a confrontation. Natty had left by choice – unless Scotland had suddenly changed from being a grateful friend into her enemy. This seemed so unlikely I did not consider the possibility for more than a moment.

But if she had left by choice, what did she plan to do? Explore the island? Not in darkness. Escape with Scotland? Impossible. Although I knew an affection had sprung up between them, it was not of this kind. Would they, then, have devised a plan they thought might do some good for the rest of us? This seemed probable – and impetuous, to say the least.

I told myself it was only a matter of time before they would reappear through the undergrowth, and we would be happy again. But when Captain Beamish came on deck he soon dashed these hopes. He did not even trouble to condemn Mr Lawson for failing to see their disappearance; he simply called him down from his position in the crow's-nest, told him to get along to the galley and feed himself, then accepted with a long face that Natty was lost in a hare-brained scheme of some kind. 'She is her father's daughter,' he whispered to me; I took his words as a sign of the trust he kept in me.

I was comforted by this, as I was by the rest of the crew now arriving on deck. They looked a ragged party in the early light, with their crumpled clothes, and their hair any old how – all rubbing at their eyes or munching on apples they had snatched from Mr Allan's barrel. But they were good fellows. The day before, they had put their lives in danger for the general good, and not forgotten their duty to one another. At the same time, I thought they would be no match for the pirates. They were men of a later time, and sailors not warriors. Unless we could establish a definite advantage, they were more likely to end their days on Treasure Island than they were to leave it with their fortune.

It was clear that when the captain had ended our conversation the previous evening, he was still considering the various courses open to us. We might negotiate with Smirke and his men. Or we might attack them. Now it seemed there was no alternative; Nat was at risk, he announced, and must be rescued.

The decision provoked a cheer from the men, although when I saw them clapping one another on the back they seemed more concerned to bolster their courage than show how warmly they agreed with their commander-in-chief.

'Bo'sun Kirkby,' said the captain – at which their noise immediately stopped, and so confirmed it was not quite heartfelt.

The bo'sun stepped forward, pulling his beard straight and standing to attention as well as he was able. His cap was pushed back on his head, showing a white line on his forehead where the sun had not yet ebonised him.

'Yes, Captain.'

'Bo'sun Kirkby, I want you to hear what I have to say, and

tell me whether you agree. This is not the time for any of us to harbour doubts.'

I thought this was clever, since it gave an appearance of democracy to what was in fact an order.

'I want you to agree,' the captain went on, 'that in all probability Master Nat has fallen into the hands of our enemies, along with Mr Scotland.'

'In all probability, Captain,' said Bo'sun Kirkby, seeming rather surprised to find so large a word fitting into his mouth.

'I want you to agree that although we do not know the conditions in which they are held, they are probably dangerous.'

'Most likely dangerous, Captain.'

'I want you to agree that we should visit the stockade with a view to rescuing Master Nat, by force if necessary.'

Bo'sun Kirkby, whose face was now reddening with the effort of standing to attention for so long, replied very determinedly to this. 'By force, Captain,' he barked.

'I want you to agree that if Master Nat is not in fact a prisoner inside the stockade, we shall have other duties to perform there.'

'Other duties, Captain.' Bo'sun Kirkby said this in a more pausing voice, as if he did not entirely understand what he had heard. The captain evidently thought he had not been sufficiently clear, at any rate, and interrupted his catalogue.

'By which I mean the following,' he said. 'The courts may not yet have abolished the dreadful trade of slavery, but they surely will, and we can surely anticipate their actions.'

Bo'sun Kirkby brightened considerably, now he caught the drift. 'Anticipate very firmly, Captain.'

'To be specific,' the captain continued, 'I want you to agree these other duties will be to set free Mr Scotland and his friends, and to oppose our enemies if they oppose us.'

'Likewise oppose very firmly, Captain.'

'And once we have achieved our objective in this regard, we will continue our search for the silver – assisted by Mr Scotland.'

'Very ably assisted, I am sure.' Bo'sun Kirkby looked to heaven as he said this, wearing a very gleeful expression.

'And I want you to agree that this will be done with all possible speed,' the captain went on.

'With all possible speed,' said the bo'sun, lowering his gaze again and looking the captain in the eye.

'But not with so much haste that we run unreasonable risks.'

Another look of bewilderment clouded the bo'sun's face, and his shoulders drooped. It was a signal for their conversation to take a new shape. Hitherto, as I understood it, the captain had tried to rally our spirits by addressing our difficulties in a way that smacked somewhat of comedy. From this point onwards, reason and gravity were the order of the day. The change must have altered the atmosphere of the *Nightingale*, since Spot, who had been listening in silence from his perch in the roundhouse, now suddenly remembered to grieve for his mistress by shouting, 'Take me back! Take me back!'

The captain did not so much as glance in his direction, but pulled us into a tighter circle and reminded us what we had learned from Scotland the previous night, and what had since been spread among the men more generally. In addition to Smirke and Stone and Jinks, there were ten guards who had survived the wreck of the *Achilles*, making an unlucky total of thirteen. Although Scotland had thought they did not have much in the way of guns and gunpowder, it was clear that a small amount had been held in reserve – and this, when combined with the strength of their defences, their knowledge of the island, and the arms they had dug out of the earth, could be said to amount to a considerable armoury.

The captain did not want to admit how this compared to our

own situation, but a glance round the deck, and especially towards our useless gun, for which we had no ammunition, made it clear as day. Our numbers were almost the same as the pirates', but we were men (and a boy) who had never shouldered arms, and had little appetite for fighting. Our weapons were few. Our knowledge of the island was paltry. We lacked the element of surprise that might have been our one advantage before Natty embarked on her adventure.

A silence fell as the captain asked us to reflect on these things – a silence interrupted by the creatures that continued their lives around us: their jabbering and screeching echoed off the surface of the river as it squeezed out to sea. But when I looked into the faces of my fellows, I did not find any hesitation or uncertainty, only resolution. I wished my father and Mr Silver had been there to see it as well; the story unfolding before us was so like their own, and yet so different. The captain's plan pitched a new expectation of happiness against the brutal fragment of the old world that still remained on the island.

Not that Captain Beamish would have admitted this himself; it was purely my conception. He was entirely matter-of-fact when he continued speaking. It would be foolish, he said, to approach the stockade in broad daylight, when the pirates could very quickly organise against us, and the prisoners were likely to be scattered. Better if we made a sensible delay, and arrived at first light.

'Who shall go?' now became the question, with the loudest voices suggesting it should be all of us – until the captain brought us to order again. Rather than make a single rush, he said we should divide into two parties: one for the expedition (as he called it); the other to guard the *Nightingale,* then sail her out from the inlet and back along the coast towards the Anchorage, where she would collect the prisoners after their liberation. He said this so easily and so fast, it sounded like a thing that had been ordained, and not something fraught with dangers. Mr Lawson, he said, would stay on board with five other shipmates necessary to man the ship. The rest of us would cross the island under his own command. As the words left his mouth he looked directly at me, by which I knew I would be with him. I wanted nothing else.

When these arrangements were settled, and further details had been added to our plans, and more breakfast taken, and pipes smoked, and ropes curled, and sails examined, a large part of the morning was already passed. Yet the remaining hours of the day seemed to stretch very long and vacantly ahead of us.

In such emptiness it was impossible not to encounter Natty at every turn of my mind. One moment I saw her safely hidden in some cranny of the island – asleep and ignorant of all our worries. The next, she was a prisoner in chains, and subject to terrors I could not completely imagine. In either case – and in all the variety that lay between, where I saw her lying injured, or eaten by wild animals, or lost – the effect was to make me very melancholy. While the crew attended to their tasks of ordering and reordering materials around the deck, and Mr Stevenson returned to his place in the crow's-nest, from where he kept a lookout over the estuary, and Mr Allan shut himself in the galley to prepare the fish he had pulled from the river for our supper, I went to the prow of the *Nightingale* and climbed along the bowsprit until I sat with my legs dangling either side, staring ahead as if we were sailing into the jungle and its leaves were parting as easily as the sea.

I would have been willing to moulder there for a while, dreaming and drifting; I was used to my own company, and had learned to enjoy it. But the captain had other plans for me – plans that might have been provoked by pity, or by his own restlessness. He called to me on my perch, saying he needed my help with a task he had to perform. He added that in the process we would see different parts of the island, and discover what God had given us to enjoy.

This seemed a privilege, in view of my youth, and another proof of his kindness – by which I mean that I understood the captain must have a good independent reason for proposing our expedition, but was also determined to distract me from the crisis that lay ahead. I did not hesitate. I crawled back from my retreat and walked straight up to him. He was holding two small wicker baskets, each of which had a narrow cap or lid, and two long wooden thumb-sticks. One of the sticks, and one of the baskets, he gave to me.

'Come on, my boy,' he said with a gleam in his eye. 'We have important work to do.'

CHAPTER 25

I am Rescued

After we had announced our departure and left Bo'sun Kirkby in command of the *Nightingale,* the captain and I were rowed ashore and disappeared into the vegetation. For a while it was impossible to see more than a few inches in front of our faces, and difficult not to feel the baskets and the sticks might be torn from our grasp – but I kept my sense of direction. We had set our course north-west, which was the way the captain had taken yesterday, towards the site of the silver.

We soon reached a part of the same pine forest that grew across the central part of the island, except the trees were smaller here, and in many cases bent into writhing shapes because of the wind. This would have made the area seem desolate, had it not been for the fact that a thin canopy allowed more sunlight, which had bred an extraordinary richness of flowers. Some of them I recognised; there were large drifts of convolvulus, for instance, and clumps of honeysuckle and bougainvillea. Many varieties, however, were entirely unknown to me.

Now and then I stopped to collect a specimen, thinking the captain had given me my basket for this purpose. When he told me not to fill it completely, I realised he had some other kind of storage in mind, and was surprised not to hear immediately what it was. Surprised, but still so absorbed in the pleasure of finding new species, and so happily neglectful of the dangers that awaited me, I said nothing and continued my botanising. I was especially pleased to discover a new variety of lily (lilies have always been a favourite of mine). It had a delicate flower-head shaped like an infant's pouting mouth, but the petals were striped in bands of black and yellow as regular as the body of a wasp. In a fantasy of ownership, I named it the 'Hawkins Lily'.

Because there was no definite path through this garden, we found ourselves trampling beauty at every turn. It was very agitating, but not a torment we were allowed to suffer for long: Nature is never so careless with her gifts. Within a few hundred yards the earth was almost bare again, and strewn with heavy boulders in which the wind had carved a number of large holes. Here, however, were other sights that made us stop and wonder. The most remarkable was a plump bird about twice the size of our fulmar in England, which had decided these holes were very convenient places in which to rear young.

The birds had been silent while we were out of view; now they began accusing us of coming to murder them. Several launched from their rocks and attacked us as boldly as soldiers, waddling on short legs (with bright *green* feet), and pecking our knees and hands. While we were busy defending ourselves, it was impossible to notice much detail in their appearance – only the colour of the feet, and that the adults were covered in shiny feathers the colour of tortoise-shell – and to reflect that these birds were unusual among the inhabitants of the island in seeming aggressive. I silently told myself that although their rage was disagreeable, it showed they possessed greater powers of self-preservation than any of their more trusting fellow creatures.

On our right-hand side, where the colony continued up a slope that ended in the northern cliffs of the island, I saw several birds stumbling towards the precipice and preparing to launch themselves off it. I realised this must be how they became airborne – and understood we would therefore soon be attacked from above as well as on the ground. After I had mentioned this to the captain we made a rapid retreat, tacking south-south-west, and so leaving the birds to resume their bad-tempered existence.

Our retreat brought us back among the flowers, from which we now set out a second time, following a more westerly route that led round the edge of the birds' territory, and so to a region of the island the captain had already seen. The soil here was sandy, with some yellowish clay mixed into it; because it was protected from the sea-wind, the pine trees grew straight and to a proper height. It was the site of the silver.

'They set less store on this treasure,' the captain said as we drew near. 'Less than they did on the rest, at any rate.'

I asked how he could be sure.

'Did your father not tell you?' he replied, and let the question dangle for a moment. Although he had previously spoken no more than a few sentences to me about my father, he knew my lineage very well, and understood how I had come by the map. In this respect he had treated me with the same tact that he had shown to Natty throughout our journey – in order to spare us being continually compared to our parents. Hearing this silence suddenly broken, and my father's name spoken aloud, was very affecting. I could not immediately answer.

'When they found the other treasure . . .' the captain went on. 'That is to say, when *your father* found the other treasure, which Ben Gunn had discovered before any of them, and had moved to his cave, they also found Captain Flint's – . . .' his voice faltered, then hurried on – 'Captain Flint's *direction*.'

By now I had regained my composure. 'My father did tell me,' I said. 'You mean the *direction* that was a dead man lying on the ground and pointing like an arrow.'

'That is exactly what I mean,' said the captain with a smile. 'Old Flint left no such instructions near the silver – which shows what he thought of it.'

'Or perhaps because he valued it so much.'

'Explain?'

'Perhaps he wanted to leave no visible evidence of its existence,' I said. 'We shall only know how much we think of it, when we see it with our own eyes.'

The captain clapped me on my back. 'Right enough,' he said cheerfully. 'We shall know when we see it and not before.' Then he paused again, and a distinct look of mischief came into his face. 'Just for now,' he said, 'I ask you to think of this and nothing else: what kind of hole do you think it would make in the earth, this silver, if it were to be buried? What kind of *capacity* would be required?'

I did not immediately understand the captain – until I turned away from him. We had reached the lee of the highest part of the hillside, where the yellowy ground was covered with a black dust more like ash than earth. This dust had collected in a wide and shallow crater that was crossed by a chain of stagnant pools, each of which was covered by a rainbow-scum; I thought it must be produced by minerals in the earth beneath. The colours might have made the place look joyous, since they were as bright as peacock feathers, but their effect was entirely the opposite. The shimmer was revoltingly bright, and a sickly counterpart to the bare earth round about.

'Tread carefully,' said the captain, tightening the grip on his thumb-stick, and poking it into the earth before he took a step forward. 'We are close now.'

'Here?' I asked uncertainly.

'Not here precisely,' he said, very watchful. 'Follow me and you will see. We avoided this part when I came here recently; now we must enter it. Be careful!'

I did as I was told, treading in the captain's footsteps as he set off across the crater. Every time my foot touched the earth, it produced a puff of black dust that coated my shoes and ankles, and floated so easily on the air it even crept into my nose. My eyes watered, and I began breathing in shallow sips to keep the stuff from entering my lungs.

When the captain stopped a moment later, and crouched to put his basket on the ground beside him, my first thought was: we had reached the treasure site. Then I saw, by the way he hoisted his stick like a spear and pointed the V of the thumb-rest towards the ground, that whatever was happening now had nothing to do with silver. We were standing where Scotland had told us we would find the snakes – the kind that made this miserable ash their only home on the island, and had killed his friend with a single bite. The captain was endeavouring to catch one. That is why we had brought the baskets. We were going to catch the snakes and bring them back with us to the *Nightingale*.

These thoughts slithered into my head very suddenly, confusing me and unnerving me. I took a breath and swallowed; I remembered the marshes at home, where I had crawled up to spy on unsuspecting creatures without a fear for my life. Why should I not be as fearless now? The question steadied me so much, I was able to peep over the captain's shoulder and watch how he managed his work.

The snake in front of him was a foot long, and grey as the dust that now almost enveloped it, with its neck pinned in the V of his stick; its slender body lashed viciously from side to side, and it made a fierce hissing noise like a kettle on a hob. Moving very gingerly, the captain bent forward and took hold of it close behind the head, using his thumb and forefinger to lift it into the air – whereupon the hissing stopped and the creature hung limp as string, before he dropped it into his basket and swiftly replaced the lid.

'One!' he said to me, or rather shouted. His wide face was shining with sweat. 'Now you.'

If there had been a minute to think, I might have asked him to continue as my teacher. But when I opened my mouth to say this, I noticed a second and smaller snake coiled an arm's length away from me, its shiny tongue already darting between its lips as though the prospect of my leg were delicious. Without any delay, I plunged at it with my stick – which produced another explosion of dust – and found that I had trapped the creature as I wanted, and was able to lift it as the captain had done. The skin felt absolutely cold and lifeless, like the tallow of a candle that has long since been blown out.

Because we had caught these first two snakes very quickly, the captain and I then decided our work was easy – and set about finding ten or a dozen more, which we stored in our wicker baskets, where they lay coiled around one another's bodies without any fuss. 'Our security,' said the captain as we finished our work. 'Our "arms", you might say.' I nodded at this, to show I knew what he meant without him needing to explain. We would use the snakes as weapons, since our firepower on the *Nightingale* was so limited; it pleased me very much to think the native spirits of the island were turning against the men who had defiled it.

We set off north-west again, and within a few minutes found ourselves on the slope of a crisp little ridge that seemed insignificant in itself. It turned out to mark the beginning of a long sweep that ran towards the north-western shore of the island; the ground here was lush as an English park, being lightly covered with pine and live oak. Two especially tall pine trees stood directly in front of us, making an obvious landmark – so in this respect, at least, it was no surprise to see the earth between them had been torn up and thrown about.

'Here is where we discovered our loss,' said the captain, very heavily. I felt so determined not to say anything my father might have done, such as what a desecration it was, that I did not immediately reply. All the same, and using the strange sort of measurement the captain had suggested a moment before, when he had spoken about the earth's *capacity*, I calculated the emptiness before me must be a very valuable one. It was not, perhaps, a vault to hold as large a fortune as the £700,000 my father and the others had removed from the island. But it could have contained at least half as much, which would have been a pretty amount for all of us.

We stood in silence – our heads bowed with the weight of failure, but also I suspect with *guilt*, since the sensation of being thwarted had exposed us to the consciousness of our own greed. In a short while, however, I found that my concentration was not directed where I meant it to be, but fixed on a succession of irritable *click-clicks*, quickly repeated, that came from one of the two pines that grew nearby. I recognised these as the sound a squirrel makes when defending its territory, and when I looked up I found that two pairs of eyes were regarding us from a large ball of twigs and moss. I supposed this must be a nest, and contained young the parents were anxious to protect – which was why they had raised their voices in our direction, and were determined to leave us in no doubt we were not welcome in this part of their parish.

This sight alone was enough to make us want to move our ground. Another reason was a second noise – much fainter – which I had never heard before, and which quickened my curiosity. It was a mixture of sighing and whistling, but sometimes broke into a sort of bark. Not a dog's bark but something more drawn-out, and more amused than affronted. It appeared to originate on the coast below.

The captain heard it too, which he showed by cocking an eyebrow and indicating we should walk on, and discover the origin of this strange music. It seemed a simple decision, but it marked a profound change in our mood. In fact, I might even say that while I could not entirely forget my fears for Natty, the next several minutes were the happiest of any that I spent on the island. The wind pressed gently against my back and drove me forward. The sun was warm as an English summer. The downward slope was easy. The talk . . . I cannot remember the talk, only that the captain and I were together, and did not say anything to break our mood of exaltation.

As we came towards the coast at last, the trees ended and the land began to dip more steeply, but in a succession of shallow natural steps, which must have been carved by the wind as it carried off the soil from one layer of rock and laid it on the one adjacent. This rock was pure black, and inhospitable to all but the smallest plants, such as sea-campion and harebell; these had seeded in crevices, and now clung quivering as the wind blew across them.

When we reached the foot of the cliff we instantly recognised our sirens. The beach was narrow, and made of stones that had been rolled by the sea until they were almost perfectly circular. And reclining on these stones was a colony of sea lions. Several were fully as large as the captain himself, with skin that was wrinkled and dark brown around their heads, but greenish as it became sleek on their bodies. The large males had whiskers that made them look very fierce, yet they seemed completely accepting of our approach; the females and especially their pups wore the most appealing expressions, with mouths set in a continuous smile, and eyes – large and clear – gazing into my own with remarkable kindliness.

When I say they were *reclining*, I hardly do justice to the posture of these creatures, since although each was forced by its lack of arms and legs to remain horizontal, each was nevertheless marvellously active with its flippers, and lumbered gleefully towards us as we approached.

'I reckon they've not seen anything like us before,' the captain said. He spoke quietly, since he did not want to alarm them, but was so obviously correct in his assessment, there was no question of us seeming a danger, even to the males. They trusted us completely, and sometimes even nuzzled us with their noses as we began walking among them. I could not help feeling this was one of the great privileges of my life, and wanted to praise God for granting it to me. I suspected the captain would think this excessive, so I confined myself to patting their tight flanks, and occasionally their heads, which always produced an eruption of barks and honks among the pups. Whether they thought we were very fine or very ridiculous, I did not want to decide.

The encounter gave us such a powerful sense of contentment, we continued strolling up and down the beach until we had greeted every family, and allowed every parent to introduce every child. And when we had finished our diplomacy, we still felt no appetite for a swift return to our own world and the troubles it contained. Without either of us needing to explain to the other what we were doing, we sat on a rock with our baskets and sticks at our feet, and stared out to sea. We had no reason to do this, beyond watching the waves roll towards the shore, and feeling our minds turn into stones as smooth as those around us, and noticing how the sun kept its heat longer today than yesterday, and how the sea-birds fished, and other such important trifles.

When I had dallied in this way for long enough to wonder whether I might turn into a statue unless I moved, I suggested to the captain that we might like to swim and refresh ourselves. He looked at me sideways. When I asked him why, he told me (in a manner that was surprisingly awkward, considering our relative positions in the world) it was not because he feared any dangers in the water, but because *he could not swim*.

I told him I had heard this was common among sailors, which he did not deny, though neither of us liked to mention the reason or to think of Jordan Hands, and how he had proved the adage. But after sharing this embarrassment for a moment, and remaining beside him in silent contemplation of the waves, I nevertheless asked for his permission to go alone.

It was only when I had hobbled over the stones and reached the edge of the water that I noticed I had not seen any of the sea lions do as I was about to do. This, I told myself, was because their day was divided into separate activities, as a human community's might be, and our arrival had coincided with their time for resting and not for hunting or playing. The minute I stripped off my shirt, however, and limped into the water, one of the larger pups – an animal about the same size as myself – decided I was proposing a game we might play together, and squirmed off his stones to join me.

It is a commonplace to say how creatures that are cumbersome on land are capable of great dexterity in their own element – and so it was with my companion. A body that had been heavy in rest now became acrobatic in play, and a brain that had been sluggish or idle, now seemed very agile. My own body, by comparison, felt extremely *incompetent*. This was because I was suddenly drawn into a powerful undertow, that ran where the waves drained back into the deep again, once they had broken on the beach.

Within a minute of entering the water I was at least thirty yards offshore, and doubted whether I had the strength to return. The change was as quick and shocking as that. I began to struggle hard, with no more result than a good deal of salt water flooding into my nose and panic squeezing my heart. For a moment, I really believed the price I would have to pay for my glimpse of paradise would be to see nothing more in this world. I began to say goodbye to my father and to Natty, and to revisit for the last time some of the places I had loved, such as the marshes behind the Hispaniola, which now appeared to me in vivid glimpses, tinged with their authentic blue light.

I supposed this was proof I must already be drowning – which was confirmed by what I could see of the captain. In a hazy distance that greatly diminished his height and bulk, he was running along the beach, flinging his arms about and shouting. This alarmed the sea lions so much, they began a formidable honking, which I heard in snatches whenever my head bobbed above the waves. He later told me he had been saying: *Let the current take you; don't fight against it –* because he believed I would then be swept round the northern tip of the island, as my father had been in his coracle, and eventually come to a place where I might easily swim ashore. At the time, my confusion and fear were so great, I was not able to follow this sensible advice, but continued to pitch all my strength against the sea, although I knew it must soon drag me down.

By now I had entirely forgotten the fellow creature that had come with me into the water. But as my body began to tire, and a film covered my mind, his shining head rode through the waves beside me. To judge by the friendliness of his expression, and the mewing noises he made, he found the game that I was playing to be highly entertaining – but at the same time sufficiently alarming (being accompanied by a great deal of splashing) to persuade him to keep at a respectful distance.

As my movements slowed, this fearfulness disappeared and he swam closer. I saw his eyelashes were beaded with water-drops, and heard his breath snuffling in his nose as his nostrils opened and closed. These, I genuinely believed, would be my last sights of the earth, apart from the dark-blue water into which I was sinking.

Except, as my descent began, and I lost my connection with everything in the light, my companion was no longer content merely to watch, but wanted to position himself underneath me. In fact, he had managed to stand *upright on his tail* in the water, with the whole length of his body pressed against my own. His skin felt slippery, but not so much that it was impossible for me to hold and grip him. I understood that he meant the next part of our game, which he had only this minute invented, should involve me putting my arms around him – which I did. He then gave another flick or shrug as he passed from the vertical to the horizontal, and I found that I was lying on top of him, with my head resting on his back, my body trailing along the ridge of his spine, and my arms joined round what I would have called his chest if he had been a man.

During the minute it took him to carry me back to shore, I was so preoccupied by coughing the ocean out from my lungs, and sucking the air into them, I was hardly able to notice anything about the journey. I do recall, however, that on the beach ahead of me the other pups were giving loud barks, which I took to be encouragement. Even more clearly, I remember the feeling of wonderment rushing through me in successive waves, each of which had their own peculiar feeling of buoyancy.

I have called my rescuer a companion. Had he been such a thing in the usual sense, I should have thanked him with all my heart, and promised to do as much for him, should the need ever arise. As it was, no such things were possible. When he had brought me a few yards from dry land, where I could easily reach the stones again, he gave another quick shudder which released me into the shallows – while he withdrew into the deeper water. There was no particular look in the eyes, only the same blank friendliness for as long as the head stayed in sight, then the empty waves when it slid below. The action that to me meant life to my companion meant nothing – or nothing that I could understand. It was therefore not his but the captain's chest I leaned against as soon as I was able, and into which I sobbed my relief and thanks.

CHAPTER 26

My Life Before Me

The question is one of accommodation. How does a mind *create space* for so large a thing as the clear sight of death? It was not a question that troubled me while I lay on the beach, hauling the life back into my lungs. I was too exhausted for thinking. But as my breathing steadied, and the world became clear again, my thoughts began travelling in two different directions at once. One part searched for significance in what I had endured, and longed to know how it fed my affection for life – and especially my feelings about my father and Natty, who had appeared so vividly to me. Another part of me wanted to fix entirely on matters at hand – and for the time being, at least, this approach seemed best. The captain and I had work to do, and attention to detail was an essential part of it.

After we had retraced our steps to the *Nightingale*, the captain's first duty was to store our baskets and their contents in his cabin – in the same chest where he kept our pistols, which had a lock and key. Then he summoned me, along with Bo'sun Kirkby and other shipmates, to parley in the roundhouse. The history of my recent escapade did something to lift spirits, but once I had turned myself back from a fish to a man for the third or fourth time, the miracle of my rescue seemed commonplace; the unhappiness of losing both our treasure and Natty flooded over us again.

I had never seen the men so listless and miserable as they were now. The cook, Mr Allan, whose talk generally bubbled like a boiling pot, stood by one of the windows and said nothing, but watched the rain-clouds that by now were sweeping across the wide grey mouth of the river. Mr Tickle even forgot to light his pipe, although he did sometimes pat his beard, as if fire might have broken out there by spontaneous combustion.

To give my friends the credit of seeming anxious as well as thwarted, I should also say they were preoccupied by thoughts of tomorrow, and how they would perform the roles allotted to them. Although the captain was very decisive in reminding everyone of their duties, we could not safely predict their result, nor entirely reconcile our wish to recover the silver with our wish to right the wrongs that had been done on the island. Maybe we would become barbarians ourselves, if we punished the barbarity of the pirates? Maybe we were no better than them, in wanting to gratify our desire for wealth?

Such questions, not always spoken aloud, passed between us as the day waned, and the afternoon downpour thickened into the customary evening storm, and candles were set on the table in the roundhouse that allowed us to look one another in the eye (or to avoid this sort of directness if we preferred). In several instances, and especially in the matter of how to divide the silver supposing we obtained it, there was a great reluctance to reach firm conclusions; all our conversations ended in 'We'll see what happens', and 'It may not come to that', and 'God will decide'.

As night fell and I continued listening to my shipmates, I realised my own opinions about how our story would end were equally vague. When I gazed into the darkness I could see myself walking through the pine woods towards the stockade, see us approaching the outer wall, see Smirke rolling towards me – but after that, nothing. Not the dead men who lay around me, nor whether I might be among them. The question *were we liberators?* would be answered by our enemies and not by ourselves. The future depended on their reactions to us, not on the actions we took against them.

It was an uncomfortable truth, which I could not avoid remembering when the wind rose at last, and the rain eased, and the captain dismissed us with the opinion that we needed our beauty sleep, because we would be rising in just a few hours. He wished each of us to go directly to our cabin, but I pretended I had not understood and remained on deck for a while longer. I suppose our nightwatchman was at his usual place above me, gazing across the shining undergrouth – but as far as I was concerned, I was alone with my questions.

A few hours before, I had looked Death in the eye. A few hours hence – who could know? For the second time in the same day, my mind proved to be too small for the thoughts it contained, and I turned to look at the world instead: the river thrumming along our hull; the pine trees leaning away from the wind; and the moon buffeting the clouds, which seemed made of saffron and ebony.

All these things kept themselves to themselves, and had nothing to say to me. Nothing until, with no warning and no noise, a large bird broke out of the vegetation opposite, and floated directly over my head, turning down its face (which was like the face of a kitten) to examine me before veering downriver towards the open sea. I thought it must be a species of owl, since the shape of the body and head resembled a barn owl, which I had often seen ghosting over the marshes at home. But this bird was larger, and shone bright silver, and seemed not in the least shy. In fact it turned to look at me again before it disappeared, like a person peering over their shoulder, and seemed to expect that I would immediately sprout wings myself and follow.

CHAPTER 27

We Reach Our Destination

I was woken by the captain's bell clanking two o'clock through every part of the ship, and clambered on deck still wiping my eyes. However poorly I had slept did not matter now; I was ready. The rain had drifted away, the clouds were thin, and the moon sat high in the west – all perfect for our plan.

'Fit as you look, Master Jim?' This was the captain, who did not wait for an answer but led me to the roundhouse, where the rest of our party had already gathered: Bo'sun Kirkby, Mr Tickle, Mr Stevenson (who for the time being had bequeathed his crow's-nest to Mr Lawson), and also another sailor I hardly knew – a little, quick, dark-haired man like an eel, by the name of Mr Creed.

'This is for you,' the captain said, as he gave each of the men a cutlass he had broken out from his cupboard; he kept a doughty old pistol for himself, which he tucked into his belt. When it was my turn, he handed over a *dagger* – which I thought slightly insulting. Seeing my disappointment, he clapped me on the shoulder and said, 'That will do you very well, my lad; it will be everything you need' – then ran his thumb approvingly along the edge of the blade and recommended I do the same.

While he did this, I took the chance to wonder whether we would also be taking our 'baskets' with us – and gave him a significant look. He seemed surprised, as if I had challenged his judgement or misunderstood his intention. 'We shall leave them on board,' he told me quietly.

'But if –'

I had wanted to suggest the pirates might not be so reasonable as he was himself, and might attack us without warning. But I was not allowed to complete my sentence. 'I have told you already,' the captain said. 'They are a security, nothing more. They may not prevent an attack, but at least they are a weapon of a kind. A last ditch.' This was enough to show I could no longer expect him to show me the same fatherly warmth as yesterday; I was his soldier now; I must obey orders.

'Now gentlemen,' the captain continued, addressing everyone with the same air of command he had just used with me. 'Remember what we decided. We are for rescue and parley – we are not for murder. We shall make our country proud.'

As the captain finished speaking, a murmur of approval rose from us all. Although we were very few, it made us brave to know we had a common purpose, and were led by an honourable man. When his broad face looked at each of us in turn, I felt the night had somehow been replaced by sunlight. My companions were brothers to me. And as they clambered over the side of the *Nightingale*, and into the jolly-boat that rowed us ashore, I knew they were brothers to one another.

Our first task was to hack a way up from our valley. The captain passed me his satchel (filled with extra powder for his pistol) so that he was better able to lead us, then set off swinging his cutlass from side to side, with his shoulders heaving and his cocked hat pressed around his ears. The rest of us were grateful for his efforts and pleased to follow. Two, including Mr Stevenson, had experience of this kind of work, since their earlier lives in His Majesty's Navy had included spells on shore in India and elsewhere. But the rest were sea-men through and through. Had it not been for the distant prospect of silver, which cast a gleam over everything, I am sure they would have preferred to return to the *Nightingale* and perform their duties on deck.

Although I had tramped this part of the island already, and was beginning to feel familiar with its moods and geography, my midnight journey almost persuaded me I was seeing the place for the first time. Creatures that had previously spied on me were now asleep – and others I had not previously met came forward to intro-duce themselves, including dozens of bats that began plunging round our heads when we reached the edge of the pine woods. Mr Stevenson in particular found this disgusting, and swiped at them with his sword now and again, without ever harming a single one. The rest of us found his antics more annoying than the creatures themselves, and were relieved when we came to the higher ground, where the bats were not so interested in following. Here, I am bound to say, I found something I enjoyed much less than their squeaks and peeps, which was the familiar sound of the surf beating on the rocks below. As we marched south-west it kept up a continuous barrage – a tragic sound, which reminded us the waves were patiently tearing away the earth and returning us to chaos.

It has been said that time passes differently at night – often more slowly than during the day, then suddenly fast. So it was during our tramp towards Spyglass Hill. For a long while the horizon was nothing but pine trees and tumbling clouds, then in a blink we found ourselves on the open shale beneath the mountain. Moonlight made it seem nothing but a monstrous heap of ash, and therefore a part of the desolation we had come to overthrow. Here and there bands of mist drifted across its high fissures, like gasps escaping from a body. Sometimes shadows turned one of its faces into the profile of a savage, or a man in hiding, or a runaway horse. Otherwise it simply glowered, and darkened the night around it.

The next part of our journey seemed infinitely long. Our least burden (a sword, a water-bottle) was nearly intolerable. The smallest stone turned treacherously under my shoe. Thorny shrubs scratched at my clothes, or tore my hands. And gradually exhaustion began to creep over me – until the ache in my bones, the sweat in my eyes, and the knocking of my heart against my ribs made me think I might prove incapable in the fight to come. When I looked at my friends, I tried to convince myself that I saw no such weakness in them – more to bolster my spirits than to establish the reality of things.

At last the captain, with no warning except that he had recently been gazing more carefully at his compass, held up his right hand: we were close to our destination. This was the region where black rock had given way to rhododendron bushes with azalea and other shrubs spreading among them. Their flowers – red, and yellow, and purple – were very prolific, and the scent hung about us very heavily.

These plants grew in a sprinkling where we first encountered them, but as we continued downhill they pressed closer until with every step we were stroked or prodded by branches – though never so much that we turned from our course. Moreover, the ground here was generally firm, with little winding paths between the bushes, and we were able to make good progress, always provided we did not fall into a trap. The captain took care to avoid such a possibility by slicing off a handy branch, stripping it, then using it as a kind of antenna to explore the ground in front of him.

When we had walked for several minutes in this careful way, breathing as quietly as possible and feeling grateful to the wind for buffeting the leaves (and so disguising any noise we did make), the captain held up his hand again. In the silence that followed, I heard a dim crackling sound, which I recognised as flames, and noticed occasional fiery gleams and slivers whizzing into the sky. These made us advance even more cautiously – creeping up beside the captain and peering through the leaves in a gap he made for us.

The stockade stood a mere hundred yards below, giving the same confusing impression of cheerfulness and menace that we had first noticed from the *Nightingale*. In the central meeting-ground, a huge staggering bonfire sent an everlasting stream of sparks into the heavens. Much smaller dabs of yellow candle-flame glowed through the windows of the pirates' log-house; the prisoners' cabin, being entirely window-*less*, was dark as a rock. I imagined Scotland and the others lying inside it as quietly as fossils.

Late as it was, several pirates were still moving round the camp – though whether any of them were the original maroons, or guards they had recruited from the *Achilles*, I could not be sure. It was evidently still their time of pleasure. A few were stretched on the veranda outside their cabin, the tiny red eyes of their pipe-bowls sometimes glowing in the darkness. These were obviously drunk or incapacitated in some other way.

Occasionally the wind carried up coarse bursts of their laughter, or the smack of wood on flesh; at other times, and from parts of the stockade where shadows were too thick for us to see anything in particular, voices sometimes cried out in protest or distress, then others subdued them. The thought that one of these victims might be Natty was too horrible to contemplate. I needed to believe she was alive and elsewhere, in order to do everything expected of me.

'They will be sleeping soon,' said the captain softly. 'We shall watch them, and keep to our plan.' Although I saw the logic of this, I could not help asking how long he thought our wait would last. He held up the fingers of one hand to show he reckoned we had two hours until dawn – then whispered that I should use the time to make up some of the sleep I had lost. I would rather have kept watch, but understood this was an order – and began to look for a patch of ground where I could stretch out.

While doing this, I glanced out to sea and realised that instead of resting I was going to have to look sharp: a whole army of new clouds was even now arriving over the horizon, and a wind that buffeted the water until it turned a creamy white. The pirates evidently saw this too, to judge by the way their shadows darted around the compound then suddenly vanished, leaving the bonfire spitting like a devil as the rain arrived.

We had no choice except to make do – retreating to what we reckoned was a safe distance, chopping branches from the bushes round about, then arranging them into a kind of tent with a ragged opening in the front. This gave us shelter, and also a fine view of the storm. The clouds' first assault proved to be the opening gambit in a campaign that lasted for the next half-hour or so. A storm now began that produced an even more torrential kind of rain; lightning flashed and thunder-rolls shook, that might as well have been the start of a second Great Flood: the hillside itself was soon complaining, groaning as it struggled to shrug off or swallow the great weight of water that was thrown onto it.

When this downpour was over, a third kind of battery began,

with the sound of an enormous wind bursting through the gates of heaven and letting them slam shut behind. This bang shook raindrops from the oak leaves all around us, and seemed to dry their tops in an instant. Very soon, however, the same wind erupted out of heaven again and returned to earth in a fury: a few of the trees that had previously bobbed and curtsied now actually collapsed, making very dismal groans.

Nature could not endure such an attack for long – and when it stopped, it did so with such suddenness I thought a higher authority might actually have taken pity and intervened. The clouds lifted. The wind switched from the east to the south-east and became mild as a lamb. The moon appeared – and shed a soft glow that would not have looked out of place on an English summer night. This allowed me to see that one of the uprooted trees lay directly below us – and its fall had opened a clear view to the stockade.

The captain also noticed this and immediately screwed his telescope to his eye, frowning with concentration. After satisfying whatever questions were in his mind, he passed the instrument to me and pointed where I should look.

The instant I had my range, I gasped and winced away – then focused again. I was looking exactly at Smirke, who seemed so close I might almost have reached out and touched him. The villain seemed hardly to have noticed the storm that had nearly torn the island in two, and was crossing the veranda of his log-house with a swaggering bow-legged gait. I followed him onto the meeting-ground, where he stopped to caress the back wall of his court before strolling on towards the prisoners' hut. Here he stopped in front of a figure I had not noticed until this moment, but now saw was Jinks, who had exchanged the role of prosecutor for that of guard, which he performed by lolling in a chair with a tankard at his side. As Smirke began speaking, which was of course inaudible to me,

Jinks convulsed and scrambled upright, as if he had been repri-
manded. Smirke then turned away and pounded a few times on
the prisoners' door – for no better reason, I guessed, than to
frighten those inside, and to disturb their sleep. The sound of his
blows reached me only faintly, but nevertheless felt like a fist against
my heart.

Was Natty one of those he had just terrorised? When it came to
imagining, I would only allow myself to see Scotland. He lay on
the floor of his cabin with his eyes wide open, as if the darkness
might split apart at any moment and dazzle him with some new
and atrocious violence. I heard the planks creak as he shifted his
weight. I felt the splintery wood chafing his shoulders. I sensed the
heat like cloth across his face. I did all these things – and it made
me ashamed to know that I had been jealous when I had thought
of him with Natty.

I returned to myself in time to watch Smirke amble back to his
own cabin and disappear inside – where I suppose he must have
fallen asleep. At any rate: a torpid silence settled across the camp.
Even the doo-dahs were quiet, all standing in their pen among the
other creatures, with their backs turned to the breeze so their tail
feathers were blown about like broken fans.

When I handed the telescope back to the captain he said nothing,
but gave me a narrow smile. It was a small act of kindness, but did
my heart as much good as if he had shaken my hand – and woke
in me a mood that was close to contentment. When I looked
round at the others, I knew they felt it too, thanks to the spirit of
brotherhood that existed between us.

Although daylight was now so close, the captain again ordered
us to rest – to sleep, if possible. I therefore lay down at the edge of
our shelter, where its leaves were almost touching my face. Here I
swam into a strange in-between state that was neither fully conscious

nor quite unconscious, but a cousin of both. And when I did manage to doze a little, my dreams were mostly of losing my way. In one I blundered through a forest of grotesque shapes and sudden noises, until I discovered Natty lying on a bed of moss like a princess in a story. In another I came across a scene of pirates round a fire, gnawing on something hideous and steaming. In a third I found my father on his bed in the Hispaniola, as I had seen him on my last night in my old home. He had the look of death in his face, and the shock of this was enough to wake me – whereupon the cycle of staring and snoozing began once more.

It was during this spinning time, when I was sometimes in my right mind and sometimes not, that I came closer than ever before to thinking what it would be like to vanish entirely from the earth. All through my childhood, and especially when left to my own devices on the marsh and other solitary places, I had made myself familiar with the facts of our mortality. In particular, I found that as I studied the lives of creatures while they preyed on one another, I was always led to thinking about my mother – whose own life, or rather whose *end* of life, was the foundation of everything I knew about the world.

Since leaving home I had seen the face of Death and studied its expressions more closely – in the tragedy of Jordan Hands and his victim, Mr Sinker; in the work of Smirke and his crew. None of these had actually made me fear for my own life, not even when I had taken my swim, and the sea had shown me the way to heaven. Either I had been too surprised by my peril to assess it properly, or I had expected a miracle to save me, which indeed is what seemed to have happened. Capture, I feared. Pain, I feared. Cowardice – I feared that too. But in my youth and conceit I had thought I was immune to injury. In all my imaginary scenes of disaster, I was always the survivor.

Now, with rain-drips squeezing inside my clothes, and the wet foliage knocking against my cheek, my belief in myself wavered. Because I was my mother's son, I was Adam's son. I was bound to die – perhaps this morning, when Smirke might snuff me out like a mosquito. I would never find England again, or hear the river beneath my window. I would never be reunited with my father, or walk on the marshes under the wide sky. I would never see Natty, or know what had become of her.

CHAPTER 28

Into the Stockade

When Captain Beamish shook my shoulder I lay still, staring without blinking so he might think I was already awake. 'Well done; good fellow,' he said – which allowed me to look around without losing any dignity. A confused light was soaking into the sky, mostly pale green and purple; several minutes would pass before it lifted into blue.

'Are you ready, lad?' the captain went on; he was speaking so close, I felt the heat of his breath.

I nodded eagerly, to show sleep had not destroyed my good sense, and climbed to my feet. To tell the truth, my thoughts were still fixed where they had been a moment before, on Natty and on Scotland, though my eyes were turned towards my friends. Bo'sun Kirkby and Mr Tickle, Mr Stevenson and Mr Creed. All stout hearts – but, with their hats pulled down, and their collars turned up, and smudges of the forest on their faces and their clothes drenched, as ragged-looking a crew as the pirates below. I took this to be a kind of encouragement, should it come to fighting.

The captain touched my shoulder again, and pointed down the slope. There was now enough light to see the stockade clearly. None of the pirates had broken their habit of sleeping late; even Jinks, whom I had seen Smirke berating, was slumped forward again in his chair outside the prisoners' door. I wanted to think this must be a good sign – for surely if they had captured Natty, her guard would be more vigilant?

The captain took a long look at each of us in turn, then set off downhill and expected us to follow. We very soon reached the bushes where we had made our reconnaissance earlier. Then we had walked upright, knowing we could not be seen as long as we were silent; now we hunched as though a bullet might be about to buzz through the leaves. None of us quite believed what Scotland had said about the pirates' powder being in short supply, even though reason told us it must be true.

The captain gave us a second once-over, staring into our eyes as if a part of his own courage might enter us that way, then whispered, 'Come on, boys,' and set off again.

Making ourselves as much like ghosts as possible, we swooped and soon faced the stockade. The captain went over the fence first, which I knew would always be his way – though the effort of hauling his large body over the obstacle, and the oath that escaped him as the tail of his coat snagged on one of the pointed timbers, causing it to tear as he dropped down on the farther side, somewhat spoiled the effect. My own climb was easy, which he acknowledged when I landed beside him. 'Well done, young man,' he whispered, and cast a rueful glance at the gate in the southern wall, which he had chosen not to use.

The others arrived beside us with such a performance of jangling and thudding, I thought it would be loud enough to raise the dead as well as the drunk. But only silence followed – silence of such peculiar density, we seemed to have dropped into a different universe, where the inhabitants did not breathe the same air as ourselves. This sense of *weight* was caused by the pervasive sweet smell, drifting from the distillery the pirates had built alongside their cabin. And also by the degradation we found everywhere. Grass, that here and there had attempted to sprout across the middle part of the compound, sprawled as lank and flat as unwashed hair. The vicinity of the cabins was strewn with filthy tankards, and scraps of clothing, and broken utensils, and fragments of glass. The surfaces of the court had a repulsive shine, which was actually dew but looked as sticky as sweat.

The captain paid no attention to any of this. Moving with remarkable speed for so large a man, he flew towards the prisoners' quarters. Being directly behind him, I saw his right hand drop to his side as he went, and slide his knife from its sheath. In the same instant, I noticed the twisting pattern of a snake engraved along the blade – and felt it told me something I had not known before. The captain seemed so peace-loving and composed, it was shocking to find he had a knife that was *decorated* – as though he had a secret relish for the violence he professed to deplore.

As we rushed past the court, the captain appeared to swell – which must, in fact, have been his long coat billowing away from his body. Whatever the reason, I lost sight of Jinks as we drew close to him – but I guessed from the captain's suddenly even greater acceleration that the rogue had woken, and noticed our approach, and was beginning to struggle to his feet. All I know for certain is: the captain straightened to his full height without a pause, lifted his right arm as if he were about to make a declaration, then plunged it down with the knife gleaming like a fang. There followed two quite separate sounds. One was a grunt from the captain, as he threw his weight into the blow. The other was a kind of exhausted whistle, as the breath left Jinks's body. When I reached the veranda myself, which was only a moment later, the fellow was still seated in his chair, with his hat pulled forward over his eyes, and his legs stretched in front of him. Nothing about him seemed to have changed – except that a red flower had been pinned to his chest.

Bo'sun Kirkby, Mr Tickle and our two other shipmates now followed onto the veranda and took their positions either side of the cabin door. Because I knew they were peaceable sailors, I was surprised none of them considered the dead man to be worth a second glance, but instead kept their attention fixed on the compound, and especially the pirates' log-house. It was a sensible precaution – but there was still no sign of alarm, just a drooping plume of smoke, which struggled from the chimney and crawled along the roof. For a moment, we seemed to be holding our breath. A crow flopped onto the ground and began prodding its thick beak into the earth. The cockerel stalked towards him, lifted his head enquiringly, then returned to his brood. Nothing else moved.

More remarkable still was the hush of our friends inside their quarters; even while the captain slid back the pole that acted as both lock and key to the door, there was not so much as a whisper from inside. And when the door opened, which happened with a squeal that froze us in our boots, a most astonishing spectacle presented itself. Herded together in confusion were the shadowy shapes of arms, chests, legs and heads – like an assortment of broken effigies.

The captain was the first to move, stepping towards the threshold of the cabin, whereupon the arms and legs assembled into human forms, and Scotland himself appeared from the gloom to seize his liberator by the hand. My first thought was: if he is alive, Natty must be nearby. But my hopes were crushed when I looked into Scotland's face. There was nothing like pleasure in his eyes. For a moment I persuaded myself this was due to the beating he had evidently taken after his recapture: the lacerations on his neck and shoulders were painful even to look at.

'Master Nat,' he whispered in his rolling brogue.

'Yes?' the captain said, leaning forward so their heads almost touched.

'He was taken with me. And brought here with me – Stone found us.'

'Ah!' the captain groaned.

'I'm sorry. I'm sorry,' Scotland answered, shaking his head miserably.

'Sorry for what, man?'

'I don't know.'

'Don't know what? What do you mean?'

'I don't know where he is. I don't know where they took Mr Nat.'

The captain lifted his right hand, meaning I think to rest it on Scotland's shoulder to comfort him, but he dropped it again because the skin was raw.

'Did you see anything?' he asked.

'Only them taking him away. Taking him there.' Scotland gestured towards the pirates' hut.

At this point I could not contain myself any longer. 'Into the hut, you mean?' I said. 'They took him into the hut?' I marvelled even as I spoke that I had remembered to say 'him', and not 'her'.

Scotland looked at the ground. 'I'm sorry, Master Jim,' he said, speaking so softly I had to crane forward as close as the captain had done. 'Into the hut? I didn't see that. I went this way, they went that way. It is all I know.'

The captain interrupted us; I understood from the sad twist in his face that he wanted more news, but felt we must drive on. 'Now is not the time,' he said sorrowfully. 'We will return to this; we shall find what we shall find.'

Scotland nodded and I did the same, knowing I had no choice – but all the anxieties that had drawn me across the island now suddenly vanished. Sadness flooded into their place. Sadness, and dread, and also determination. We would find what we would find, as the captain had said. The chance for happiness was distant, but it was still alive.

The captain evidently thought so as well, explaining to Scotland that he should lead the prisoners across the compound, with Bo'sun Kirkby and Mr Tickle to accompany him. They would skirt the Fo'c'sle Court, leave by the gate in the southern wall, then congregate on the beach. The captain would follow, keeping myself, Mr Stevenson and Mr Creed for support, in the event of the pirates coming to their senses and resisting us.

Scotland gripped the captain on the forearm; the pink of his palm was bleeding, and left a damp imprint when it touched the cloth. Then he spoke over his shoulder, passing back the details of our plan while the captain and I stood aside to form a guard as the prisoners emerged.

Scotland led the way, walking very upright and tall, with a blank look at Jinks and a glare of defiance across the open ground ahead. At his side was a woman whose only clothing was a shabby canvas sheet, in which a hole had been cut for her head, and which was fastened round the waist by a rope. Although she did not speak or look at Scotland, I assumed this was his wife. Barefoot and bedraggled, and with scabs along her arms and legs, she looked about her with an appearance of *right* – not pride, or the presumption of authority, but something akin to reasonable expectation.

After these two, their companions crept forward. The menfolk came first, many with their arms folded across their chests for warmth – even though the sun had cleared the horizon by now, and was shining directly into the compound. Some carried bundles that were all they possessed. Some propelled themselves on sticks, or supported one another with arms around shoulders. Many bore the marks of beatings: I saw deep welts across backs and foreheads, and ankles swollen by ropes that had been used to bind them. I clenched my jaw tight shut and promised I would never forget.

The later part of the exodus was more shocking still. Evidently the prisoners had made arrangements inside their quarters, whereby the men slept in the part near the door, while the women lay further off, in the blackest part of the place. This was done to protect them – although it was obvious the measure had amounted to nothing. Although I was not, at this time of my life, much acquainted with the depths to which men can sink in their pursuit of pleasure, it was as much as I could do not to cry out in sympathy as these wretches passed before me in a thin and shivering line.

The cuts on faces, the bloody wrists and feet, the broken lips, the near-nakedness spoke of cruelties that exceeded anything Scotland had told us. The looks in their eyes confirmed it. Each of these women gazed at a point in the distance – a point that moved as they moved, and seemed to hold them in a state of trance. Only one showed a spark of familiar life: a woman who clutched a book in one hand – the binding was very torn, and I supposed it was the Bible. When she stopped in the sun, she pressed her free hand against my cheek as though doubting my existence. 'I am Rebecca,' she said, and smiled at me. Her fingers were cold as snow.

When this procession had ended, the captain paused at the doorway, then took a deep breath and disappeared into the darkness to make sure no one had been left behind. Although I knew he was walking on tiptoe, I heard the unsteady scuff of his boots, and this was enough to make me imagine what sights he must be seeing – sights I pushed out of my mind as soon as he reappeared. He wiped a hand across his face like someone smearing away cobwebs, then closed the door and slid the locking-pole into position.

By the time this was finished, the head of the procession had crossed the compound and reached almost as far as the gate – our whole troop, over fifty strong, was extended across the open ground. A part of me hoped that so many people would seem a form of strength, and therefore aid our escape. Another part despaired because the majority were weak as grass, and would therefore be cut down like grass.

The conflict of my feelings kept me at a standstill for a moment. I glanced at Jinks in his chair a few paces from me and knew I felt nothing about his death, except curiosity that a man could seem so like himself yet not be himself at all. A little string of saliva hung between his sunburned lips, but no breath disturbed it. Then I stared beyond the compound towards the open sea.

Although the sun had been shining a little while before, clouds had suddenly turned the entire picture into a pattern of different greys. Grey earth inside the stockade; grey sodden ash in the ruins of the bonfire; grey barricade; grey rice-fields stretching down to the Anchorage; grey trees and rocks on Skeleton Island. The single dot of brightness was the White Rock a few dozen yards offshore, and the only definite green the tuft of ferns that sprouted from its crown. Around and beyond it, waves rolled in a melancholy succession. Grey, empty waves, on which there was no sign of the *Nightingale*.

I was never a suspicious child, or a believer in magic that had no foundation in nature. But as this scene closed and the next began, I wondered if my unhappiness had somehow provoked everything that followed. In plain English: my longing to quit Treasure Island now rushed into my mind with such force, it was equivalent to a hand-clap or a shout. Something palpable, at any rate, that was obvious to others. For when I looked across the compound again, I found the pirates had finally woken from their stupor and were bundling onto the veranda outside their cabin. This made me feel I was responsible for our discovery, even if I was not precisely to blame for it.

CHAPTER 29

The Conversation at the Gate

Smirke was first out of the hut, yawning and rubbing his head with the flat of his hand. He continued like this for several seconds, believing himself alone, then suddenly understood and began wildly swinging his arms about, roaring for his fellows to wake up. As he did this, I saw a pistol was tucked into his belt, and my heart began to beat more quickly.

'Jinks!' he bellowed, at the body still apparently sleeping where we had left it – and, when it did not move, issued a torrent of curses that I thought must have hurried his shipmate's soul on its way to hell. As he did this, I remembered that Scotland had described him as a *monster*. He seemed to overflow himself, and made the air around him seem solid with his presence.

The captain was not in the least confused by this, but continued giving orders in a clear and deliberate voice.

'Bo'sun Kirkby,' he called. 'No need for caution now. Make your way to the shore with all possible speed.'

It was sensible advice but less sensibly received. The very sight of Smirke had created panic in the prisoners, who immediately began running pell-mell towards the southern exit of the compound. This chaos made them easy prey – although I could see they might still keep the advantage, if only they could pass through the gate, since the captain would be able to defend it like a modern Horatius.

Other pirates had now joined Smirke on the veranda, all struggling into their shirts, buckling their belts, pressing on their hats, and barging into one another in a fury. I counted ten of them, which was the number Scotland had mentioned were survivors of the *Achilles*. One, I noticed, had a thick grey beard that reached almost to his waist. Another carried a toasting-fork, which he waved in our direction as if it were a broadsword. This made them seem a comical collection of villains – but their threat to us was real enough. It was nothing compared to Stone, who now floated to Smirke's shoulder as if he had materialised from a nightmare. His long face was absolutely white and expressionless, and the scar across his throat was like a neckerchief. He looked at Jinks, then back towards us, and slowly bared his teeth. Although this suggested he wanted to chew us into pieces, for the time being he stayed still, his china eyes flickering as if they were operated by a machine.

I was surprised by this – surprised that all the pirates did not immediately pursue us. But as I watched Smirke swagger around his veranda, taking long steps that made his pistol scrape against the sword in his belt, I began to understand. He might think it outrageous that his mate was dead, but he had no reason to be hasty – only the utmost confidence that he would overwhelm us in a fight. We were as defenceless as birds limed on a twig; he would wring our necks at any time he chose.

We hurried as much as we could, all the same, and as we followed the last pitiful members of our party through the gate, the captain ordered Mr Stevenson and Mr Creed to take their place on one side while I crouched on the other. In this way we were protected by the timbers of the stockade. The captain, meanwhile, had planted himself four-square in the very mouth of danger, with his feet apart as if he were on the deck of the *Nightingale* in a rolling sea.

I edged closer to him, and peered round the side of the gateway. Smirke and the others had clanked heavily towards us, stopping when they were half a dozen yards off. All of them were breathing very heavily – but more with excitement than effort, like hounds closing on their prey. Being so close, I could see their hands and faces were patched everywhere with weeping sores; their lips, too, were blackened with sunburn.

I expected Smirke to glare at us with contempt – always supposing he chose not to spring straight for our throats. But while there was an element of disdain in his look, there was a greater degree of curiosity. We were the largest collection of strangers he had seen for a long while – and although he detested our existence, he could not conceal his fascination with us. Our faces, our clothes, our hair: everything was a kind of marvel to him.

A marvel for a moment, at any rate – for within the blink of an eye, Smirke seemed to have satisfied his hunger for novelty, and to have reverted to his old ways. He put his hands on his hips. He nodded his big shaggy head. He ran his large tongue over the stumps of his teeth. He allowed himself a chuckling laugh. Had his stock of ammunition been greater, I have no doubt he would have dispatched us there and then.

'Tired of hiding?' Smirke spoke at last, with extravagant insolence, his wet mouth adding a horrible shine to the words. They were the first I had heard him speak that were not insults of some kind, yet thanks to the manner of their delivery they might as well have been.

None of us answered, which gave me the chance to look at him more closely. Beneath the creases of his topcoat, and around his cuffs, the shirt-front was stiffened with grime.

'Tired of slinking round not showing your faces?' Smirke continued, then suddenly raised his voice to a shout. 'Tired of murdering men as they sleep?' The words were intended to make him superior, and he increased their effect by glancing around for victims of his own – especially towards the shore, where the bo'sun and Mr Tickle were now herding the prisoners into a tight little group. Scotland was at the head of them, with his bare arms extended behind him as if his body were a shield.

I noticed him with admiration but also a curious detachment. Most of my attention was now focused on the captain, as I silently urged him to ask about Natty, and discover what had become of her.

But the captain was following his own course. 'No one has been hiding,' he said, with a convincing appearance of calm. 'I have merely been observing. I have been watching how you run your estate here.'

'My estate!' Smirke echoed. 'It is more than an estate, I assure you.' He was no longer interested in the shore, having satisfied himself that his prisoners were still within his reach. Instead, he was examining the captain once more – not just looking at his face to read his mind, but at his boots, his trousers, his coat, even the way he had trimmed his whiskers (which was ruggedly, but well enough). As he did this, the tip of his tongue, which was very chubby and red, continually appeared between his sunburned lips to soften them. He was, I realised, suffering a second paroxysm of curiosity; one part of him wanted to kill the invader; another longed to sit down and hear news from the wide world.

The captain understood the confusion as well as I did, and stood ready to use it for his advantage. 'Say what you mean,' he said, with commendable boldness. At no time did he make any mention of Jinks, and neither did Smirke seem interested in remembering him.

'My estate is a *kingdom*,' replied Smirke. 'And now you are here, you are one of its citizens. One of *my* citizens.'

'I belong to no one but myself and England,' said the captain, in a voice as still as a mill-pond. 'And thanks to that I call myself a free man. Free enough to take a view of your kingdom, at any rate.'

Smirke looked awkward at this; he was not used to hearing opinions that ran counter to his own. Although his instinct was to crush them immediately (as I could tell by seeing his fingers tighten round the handle of his sword), he remembered what he used to be: an ordinary sailor, who knew his betters because he had served under them.

'And what do you guess the verdict would be, Captain – once you had taken your view?'

'I do not need to *guess* the verdict,' the captain replied. 'I know it. The verdict would be that you are a disgrace. A thief, and a traitor, and a murderer. I am resolved that you will come back with us to London, where you will get the justice you deserve. You and the rest as well' – here he swept his hand sideways, to include everyone standing behind or beside Smirke.

Looking over these words now, which reproduce exactly what the captain said, I can see they are somewhat stiff and schoolmasterly. The captain had such qualities about him. But they were an aspect of his decency, not a flaw, and did not seem inadequate at the time. They sounded nothing less than the truth – and although it increased our danger to hear him spell out our purpose so definitely,

it was also a relief. We had set our course, and knew we must stick
to it.

Smirke was stung, as the captain wished him to be. But he kept
still, which the captain also intended. The longer their confrontation continued, the more time it allowed for the *Nightingale* to sail
to our rescue. 'You forget yourself, Captain,' Smirke burst out, his
lips quivering. 'Your life, and the life of all your crew – they belong
to me. If I decide you live, you live. If I decide you die, you die.
I've sailed the seas in my time, and I've come to know the land.
I've seen good and bad, better and worse, fair weather and foul,
provisions running out, and what not. And I tell you, I've never
seen good come of goodness yet. Him as strikes first is my fancy;
dead men don't bite; that's my view – amen, so be it. Dead men
don't bite.'

His words might have terrified me, but they were delivered with
such bluster and eye-rolling, they meant less than they should have
done. My mood soon changed, however, since after he had let fly
with his threats, Smirke tipped back his head and gave a great shout
of laughter. The guffaw was so loud, a group of parakeets were
disturbed from the trees nearest the compound, and whizzed off
towards the Anchorage like green arrows.

Such roaring seemed to me like absolute insanity, and finished as
abruptly as it had begun. Whereupon Smirke fixed on the captain
more intently than ever, and said in his horrible soaked voice, 'You
will die like that brat you sent ahead, you coward. That scout or
whatever you might call him. Fancy you, playing chuck-farthing
with the last breath in his body. Fancy you sending him for pork.'

By this he meant Natty, and although I knew it might challenge
the captain's authority, I could not stop myself in what followed. I
rose up from my position beside the gateway of the stockade, and
shouted at Smirke: 'What have you done?'

This was greeted by a moment of stillness, in which the captain turned to look at me, and at the same time slipped the pistol from his belt. He evidently believed my question would disturb the balance he had made, and lead more quickly to violence on one side or the other.

'What have I *done?*' Smirke replied, with a languid swivel of his hips. 'What are my doings to you, you pup? Have you lost something precious?' There was something uncanny in his phrasing, which made me think he had seen through Natty's disguise. His next words, dreadful as they were, reassured me that he did not know what he had implied.

'Your shipmate,' he said, 'won't be sailing with you again. He's walking about underground now, safe from the sea and the storms.'

When Smirke spoke these words, which squeezed my heart as definitely as if he had pushed his hand into my chest, the pirates gathered round him more tightly, muttering and fidgeting. This seemed to confirm what he said – although the precise meaning was obscure to me. I took it to be the worst, in any event, and would have begun my grieving instantly had everything else allowed it. But as Smirke finished his little speech, and folded his arms across his chest, which made him look delighted with his own wickedness, his henchman Stone at last stepped forward. There was a listlessness about Stone that showed he cared nothing for anything or anyone – yet at the same time made him seem implacable in the pursuit of his own aims. He had decided that he was weary of Smirke's methods, and wanted a more direct route to the end of things.

This made me crouch down again, and peer as before round the edge of the gate-post as before; I felt I was seeing a dead man who could feel no more pain, but only inflict it on others.

The captain was still determined to drag out the encounter for as long as possible. 'You are mistaken,' he said, ignoring Stone and speaking only to Smirke. 'I have given you the chance to recognise the evil you have done here, and to submit to justice. If you will not, I have no choice except to take you prisoner – you and all your fellows.'

This provoked another great roar of laughter. 'Do you hear that, boys?' Smirke said, when he was capable of speech again. 'The captain is going to take prisoner all us fo'c'sle hands. We can clear a storm, but we're only good enough for the gallows. What do you think of that, eh, lads?'

As he expected would happen, the muttering behind him now rose into baying and yelps. I knew it would be impossible for him to restrain his men much longer, and turned for a moment to look behind me, hoping to see a sign of our deliverance. It was a most melancholy disappointment. The trees along the bay were shivering in the grey light, as if they felt the same fear as we did ourselves. Also the foliage on the White Rock, which lay half a mile off and completely encircled by water; its plume of ferns was trembling with a peculiar vigour, and beyond it the waves lay empty as far as the horizon.

When I swung back, I found our long delay was over. Smirke had finally lost patience with the captain, with criticism, with his men stirring for action – and was pulling his pistol from his belt. It was a marvellously old-fashioned and cumbersome contraption, but I had no doubt it would do the necessary. As Smirke drew back the firing-pin, he closed one eye and peered lovingly along the barrel; like much that he did, it was an act performed with the most disgusting sort of insinuation.

This gave our captain the chance to raise his own weapon, which Smirke did not seem to mind or even notice; he evidently believed the captain would not have the determination to fire first, and – in the long debauch of his life – had come to think of himself as immortal. When this performance was finished, both men stood with their weapons pointed at one another's hearts.

I am ashamed to say it was only now that I fully understood what I was seeing. I had always known our adventure would be perilous. I had seen two lives lost at sea. I had feared for Natty and expected soon to be mourning her. I had almost lost my own life and been made to contemplate Last Things. But I had never believed my existence would lead to *this* moment. Not to *the captain* in mortal danger. The captain, who had led us through difficulties of every kind. Whose kindness seemed a match for all the cruelties in the world. Who had taken care of me as considerately as if he had been my own father.

With this thought – *he had been like a father* – I jumped to my feet again, and the single word 'No!' burst from me as uncontrollably as if I were indeed a child. No sooner had I spoken than I saw my wish to protect the captain had in fact put him at greater risk – because he now had to push me further behind the shelter of the stockade for my own safety. And when he straightened from doing this, and began to aim his pistol again, Smirke tightened a finger round the trigger of his own weapon and fired.

The two men were no more than ten feet apart: the captain was certain to be killed. That was my instant conclusion, swept into my mind on a torrent of confused feelings – dismay, guilt, shock, dread. But this turmoil immediately subsided, or rather *changed*. Instead of producing an explosion, the chamber of Smirke's pistol – which had been kept too long in readiness, and was useless with damp or some other infection – smoked, and spluttered, and that was all.

I expected the captain to say something about this, if only as a means of filling more minutes. But he knew the time for talking had passed. Accordingly, and with a courage I thought exceptional, he refused to acknowledge what had occurred, and merely continued pointing his weapon. Smirke lost his energy and hung loose in his clothes like a large puppet. The captain, by contrast, seemed to intensify and harden, even leaning forward a little to make sure his bullet found its mark.

He fired – a hard sound, like two short lengths of wood clapped together, and the echo bounced back from the surrounding trees.

Did Smirke fall? Did his crew support him, then furiously spring forward to cut us down? I imagined all these things – but saw none of them. For in almost the same second that Smirke reeled backwards, yet another sound had occurred, which at first I did not notice. This was a sharp clang, such as you might hear in a blacksmith's forge. I stared wildly at Smirke, searching for an explanation. Although his face was twisted like a gargoyle, he remained standing. His wide mouth had opened not to breathe his last, but to release another hideous bellow of laughter.

'You think . . .' he shouted, as he caught his balance again, and the mirth in his face curdled into hatred. 'You think you can quench old Smirke so easily, Captain? You think you can tear the crown from the head and possess the kingdom? Or creep here with your crew of fools and children, and take me away over the sea where I've no wish to go?' He paused to catch his breath, glowering like a Goliath; the captain, I was dismayed to see, no longer met him eye to eye but was fumbling with his pistol, and then with the satchel I threw towards him, so that he could begin reloading. It seemed a singularly forlorn tactic, and did nothing but fuel Smirke's fury.

'Damn you for a coward, Mr Captain,' Smirke roared on. 'Damn you for a fool, and an imposter, and a puffed-up, bragging, tedious . . . I'll split you to the chine, I'll . . .' His excitement was so great, his words piled on top of one another, struggling for space, then shrivelled into sounds that were like gasps or grunts until they ceased entirely – at which point he began grabbing at the buttons of his topcoat, where the mark of the captain's bullet showed clearly over his heart.

A strange clumsiness now hampered his movements – unless it was the sluggishness of my own mind, which did not want to understand the things it began to see. Smirke slowly lifted the cloth of his coat – which he persisted in wearing (as a sign of his authority, I suppose), despite the rising heat of the day – and then his shirt. Beneath it was a square of thick brown metal, hung round his neck on a length of tarred string; it was covered in the silvery marks of hammer-blows, and I thought was probably the base of an old skillet that had been cut and altered. The remains of the captain's bullet were pressed neatly against its surface, looking as wrinkled and harmless as the pupa of a butterfly.

The captain groaned when he saw this, and his shoulders drooped. There was something in this loss of confidence that shocked me more deeply than anything that followed, yet also made me love him more deeply. He flung his pistol to the ground, where it bounced towards me across the turf as though it had a life of its own; I snatched it up and felt the handle damp with sweat. My intention, of course, was to reload it myself, but fate was taking our authority away from us. My fingers shook as they set about filling the breech, and I glanced up expecting to make an apology for my delay.

There was no need. The captain had forgotten his pistol and was pulling his sword from its scabbard. Once this was done, he flourished his blade bravely enough in the face of our enemies, daring one of them to advance. Yet it was not a convincing performance, and seemed done more in sorrow than anger. Smirke was unimpressed, at any rate. He took a long stride forward, drawing his own sword and prodding his breastplate with a dirty finger, so the metal gave a muffled chime. His clothes no longer seemed to hang on him, but were tightly filled with his heavy arms and legs.

'You'll kill me with that needle now, will you, Captain?' he said. 'You'll murder me with your pin, like you murdered my shipmate Mr Jinks, God rest his soul?' He threw a glance across his shoulder, more by rolling his eyes than turning his head. 'I've sailed the seas with my friend Mr Jinks. I've shared more solitude with him than I want to say. And you murder him in his sleep? Now, I ask you, is that the action of a Christian gentleman, Mr Captain? Is that the example to be setting your young friends and mess-mates?' He paused here, to swallow and give me a leering smile, then continued with his deliberate slowness. 'You a murderer and me a murderer, Captain, that's the way I see it. What's the difference between us? Nothing. No difference between us. Except I might be a little more . . .' – here he shrugged his shoulders, so the breastplate heaved on his chest – 'a little more *comfortable*.'

Smirke was holding his sword low now, tapping the ground sometimes with the tip as though flushing out game. And while he advanced on the captain, his crew moved up behind him like his own shadow; they were so packed together I thought they might not fight us with blows at all, but instead smother us to death.

Then the picture changed again. Whether it had always been his intention, or whether it was a whim, Stone broke from the throng and stepped in front of them all. Smirke seemed a little surprised, and ready to divert his flow from the captain in order to assert his command. But when he looked into Stone's blank eyes he changed his mind, and closed his mouth, and nodded – before beginning to suck his teeth with a disgusting relish.

Stone brushed his long wisps of white hair away from his face, then with great deliberation lifted his right arm, holding it very straight and apparently pointing out to sea. But he was not pointing with a finger. He was pointing with a gun. A little silver pistol. And it was not directed towards the ocean, but at the captain's forehead. Stone did not say a word, and his eyes never blinked. They merely gazed at their target as his finger tightened, then narrowed a little as the explosion sounded.

Because I had seen Smirke survive a similar threat, I thought for an instant there would now be a similar reprieve. But this was impossible. The moment Stone fired, the captain fell backwards, straight as a tree; when his body hit the earth, it sent a hard ripple of shock into my own hands and knees where I knelt on the grass. His face was a yard from my own, with his old cocked hat, green with mould along the seams, knocked away behind. I saw him more clearly than in my life before: the freckles across his nose and cheeks, the sandy-coloured eyelashes that darkened where they met the lids, the silver whiskers along his jaw. In the centre of his brow, which I had admired so often for its candour, was a neat black hole with a fringe of smoke clinging to its edges.

'Oh, sir,' I heard myself say, in a voice I scarcely recognised as my own. It was the first sound to break the silence, travelling through the heavy air like a crack through ice – and suddenly, to my great astonishment, producing an echo from the shore behind me. No, not an echo. A loud cheer – which I could not understand until I turned and saw the *Nightingale*, looking as pretty as a ship in a bottle, carving through the waves at the tip of the headland and sailing towards the Anchorage.

CHAPTER 30

The Battle on the Shore

I wanted to stay still and grieve. I wanted to creep into the earth, and pull the grass over my head like a blanket, so that I could lie unnoticed beside the captain. My mind was not ready to leave his protection. My instincts, however – my instincts were interested in nothing but saving my life. With despicable energy I jumped up, seized the captain's sword where it lay in his open hand, turned tail, and began running fast towards the shore. In the corner of my eye, I saw Mr Stevenson and Mr Creed follow suit – Stevenson pulling his hat from his head, to prevent it being swept off in the rush. The skin of his forehead was extremely white, and made a strong contrast to his weather-beaten face.

At every step I expected a musket-ball or the edge of a blade to slash into my shoulders. But either because they reckoned we were easy prey, or because they were distracted by the appearance of the *Nightingale*, Smirke and his men did nothing. As I continued running, and my mind reassembled itself, I heard them calling to one another – saying how pretty our ship looked, and how they would be home soon. When I threw a glance over my shoulder, several of them were pointing and clapping one another on the back; only Smirke and Stone seemed less than excited – Smirke because he was gloating over the dead body now stretched before him; and Stone because he was intent on reloading his pistol.

The ground I ran across – it would be better to say *flew* – was the old marsh that Scotland and the other prisoners had turned into rice-fields. Even at speed, I was conscious of how neatly everything had been made: the rows of young plants, and the low walls that created a terrace leading down to the shore, where fertile earth gave way to sand. It made me pick up my feet in a high-stepping gait, because I did not like to destroy what they had so carefully created, even though I was fleeing for my life.

As the three of us reached the shore, Bo'sun Kirkby and Mr Tickle ran forward – Mr Tickle with his unlit pipe still clamped between his teeth. For all that he was not my captain, I was mightily relieved to see how determined he looked, especially since the prisoners – whose tight formation on the sand behind him had now broken up – were extremely confused. One or two had dropped down and pressed their faces to the sand, mumbling prayers that were inaudible to everyone except Mother Earth. Others had tramped into the water and stood with waves breaking round their knees, unable to decide what most deserved their attention: the pirates behind them or the *Nightingale* – which was now a few hundred yards offshore and putting down her anchor.

Our friends' distress, combined with their near-nakedness and shivering, was miserable to see. Only Scotland had kept his composure – still standing beside the bo'sun, with his arms held out so that his wife could shelter behind him. It was a brave defence but also very desperate and pathetic, since he had no weapon except his courage. Or none until I handed him the captain's sword, still warm from my grip, and drew my own shorter weapon. Our two blades clanged together, which seemed to seal the brotherhood between us.

'Thank you, Master Jim,' he said, very grim-faced – then added with a touch of poetry that was never far from his speech, 'We are all the captain now.'

'We are indeed,' I said.

'We will make him proud of us.'

'We will indeed,' I repeated – although, when I looked inland again, I felt less than perfect confidence. Smirke had now ended his gloating over the captain, and was slowly leading his men down from the stockade; they had spread into a crescent, to prevent anyone slipping past them. None were talking, not even to curse us, but instead they kept a very menacing silence, swinging their swords lazily from side to side as if they were mowing grass.

The most terrible thing about this approach – more terrible than the fact of massacre it seemed to anticipate – was the appetite it suggested. Every swish of steel spoke of how the pirates would enjoy dispatching us, and of how they saw this enjoyment as merely the prelude to other pleasures now lying before them – namely, commandeering the *Nightingale*, and escaping from the island to whatever life they wanted.

At this point, when the likelihood of disaster became very clear to me, I found my terror had suddenly evaporated and my head was clear. It was not that I reconciled myself to death, rather that I found a way to keep my dignity – by deciding to end my life in a way that made me unlike my murderers. I would fight as myself, in the best way I could. I would not allow my courage to weaken because I was a long way from my home, and because I had lost Natty and seen the captain die. I would not allow Death to think he had gained the upper hand because I had done wrong in my life – by stealing the map especially, and betraying my father. I would believe I might be forgiven my sins. I would accept the second life I had been given when I was rescued from the sea.

I did not express these thoughts as words – of course not; they were a surge of authority, of *possibility*, that I have since captured for myself in these terms. I cannot otherwise explain the change that came over me in those moments on the beach. Behind me I heard shouts from the *Nightingale* as men lowered our jolly-boat into the water and began rowing towards us. This settled my nervousness. Around me I had the beauty of the world – the white spray whipping off the grey waves; the shivering tree-line around the pedestal of Spyglass Hill; the glimmer of birds flitting between trees in the forest. This stiffened my resolve. But the principal inspiration came from myself alone. I was transformed for as long as necessary into a belligerent angel.

Bo'sun Kirkby and the others in our troop, which now included Scotland, had fallen into a line along the beach with the prisoners milling in the shallows behind us. They were in no condition to come to our aid, and without them we were only a handful, outnumbered by the pirates bearing down on us. It was therefore strongly in our favour to delay the fight until the jolly-boat arrived – as the pirates also understood.

They crossed the last few yards very swiftly, tramping through the rice-fields, then thudding over the firmer sand. The bo'sun was at the further end of our defence, and opposite him was Smirke. Next to the bo'sun was Mr Tickle, still chewing on the stem of his pipe, squaring up to one of the slavers – a hideous-looking man, with staring eyes and a coat that seemed to be made of twigs and patches. Scotland stood in the middle facing Stone – and although it was not the moment to reflect on the inequality of this contest, I did notice with relief that Stone had put away his pistol and was preparing to go at it sword to sword. Mr Stevenson was fighting close to Mr Creed, opposite a gaggle of slavers who could not decide which among them was in the vanguard and which was not, and so flashed their weapons together in a noisy tangle. My own adversaries were two characters I had not much noticed before in the camp – both of them also slavers from the *Achilles*. One was a little stooping monkey, who now began passing his weapon from hand to hand with great agility, and the other a taller, older, heavier oaf, whose face was so thickly covered with sores, his eyes were almost closed.

I went for him first, shutting my mind to the sound of clanging and scraping and cursing that now broke out around me. The monkey fellow (exactly as a monkey might) seemed to sit on his friend's shoulder, chattering continuously: 'Hit him low, Turner, hit him low. There in the vitals. Stick him; stick him.' Almost none of this advice was taken by old Turner, who lumbered towards me with his sword pointing towards the sky – planning to bring it straight down on my head and end things that way. Whether he stumbled in the sand, or whether I actually did outwit him, I am not certain. What I do know is: while his weapon was still high in the air, mine found its way into his belly, entering (because I was smaller) in an upwards direction beneath his ribcage, then sliding on towards his heart. The texture of his body was thicker than a pig's, and the great quantity of blood that began to pour from him was about the same as a pig would produce. It ran down sticky and very warm over my hands, until I quickly tugged out my blade as if I had been scalded.

The monkey fellow now sprang forward, screeching and flashing his teeth as if he meant to nip me and not fight me. We circled one another a few times – and in this interval I had the chance to see Turner finally lower his sword. Not, as he had intended, in a cleaving blow, but with a heavy and useless swoop, which ended in the sand as his body collapsed on top of his weapon. His face was drained of all colour, except for the sore places on his cheeks and forehead, which remained bright red.

'Kill me, would you, you pup?' the monkey nattered. 'Put away old Turner, would you, and leave a widow in the world? Orphans too, I shouldn't wonder – orphans in the ports here and there with hungry mouths.' With my new sense of purpose, none of this had the slightest effect on me. Once I had followed him round in a shuffling circle a few times, and got the measure of things, I made a direct jab that seemed to amaze him. His sword fell from his hand as he parried my strike – and the tip of my blade entered his throat, in the hollow below his Adam's apple.

'Ah!' he said, in the thoughtful voice of someone who has found the answer to a mystery that has long eluded him. Whatever this knowledge might have been, he kept it to himself. For as his sigh ended, his life left him. Then he too toppled onto the sand, where his head rested against the thigh of his friend Turner; they lay there together like two men sleeping after a meal – Turner blubbery and elephantine, the monkey still quite young, but very bald. As I looked at them, I waited for a shock of pity or revulsion to break through me. I felt nothing of the sort. Instead a calm voice spoke in my head, saying, 'You have killed a man. You have killed two men.'

At other times in my life, such a sentence would have been monstrous. In the strange state I had now entered, it seemed nothing other than a statement of fact; I did not pause to consider what it implied, in transferring me from one sort of existence to another. My only concern was my friends, whose contests were more evenly balanced than my own had been. Furthest away from me, Smirke and Bo'sun Kirkby were both standing at their full height, swinging their cutlasses with methodical ferocity. (Smirke, I noticed, was puffing a good deal and sweating very heavily.) Mr Tickle, Mr Stevenson and Mr Creed were also standing their ground – Stevenson with his chin held high and a disdainful expression on his face, as though he considered the whole business of fighting to be beneath him; Creed hopping quickly from foot to foot. Mr Tickle stood solid as a yeoman, chopping and thrusting as if he were demonstrating a means of signalling – with swords, not flags.

The battle between Stone and Scotland was more subtle. Scotland had evidently decided his long incarceration put him at a disadvantage – which it certainly did, in terms of strength and stamina. He stood well back from his enemy, up to his ankles in water, making occasional lunges. The scars across his shoulders, and one raw gash across the crown of his head, made it appear he had already been struck several blows. In reality these were earlier wounds he had received in the stockade – for Stone was also reluctant to fight close-to.

This hesitation seemed strange, until I noticed that, with crab-like manoeuvres, Stone was in fact not especially interested in Scotland himself, but what lay *behind* him. This was the woman who had walked at his side when he emerged from the log-house His wife.

I am writing these words as though in the midst of battle I had time to stand easy, and observe, and think. There was no such time – only a brief pause before I began fighting again – but in such moments as did exist, I noticed this woman with peculiar clarity. She was almost the same height as Scotland and the same age, with loosely curled hair, skin as black as ebony, and an upright way of standing that made her Scotland's equal. I was yet to hear her speak, but the blank fury in her eyes made speech unnecessary. It was clear that she wanted much more than Stone's death. She wanted him killed and all trace of him entirely removed from the face of the earth.

In the same instant that I felt the power of her rage – seeing her stand up to her knees in sea-water, with the waves plucking at her – my horror of the stockade and everything it contained reached a new intensity. Smirke was heartless enough, but my instincts told me it was Stone who had instigated the worst obscenities. The coldness of the man was a kind of petrifaction – the lizard stare, the carved mouth, the dead pallor of his face. Although I wondered whether any earthly weapon could put an end to him, since he had already survived the slash across his throat, I nevertheless threw myself forward to join Scotland, where I might strike a blow for justice.

As I did so, I saw the jolly-boat had made less progress towards the shore than I would have expected. To judge by the way some of the rowers were struggling, while others bailed the water breaking over the sides, I assumed they had encountered a current running offshore – produced, no doubt, by the powerful stream that entered the bay near to where they were arriving. It was obvious that we needed to hold our ground for another several minutes. Or to put it a better way: I thought we had several minutes to win the battle ourselves.

It was not to be. Although I did not flatter myself by thinking Stone wanted to avoid me, the sight of my approach did accelerate the matter he already had in mind. Rather than engaging with Scotland and trying to finish him, he now backed away entirely, scrambling to the top of a little sand-ridge that divided the rice-fields from the shore. Here he paused, one minute looking down the slope to where Scotland and I stood side by side, and the next out to sea, where the shouts of my shipmates were clearly audible above the slop and crash of waves.

I blame myself for failing to understand what he had in mind; I have criticised myself ever since. If my wits had been about me, I would have rushed forward regardless of any risk – and really believe that, with Scotland to help, we might have overpowered the wretch. As it was, I waited like a fool for Stone to come down to us again. This gave him his opportunity. Without so much as a blink, he coolly struck his sword in the sand (which it entered with a hiss, as if the blade were hot), then reached a long hand inside his coat and produced from it his silver pistol – the same he had used to kill the captain. This he raised with a straight arm, pointing it not at my heart, or at Scotland, but between and beyond us – at Scotland's wife. It was simple cruelty that made him do this, because he knew the grief it would cause.

Scotland's misery began as Stone squeezed the trigger; he saw immediately what must happen. Therefore, instead of flinching or leaping aside, he turned round to discover what he already knew – his wife straight on her back in the waves. His wife with the waves splashing over her, making a continuous rocking movement, such as might send a child to sleep. The spirals of her hair swayed lazily about her face. Her blood, too, where it flowed from her breast.

I saw this in the second before I also saw Scotland run out to her, kneel, heave her upright and dripping, and begin calling her name. It was a terrible, loud wail; the saddest sound I ever heard. And the sound of it was all I needed then, to make me begin labouring up the slope towards Stone. I thought he would be reloading his pistol, or at least be pulling his sword from the sand, to send me on my way to the afterlife by one means or the other. In fact he seemed not in the least bothered with me, or with what he had just accomplished. He was staring over our heads and out to sea – not in the direction of the jolly-boat, and not towards the *Nightingale* either, but towards the feathery mound of the White Rock, which lay midway between our shore and Skeleton Island.

It was the only time I saw his expression change – his blank mask melting like wax and wrinkling into a grimace. Blood surged into his cheeks and along the scar round his throat, so that it seemed like a fresh wound. 'Smirke!' he called, in a high-pitched whisper. 'Smirke! Smirke!' Further along the sand, his captain broke away from Bo'sun Kirkby, and looked where his lieutenant was pointing – and also changed colour like a chameleon.

'Mr Stone,' he called back in an unsteady voice. 'With me! With me!' As soon as the order was given, they both galloped away from us, disappearing across the rice-fields and into the undergrowth that lay alongside the stream whose current had delayed our friends.

CHAPTER 31

On the White Rock

My relief at seeing Smirke and Stone disappear was so great – and all the greater when their subordinates from the *Achilles* also spun on their heels and followed them into the undergrowth – I did not yet ask what had suddenly provoked them. Only when I was sure they were gone, and we were no longer in immediate danger, did I begin looking out to sea and searching for an answer. For a moment I saw nothing but the grey sea and the *Nightingale*. Then I looked again towards the White Rock. Then I saw the ferns crowning the White Rock. Then I saw a shadow among these ferns. Then I saw this shadow harden into a shape. Then I saw the shape change into a person. Then I saw the person had a face. Then I saw the face had eyes and a nose and a mouth. Then I saw Natty.

My first thought was: it must be a vision. A compensation for the fright and giddiness of battle. I shielded my eyes to look more clearly and be sure. Not even this could convince me entirely, given the dimness of the day and the distance between us – until I remembered the pirates' look of astonishment. They were aghast because they also thought Natty was dead. Their surprise was proof of her life.

My first instinct was natural enough – to shout her name, to point, to leap up and down on the sand, to open my arms towards her and show her the happiness I felt. But I stopped myself. The ghost of the captain still stalked about my heart, and made anything like rejoicing seem unnatural. Unkind to Scotland as well, who was still kneeling in the water beside his wife, touching her face and hair and murmuring words she could not hear.

This sight, coming so soon after my glimpse of Natty, brought sorrow and delight so strongly together in my mind, I felt rooted to the ground. But to tell the truth, I never doubted where I must turn first. After hesitating for only a minute, I splashed out through the waves to help Scotland carry his wife onto dry land. I did not so much as mention Natty. Instead, and with as much dignity as possible, we took the weight of the dead woman, and raised her, and came ashore, and laid out the body on the sand while our friends gathered round us in a tight group. Scotland held his wife by the hand and ran his fingers up and down her own, as though he might be able to preserve the warmth in them.

'Leave us,' Scotland said after a while – and when he saw we were reluctant to go, he told us a second time, more firmly: 'Leave us. Please.'

Our delay had only been a form of kindness, but we did as he asked, scattering along the shoreline and talking quietly to one another. I came in between Bo'sun Kirkby and Mr Tickle, so that I could point out my secret.

At first they were disbelieving, as I had been; having accepted the likelihood of Natty's death, they could not easily reject it again. But when their cautious signals across the water were greeted by the voice we all recognised, they were convinced – and felt some of the happiness I knew myself.

'I'd given him up,' said the bo'sun, which was more than he had previously admitted. Mr Tickle would not go as far as this, but kept saying, 'Nat's a good lad; Nat's a good lad; Nat's a good lad,' as if he had taken a lesson in conversation from Spot. To celebrate, he then lit his pipe for the first time in a long while – whereupon the breeze promptly blew an unusually thick shower of sparks into his beard.

The same breeze was also bringing our little gallipot of a boat towards us more speedily, since it had now escaped the drag of the river-current. It made a cheerful sight cresting through the surf, although there was not enough room on board for more than a dozen of us at a time; there would have to be five, if not six, separate journeys between the *Nightingale* and the shore until we were all safely on board. The prospect of this delay was troublesome, since we felt Smirke and the others might return at any moment. Although one of the men in the boat had brought a rifle, and the other three swords, we barely matched the number of our enemies – which I calculated was ten, including Smirke and Stone, and who owned more weapons than they had so far used against us.

When our jolly-boat finally slid up the sand, I therefore set about handing our charges aboard with the utmost haste. But this was not easy. Every one that I helped had been frail to the point of exhaustion when we first released them from their quarters. Now, after cowering in the open, witnessing further cruelties, and thinking they might be exterminated at any moment, many were unable to stand. Fear had turned them into rag dolls. Some were so confused they even mistook their rescuers for enemies – and feebly resisted us, scratching and moaning; one bit Mr Tickle on the chin (which he scarcely felt through his beard), and I myself had to chase through the waves after a young woman who cringed from the hand I had raised to help her; she shivered in my grasp as I led her back to the boat.

Faced with these difficulties, Bo'sun Kirkby decided that Scotland and Mr Tickle and I should accompany the first party to the *Nightingale*, before returning for the second. Myself because I would then be able to rescue Natty in person, as we stopped en route at the White Rock; Scotland because he could reassure our friends in a language they understood. As soon as the boat was filled, I ran back along the beach to persuade Scotland he must do this.

I expected some difficulty, because I assumed Scotland would be concentrated on his grief. In fact he hesitated for no more than a moment – a moment in which he stared into his wife's face, and touched her hair with a most lingering tenderness. Then he rose to his feet.

'I have seen Master Nat,' he said – which took me aback, since I did not think he had been looking at the world.

'She . . .' I began, meaning only to state the obvious: that she was alive. But in my excitement I had misspoken.

'She,' said Scotland, with a grave bow. It was not a question. It proved that he knew the truth of Natty's situation, and had considered it a secret worth keeping.

'Yes,' I said quietly. 'She.'

'I have always known,' he said. 'But I saw she had her reasons for keeping herself in disguise. You both did.'

'Thank you for understanding,' I told him, and gave him my hand. Once again his palm felt very rough against my own.

'Well,' I went on, 'she is safe, at any rate.'

Scotland sighed, then narrowed his eyes and looked towards the White Rock, where Natty now appeared to be sitting among the ferns. He seemed about to speak, and because I thought he would make a comparison between his situation and my own, I interrupted in order to spare us both.

'We can collect Natty on our way,' I told him. 'She will be safe on board the *Nightingale*, while we finish here.'

'She will have something to tell you,' he replied.

'She will,' I said, assuming he meant we would be pleased to be reunited.

Scotland shook his head. 'You will see,' he said – and almost smiled. Then, evidently feeling he had strayed too far from the one thing he wanted to think about, he turned again to gaze at his wife.

After a moment of silence, he called to a friend in the group of others now milling around the jolly-boat. This was a grizzled fellow about twice his age, whose bowed shoulders, and scarred face and hands, showed the sufferings he had endured on the island. In spite of this, he lolloped across the sand in loose and easy strides, and spoke very affectionately with Scotland. I could not understand what he said, but guessed the gist of it when he sat down at the feet of Scotland's wife, with his hands on his knees. He was to keep guard, until Scotland returned. Scotland thanked him, then bowed and crossed himself, and walked away beside me without once looking back.

As we scrambled aboard the jolly-boat, it was obvious that unless we remained very still in our places, and kept the balance, we would all soon be tipped into the sea. Even as it was, waves grabbed at us hungrily, so we were soon ankle-deep in water. Mr Tickle, who had appointed himself leader of the oarsmen, kept up a low rumble of curses.

I was squeezed between Scotland and Rebecca, the prisoner who had introduced herself to me when she emerged from the log-house holding her Bible. The Good Book was now clasped tight between her hands, as though it could be relied on for buoyancy, and her chin was resting on her chest. In spite of this, I could hear that she was singing – if a whisper can be called a song. I recognised it as that fine old hymn 'The Shepherd's Hand':

> When I put myself in the shepherd's hand,
> He leads me to the Promised Land:
> Sweet Lord, guide me home.

> When I hear the word the shepherd says,
> I shall know the number of my days:
> Sweet Lord, guide me home.

> When I find the warmth of my shepherd's fold,
> I have no need of silver or gold:
> Sweet Lord, guide me home.

I listened to these verses in a respectful silence. Scotland, who surprised me in almost everything he did, was not so patient. Even before the song was done, he lunged forward to one of the oarsmen recently arrived from the *Nightingale* and asked a question. What with the hubbub of wind and the waves, I did not hear the answer exactly – only that it contained the phase 'to avenge us'; Scotland's response, however, was clear enough. Muttering, 'Very good; very good,' he rummaged in a little cabinet under his seat, and took out an object the size of a man's head, which had been covered with a thick cloth then tied with string.

As our oarsmen worked the boat round in the water, until the prow faced towards the White Rock and the *Nightingale* beyond, I asked what the parcel contained. Scotland placed it cautiously on his bare knees and stared at me with his head held sideways, like a blackbird listening for a worm in the ground. 'It is our weapon,' he said, then added in a whisper: 'Look over by the Rock'.

I did as he asked – and was astonished he had spoken so calmly. Not a hundred yards away, emerging from the mouth of the largest of the streams that poured into the Anchorage, was a roughly made canoe in which sat Smirke and Stone, paddling very hard and efficiently and heading in the same direction as ourselves. So long as they remained in the smooth freshwater, they made rapid progress, carried by the strong force of its current. When they reached the open sea, however, their speed was not so great – although both bent to their work furiously, and dug their paddles into the water as if the devil himself were chasing them.

Except: it was not fear of what lay behind that drove them on, so much as their desire to reach what lay ahead. I assumed this must be Natty, who was now clearly visible in her strange little fort. Cowering among the ferns with her hat squeezed down onto her head, and her knees pressed tightly together, she looked more like a child accused of a misdemeanour than a young woman in danger of losing her life. The sense of her innocence made my heart fly towards her like an arrow, and I heard myself call her name aloud repeatedly – 'Natty! Natty! Natty!' – as if this would somehow quicken the rhythm of our oars.

But the jolly-boat was not built for speed, and continually shipped water. The prow laboured through the waves. Spray spattered in our faces. Everything about us seemed heavier, and slower, and more cumbersome by the minute. And more nearly helpless, too, which I could measure by watching how Natty gradually sank down further and further among the ferns – but still could not make herself invisible.

I could do nothing but sit in my place as Smirke and Stone raced their canoe alongside the little island with a final surge of strength. And nothing again as I watched them make a deft manoeuvre whereby Smirke stayed aboard, keeping things steady, while Stone leaped to capture their prey. I saw the tall ferns shake at one end of the Rock, then in the middle, then at the other, then back in the middle again, as Natty played a quick and humiliating game of hide-and-seek. Eventually there was a violent trembling of the long stems, and a cry as Stone fell on her (so I imagined) like a hawk on a lark.

At this point we were still a few dozen yards off the Rock, but the sight and sound of the capture was so alarming, it produced an even greater effort from my shipmates. We ploughed through the last stretch of water with a terrific splash, and scraped against the pale boulders exactly as Stone dragged Natty into the canoe and Smirke began to paddle them all back towards the shore.

He could not easily do this, thanks to Natty – who was struggling very fiercely. One of her feet kicked out sideways and caught Smirke such a blow across the knuckles, he took his hand off the paddle for a moment, and shook it. Stone, meanwhile, was aiming to land a clout on her head with his own paddle, like a man trying to stun an eel – but the more determined he became, the more she wriggled, and the more their boat wobbled, and the more inclined he was to use a different kind of force.

I knew this because I saw him suddenly shrug, and straighten, and reach one hand inside his long coat – towards the pocket where he kept his silver pistol.

'Strike them amidships!' I shouted to my mates, urging them to make a collision that would knock Stone off balance. The oarsmen needed no further encouragement. With every ounce of strength they could muster, and all the weight of our passengers combined, we hit the canoe dead centre. Stone did indeed lose his balance and fell down very smartly, with his legs over his head in a most ridiculous posture. Smirke was more composed, if a man can be called such a thing when his face is buckled with rage.

I assumed the canoe would sink – which had been my intention. But nothing behaved as I thought it would. The canoe merely creaked, and staggered, and spun sideways, then began dragging alongside us, making our gunwales squeal.

The faces of all three on board were now inches from my own – Stone once more expressionless as his name, Smirke with his eyes rolling and large mouth gaping like a water-spout, and Natty imploring. 'Jim!' she called, in a voice I cannot forget; it was the moment I felt sure she had never forgotten me, and the moment I thought I had lost her for ever.

It was not my voice that reassured her, although I believe my eyes looking into her own told her everything she wanted to know. It was Scotland's voice. While our two boats were still locked together, he sprang to his feet, causing us to sway violently in our seats.

'Jump!' Scotland shouted, and flapped his left hand – meaning that she must leap into the open sea, rather than into our boat – while with his right he lifted the parcel he had been balancing on his knees. The cloth had now been removed, and I saw what had been concealed. One of the baskets the captain and I had brought back from our expedition. A basket made of plaited grass, topped with the small cap. A basket that contained the snakes.

While Scotland continued to hold his arm high above his head, the cap began to fidget as if the contents were boiling; then it slipped off and fell into the boat. Scotland said nothing. He did not look up – so did not see the glistening bodies that began to uncoil into the air. But their effect was extraordinary. Although the creatures themselves seemed calm, with stiffened bodies craning from side to side with great curiosity, everyone who saw them began to panic.

Some of our passengers were so frightened I thought we might capsize. In fact there was a quite different kind of catastrophe. Scotland's right foot was planted on the bench that ran around the jolly-boat, while his left was on the gunwales; beneath him, the faces of Smirke and Stone were twisted in horror, as they understood what a pestilence he was about to bring down on them. They seemed paralysed. Natty, whom I glimpsed in a blur, was more nearly in control of herself, and had already started to wriggle overboard.

I told myself this is what Scotland wanted her to do, before tipping the snakes onto her persecutors. But in the unsteadiness his own courage had produced, he lost his balance. He was himself pitched into the canoe along with the basket, instead of throwing nothing but the snakes.

Wind and waves shrank to a murmur. The sobbing in our boat became a sigh. The roaring of the pirates was nothing. As far as I was concerned, the only sight in the world was Scotland's long body tumbling through the air and sprawling onto our enemies. The only sound was his voice calling again, 'Jump out, Nat! Jump out!'

This seemed so complete a scene, I did not immediately notice it contained other elements. One was Natty slithering over the side of the canoe and already splashing in the water before Scotland's fall had ended. She then swam very quickly towards the jolly-boat, and reached the side opposite from where I was sitting; I lost sight of her as other hands stretched to lift her in. The next was Scotland's basket jarring against the inside wall of the canoe, and four or five snakes spilling out like locks of curly grey hair.

Because Scotland himself, the snakes and the pirates were instantly tangled together, I could not see precisely what happened next – though its effects were clear enough. The canoe slid a little further away from our boat, and began rocking violently as its occupants heaved and convulsed. Smirke tried to follow Natty's example, dragging his large body upright in order to hurl himself into the waves – but then falling back down very sharply, as he realised the snakes had already done their work on him. Stone I never did see again as a living thing, for the reason that Scotland was actually lying on top of him with two or three snakes in his hand, appearing to feed them into the body that had caused his own so much misery.

It was this action, so deliberate and so intent, that made me change my mind and think Scotland had not lost his footing, but had always intended to leap into the canoe. In the excited lifting of his arm, with the snakes writhing between his fingers; in its eager plunging downwards onto Stone; in his furious dabbling; in the way he spread himself with legs apart, to prevent his victim from moving – in all these things I saw a purpose that was not so much desperate as passionate.

Smirke meanwhile continued to sit bolt upright, glaring and spewing curses as the canoe drifted further away from us. When the poison began to nip through him, this blaze of rage dimmed – turning first into puzzlement, then into something rather pathetic and child-like. His curses stopped, and were replaced by thoughts that became less orderly as his mind faded. 'Damn you, Jim Hawkins, and you, John Silver,' he said, in a choking voice. 'Damn you, Captain Smollett and Dr Livesey and Squire Trelawny. Damn you all for leaving me here to rot.' Here he broke off and spread his arms wide – then continued more moderately: 'Why would you never take me home again? Why would you never take me home? I have done nothing but dream of old England. Green fields and safe harbours. Nothing like old England. Oh –'

Here his arms dropped to his side, and he sagged off the bench on which he was sitting, until he was kneeling. He achieved this

manoeuvre without making a sound, so he must have been cush-
ioned on the bodies of Scotland and Stone. All of us in the jolly-boat
were staring at him now, though whether willing him to stop or
continue I could not be sure, so extraordinary was his performance.
As if acknowledging this, he raised his arms again, high above his
head this time, which I remembered my father saying he had done
years before when beseeching the *Hispaniola* to include him in the
last exodus from Treasure Island. 'Take me with you,' he said, in
tones of the most earnest supplication. Then again, more quietly:
'Damn you, Silver. Take me with you. Take me with you.' When
he saw none of us move, but only sit and watch, his mouth snapped
shut and he toppled sideways like a sack of grain.

For a moment it seemed the canoe would be able to withstand
this change of weight and stay afloat. But the body was too heavy
– and soon, as though deliberating whether to live in this world or
the next, the little craft leaned a little, then a little more, then capsized
in such a way as to tip all its occupants into the water rather than
trapping them underneath. For a minute or more the three dead
men rode the waves face down, while around them the snakes sizzled
like flakes of fire. Then everything was still.

By this time Natty had been dragged on board, and I was able
to embrace her safe and sound.

CHAPTER 32

Bar Silver

I did not expect to hear Natty's story immediately, nor for her to hear mine. One thing, however, could not wait to be told. When she was finally dragged from the waves with her battered black chapeau knocked from her head, and her clothes clinging to her body, she was at last revealed to all and sundry as her own true self – no longer Nat, but Natty. Mr Tickle, whom I knew best of the oarsmen, spoke for them all. 'Glory be!' he exclaimed, pushing his own cap back from his forehead. 'You've been eating mighty strange fruit since you ran off from us, Master Nat. Either that or you've fooled us all along.' He did not seem offended by the fact that he had been misled, only pleased to have saved a soul.

Natty herself seemed more put out, struggling to stand in the crowded boat, but looking around defiantly. 'I am Mr Silver's daughter,' she said, as if the spectre of her father had come to stand beside her, and was ready to crush anyone who mocked. 'I did what I did. I disguised myself in case . . .' But here her courage seemed to run out and she looked to me. Exhaustion was to blame, I understood that. And shock, too, at everything she had seen. But I suspected something else as well. Natty had grown used to her disguise, and the opportunities for freedom that it offered; now she was herself again, and felt constrained.

The least I could do was admit that I had been privy to her trick. 'Natty thought it would be for the best,' I said, from the place I had taken on the bench beside her. 'It was her father's idea – in case of *accidents*. Our captain knew, didn't he, Natty? Captain Beamish also thought disguise was right for our journey.'

At this Natty suddenly rallied and clapped her hands. My first thought was: she wanted to fix our attention on the remaining buccaneers, because they might reappear from the trees at any minute and launch another attack against us. Our friends were certainly concerned about this, and glanced continually towards the shore, where the remainder of the slaves stood in a ragged group, still guarded by Bo'sun Kirkby and the rest. Instead, she meant us to look towards the place she had recently been hiding.

'The White Rock!' she called out.

I did not understand what she could mean, beyond naming the place.

'What of it?' I asked.

'We must go there,' she said quickly. 'We must go there and you must see, you must all see.'

Such insistence surprised me very much. Natty had admired Scotland and inclined towards him. Yet now his corpse was floating in the waves a matter of yards away, she did not so much as acknowledge him. I could not comprehend this – except by supposing her mind was injured by the dangers she had recently confronted. It was not that she felt nothing; rather that she felt too much.

As Mr Tickle and the others began to pull the dead men closer to our boat, I thought this must indeed be the true state of things – because Natty could not prevent her eyes swelling into tears when she turned and looked down into the water. Scotland's body had rolled onto its back so that his face was plain to us, very calm and smooth. All the fury of his last few moments had vanished, though not the longer grief of his life. The scalp and shoulders were still deeply scarred, and here and there on his chest were hard lumps, each with a darker V-shape at the centre, which showed where the snakes had bitten. As Natty saw all this, and choked back tears that still threatened to fall, she pressed her hand hard enough against her mouth to leave a bluish mark when she removed it again; she then let her fingers trail in the water where they could dabble against Scotland's neck and chest.

There was a pause and a silence, broken only by the splash of little waves as they appeared to lift Scotland towards us. In reality they did no such thing; we took responsibility for him ourselves, hoisting him into the boat with all the gentleness we could manage, and laying him at our feet. We showed no such respect for Smirke and Stone, however, but tied a rope around their ankles and dragged them roughly through the water behind us. I could not see this, because my view was blocked by friends who sat in the stern; I did notice, however, that occasionally they turned to spit at them, after my shipmates had taken up the oars again.

Natty now wiped her face and remembered to finish what she had begun a moment before.

'The White Rock,' she repeated, pointing to where she had just left. Mr Tickle, who was setting the rhythm for rowing, looked at me with a raised eyebrow, which meant he was asking my advice.

This sense that I had some authority, now the captain was no longer able to provide it, was new to me – but I did not hesitate. Although I understood our friends on shore were still at the mercy of the slavers, should those devils return, I calculated that the men we had left as guards would be able to protect them. Indeed, the miserable cargo dragging in our wake convinced me that for the time being we were invincible – which may have been the hubris of youth.

'Thank you, Mr Tickle,' I therefore said, with as much command as I could muster. 'Back to the Rock, if you please.'

Our boat swung round, banging heavily through the waves. This change of direction produced a good deal of whispering among the friends sitting close to me, which at first I thought must be complaints that they were frightened, and cold, and weary of being cooped in our boat. When I looked at them more carefully, I saw they were in fact sharing glances of excitement, not anxiety. They knew what we were about to find.

As we made our approach, I could not help reflecting it might have been easier if we had jumped overboard and *waded*, the tide had now withdrawn so far from the Anchorage. As our oars struck the water, they disturbed small puffs of sand on the seabed. It gave an impression of quietness and safety, which was at odds with the sky above: whereas previous mornings on the island had been sunlit, today had never shaken off the storms of the previous night. The expanse of sea stretching towards the *Nightingale*, where she rode at anchor in the middle distance, was still as grey as pewter.

'Hurry!' said Natty, as if she had once again forgotten Scotland and the captain. It seemed almost heartless, although I forgave it by reminding myself of the reasons and turned in my seat to look where she was looking. Thanks to the low water I could now see the lowest part of the White Rock was in fact *black* rock: a blunt tooth of the same granite as Spyglass Hill, which loomed over the island. The repeated washing of the tides had carved its lines of weakness into fantastic shapes, such as the inside of an ear, or a shell. Where it stood proud of the sea, the burnishing of salt and sun had produced a comparative pallor. Not exactly white as in its name, more a pearl grey, and very smooth, as though waves were in fact sandpaper.

Had the Rock been domed or even flat, I doubt it would have supported a single seed. But now we were about to draw alongside, I could see its whole length (about twelve foot) was in fact sharply concave. Over the centuries the edge of this bowl had been coated with all manner of dust and vegetable matter, including the fertilisations of birds, and had become a circular garden in which the ferns I have mentioned had taken root and flourished. The collection was immensely varied in so small a place. Some had leaves like slender green tongues, some were coiled like English bracken, and others were deep red, or almost black, or mixed green and yellow.

Natty cared nothing for the flora. As soon as the nose of our jolly-boat ground against the side once more, she grabbed the rope in the prow and jumped ashore, clinging to the slimy roots of a plant that hung down over the bare stone. While she secured us, I followed – and was again surprised by the behaviour of our friends in the boat, who suddenly gave a long musical sigh.

By the time I found my balance, Natty had almost disappeared into the ferns – where I immediately followed. We were now standing on the rim of the little volcano-shape, and could not go any further without slithering down its slope.

When looking from the jolly-boat, I had supposed this middle part of the Rock to be covered with the same plants that formed a kind of barricade round the edge; in fact the centre was a clearing, overhung by foliage, with a floor of dead leaves. Beneath these leaves

– showing in little gleams and fragments, where their covering had been disturbed – were dozens and dozens of bars of silver. They reminded me of something I had seen as a child, when fishing with my father near the mouth of the Thames; we had looked over the side of our boat and found a big shoal of sea bass, dawdling six feet beneath the surface of the water. With the shadows playing across, and the varying light this created, I saw the same ripple, and dapple, and silent suspension.

'Our treasure,' said Natty in a deep voice of reverence. 'This is where they brought it for safe keeping, where they could watch it from the camp. This is their silver vault.'

'Did you know?' I asked in a whisper.

'Not exactly,' she said.

'Scotland told you?'

Natty shook her head.

'What, then?'

'I cannot say exactly. It seemed to find me.'

'The silver found you?'

'Yes, the silver found me. Scotland told me it would.'

I did not reply, but looked into her eyes and saw a cold light reflected there. It was the same that I had seen in her father's eyes, when he first explained to me what I must do; I knew she must be thinking about him, although neither of us spoke his name. In my own eyes, I think, there was the glitter of a question: was this what we had come for, so far and with so much loss? There seemed very little of it – or too much. I could not decide.

CHAPTER 33

The Burial of the Dead

When Natty and I clambered down from the White Rock and into the jolly-boat again, several of our friends gave shouts of congratulation: these were the men who had carried the silver from its original site, and understood its value. By this time my shipmates also knew what we had seen, and so abandoned their oars to share in the discovery: we soon heard them whooping and laughing among the ferns, which shook in a kind of ecstasy. When they returned, Mr Tickle was carrying an ingot – a lovely old piece of silver the size and shape of a cottage loaf. He laid it in the bottom of the boat, beside the body of Scotland, with so much reverence it might have been a holy relic. Then he took his place beside the other oarsmen and together they set about their work.

Natty placed her hand on my arm; it looked somewhat wizened

after her plunge in the sea. 'I'm sorry about the captain,' she said, as though suddenly remembering what she observed seen from her perch on the Rock. 'I saw it all; I watched everything.'

I nodded, thinking I must be patient with her distractedness, until her mind had healed. 'And I am sorry about Scotland,' I said.

'Perhaps he did not want to live any longer,' she replied.

This seemed blunt, even allowing for Natty's distress, which I showed by frowning at her. When she returned my look without flinching, I reminded myself how often she used boldness as a way of concealing her more delicate feelings.

'Because of his wife?' I said.

'Because of his wife,' she repeated. 'Because of his poor wife' – and that was the end of it. By mutual consent we shifted to more practical matters. In particular, we decided that we should return to the shore, and not continue to the *Nightingale*, so that we could lay Scotland to rest beside his wife as soon as possible, and then attend to the captain's body, and to everyone else who had been killed. Once this was agreed, we completed our journey in silence, with Natty smiling to herself as she remembered her safety, and frowning as she reflected on its cost. Despite this self-communing, or perhaps because of it, she collected herself very quickly when the prow of our boat rasped into the sand, seizing hold of the rope and urging me to follow. We climbed into the water together and set about helping our passengers onto dry land.

To return to the island, and not to be on board the *Nightingale*, must have been a bitter blow for them. None showed this, however, but instead they hobbled, or ran if they were able, to join those they had recently left. Once they had greeted one another, which was done with great enthusiasm, as if they had been separated for months, they began to discuss everything they had seen: the pursuit of Smirke and Stone, the bravery of Scotland, the recovery of the silver. Although the detail of what they said was lost on me, the subjects were easily identified – thanks to the vivacious waving of arms, or melancholy head-shakes.

Whenever this talk appeared to relate to the slavers hidden in the forest, there was no sign of anxiety – only a few wondering looks towards the trees, and a few fists shaken in the same direction. I took this as proof of their confidence in our bravery, and also of their estimation (which I shared) that our enemies had been so demoralised by the death of their leaders, they had no more stomach for a fight. Certainly, when I stared towards the slopes of Spyglass Hill myself, and pricked up my ears for any sound, I heard only the sigh of wind, and the occasional squawk of birds.

As for my shipmates: a few were heartless or foolish enough to think that because they were now wealthy men, nothing but good had come of our efforts; a couple even went so far as to dance on the sand, with their old caps bouncing on their heads. Others, including Bo'sun Kirkby, continued to balance their pleasure against their sadness, as I could see from the way he sometimes began to smile, then fell into a study, then smiled again.

Our captain's death was undoubtedly one reason for this. Another, I conjectured, was the fact that he had been so used to working under a superior all his life, he was not used to taking complete command of a ship.

I suppose the same thought must suddenly have dawned on Natty, for what we said next had an uncanny symmetry.

'Bo'sun Kirkby, Mr Tickle,' we called in unison. 'Bring Scotland ashore and carry him to the stockade, then we shall make a plan.' There might have been a small difference in the last sentence, such as Natty saying, 'Then we shall decide what to do' – but this was negligible. Much more important was the fact that Natty and I had both decided we must take some responsibility for our adventure.

The fact that our bo'sun accepted this, which he showed by smoothing his beard and wading out to the boat immediately, seemed quite remarkable. Or rather, it seemed remarkable until I remembered that it would never have happened without the invisible authority of our two fathers. Natty and I thought we had sailed to Treasure Island to escape their influence; instead, we had found them waiting for us.

'Begging your pardon, sir,' said Mr Tickle, straightening his cap; being made of carpet, and now wet with spray, it drooped down heavily on one side of his head. 'What do you think to those other swabs? I reckon we've seen the last of them.'

It occurred to me that he wanted my reply to convey a captain-like sense of certainty, which I duly endeavoured to give. After pausing for a moment, and squaring my shoulders, I told him the slavers were degenerates who preferred to watch us leave the island with their treasure, and take their chance as maroons, than die in opposing us. We would, I assured him, have no more trouble from them.

Mr Tickle was evidently satisfied by this; he grinned, and patted the sword at his belt to show they would be foolish to consider any other course. 'Very good, Master Jim,' he said simply, when I had finished my answer.

'Yes,' said Natty, seeming equally adamant. 'We're ready for them – ready while we go about our other . . .'

Without finishing her sentence, and to show she did not think our enemies worth any further thought, Natty then began directing the mates who had been our oarsmen to lift Scotland's body from the boards of the boat. It was an awkward task, which involved a great deal of splashing and bending and adjusting, while all the time giving a proper impression of respect and sorrow. Natty and I both stood in the shallow water with our heads bowed as the men hoisted him onto their shoulders at last. I did not look into Scotland's face as he passed me, but only saw the water dripping from his body, and the footprints of the sailors in the sand; they left very deep clear marks, owing to the weight they carried.

Our friends had collected to wait for us at the edge of the old marsh, and formed an avenue through which we passed before they fell in behind. We then proceeded inland at a stately pace and, as the pall-bearers reached the entrance to the stockade, slowed down still further. At this point, I moved forward to speak to Bo'sun Kirkby and Mr Tickle. It was not an easy thing to do, since they were both stooped under Scotland's weight, supporting him at either shoulder; the man's head hung down between them with his mouth open and horribly smeared with blood. To make matters worse, I realised the spot on which I was now standing was exactly where the captain had fallen. The memory made me feel the ground was screaming under my feet.

Natty came to my rescue. 'This way; this way,' she said, trotting up beside me and pointing towards the graveyard that lay adjacent. It was what I should have said myself, if I had not been so bemused by the occasion – and when I looked, I could see that several of our shipmates were already standing among the old crosses and head-stones, with the bodies of everyone killed in our battle, including the pirates, laid out before them. These had been brought together very quickly by our friends, who only a moment before had been watching our sea-fight from the shore. The corpses made a wretched sight, lying among the memorials to poor Tom Redruth, the sullen gamekeeper; and Joyce, shot through the head; and the Irish man O'Brien; and the others who got their rations in my father's time. Then the slaves who had not survived their hardships, laid out in rows: I counted more than a dozen graves, including some no longer than my arm, which must have been children.

When our cortege had walked forward a few more paces, Scotland's body was tenderly set down beside that of his wife, with the captain on his other side; the first part of our work to restore order and decency was complete. At this point a heavy silence fell, disturbed by the hiss of wind through the pine trees on the rising ground ahead of us, and the boom of the surf behind.

I shall not mention everything I might about the work we did next. It is too melancholy to remember. But I will report that we were conscientious enough to dig separate graves for Smirke and Stone, whose heads I noticed were very bloody and disfigured, having bumped across hard earth when their bodies were dragged to the graveyard. Scotland and his wife we buried together, as we knew they would have wanted. Finally, we set above each fresh mound of earth a wooden cross that was carved with a name – where we knew it.

The captain was the last we buried. By this time we had devised a little service to accompany our proceedings. Rebecca, the prisoner who could not be separated from her Good Book, and who spoke a little English, would read a passage of scripture; I would say a prayer; and the whole congregation, gathered in a ring, would give an 'Amen' before those who had shovels began piling back the earth. My role in this was often difficult, since when I looked upon Smirke and Stone, and upon Jinks with his baldness and blisters, I could find very little compassion in me. They therefore went to their everlasting rest with a perfunctory hope for their life hereafter, and not much wish that it should contain the kindness they had denied to others. Monkey and old Turner, the two men I had killed myself, I did not look at.

The captain, however, I wanted to bid farewell in a way that showed the particular affection I felt for him. Although I had the eyes of some fifty people watching, I knelt beside his body and spoke to him as if he could actually hear. I thanked him for his care of us during our voyage, and for the fatherly way he had looked over me. I said I did not doubt that he had behaved with a similar generosity in the earlier parts of his life, of which I knew nothing. I promised that when we returned to England, we would give a good account of him, and seek out his friends so that we could tell them how bravely he had died.

All the while I spoke, a low murmur of assent came from everyone around me – although I dared not look at them, thinking that if I saw how much they sympathised, I would lose my self-control. I did not dare to look at the captain's wound either, though I glimpsed it was very black and surprisingly precise in the centre of his forehead. Instead, I kept my eyes fixed on his brown hair and his freckles, and the lines round his eyes that showed where he had narrowed them to stare into the weather ahead.

When I had finished my eulogy, and heard Rebecca recite her passage from the Bible, and said my prayer for his soul, I leaned forward to touch him for the last time. His cold face, then his shirt-front, where the linen still seemed to hold a little warmth. As my hand pressed down, I realised it was not his skin I was feeling through the material, but something unyielding. I did not have to think, in order to understand. It was my father's map, which the captain still kept in its little satchel around his neck. Before I was fully aware of my own actions, my fingers had fumbled at the buttons, thinking I must recover what belonged to my father, so that I could return it to him. When my mind caught up with my instincts, I stopped. I knew the map should be buried with the captain – so that the directions it contained would not be seen again. The world would have been a happier place if Treasure Island had never been found.

No one saw what I had discovered and decided. They thought I had merely laid my hand over the captain's heart, which in a manner of speaking I had done. As I withdrew my weight, I pulled his coat straight, then climbed to my feet and told the gravediggers to complete their work. They slid ropes beneath the captain's body, hoisted and swung it, then lowered it slowly enough for me to watch his face sinking into the darkness. When the ropes had been pulled out again, I picked up a handful of the island's sandy soil and threw it down – hearing it patter on the captain's clothes with a hollow sound, like rain after a drought. With that I turned away and walked to the edge of the graveyard, where I could look on the open sea beyond the *Nightingale*, and contemplate the grey waves as they folded over one another.

CHAPTER 34

The Conflagration

I remained in this state of reverie for a decent interval, which ended at last with a silent promise to the captain that I would never forget him. Then I returned to my work.

'Bo'sun Kirkby,' I said, no doubt interrupting his own private meditations at the captain's graveside. Like the good fellow he was, he immediately stepped up to me, encouraging the rest of our shipmates to follow suit. We stood apart from the others, which I regretted since our discussion affected them directly. But they were not accustomed to determining their own fate, and I was not yet bold or considerate enough to include them.

'Begging your pardon,' said the bo'sun, using the polite phrase that nevertheless told me he knew exactly what he wanted to say and do. 'Begging your pardon, sir, we need all hands on the

Nightingale before sunset, in case we've made the wrong judgement of those villains presently hiding from us, and they decide to have another dart at us after all.'

'And in case they have another of them *canoooes*,' added Mr Tickle, elongating the word to show he thought they were ridiculous contraptions. 'We don't want them boarding our beauty and sailing clear away. There's only Mr Allan and a handful more on board.'

Although it seemed unlikely to me that a second canoe was lain up for such use, in view of the maroons' great idleness and complacency during their sojourn on the island, I reckoned it was wise to be cautious. I repeated my opinion that the slavers were cowards, as well as villains, and would therefore not bother us – but agreed we should take sensible precautions. Natty evidently thought the same, and now joined in.

'We must be smartish,' she said in her own voice – the one she had tried to deepen in disguise. Bo'sun Kirkby had never taken orders from a woman before, but seemed to accept that a revolution had occurred in his existence, and smiled broadly enough to show twice the number of tooth-pegs he usually revealed.

'Thank you,' he said, and with no more to-do began instructing Mr Stevenson and Mr Creed to divide our friends into parties of a dozen each, which would then be ferried out to the *Nightingale* one after the other in our jolly-boat. Mr Tickle and Natty and I volunteered to stay on the island until everyone had been safely taken away, so that we could stand against our enemies if they proved me wrong and decided to reappear.

During all this discussion, no mention whatsoever was made of the silver, and when we would take that aboard. Common sense told me it could not easily be stolen away from us now, so might as well stay where it was until our other work was finished. The silence of the others on this subject seemed to prove they agreed

– although Mr Tickle, I saw, had removed his ingot from the jolly-boat and was carrying it with him wherever he went. When I asked him about this, he told me it was 'for safe keeping', and would be shown to Mr Allan and the rest as proof of our good fortune when he returned to the *Nightingale*. All this was said with such child-like enthusiasm, I could not resent it.

My second thought was more tactical. I reckoned that because it was now towards the middle of the afternoon, we might already expect rain to be blowing in from the east – as was usually the case. But a day that had begun by refusing us any sunlight in the morning was now sparing us torrents as the evening approached. This might have been a relief, except that grey clouds and sticky wind were hardly a pleasure; we needed to finish our work as quickly as possible.

As the jolly-boat set out – with Mr Stevenson in charge, and the remaining friends waiting as near as possible to the water, which showed how anxious they were to depart – Natty and I decided to return to the compound. This might appear strange, given how much we deplored everything that had happened there, but at the time it seemed a completely natural decision. We wanted to satisfy ourselves that recent ghosts had all been banished, and also to prove that its older spectres – our fathers – had been set free.

I had already noticed in my travels across the island how its scenery seemed to change according to my mood. As we came in through the southern gate, the same thought struck me again – but more strongly. While Smirke and his crew had been the kings of their empire, everything they owned had acquired a look of significant evil. Now they were dead, even their most terrifying instruments of oppression seemed merely gimcrack. The Fo'c'sle Court, for instance, with its peculiar fan-shaped wall, its creaking chairs and jury-seats, turned out to be an utterly inept piece of carpentry. When I leaned against any part of it, such a groan rose from the joints, I almost expected it to fall to the ground. I might have leaned harder and made this happen, had the sound of its imminent collapse not planted a more ambitious idea in my mind.

As we continued towards the pirates' log-house, Natty told me more about the time we had spent apart, including her miraculous descent and escape along the ravine. She said she did not want to dwell on any particulars yet, but would lead me to the places where she had suffered, since they would be eloquent enough. When I saw the scrape-marks her heels had made in the soil by the 'staging post', which showed where she had struggled as Smirke threw her down or dragged her to her feet, I seized her hand and held it tightly in my own. When we reached the shack containing the distillery, and peered into its dizzying smell of rot and fermentation, I felt her faintness as if it were my own.

I had thought we might look into the log-house after this, to get some idea of how the pirates had lived, and see where our fathers had made their negotiations with Squire Trelawny in the old days. But even as we stepped across the dingy little stream that ran from beneath its veranda, I felt sickened by the idea. There was such a hideous confusion of stains and gouges in the floor, and such a tide-scum of torn clothing and trinkets (including a piece of scrim-shaw, that showed a naked woman sitting astride a dolphin, which I put in my pocket and still have in my possession), I could easily imagine how revolting it would be to go further.

The open door showed I was right. In so far as the greasy light allowed me to see anything, it was all suffocating squalor – the floorboards entirely buried under rubbish, the beds rancid, the air choking with the stink of sweat and alcohol. Very bizarrely, the slender branch of a tree was propped in one corner, which I think must once have been covered in blossom, and been introduced as decoration; now it was leprous with the same mould that also flowered across the roof, like a corrupt imitation of the stars that are sometimes painted on the ceiling of a chapel.

Everything I saw quickened the idea still hatching in my mind. It also explained why Natty, in a rage of disgust, pulled me away from the door and further up the slope towards the northern end of the compound. We did not need to see the quarters in which our friends had been kept – the captain had already shown me what to think of them. Instead we left the compound and followed a narrow path where fragments of black rock were scattered like coal; Natty explained it was the way she had been driven by Smirke and Stone.

There was a note of excitement in her voice, and not the dread or terror I might have expected. 'Come and see! Come and see!' she called like a child, running ahead of me and sometimes brushing her hand through the tops of the bushes, until she suddenly stopped and told me to be careful. When I came up beside her, I found we were at the edge of the same ravine I had discovered on my first visit to the stockade. I planted my feet as firmly as possible on solid ground and leaned forward – far enough to see the pine tree wedged between the two walls as she had previously described it, and to feel the cold breath of the deep earth rippling against my cheek.

I also saw – and wished I had not – rags of flesh and clothing, as well as some white sticks of bone, lying on the bottom of the ravine some fifteen fathoms below. These were the remains on which Natty might have fallen – and although we both stared at them for a full minute, neither of us said a word.

In my own case, I could not think of anything to express the shock and pity I felt. As for Natty, I assumed she did not want to think about the death she had so narrowly escaped. Later, when I remembered her tight-lipped face, and set it in my mind beside the sight of her gazing at the silver on the White Rock, I thought her silence might in fact be further proof that a seam of her father's coldness ran through her. This did not make me feel any less fascinated by her; it only made me realise that I should be open with myself about what I liked in her personality.

When we had gazed long enough, Natty and I turned to look at the Anchorage. Daylight had softened a little by now, and the first purple traces of evening enriched everything we saw – the straggling mound of Skeleton Island, which cast its shadow across the wreck of the *Achilles*; the feathery stump of the White Rock; the *Nightingale* at anchor; and the paws of wind making their scratches across the mirror of the sea. If I had not been so complacent about my safety, and so absorbed in my happiness with Natty, I should have paid more attention to the streaks of yellow that had crept into the clouds on the horizon, and realised our difficulties were not yet over.

As it was, my attention was distracted by our jolly-boat, which we could see continuing its work in the distance below. It seemed that only one group of friends, including Bo'sun Kirkby, remained to be taken on board – and because the tide was now at its lowest ebb, these had walked out as far as possible towards the retreating shoreline, where they stood waiting for their deliverance. Mr Tickle was fussing round them like a sheepdog, keeping them compact and tidy; I could not help thinking he would have moved more nimbly if he had not been so hampered by the weight of his silver bar.

Everything about our mood and the occasion had now run down so far into quietness, it was almost a shock to hear Natty say she thought Mr Tickle must still be anxious the slavers would suddenly appear, despite his own assurances to the contrary. I told her again I did not think this would happen, since they knew they would be hanged if they returned to old England, and would therefore prefer to take their chance on the island like Smirke and Stone and Jinks before them. Whether or not Natty agreed with me, the silence that lapped round us seemed to prove what I had said. There were no human voices in the foliage – only the metallic cries of parrots, and the chatter of small insects, and occasionally the deeper and more definite *click-click* of squirrels as they guarded their particular patches of ground.

After we had listened to this unpeopled noise for several minutes, which was long enough to convince Natty even more deeply that we were not in danger from the maroons, I put to her the plan I had been devising. I told her I wanted to destroy the stockade before we left the island – to burn it until it had been obliterated, and could not be revisited or even recognised. I had expected this to surprise her but she replied quite calmly.

'Why would you do that?'

'Is it not obvious?' I said. 'To destroy all memory of the evil here. To make the place whole again.'

'Our fathers will be sorry,' she said.

I looked at her in astonishment. 'Surely our fathers will be glad? Your father is a reformed character. Mine had no need of being reformed. Why would they want to preserve the relics of so much suffering?'

Natty hesitated for a moment, frowning as she stared down at the Anchorage and the miniature figures that remained on the shore.

'I dare say you are right,' she said eventually, her voice very gentle. 'And yet we cannot destroy it entirely. We can remove the evidence but that is not the same thing. What has happened has happened, and we are a part of it. It is a part of us. For ever.'

Although Natty's words seemed logical, and followed from what we had been saying, there was an element of mystery about them that made me turn towards her. As I did so, she pushed her hand into my hair and pulled down my face to kiss me. I felt her lips on my own, very warm and soft, and when our teeth touched there was a jolt in my brain.

'Don't you have a reply to that?' she whispered – although her voice sounded enormous.

My heart was beating too fast for me to think clearly. 'I do have a reply,' I said, hoping that I was answering the right question. 'My reply is: you are right. For ever.'

'Very well, then,' Natty said, and stepped away as suddenly as she had taken hold of me, looking directly into my eyes. 'Provided we are agreed about that. For ever. And yes, we should destroy the evidence. We should destroy it now.'

With that, and no more to prove what had passed between us than a smile, she led me back down the stony path towards the stockade and the shore.

When we reached Mr Tickle, the sight of his anxious face peering into my own for orders, and perhaps even for comfort, reminded me I should concentrate on matters in hand. There would be time to study the larger horizon, and the place Natty and I might take in the world, when we were safely away from the island. When we were travelling home.

I therefore became as pragmatic as possible, and explained that our plans had changed: we would now send the last of our friends and the bo'sun ahead to the *Nightingale*, and ask the jolly-boat to return one last time in order to collect the three of us. The oarsmen grumbled a little when they were given this news, but soon brightened when Mr Tickle told them they would eat well as a reward for their labours, because he had in mind 'a certain piece of work' he would perform in their absence.

As soon as the boat had departed with the bo'sun and the last load of friends, Mr Tickle led us inland through the rice-fields again, and we came to the little compound that Smirke had used as a pen for animals. In the rush and confusion of the last several hours I had become so used to the sounds arising from the creatures it contained, I had stopped paying them much attention. But when these animals heard us approaching now, their voices rose to a new pitch of excitement, and made a tremendous orchestra of squeals and bleats.

When we looked over the wall of the pen, we found the maroons had been as cruel here as everywhere else: the place was crammed with emaciated things trampling hock-deep in their own filth, which included the bodies of those who had not survived their deprivations. The stink was horrible. More touching still, because more surprising, was the sight of at least a dozen doo-dahs waddling among the pigs and goats and suchlike: the subtle blue of their breast feathers had been dulled to a plain grey by the squalor in which they lived.

Mr Tickle (who had continued to carry his silver ingot throughout this excursion) now slid his treasure into a pocket of his topcoat, where the weight of it almost pulled this garment off his shoulder; he then pressed both his hands over his nose and mouth. Although he would not remove them when he spoke, and therefore muffled everything he said, I understood him well enough. He had brought us here in the expectation of selecting some specimens to take on board as a reward for our labours, but had taken pity on everything he had seen.

I agreed with him, and did not need to look at Natty to know she would feel the same. We therefore continued to walk round the wall of the pen until we reached its gate, which I took great delight in opening, before I stood to one side and prepared to watch the creatures returning to their kingdom.

I had expected this exodus to begin with the kind of glee that makes animals dear to us. But these creatures had become so used to living in fear of their lives, they did not immediately know what to do. There was some inquisitive grunting, some doubtful bleating, and a few flouncing leaps from doo-dahs who seemed determined to remind themselves they could not fly.

By slow degrees, this randomness and uncertainty acquired a sort of purpose, whereby all the creatures fanned into a crescent inside the open gate, in order to gaze at the wide world that lay before them. None of them knew whether they were allowed to live in it. The emptiness of space seemed to hold them back. Or did, until one little pig, which must have known nothing but captivity all his life, came forward with the appearance of extreme caution, since he seemed to be walking on tiptoes, and passed before us into the wilderness.

This example persuaded the rest to follow – pigs, goats, doo-dahs, one or two geese I had not noticed in the melee, and also a curious furry creature the size of a badger, but walking upright with large baleful yellow eyes, which bounded past making a high-pitched whimpering noise. Apart from this fellow, who seemed really desperate to vanish, none of them went quickly, but rather sauntered, glancing around as if reacquainting themselves with what they had forgotten, or had only dreamed, and making occasional comments to one another.

Because the ground here had been cleared to the distance of about twenty yards, it was possible for us to watch this progress in a leisurely way, and to marvel at how nearly human it seemed. At the same time, the ties that originally bound the creatures into a kind of community gradually began to loosen, so that before they had reached the edge of the trees surrounding the compound, each one had made a particular association with its own kind – the pigs forming herds, the goats flocks, the doo-dahs a gaggle, and so on. When this had been accomplished, there was a final burst of what sounded like conversation – which it was difficult not to think must be a farewell. Then they strolled purposefully into the shadows and vanished from us.

Mr Tickle, who had recently seemed very tender-hearted about the animals, now became less sentimental – as I discovered when I turned round to make sure the pen was entirely empty. It was not. Slumped along one wall was a middle-sized sow, apparently unable to move. On closer inspection it transpired that both her back legs had been broken, though in what way and how long ago I did not like to think. In any event, Mr Tickle was determined she should not suffer any longer – and the knife he pulled from his belt proved we could be sure of our dinner, before Natty and I turned to the last part of our work and left him to complete his own.

This work of ours began with a hunt through the stockade to collect every scrap of loose and combustible material – logs, dried grass, sticks – which Natty and I then took turns to lean against the Fo'c'sle Court and along the sides of the two log-houses. The longer we toiled in this way, the more fiercely my heart beat within me. At first I thought this must be a sign of excitement – I might almost have been a liberator about to burn the Bastille! But as I continued gathering and stacking, I realised it was anger I felt, and nothing else. Anger at what had been done in these places, anger with myself for thinking a journey to Treasure Island might have been a simple thing to undertake, and anger with my father for raising me in the shadow of stories I had not been able to resist. These were the things I wanted to destroy. These were the memories and grief I had to abolish.

We did this work so carefully, it took us almost a whole hour – and by the time we were finished, the sun was melting its first long bars of crimson along the horizon, as if encouraging us in what we were about to do. After I had stared into this cauldron for a moment, I asked Mr Tickle to lend me the tinderbox he usually kept with him to light his pipe – and laid it against the base of the Fo'c'sle Court. I had half a mind to move at once to the log-houses and repeat the action there, but Natty prevented me.

'One at a time,' she said with a slow delight, and together we stepped backwards until we were leaning against the timbers of the stockade, where it abutted the graveyard. In this sense, I felt we were allowing the captain to stand alongside us, and admire our handiwork.

For a minute I saw nothing more than a plume of oily smoke twisting from the rubbish we had assembled. But just when I thought we might need to encourage it somehow, a breath of wind came from the sea and buffeted the smoke into flames. These snarled very rapidly across the bench where Jinks had made his travesty of justice, and the chair in which Smirke had sprawled with such contempt, and the dock where Stone had laid hold of the accused. It seemed the fire had a particular appetite to destroy these things – seizing the timbers and scarring them with deep black corrugations before they raged into scarlet.

By the time these flames had spread across the entire construction, the heat was tremendous – as if I were looking into an oven. The word 'Mercy!' squeezed out of me, not because I wanted the fire to die down, but because it was much more furious than anything I had imagined – showering sparks and flashes and ribbons I thought might soon fly into the trees, and afterwards incinerate every leaf and twig and branch and trunk on the island.

I looked out to sea, gulping a lungful of cooler air, and saw the reflection of what I had done was shaking over the Anchorage. Every wave was tipped with gold, every hollow a seething mirror. There seemed no end to the extravagance. It rippled round the boulders of the White Rock and Skeleton Island, then quivered as far as the *Nightingale* – so that she seemed to be tethered in fire, but unharmed – and on towards the horizon itself, where the flames were renewed in the sunset.

When I looked inland again, I found the thing I had thought was mine now had a life of its own. Several long flames had jumped from the court onto the roof of the two log-houses, where they were feasting on the dirt between the pine trunks. The material we had laid against the sides was unnecessary – because the buildings themselves were so hungry for their own destruction. They seemed to will themselves to be ablaze, then wrecks, then nothing. As the roofs began to show holes, and the air rushed inside, a loud woofing roar broke out – which was the fire admitting that everything it had done so far was child's play, and now it would show its true appetite and authority.

I thought of the tousled beds I had seen, and the blankets, and the packs of cards, and the empty tankards – all the flotsam and jetsam of the pirates, all the humdrum apparatus of their lives, that had been made sinister and frightening. I thought of how my father had stood inside those walls as a child, and Mr Silver, while they wriggled round the truth of things, lying and making up and lying again. I thought of their clothes, long since turned to dust, and their living flesh, and saw everything vivid, and crisp, and pure for a moment, then disappearing completely.

This would have been enough for me, this ferocity of destruction. But I had not bargained on how the distillery might affect the flames. As they began to caress its walls, and jerked the latch of the door, Mr Tickle laid a hand on my arm, and on Natty, and pulled us further down the slope until we were outside the stockade.

From here I watched the fire pause for a moment, with all its scintillating scarves, its cloaks and ruffles and laces hanging suspended, as if the body inside them were gathering its strength. Then it lunged. Then it exploded. Splinters of blazing wood, whole logs, fragments of barrel, glass and metal, a piece of wall the size of a bed: all these leaped into the air as if they weighed nothing, while a blast of scorching air rushed across our faces and burned into our lungs.

'Ah! Ah!' cried Mr Tickle, whose face in the glow seemed almost like fire itself.

I was not sure whether this was a laugh or a cry, but I echoed it nonetheless – 'Ah! Ah!' – while the debris that had been flung upwards continued to hail down, some pieces sizzling on the grass of the compound, and others thudding onto the fresh earth of the graves we had dug.

I will not say that was the end of things; the fires were still burning when we turned towards the shore at last, where our jolly-boat awaited us, and stepped aboard – Natty and I with empty hands, Mr Tickle carrying his silver. I would say, however, that it was the end of *something*. As we set out across the red water, the scene we watched shrinking into the distance had a strange peacefulness. The embers of the court and the log-horses still glowed very fiercely, and showed the shape of how things had been. But now the shadows of trees seemed to lean forward until they were almost touching the stockade. The island was already beginning to take back the darkness that had been stolen from it.

PART VI

THE WRECK

CHAPTER 35

We Leave the Island

There was less than a sea-mile between the shore and the *Nightingale*; with our shipmates hauling strongly on the oars, the jolly-boat took us across in a matter of minutes. Brief as it was, this journey transported us from one world to another. Behind us everything was wreckage and death. When I stood four-square on the ship again, all I could see was stoicism and life. Bo'sun Kirkby and Mr Stevenson had arranged for several of our passengers to find quarters in the cabins below, where they were already asleep or resting. The majority, being reluctant to enter any confined space, preferred to remain on deck – where they sat, or stood, or leaned together, with their faces touched into red and gold by the fires still burning on the island.

Mr Allan and the rest had hung lanterns in the windows of the roundhouse, and also along the yardarm, which allowed me to see that care had been taken of everyone as they came aboard. A large tin bath stood in the prow, and to judge by the amount of water slopped round about, and the number of wet footprints leading to and fro, it had already been used and refilled several times. In addition, our crew had given some articles of their own clothing to our guests, which I knew because several of those I went to greet were dressed in a strange assortment of nautical shirts and trews, as though they had been sailors all their lives. Despite the fact that the *Nightingale* was now very crowded, and that as I walked from prow to stern I frequently had to step across curled-up bodies, or bodies flat on their backs admiring the stars beyond our rigging, this evidence of kindness brought a sense of order to what must otherwise have been chaotic. Despite the misery still evident on so many faces, I felt the beginnings of contentment spreading among us.

As I shall soon explain, this mood turned out to be a deception – but we did our best to enjoy it, and told ourselves that our luck had changed at last, because our course was set reliably for home. This was confirmed when Mr Tickle vanished into the galley with the carcass of the sow we had brought from the animal-pen. His arrival provoked a great deal of busyness there, and the assorted cooking smells that were already drifting around the deck soon became delicious. In truth, this fragrance must have been a kind of torture for our friends, who had been kept in near-starvation by Smirke, but they accepted their pain with good humour, because they knew it would soon end. One fellow I noticed, who grinned broadly as I passed him, had found our apple barrel: he held a stripped core in one hand, and a second apple already half-eaten in the other. I was surprised that others had not followed his example, and entirely finished our supply.

When Mr Tickle reappeared, he carried his silver ingot on a tour of the whole company. His fellow shipmates showed an exceptional interest, calling it names like 'my beauty', as if it had been a pet, but the Negroes were not so fascinated. One or two gathered round to admire, but the majority remained where they were on the deck, showing that peace and quiet were more valuable to them than all the riches in the world. After a while, this judgement seemed to affect Mr Tickle, for he gently placed his treasure on the table in the roundhouse, and left it alone there.

If anyone doubted the safety of our remaining store on the White Rock (which I admit Natty and I both did, now and again), we were easily reassured. As we waited for our meal, we wandered to the port side of the *Nightingale* and gazed in the direction of the little island. Its dark mass seemed to shine even when the sunset disappeared, as though the silver nestled inside its crater had suffused colour and warmth throughout the surrounding stone.

When our feast arrived – with the carcass of the sow already dismembered by Mr Allan in his galley, and the glistening pieces carried above deck on several large plates with great ceremony – a satisfied silence fell over the *Nightingale*. This was the sort of hush I had never expected to hear on Treasure Island, or in its vicinity, and I felt my heart swell in my chest when Bo'sun Kirkby banged his shoe on the deck and demanded our attention so that he could say grace before we began eating. As he spoke, I looked round the circle of faces, all now smoothed and softened by the light of the lanterns, and felt certain for the first time that our adventure had not been in vain.

The mood I am describing here could be called happiness, but it was mixed with sorrow about everything we had lost. Even as we found places to lean against the bulwarks of the ship, or looked across the dark water with pieces of pork shining between our fingers, it was impossible for our guests suddenly to forget their suffering, and for the rest of us to feel we had saved ourselves completely. Conversations were hushed around the lanterns, out of respect for the ghosts that hovered close to us. Songs, when they began as our meal ended, lifted into the sky above the Anchorage with more frequent reminders of sadness than joy – including one that I sang myself, which my father had taught me:

> I met a maid from a far country
> And she was passing fair –
> The prettiest maid I ever saw
> But fleeting as the air.
>
> I walked her through the land nearby,
> And showed her streams and trees
> I'd known since I was just a boy –
> All close and dear to me.
>
> I saw their peace and beauty set
> As clearly in her mind
> As sunlight in a river's ice
> Or rain along the wind.
>
> And still she said, 'I cannot stay,'
> And still she told me, 'Love,
> Your country is the earth below;
> My own remains above.'

To judge by the height of the moon in the clouds, it could not have been much later than ten o'clock when Natty and I realised we were almost the last awake – and went towards the place we had habitually taken during our voyage, which is to say the roundhouse. Here we found Spot waiting for us in his cage; he glared at Natty with such intense interest, his pleasure at seeing her might have been mistaken for anger. Then he tipped his head on one side and seemed to murmur, 'Always too late, always too late' – which to me was entirely meaningless. If Natty understood, she did not explain, but blew gently across the bars of his cage so they made a noise that was at once dull and musical, like a muted harp. Spot seemed to enjoy this, and soon began preening his feathers very contentedly.

Natty and I then took our places side by side at the little table. Most of the candles previously set there by our crew were drowned in their wax by now, though enough remained for us to see one another's faces, and also the silver that shone between us. Natty ran her hand along its length as if she were stroking a cat.

'It's warm,' she said, and for a moment I saw again the gleam in her face that I had noticed when we stood on the White Rock.

'Warm as blood,' I replied, which was a little theatrical of me, but showed we should not forget the price of our good fortune.

Natty then leaned backwards until her head was resting against one of the curved windows of the roundhouse, and turned towards the island. Beyond the creamy waves breaking along the shore, cinders of the log-houses glowed with a strange pulse as the wind rose and sank across them.

'Scotland saved my life,' she said; her voice was expressionless, as though she might be asleep.

'He did.' My reply was also soft, since I could tell that she was still wandering in the trance she had entered a few hours before; I thought in this condition she might speak more easily about things she usually kept hidden.

'Do you think he meant to sacrifice himself?' she said.

'His foot slipped,' I told her. 'I saw that. He slipped as he jumped. But there's no doubt what he meant to do – which was to save you.'

'His wife died,' Natty said, in the same empty voice.

'You mean he had nothing more to lose?'

'I do mean that,' Natty said, and swung round to face me so suddenly that the glass creaked as her head pressed it. Her eyes were wide and full of tears.

'Imagine,' she went on. 'Loving a person so much, your own life is worth nothing to you.'

I did not reply to this, but placed my hand on hers, where it lay on her knee, and kept it there. The fact that she did not move away, but tightened her fingers around my own, gave me confidence to ask for the complete story of her adventures after leaving the *Nightingale*. Her answer was the longest speech I had ever heard her give, and by the end we were seated in complete darkness, because our candles had entirely burned down, and the moon was obscured by clouds. I could not even see the bodies sleeping on the deck all around us.

Everything Natty told me was very candid, and very affecting, and very reassuring – except that in conclusion she said Scotland had reminded her of her father. I asked in what way. 'Age,' she replied. 'Their age. If you cannot understand, you understand nothing.' I took this to be a reproach, although it was spoken gently – and so said nothing more, but unwound my fingers from her own and sat still for a moment, looking into the night.

Throughout our long voyage together I had avoided questioning myself about my feelings for Natty – fearing, as I have said, that it would lead me to conclusions I could not easily bear, because I could not easily act on them. Now that our adventure seemed almost finished, I indulged myself a little – by wondering whether I might lose all connection with her after we had returned to London. The thought was unendurable. I had loved her from the moment I first saw her, despite the silence I had kept. The sights we shared on our journey to Treasure Island; the revulsion we had both felt when we discovered the stockade; my jealousy of Scotland; my dread when she disappeared; my astonishment and delight when she kissed me: all these things had torn my heart open, and allowed her to occupy it. This very evening her descriptions of her imprisonment had seemed *particular to me*, because they allowed me to suffer with her; they had drawn me even closer to her.

Did Natty feel the same? The time for such a question would come later, I told myself, if it came at all – when we were safely home. For all that, it made me very glad when I suggested we might retire and, instead of giving me one of her cold stares, or insisting she wanted the chance to reflect on things alone, she rose very willingly, and took my hand as we walked across the deck together. It was only a short distance, but a slow and zigzag journey, since we had to pick our way carefully among the sleeping forms of our friends – some folded for warmth in one another's arms, others lying apart and straight like corpses. When I reached the head of the companionway, I felt we had travelled a long way together.

Before disappearing below decks to our cabin, I looked about me for the last time. The moon had appeared again, and a breeze was sliding in from seaward, very much weaker than on previous nights, but enough to stir the trees on the island: their shiver was like water running over pebbles – very easy and gentle, which I took to be a good omen. The sky, too, now seemed to be promising an easy passage when we set sail the next day. The clouds we had seen around sunset were beginning to lift – although outlined by a distinctly greenish light, such as you might find in a sea-cave.

I was about to point this out to Natty, when a voice called from the crow's-nest above us, giving the beautiful old sea-cry of the watch: 'Twelve of the clock and all's well.' It was Mr Stevenson, who had been keeping guard while we were thinking and talking We returned him a friendly greeting and then went below, still without the least sense of foreboding.

CHAPTER 36

Storm Coming

Our plan next morning was for all our passengers and some of the crew to remain on board, while the rest of us formed what we called 'the silver party': our task was to transport the treasure from the White Rock onto the *Nightingale* by using the jolly-boat. It was strenuous work, but we never felt it. Neither did we care when the weather took a turn for the worse. We noticed the wind blowing colder and the waves cutting up more choppily – but stuck to our labour.

When each load of treasure came on board, it was solemnly carried below deck to the captain's cabin, where Mr Tickle's piece joined it and everything was neatly stacked. This storage involved almost half a dozen trips, so that in the end our hoard was the size of a basking shark, which in general outline it somewhat resembled, and also in colour, being mostly a dull greenish grey. Although I joined several of these journeys, and was willing to take charge of the key to the captain's cabin, as Bo'sun Kirkby wanted me to do, I cannot say I felt any pleasure in the work. The weight of every bar dragged at my spirits, no matter how often I reminded myself that wealth would make life easier for us all.

When we had finished our work at last, another party returned to the island charged with the task of collecting more fresh food and water for our journey. They went carefully and armed since, despite my continued assurances, they feared the slavers might take this last opportunity to attack them. But on their return they admitted the most frightening sound they had heard was a sort of *prickly silence* – which had made them feel that perhaps they were being watched, or even haunted.

I insisted once again: our enemies had chosen to live as Robinson Crusoes, and would hope for rescue by a ship that did not know their crimes as we did. Although I said this thinking their decision was perfectly reasonable (in the sense that it could easily be justified), it shocked me nonetheless. With no shelter left in the stockade, and only one another for company, and the vegetation creeping back day after day, and the continuous pounding of surf in their ears and the scalding of sun on their heads, the future of these new maroons seemed very desperate. For my own part, I should have preferred England and the gibbet.

For this reason, it did not entirely surprise me that they decided to show themselves one final time, before we left them to their solitude. This sad episode began when Bo'sun Kirkby blew his whistle and gave orders that some of our crew must begin raising our anchor, while others should climb into the rigging and set our mainsails and topsails. As was customary, the first of these

operations encouraged the singing of an old stave – which was akin
to the chant they had made when we left London.

> Raise the anchor yarely, boys,
> Haul away;
> Fresh the wind and smooth the sea,
> Hip hooray.
>
> Raise the anchor quickly, boys,
> Haul away;
> Wives and lassies are no more,
> Well-a-day.

Just as I was thinking it was strange this song should bear so little
resemblance to actual circumstances (our crew being in a place
notably without wives and lassies), a hideous howling rose from the
trees skirting the Anchorage. Several of us, including me and Natty,
ran to the stern so that we could see what might be causing such
a terrible lamentation – which was really as desolate as the grief of
a suffering animal.

We soon had our explanation. No sooner was the anchor hanging
at the bows, and the topsails creaking overhead, than the slavers we
had marooned came bursting onto the shore of the Anchorage beyond
the White Rock, still screaming at the top of their lungs. I counted
all eight of those who had fled from us the previous day, their clothes
already very soiled by their concealment in the jungle, and their hair
flying untidily about their faces. At first I thought they must have
changed their minds about the benefits of isolation, and were begging
to be taken home to face justice. But I was mistaken. Thanks to the
violent waving of their arms, and oaths that reached me in snatches,
I soon realised they were not piteously crying for our return, but
instead furiously dismissing us – to hell, if at all possible.

My shipmates found their rumpus entertaining, and replied with loud shouts of laughter and the opinion that hell might be rather closer to Treasure Island, where they remained, than it was to England, where we were bound. No doubt they felt able to reply so confidently because by now the *Nightingale* was turning in the current, and moving further away from the shore with every passing second. It did strike me, however, that heaven itself might agree with all of us on board, since our sails began to draw more strongly, and our speed to increase, precisely as the slavers made clear their wishes for our future. My last sight of them was all eight lifting their shirts and coat-tails, or lowering their tattered trousers if they wore such things, and showing us their behinds – as if they were already part monkey, and might be preparing to clamber into the trees that provided the backdrop for their performance.

I kept my place in the stern long after they had disappeared behind the bulk of Skeleton Island; although I had not expected to fall into a reverie at such a moment, I could not help reflecting that my departure from Treasure Island was very unlike anything I had expected. Instead of congratulating myself on how well I had completed the work begun by my father, or on how I had gained wisdom through suffering, or on how I had learned a lesson in love, I thought instead about the persistence of evil, and the thousand ways in which we are likely to be disappointed when we look for a better world. To contemplate this truth after witnessing such a strange spectacle made me smile, but it felt no less urgent for its association with something ridiculous.

When I had dwelt for long enough on these miserable conclusions, which was only a minute or two, I turned to thinking how remarkable it was that no decision had yet been taken about who should be called Captain of the *Nightingale*. Instead, we had silently agreed that every necessary end would be reached by common consent, as if our ship were a little republic. Bo'sun Kirkby continued with the duties he knew well, which included manning the wheel. Mr Tickle gave orders about the setting of sails. And in consultation with them both, Natty and I decided which course we should take, with Mr Stevenson high in the rigging above us, calling down information and opinion as he thought fit. Matters involving the well-being of the Negroes were resolved by what I can only call a *natural process* – with some of them lending a hand about the ship, and others seizing the opportunity to do what they most needed – which was to sleep, and so begin recovering their health and strength. If this way of organising our existence sounds utopian, I cannot apologise for it.

Because I now wished I had never visited Treasure Island, I felt a strong need to watch it disappear over the horizon. Two miles offshore, I was able to catch the entire shape in a single glance: the black cliffs at the northern end, where I had walked with the captain; the ridge of high ground along the centre, climbing to the blunt summit of Spyglass Hill; and the sloping shoulder to the south, which ran towards the ruins of the stockade. I thought again of how my father had said it resembled a *dragon rearing onto its hind legs*, and realised he must have arrived at this comparison by staring at the map. From the angle I saw it, which was at sea-level in the fitful light of late afternoon, its silhouette appeared to be the jagged mouth of a cave, in which a person might shelter from the bare sky and the bare sea – and from which they might never escape. A cave that led to the underworld, in fact.

Only when this silhouette had shrunk from being such a cave, and had become a whale, then an eye, then a splinter, did it seem safe to turn my back. As I did so, believing it would be for the last time, I preferred to think the island had not simply disappeared, but had sunk down with all its stones and trees and plants and animals until it rested on the bottom of the sea, where it would soon become sand and mud.

By this time we were less than an hour from sunset and bowling along nicely, sailing into the Caribbean Sea, with the wind directly astern and our sails full. Such smooth progress had begun to make me think that organising a ship must be very easy, and was only made to seem difficult by men who needed to add to their authority by surrounding it with mysteries. If I had known better, I would also have understood that the greenish light I had noticed twenty-four hours earlier, and now saw burning more intensely around the fringes of a few high clouds, indicated our steady progress would not continue much longer.

The first sign that all might not be well was a sudden lowering of the sky ahead and a strange contortion in the air, as if it had been snatched and twisted like a sheet. Mr Tickle, who had climbed into the rigging to chat with Mr Stevenson about how soon they would be drinking in London, shouted down a warning I did not hear, because our sails had suddenly begun floundering in a series of loud wallops and shudders. The instant they saw this, and without waiting for orders, several of our shipmates, including Mr Creed and Mr Lawson, scrambled up the rigging to help Mr Tickle collapse most of our canvas; very soon there was only a single topsail in place. When they had done this, and scuttled down onto the deck again, Mr Tickle came to the roundhouse, where Natty and I had already taken shelter. Here he explained what had occurred. The wind had entirely changed direction and was now blowing directly into our faces; we noticed as he said this that the temperature of the air had dropped several degrees, and was laced with threads of rain.

I forget how Mr Tickle ended his speech exactly – his words were probably as simple as 'Storm coming'. But I knew from the stoniness of his face that it would not be an ordinary kind of blow. For all this, I did not hesitate when he asked me to come forward with him, so that we could stand together in the prow of the ship, where he would show me what he had seen. I almost wished he had not. The wind was already so powerful we both had to bend double as we went along the deck, and the noise in the rigging was like the shriek of the banshee. When we reached as far as the long nine, I found something more alarming still. The whole sky ahead had been turned into a colossal slab of slate – and apparently weighed as much as slate; where it met the sea, waves were buckling into monstrous troughs and peaks, all of them flicked by the raw light of the setting sun.

'What is it, Mr Tickle?' I said – and then, when he did not answer, shouted, in order to make myself heard above the wind: 'What does it mean?'

This time he heard but ignored me, and instead glanced back to where those of our passengers who were strong enough to remain on deck, and all our shipmates, had gathered around Bo'sun Kirkby at the wheel. Every one of them was staring in astonishment. Natty too. Her face was pressed to a circular window of the roundhouse as if she had been turned into a ghost.

'I reckon that's a hurricane,' Mr Tickle shouted to me at last – which was only what I had already guessed. For all that, his saying the word aloud seemed to galvanise him from the trance into which he had briefly fallen. Bellowing loudly, he summoned Mr Lawson and Mr Creed to come forward again, which they did with great difficulty – and then the two of them swung precariously into the rigging. Seeing them hang there, with hair tousled around their faces, and clothes blustered, made me think of flies in a cobweb, when the wind shudders through it.

'Down topsail!' Mr Tickle trumpeted, cupping his mouth with

both hands, and I saw our two shipmates thrill for the order, clinging fast to the rigging as the gale fizzed around them, and the *Nightingale* heaved forward through the deepening waves. Just when it seemed they might be picked from their places and flung into the clouds, the sail came down with a run, and fell half overboard among the racing foam.

Mr Tickle remained like a rock while his orders were carried out – and was still unmoveable when the men beetled down onto the deck again, and stood with their heads tilted backwards to admire their handiwork. Torn fragments of charcoal sky raced overhead, all soaked though and ragged. By now the wind seemed to have risen several further notches, and the banshee-wail made all speech close to impossible. But this did not deter Mr Stevenson, who clambered down from his perch at last, and landed beside us like a bedraggled bird in his tattered old sea-cloak. 'Too rough for me now,' he said – or rather mouthed, and left us to decipher from the movement of his lips. Then he hooked both arms though the elbows of Mr Creed and Mr Lawson, and the three of them waddled astern.

When he had seen them safely berthed alongside Bos'un Kirkby, Mr Tickle bent towards me again and laid his lips against my ear; his wet beard wagged against my skin. 'This calm weather we've had lately,' he said, with a doggedness that seemed remarkable in view of our circumstances. 'Very useful for our purposes on land, I'm sure. But very decevious. *The calm before the storm.*' He then straightened and grinned at me with an air of satisfaction, as if the phrase contained a profound truth that he had discovered for himself, which I suppose he had. In any event, it showed he thought our situation had changed from good to serious in a matter of minutes, and required us to do . . . To do what? It is still shocking for me to remember I had not the slightest idea, and must therefore have thrown him a look of very un-captain-like vacancy.

'Begging your pardon, sir,' he said, realising how much at a loss I felt.

I put my hand on his arm, to show I wanted him to continue.

'Begging you pardon, sir, but I'm thinking retreat might be a wiser action than advance at this point.'

'Retreat where?' I asked.

'Back the way we came,' he said, speaking slowly to show that he knew he was dealing with a child.

'To Treasure Island?'

Mr Tickle gave a grim smile. 'No, not to Treasure Island, Master Jim; that will not be far enough. We need to get ourselves beyond Treasure Island.'

I was so glad to hear this, I almost felt we would be spared any more suffering. But when I saw Mr Tickle's smile disappear, and watched him take his pipe from his pocket and stick it between his teeth, where he began grinding the stem as though he wanted to pulverise it, I knew better.

'Quite right,' I said, to give the impression that I had already arrived at the same conclusion myself.

'Quite right, quite right,' he repeated, making the pipe wiggle up and down between his teeth – and then, to show he forgave me my ignorance, patted me on the shoulder before running aft to speak with Bo'sun Kirkby at the wheel; his nimbleness as he did this was astonishing, since the ship was now plunging more and more wildly beneath us, and he did not seem to feel its movements at all.

I followed more slowly, making little dashes from the long-nine gun, to the mainmast, then to the second mast, clinging to each fixed thing so that I could recover some steadiness before setting off again. When I reached the roundhouse, Natty swung open the door to greet me, and I gratefully stumbled inside. As I did so, the bo'sun and Mr Tickle began giving orders that those still on deck should get themselves stowed safely below, if they did not want to be swept overboard. I had expected everyone to obey at once, since the violence around us was now so great – but several of our passengers were very reluctant: to be shut in darkness was something they had hoped never to endure again. Only when a gigantic wave suddenly clambered over the side of the ship, saturating them all and turning the deck into a mill-race, did they change their minds – several of them wailing and clasping their hands together as Mr Creed and Mr Lawson began to usher them out of sight.

'Take that infernal bird with you,' shouted Bo'sun Kirkby, as the rest of the crew prepared to follow behind; I decided this was not because he hated Spot, but was frightened of losing a mascot. In any event, Natty scowled – but obediently lifted the cage from its peg, covered it so that her pet would be quiet, then handed him to Mr Stevenson. To judge by his sour expression, our Scotsman was not at all pleased to receive him. Spot himself seemed much more than disappointed, if his parting remark was any indication. 'Here we go to glory!' he squawked as he vanished towards the galley. 'Here we go to glory!'

With the deck now clear of anyone not lending a hand, and the minimum of sail above us, we then began the very difficult business of turning the *Nightingale*. We might as well have tried reshaping Nature herself. The ship seemed to *buckle* as she floundered into the trough between two enormous waves, with a pitiful squeal of timbers and a shiver that ran from fore to aft – and shook me with a tremor of pure fear. For a moment our fate seemed to hang in the balance, and I thought we might be battered to pieces; when I looked through the windows of the roundhouse at Bo'sun Kirkby, he seemed to be holding back the force of the ocean single-handed, with rain and spray pouring off his sea-cloak as if he were standing under a water-spout, and his badger-face almost collapsed with the effort of his work. But never more than almost. The *Nightingale* was his ship, and eventually she had no choice except to do as he wanted. With another series of mighty slaps and shudderings, and waves the size of horses galloping over our sides, we came round by slow degrees – then were suddenly free and sailing back the same way we had just travelled.

At this point Mr Tickle took a length of rope and marched forward again, if it can be called a march when a man is clinging to every solid thing he can find, as the wind propels him. When he had fought his way beyond the mainmast he lashed himself to the long-nine gun, where he could keep a lookout for any dangers as they presented themselves. It was a brave act, and left me feeling I must also find some useful function to perform, rather than sit stupefied while others put themselves at risk. But when I suggested this to Bo'sun Kirkby, by gesticulating through the windows of the round-house, he shouted at me not to be a fool: I must stay put and keep Natty with me. I opened my mouth to demur as he said this, which made his usual kindness drain out of his face: he told me very sternly that we should consider ourselves lucky not to be confined with the others below deck, since we were young and ignorant. In a less dangerous situation I would have felt myself rebuked; things being as they were, I reckoned he was merely telling the truth. I decided I would not try his patience any further, and contented myself with peering through heavy curtains of rain as they flashed against our windows.

I say we were *sailing* at this point, but in truth it was more like a sort of *flight*, since even a ship as airy as the *Nightingale* could no longer skip along the surface of the sea but plunged from one abyss to another. After a few more minutes of this battering, Natty and I slithered from our bench and knelt on the floor of the roundhouse,

eyes level with the sides of the ship. This might have allowed us to
follow each rise and fall as if we were actually a part of the timber.
But the confusion of spray and wind was now so great, and the
juddering between light and dark so quick, it is more accurate to
say we felt rather than saw what happened around us. Every leap
forward was an immense labouring effort, followed by a dreadful
moment of suspension, then a vault into empty space, then a watery
crash that seemed likely to split us apart, then another colossal
labouring effort.

I cannot say how long this lasted. In the same way that everything solid in nature seemed liquid and formless, so the usual
connections of time were all broken apart. Nothing joined up,
and nothing made sense. One minute Natty and I were jumbled
together on the floor like puppets. Next we were shielding our
faces as an especially fierce wave, vicious as a punch, smashed a
window of the roundhouse and showered us with glass before
shrivelling away again. Next we were watching the silhouette of
Treasure Island rip past us, with spray silvering the dismal summit
of Spyglass Hill. Or rather, we thought we saw it; I could not
easily believe a place that had contained so much – had given so
much and taken so much – could be turned into such a quickly
passing thing. Almost into nothing at all.

Perhaps it was this idea of inconsequence that began to change
my mood. Or perhaps it was my sense that the *Nightingale*, having
survived the opening salvoes of the storm, would not easily be
sunk by any further assaults on her. In all events, as the island
disappeared behind us again, I realised I was beginning almost to
enjoy our ordeal. To see Bo'sun Kirkby clasping his wheel, while
such fury raved about him! To find Mr Tickle so thoroughly
drenched at his place by the long nine that he appeared to be
coated in silver! I thought he must be exulting, rather than

struggling for breath. I was exulting – when I should have been concentrating on humdrum things, such as how to avoid smashing my head into smithereens.

Natty was too surprised, or too frightened, to share this mood of delirium. 'Have you thought?' she shouted.

'Thought what?' I replied – and felt the words torn out of my mouth.

'Have you thought what will happen when we reach the coast?' We were side by side on the floor of the roundhouse, with our backs pressed against a bench and our feet braced against the legs of the table. Sea-water, blowing through our broken window, had saturated Natty's hair, and her face was alight with it.

I gave a sort of laugh, which was no answer at all.

'The sea around us is a kind of gigantic basin,' she went on, pushing her face against my own, to make sure I could hear what she was saying. 'Eventually we must come up against the edge.'

It seemed absurd for her to take this rational tone when everything about us was in uproar, and I could not help smiling. 'When?' I asked her.

'How should I know when?' she snapped back, as though irritated by her own tone, as well as mine. 'When we run out of sea.'

Natty's annoyance was nothing, compared to the palaver of wind and waves, but it stung me nonetheless – and made me see that I had been so relieved to think I was escaping one kind of danger, I had not realised there might be another still to come.

'It will be Spanish America,' I said, as much to myself as Natty, and hauled onto the bench again, so that I could look towards the horizon. All my hilarity left me as suddenly as it had arrived.

'Most probably Spanish America,' said Natty. The resignation in her voice surprised me – until she added: 'My father was there. My father is everywhere. Everywhere we go, we follow him.'

'We shall see,' I said, which was not helpful – but I had no appetite for wondering about fathers at that particular moment.

Natty gave me another of her fierce glances. 'Think!' she shouted at me, exasperated.

But I could not think. I could only point along the deck towards Mr Tickle. Although the *Nightingale* was still heaving through the water in very unsteady bounds, and sometimes flying above it altogether, my crew-mate had taken it upon himself to untie the rope that lashed him to the long nine, and was attempting to move further forward into the bows. He might as well have tried to wade through a raging torrent; I expected to see him swept overboard at any moment. At the same time, I realised he must have a reason to risk death in this way – and although I could not understand what it might be, I knew I must help him.

Without saying another word to Natty, I heaved open the door of the roundhouse and stepped onto the deck. The rush of wind was immediately so enormous, it was as much as I could do to drag the door shut again, and very nearly impossible to follow where Mr Tickle had already gone. I did not so much walk, or even stagger, along the deck, but crept. Every idea of family, or home, or love was sluiced out of me. Every memory of my father, of the river, of Natty disappeared. Not even the cries of our passengers, rising very faintly through the planks, meant what I would normally have taken them to mean. They were not sounds of fear or desperation, but merely noises. The entire world was myself, and my only wish was to continue living.

CHAPTER 37

The Wreck of All Our Hopes

I was so often flung back by the weight of water, or forced to stop and cling to whatever was handy, an effort that should have taken less than a minute took ten, each of which felt like an hour. When I had crawled as far as the mainmast, broken rigging snapped at me so I thought I might be blinded. By the long nine, a wave cracked my head against the old ammunition box and I lay dazed for a moment, while waves foamed over me in a continuous fury.

At last I came close enough to the bows for Mr Tickle to rescue me, which he did by flinging a length of rope that caught me in a kind of lasso, before tugging me forward so I landed beside him like a flounder. His grey beard and face streamed as if they were about to dissolve. Even the bowl of his pipe had filled with water, and trembled as he spoke.

'Did you see?' he shouted.

I was confused, and did not understand what he meant. Because the last words we had exchanged had been about Treasure Island, I assumed he was asking whether I had seen its silhouette, when we had ripped past it ten or so miles back.

'I did!' I shouted back to him. 'Very tiny and drowned!'

Mr Tickle removed the pipe from between his teeth, turned it upside down to empty the water from the bowl, then clamped it back between his teeth while raising both his eyebrows. I knew from this that I had missed my mark, and gave him a foolish smile.

This made him pat me on the arm in the forgiving way he had, then point with his thumb over the prow that sheltered us. I widened my eyes, to show I was wondering whether he wanted me to look – and when he nodded, I found a way to crouch half-upright while clinging to the bulwark. I immediately had all the breath knocked out of me, with the wind slamming into me and seeming to grab my head as if it meant to crush the brains out of me. Everything sensible begged to duck down and be safe again – but with Mr Tickle's large hand pressing into my back, I knew I must stick at my post for a moment and tell him what he needed me to confirm.

I shielded my face and tried to find the horizon, but it kept flying away from me – a bar of darkness that one moment plunged underwater, and the next launched into the heavens. Not just a single bar of darkness, but bar upon bar, all heaped in higgledy-piggledy confusion. On the island, storms at evening had allowed the sun to set in glory, with explosions of orange and gold. But this was a different end to daylight. It seemed the sun had been entirely extinguished, and would never rise again.

Mr Tickle was impatient for his answer, and bellowed up to me.

'Well, lad, what can you see?' Once more I tried to protect my eyes, peering and squinting until I could fix a fragment of the distance. But suddenly it was not distance. The horizon was a mile away – or less than a mile. And it was not simple darkness. It was a deep-green featureless wall. No, I was mistaken again. Not featureless. As I narrowed my eyes even more tightly, I saw the shape had a spine, made of peaks and valleys. And where I saw these valleys I also found a shore, with cliffs carved out of sheer rock, all lit by plumes of white spray cascading across them.

Natty's voice came back to me, no longer resigned as it had been, but hissing like her father. Spanish America, it said. Spanish America.

For the first time in my life I felt entirely at the mercy of the world – the idea of it made my legs crumple beneath me, so that I slumped down beside Mr Tickle. I felt I had been asked to carry an intolerable weight. Mr Tickle could not support it either. When I told him what I had seen, I might as well have heaped stones onto him: his face sagged and emptied. When I lolled my head against his chest, I was surprised to hear his heart still beating – loud as a kitchen clock.

I had no idea whether he understood what I said to him next – although it was nothing except a description of the coast, and an estimate that we would strike it very soon. He did not reply, and his expression did not change. I stared at him closely, willing him to speak. But again there was nothing, just the water streaming off his nose and beard. He never wiped it away. He had lost the power to feel, and even the will to care.

I took this as the final proof we could not survive. But rather than making me panic, and struggle to save myself against all odds, I accepted the idea quite calmly, as if I were a child that had been told it was bedtime. Without any exceptional sense of hurry, I looked about me with a marvelling curiosity at everything I was about to leave, until even the rage of the storm seemed beautiful: the spray breaking over the prow in flowery branches; the miniature white bubbles in the water as it drained beneath my hands; the dozens of different shades of grey cloud that swirled overhead – dove grey, and pewter grey, and charcoal.

When I had done this, and with an equally steady composure, I decided I should make my peace with my Maker, and commend my soul to Him; although I had not lived an especially virtuous life, I had at least made efforts to improve my condition, and did not want to slip back at the last. I therefore said the 'Nunc Dimittis' under my breath, and when I had finished, and felt the comfort of that phrase in which we hear about the servant departing in peace, I shook Mr Tickle by the hand and called him a good brave fellow.

It will sound from this as though I had determined to stay and die where I sat, beside my friend. But in fact all my looking and praying was a kind of preparation for what I always knew must come next (and therefore last): namely, a creeping struggle back along the deck of the *Nightingale* with the wind raging in my face. That was where I meant to die – lying beside Natty in the roundhouse.

My journey to reach Mr Tickle had almost exhausted me. My journey away from him was impossible – but I would not accept that. The gale screamed in my ears. Rain drove nails into my head and hands. The sky wrapped darker and darker scarves round my eyes. Waves tore at me, wrestled with one another, boiled in pools and streams. I defied them all. I defied them because I could imagine Natty waiting for me – and knew I must reach her. A few moments before, I had been concerned with my own survival above all else. Now Natty was the whole purpose of my existence.

Nothing I could do was enough. In my lookout from the prow, I had not been able to see whether any reefs lay offshore. After only two or three minutes of clambering and sliding, which brought me no closer to Natty than the mainmast, where I clung for a moment to recover my breath, I heard the sound I had dreaded. A sound like none I had heard before, but which I understood immediately. A tremendous *dunch* that was partly a sigh, partly a roar, and partly a scream. A hideous combination of solid and yielding. A pathetic wounding.

We had run aground. My first thought was not a thought but a question: why is there so much light on our ruin? This at least was easily answered. When I twisted my face upwards, I saw the wind had entered into a conspiracy with the sea, and suddenly blown the clouds from the sky, and the rain with them, so the spectacle of the wreck lay open to the moon and stars. They glared with a fierce brilliance – clear beams shattering across the water; lying solid over the black rock on which we had foundered, which coiled out from the cliffs ahead like a gigantic eel; and shimmering on the cliffs themselves, a hundred yards off our bow. In the space of a few leaping seconds I saw the cliffs stood higher than our mainmast, with a ribbon of gulls fraying into the sky above. The narrow shore was deserted, without any sign of a path or track that might lead us to safety, or anyone to our rescue.

While I was still gazing at these cliffs, recoiling from their desolation, I heard the timbers of our hull give another pitiful groan. This time there was no delay, no suspense, only a sudden welter of disasters. The waves took their chance like wolves, and leaped furiously over the bulwarks. The prow lurched underwater, creating a great juddery bubble of air that burst with a shine that seemed luminous. And all the while, in a chorus of misery and surrender, the rigging overhead, or such strands as remained, kept up their keening as the gale tore through.

Even now, and in a way that astonished me almost as much as the storm itself, I found my brain kept to its steady course. I can only explain this by saying that I reckoned I might have no more than a few moments to live – and so was ravening for order. I was even able to notice the end of the *Nightingale* came in separate scenes, like the acts of a play. First she slewed round on her rocky perch, until our hull lay sideways to the main blast of the gale and parallel to the shore. Then, with a laborious slowness that felt heavy even to watch, she listed towards the land. Next I heard the last small sail at our jib ripped free of its rigging, and floundering into the waves. Next I heard the hatches burst open, which allowed the water to plunge into our hold in a hundred cataracts.

Finally, in the fifth act, our terrified passengers began to appear on deck, all carved with deep and shivering shadows. Some were dumbstruck as they crawled forward, and found a boom or a rope where they might cling, and hang, and await their fate. Some railed at the top of their voices, protesting they could not believe a just God would persist in treating them so harshly. All were immediately soused, and with the moonlight twisting across them resembled maggots on a corpse.

And here I have a confession to make, as well as a scene to paint. I knew I should help my fellow sufferers, but I did not. Not even to show the least respect and kindness. I ignored them. I pushed past them, in fact, and pretended not to feel the fingers that grasped at me, or to hear the voices that clamoured. When I came to Rebecca, who was pointing towards the whizzing sky with one hand, while the other pressed her Bible to her breast, I saw a puzzlement that cut me very deep – yet made no impression. My whole heart and mind was fixed elsewhere. Fixed on Natty.

But I had lost sight of her – and when I peered ahead to the round-house I thought she must already have been taken from me. The door swung wildly, and wave after wave gushed through the empty window frame. As these torrents shrank away through the bilges, making a hideous sucking noise like a huge breath drawn endlessly inwards, the ship rose a little from the reef. Rose, and hesitated, and sent a curious shudder along her whole length. This was the moment of decision, though not controlled by any human power. When it passed, the *Nightingale* settled back onto the reef with an immense sigh, before very suddenly collapsing onto her side; the angle was so steep, every thing and every one on deck was immediately tipped into the water.

It is an easy sentence to write, but a dreadful thing to record. I heard voices shrieking as they fell, saw arms and legs scrabbling for purchase and finding none, felt the thud of bones against wood, skulls against skulls, and in a blurred glance found our entire little world had been flung aside. Bo'sun Kirkby I saw, torn from the wheel, with his mouth wide open in a scream that showed all the pegs of his teeth. And Mr Tickle I saw, with his brave red cap finally dashed from his white head. And Mr Allan, who seemed to be clutching a spoon. And Mr Stevenson, who had somehow found a way into the captain's cabin and taken a bar of silver; he held this with straight arms as he skidded into the waves, so the weight would accelerate his journey to the bottom of the sea. 'I cannot swim, I cannot swim,' he called in his gentle brogue, and then disappeared.

As for me, I should consider myself lucky to be the witness of these things, because I am their survivor. For the plain fact of the matter is this: our upending began when I had dragged myself close to the mainmast, and as it continued I was caught in a spider's web of rigging. Whether I wished it or not, I was snagged and held. I struggled at first, thinking I would be dragged underwater and drowned, but in fact the ropes supported me. This meant I was able to lie in a sort of cradle as my companions slithered into the sea – able to lie; able to turn; and able to search for Natty with a last desperate scouring – and miraculously to find her. As suddenly as if I had actually *invented* her, I saw her hurtle through a window of the roundhouse with her arms crossed over her face. She bounced on the deck like a toy made of Indian rubber. She ricocheted into the waves. She sank, then immediately shot back to the surface, where I saw her face clenched in what seemed to be fury. She sank again and I saw her no more.

I writhed in my trap of ropes, kicking with my legs until I was free enough to wriggle around and follow. But follow where, exactly? Even with the moonlight falling in a steady wash, the surface of the sea was now so churned with arms and legs and heads and whole bodies and ropes and barrels and pieces of clothing and spars of wreckage, it was impossible to be sure exactly where she had vanished. But this did not deter me – how could it, when the thing I most valued in the world was on the point of leaving it? I marked a spot which I thought might be her place – a few of our apples had collected there, looking as red as starfish in the white spume. I took as large a breath as I could, and dived down.

The quiet that followed was uncanny. After the screams, and the curses of some men, and the prayers of others, and the continuous boom of the wind, and the crash of the waves, there was only the drum of my pulse, and the gurgle of bubbles as they trickled up from my lips and across my face. Could I see anything? Darkness. Could I feel anything? Only the soft nudging of flesh that I burrowed past into deeper water.

Nothing. When I burst to the surface again I struggled wildly, attempting to gauge by my distance from this piece of jagged timber, or that rag of sail-cloth, how far I had drifted from the spot I had tried to hit. But the sea does not allow precise calculations of this sort. Everything drifts – as I remembered Natty and I had said to one another, after the death of Jordan Hands. Nowhere remains steady. All I could do was dive again, and then again, and then again, with each plunge more desperate than the last.

Whenever I swam beneath the waves, I might as well have been blundering through a dream. When my head was above water, and I was gasping to fill my lungs again, my dream became a vision of hell itself. There was never a trace of Natty – only devastation, revealed by flashes of moonlight. At one point I saw Spot, still in his cage, dragged in a cartwheel as the current bowled him through the foam; his small wings raggedly opened and closed, but there was no life in them. At another I found Mr Tickle and Bo'sun Kirkby, their limp bodies snared in the ropes of a cross-mast. Mr Allan I noticed, still alive. 'Stay there, old girl,' he was calling, speaking to the *Nightingale* as his arms flailed to keep himself afloat. 'Stay there and we'll come and empty you.' His voice was full of foam, and his words bubbled.

In my fifth or sixth dive I was able to stay underwater for no more than a few seconds at a time. After that, my efforts were pure instinct, and had nothing to do with hope or reason. I was certain I had lost Natty. If my heart had not been frozen already, it would have broken there and then.

This is when I surrendered to the forces of the world. When it did not matter to me any longer whether I sank or swam, breathed air or water, lived or died. I was not even concerned to notice the storm, still less the moon sailing above me, or the stars. Sleep was all I wanted; or rather indifference; or rather unconsciousness. I therefore let the waves turn me onto my back, and spread my arms and legs wide so the current would take me wherever it chose.

My preference (supposing I had the will to make any choice at all) was for oblivion. My fate, which the numbness of my mind and body allowed me to understand only very gradually, was to live.

To survive, at any rate. For while others struggled and died in the lee of the ship, I was lifted and carried – swept away from the furious battering of the waves, and along the edge of the reef which had been our undoing, until I was brought into a stretch of water that lay cradled between a crescent of rock and the shore.

I did not immediately see what sort of place it was, or what a safe harbour it must be. But as warmth and stillness restored feeling to my body, as well as wits to my head, I began to realise that within this shelter the sea was calm as a lake. Like a man raised from the grave, I lifted my head and looked about me. On my left, a hundred yards out to sea yet apparently in a different world, I saw moonlit waves continuing to pound the *Nightingale* – as remote as if she were an etching on glass. Looming close on my right were the black cliffs I had thought entirely featureless, but which I now saw were incised with little paths here and there, which had steps cut ingeniously into the stone, and hand-rails made of rope. At their foot lay a narrow and gently sloping beach. As I continued to float towards it, I heard waves that were really no more than ripples, making a peaceful silvery clatter.

I had been saved, as surely as if the sea itself had chosen me. I had been saved – along with another who was already waiting on the shore. I could not tell who this was, only that they appeared slim and youthful; the head was covered with a shawl and the face was invisible. When I had drifted closer still, and felt my shoulders brush against smooth stones, this figure lifted one hand in a solemn salute and a voice spoke. 'Are you there, Jim?' it said, with a sweet note I recognised. 'Is it you?'